The Final Witness

By

Cary R. Bybee

Published by Bybee Books
Lebanon, Oregon
U.S.A.

This book is a work of fiction. While I strived to keep history, science, geography, and Biblical truths true and accurate, any resemblance to real events or situations or actual persons, living or dead, is coincidental.

The Final Witness
Copyright ©2003 by Cary R. Bybee

Published by Bybee Books, January 2004

Edited by Bea Kassees and Tina L. Miller
Page layout by Tina L. Miller
Cover art and design by Steve Gardner
Copyright ©2003 Bybee Books
Cover Photos Copyright Photo Spin, Digital Stock, Digital Vision, PhotoDisc

ISBN: 0-9744398-6-x (soft cover)
         0-9744398-7-8 (hard cover)

Library of Congress Control Number: 2002095844

Previously published in March 2003 by 1st Books Library.
Previous ISBN's:
         1-4033-8659-5 (soft cover)
         1-4033-8660-9 (hard cover)
         1-4033-8658-7 (ebook)

Printed and published in the United States of America

This book is printed on acid free paper.

Dedication

This book is dedicated to my Grandmother
Olive Marie Bybee (1912-2002)
One of my dearest treasures and a woman who
had an enormous influence in my life and upbringing.

Grandma, I love you dearly.

Other books by Cary R. Bybee:

The Last Gentile
Deacon's Horn
The Library Man

Acknowledgements

Bea Kassees of Millennium Christian Shows—Thank you for your tireless dedication to this ministry and your many thoughtful prayers.

Tina L. Miller of Obadiah Press—Thank you for helping us make our work more worthy of God.

Steve Gardner—Thank you for the wonderful cover designs.

Dustin and Melissa Mitsch of Written Communication.com—Thank you for the terrific web site.

Chapter 1: The Day After

Day 1261, December 26: The sky was an ugly gray with an eerie red hue as the sun tried desperately to burn through the dust and ash. Though it struggled, the sunlight would never make it through the residue left behind from the massive asteroid that crashed into the earth's surface.

Calvin Fraser's stocky, black body stood looking out at the desert before him. *What a terrible sight,* he thought, as tears rolled down his rugged jaw. The desert floor looked very much like the surface of the moon. Literally thousands of small craters were strewn over the land as far as Calvin's eyes could see. Small pieces of rock and asteroid, commonly referred to as tektites, had peppered the earth's surface on nearly every part of the globe. Calvin did not know it yet, but millions of people had perished earlier that morning as the two-mile-wide death star fell into the heart of the U.S.A.

As the crowd of 150 gathered around Calvin, he began to speak softly. "'In the beginning was the Word, and the Word was with God, and the Word was God. He was with God in the beginning. Through Him all things were made; without Him nothing was made that has been made.'"

Leasa Moore stepped up next to Calvin's truest friend and faithful companion, Cory Parker. She slid her small black hand into Cory's huge palm and squeezed it lightly. He smiled at her through his own tears, but said nothing. What could he say? What could any of them say? The damage was done. Life had changed so drastically over the last three and a half years, and now it was only going to get worse.

"People," said Calvin, "from today forward we have one task, and that is to find every person we can who has not taken the mark of the beast, Carlo Ventini's ID tag. We need to organize and break into smaller groups and scour the United States in search of other believers and unite as we preach God's Words. We are His final witnesses to the world. The end is coming soon."

The air around Calvin and his group of followers was boiling hot, but this too would not last. Soon the earth would cool down to an unbelievable level. The air was acidic, and it left a bitter taste in their mouths as they walked back towards the mine's entrance where they had been so graciously protected from the barrage of hot, explosive pieces of asteroid debris.

******

Simon awoke in his private chambers at the United World Organization building just north of Rome. What a tremendous night's sleep, he thought with a smile. The only thing that was missing was a woman. They had gotten back from Jerusalem so late that he did not have time to order one, but he would correct that situation tonight. "We are gods," he spoke loudly to himself. Oh, how sweet it was to see Joseph and Yvette's heads lopped off at the altar. Simon smiled at the thought. *Deacon's Horn* had been a real nuisance and a thorn in his side, but that was ancient history.

This morning only one thought perturbed his mind and that was of Peter Bastoni, Joseph's brother. This man had developed an antidote to fight off the plague that he and Carlo had planted around the world. Peter had stolen their glory. It was they who were supposed to come to the rescue of the sick and dying, but now even this fact had been turned against Peter. Simon made sure that the world saw all that Dr. Bastoni and the other scientists did as evil.

He had created a huge deception, blaming them for the plague itself and suggesting that they had developed their own antidote to make themselves look like heroes. This lie of Simon's really had worked well, and now not only were all the Christians of the world hated, but also any associated scientist was hated, and maybe even more so. The thought reminded Simon that he had two other scientists to go in search of as well.

Tommy Glover and Dr. Sara Allen had escaped from him in Rome, but not for long. *Now that this simpleton, Pope Peter John, is dead, I can do this myself,* thought Simon with a laugh as he remembered Peter John's headless body draped over the small golden table.

"Today I will assume my new role as second only to Carlo, the god of this planet, and I will find and kill Peter, Tommy, Sara, and every Christian and Christ-professing scientist on earth!" said Simon with a roar.

But first, Simon thought, *I need to get organized.* His mind was spinning with so much to do. *I need to call in the media for an interview with Carlo and me on the future of this planet and how we intend to run things.*

"Also," said Simon in a whisper, "I need to develop a special security force that I can use to seek out and destroy all Christians and any other opposition."

Simon was deep in contemplation as his body began to twitch at the thought of supreme power over the world. He would have to bow down to Carlo, of course, but maybe someday he would be Carlo's equal. "Maybe—someday—I'll be the greatest," Simon supposed loudly.

Simon was startled as Carlo came through his bedroom door dressed in a 3,000 dollar suit. Simon stood but said nothing. Carlo seemed to have a different look about him that Simon was not sure about. Somehow he looked older—as if he was from a different era—yet he still appeared to be a young man in his mid-30's, tall, and handsome.

Simon was, on the other hand, not a handsome man—being short, fat and bald—but he figured that it didn't matter in the least, at least not any more.

"I want some information!" Carlo demanded. "I want to know what happened to the United States and how this will impact the world."

"I will find out this morning as soon as I can." Simon smiled, but Carlo did not acknowledge this gesture and turned to leave.

Without turning around, Carlo spoke to Simon. "By the way, now that the Pope is no longer among us, I guess you can have Vatican City and the Papal Castle as your new headquarters if you want." Carlo walked out of the room without shutting the door.

Simon nearly danced off the floor at the thought of his own city and his own castle, especially one with so much Roman history. He couldn't wait to go and check it out. *I'll have servants in every room and my private security force living in the castle. It will be my headquarters for the campaigns I launch,* Simon thought cheerfully.

******

A few hours later Simon went in pursuit of answers for Carlo. He entered the old, downtown building with six security guards by his side. Unlike Carlo, he liked having these men around him at all times. It made him feel important and safe simultaneously.

Instantly a small man hurried forward to greet Simon. "Hello, Mr. Koch," said the director of the Spaceguard Foundation nervously.

Simon smiled at this obvious show of fear. He loved his ability to intimidate others. "Good morning. Do you have the answers I have requested?" Simon asked as he looked around at all the pictures of comets, meteors, and planets plastered along the wide corridor. The building looked more like a converted old hotel than a scientific facility, with the original architecture and marble floors one would expect in an Italian hotel, especially in Rome.

The anxious man pointed to a room further down the hall. "There is someone here that I think you should meet. He is a scientist from America and he is—or I should say was—the scientific advisor to the President of the United States.

Speaking of the President of the United States and his loyal dominion, Simon thought, *I wonder what happened to them. I guess I'll have to check that out later as well. So much to do!*

Simon waved his hand motioning the group forward. *Another scientist, just what I need,* he mused sarcastically.

Simon's security escort entered the room first. He and the foundation director stood outside the large mahogany door while a security guard searched the surprised man in the center of the room. Simon had an excellent ability to recall faces he had seen before. As he looked at the young man with outstretched arms, he recalled that he had seen him on television playing down the effects of the asteroid that was heading directly towards Kansas at six miles per second.

After a nod from his security officer, Simon entered the large meeting room. With a broad smile he extended his hand like a politician. "I am Simon Koch. Who might you be?"

The intimidated, young scientist spoke softly. "I am Dr. Raymond Hyder."

Simon shook the man's hand firmly. He noted the tall, handsome man's firm grip and the intelligent look in his eyes. Simultaneously Raymond noted the cold, clammy hand and lifeless eyes of Simon Koch.

"What are you doing in Rome?" Simon asked. "I thought I saw you on television just the other day telling the people of your country not to worry about the incoming asteroid." Simon grinned hideously as he spoke.

Dr. Hyder's heart sank at the thought of all the innocent people he had betrayed and lied to as he followed directions from the President of the United States.

"I was under orders not to start a panic," Dr. Hyder alleged.

"Yes, well I guess it would not do for all those people to run away from the epicenter of a massive megaton explosion. After all, they could be hurt if they tried to move to a safer place like Rome, I guess!" Simon beamed as he opened his arms wide as if to embrace the country of Italy.

Raymond was speechless. He knew Simon was right. The people should have been told the truth, but he hated the man's cruelty just the same.

"I need some information from you," said Simon. "However, I need factual information, not fictional stuff like what you spoke of on national television." *One last blow for good measure,* Simon thought as he concluded.

"What do you need?" Dr. Hyder asked flatly.

"Carlo Ventini, the leader of the United World Organization and the benevolent god of this planet, would like your educated assessment of the damage to America caused by the asteroid and a summary of what we can expect as a result."

Dr. Hyder felt the urge to strike back at Simon by asking him why his benevolent god, Carlo, didn't have the answers himself, but Hyder didn't get to be a scientist by being stupid, so he kept his mouth safely shut. "Let's go into the computer room, and I will show you my model simulation," said Dr. Hyder.

Simon and his entourage followed Raymond down three flights of stairs and into a very cold, dimly lit room in the basement of the old building. Along the wall was a series of green and red LED's. There were magnetic tape drives and huge rectangular metal boxes full of electronic components. "What is all this, and why is it so cold in here?" Simon asked inquisitively.

"This," said Dr. Hyder as he turned towards Simon and smiled, "is a Teraflops Supercomputer, just like the one at the Sandia National Labs in New Mexico, and we have to keep the room cool or the system will overheat and slow greatly.

"What can a supercomputer do?" Simon inquired while trying not to be impressed.

"This particular computer can perform over one trillion mathematical calculations every second. It was designed to predict the outcome of a nuclear war, but we at the Spaceguard Foundation have modified it to predict NEO effects."

"What are NEO's?" Simon asked bluntly.

"They are near earth objects. We assume for an instant that they might enter the earth's atmosphere at certain locations. Then based on the composition of a particular NEO-comet, asteroid, or meteor, we can simulate the effects on the planet."

"And you can do this accurately?" Simon asked doubtfully.

"We can calculate the destructive forces of a solid object based on mass and velocity, but we cannot entirely predict the effects of an asteroid with volatile components such as hydrogen. We have only now, over the last 15 years or so, learned enough from the K-T extinctions to predict what might happen. So far our only scenarios have been based on what we call *Nuclear Winters*." It was obvious by the look on Simon's face that Dr. Hyder needed to give a better, much simpler explanation.

"Mr. Koch, K-T stands for *Cretaceous* and *Tertiary* period. Over 65 million years ago nearly all life on land and sea was mysteriously destroyed. Many think an asteroid of significant mass and composition hit the earth and caused this extinction.

They even go further in presuming that they have found the actual site of the asteroid impact somewhere in the Yucatan Peninsula region of Mexico, evidenced by a 100-mile wide crater below the sea. Others believe that the destruction of the dinosaurs came from within, specifically citing the *Deccan Traps* volcanic eruptions—especially those of India and Iceland—as the culprits."

Simon was getting bored with the explanation. "What does it matter which type of disaster caused this extinction 65 million years ago?"

Raymond Hyder turned and looked into Simon's frightening eyes. A shiver ran through his body for a moment. "Mr. Koch, it is the mechanism that eludes us today, and it is extremely important in order for us to predict the outcome of a disaster. Our lives may depend on it some day. A nuclear winter results from a dust cloud blocking out the sun's rays— in effect, dramatically cooling the planet. This causes massive snowstorms initially and eventually kills all plant and animal life everywhere. However, the *Deccan Traps* disaster would not have caused a nuclear winter. Instead it would have raised carbon dioxide levels to the point of triggering the greenhouse effect. So you see, the dinosaurs, plants, and sea life died from either the cold effects or they died from the warming effects— two completely different mechanisms with scenarios and complexities of their own."

"Or possibly," an irritated Simon snapped, "they died off naturally over a short period of time or by disease." Simon hated the way Dr. Hyder made him feel ordinary, if not downright stupid.

"Possibly," said Dr. Hyder. "In any case, since we have an actual asteroid that hit earth, we can now predict what will happen next." Raymond stepped over to the screen and pulled up the simulations that he had been working on for the last week since he had caught a military hop over to Rome.

Dr. Hyder pulled out a chair so Simon could sit down next to him and view the screen. "We know the diameter of ED14—the asteroid that hit Lebanon, Kansas—was approximately two miles. We also know that it was partially full of volatiles like hydrogen. That is why it reduced in size dramatically as it entered the earth's atmosphere.

We can now confidently classify this extraterrestrial as an S-type asteroid, which means it is metallic—probably nickel and iron—with a large amount of silicates. We know its initial and terminal velocities, so we can calculate the impact forces of at least 500 gigatons of TNT which is more explosive power than all the nuclear weapons of the world combined, even at the height of the *Cold War.*"

The last statement impressed Simon. "So then something bad is coming, right?"

Dr. Hyder didn't even look at Simon but instead clicked the right mouse key and the computer screen came to life. Simon stared at the images in disbelief as they flashed across the screen. With each view came a statistical chart of effects and casualties, along with geographical pictures of locations around the globe. "Interpret for me," said a panic-stricken Simon.

"What we expect is that 80 to 100 million people died last night in the United States and Canada." Dr. Hyder felt nauseated as he spoke these words. "Next we will see the sky darken around the world. Temperatures will decrease uniformly until they reach as much as minus 13 degrees Fahrenheit on average and much colder at the extremes.

This, of course, goes back to the original nuclear winter scenario. We have no way for certain to predict this. From these estimates what you see on the screen is the virtual elimination of all plant life and the reduction of heat in the oceans and seas to the point that they will freeze and reduce in height by as much as 500 feet or so. The death of fish and mammals and, eventually, the starvation of the world will follow." *As if they were not already starving to death,* thought Raymond to himself.

Simon swallowed hard and whispered, "Are you sure?"

"Unless the earth shifts orbit and draws closer to the sun, at least long enough to burn through this dust cloud, there could be no other conclusion," said Raymond solemnly. "Additionally, unless we discontinue the use of motorized vehicles, planes, and all factories that pollute the atmosphere, we will very quickly pollute our air supply to dangerous, if not toxic, levels. As the temperatures come down, people will undoubtedly burn more oil and wood which will destroy our limited fresh air supply more rapidly, so either we freeze to death or we suffocate. Take your pick."

"There must be an answer," said Simon. He had not struggled through life to achieve his present status just to lose it all because of some dumb asteroid impact. "What about rain? Yes, maybe if it rains, it will pull this dust down and allow the sun to penetrate our atmosphere."

Dr. Hyder could sense Simon's growing desperation and, for some reason, he almost enjoyed the fact that Carlo Ventini's right-hand man was worried and even scared. It showed that he was human after all.

"It will not rain, Mr. Koch. The dust will cover the surface of the oceans, rivers, and lakes. It will insulate the atmosphere from the moisture, so no exchange will take place. No rain clouds will form under these conditions. There may be some initial snowstorms from the existing moisture in the air and the plummeting temperatures, but after this, we've seen the last of the rainfall.

In addition, I believe this dust cloud has already risen and penetrated out into space hundreds—maybe thousands—of miles, which means satellites used for weather tracking, nuclear rocket launch detection, and NEO tracking will most likely encounter this debris. And, moving along at four miles per second, they will be destroyed. Even the International Space Station—ISS—will likely hit this debris and be destroyed, along with the six member team up there at this moment."

"Are you sure of this?" Simon asked as sternly as he could.

"Yes, Mr. Koch, I am sure. The only thing I don't know is how long it will last and whether or not the human race can endure. Will we become a thing of the past like the dinosaurs? The world has been warned for years to prepare for a large-scale catastrophe, but these warnings have gone nearly unheard. Due to this disaster, there will be no plant growth. Your Agripods will not be sufficient for feeding the world. There is no more than a 90-day supply of food worldwide. The dust from this asteroid will damage all the fresh water supplies soon, if not destroy them completely."

"What can we do to ensure we survive?" Simon asked with little composure.

Dr. Hyder stood and towered over Simon. "Mr. Koch, I am not even certain that there are not more asteroids on their way to earth at this very moment. The Jet Propulsion Laboratory in California didn't even see this one until about two weeks ago, and now that all of the satellites and cameras in space will likely be destroyed, we will be blind to what may be coming our way."

The thought caused Simon to shiver. He so wanted to live. Why had he and Carlo not taken actions of their own—sent up a nuclear weapon or something to destroy the asteroid before it hit the earth? At the time it looked like a convenient solution to their problem with the United States, but now it seemed that the destruction of America might also destroy their own empire. "I need you to come with me and report all this to the benevolent Carlo Ventini."

Now Dr. Hyder shivered at the thought of meeting the exalted Carlo. "What can I do?"

"You can help us prepare to survive this nuclear winter. We will give you a job working directly for his highness and me. You can even live at the World Headquarters," Simon smiled.

Dr. Hyder had read the latest on the Christian resistance against Simon and Carlo. He had even seen televised clips of Simon torturing young children to death in Australia, and although he was not a Christian, he knew the danger of refusing to support Simon's cause. Raymond Hyder simply nodded compliantly without saying a word.

"Good then" said Simon. "You will be in charge of the survival of this planet while I work on ridding it of the unwanted element." Simon wore an evil grin as he spoke these final words.

******

One by one, hundreds of miles above the earth, each satellite flew by the massive, free-floating cloud of dust. Much of this dust was composed of particles no larger than grains of sand with others as large as a quarter. As the satellites moved through space at four miles per second, every piece of debris was potentially catastrophic, and within 16 hours time every satellite in orbit was completely destroyed.

The ISS ship had been warned days earlier to alter its distance from the earth and to hold its rotational speed down with thrusters. The team of three American and three Russian astronauts struggled with the ailing station for as long as they could.

If only they could hold out until the asteroid debris had time to clear their flight path, everything would be okay. They could stay in space for the next couple of years or so without any trouble.

The ISS commander was a 52-year-old man named Petra Sverdlov, the grandson of the famous Yakov Sverdlov, a comrade of Lenin and the first titular head of Communist Russia. Petra was facing a brilliant career after his military service concluded, but unfortunately for him, the U.S.S.R. could not hold together after their lengthy and fruitless battle with Afghanistan. So in the early 1990's Petra made the decision to stay with the space program in hopes of maintaining at least a reasonable income for himself. Since he never married, the space program's demands did not greatly impact his personal life.

Petra had two others on his Russian team—a frail but brilliant 42-year-old man named Samuel Pearlman, and a very plain-looking, young Romanian woman, Shila Torpof. Samuel was on his second tour aboard the space station. He, too, had no other family to concern himself with. Samuel was no more than 5'4" at best and probably 120 pounds dripping wet. He nearly failed out of the space program because of his many physical weaknesses, but he was brilliant and useful. In addition, the Russians had a necessary quota to fill and, since Samuel was Jewish, he fit that qualification.

This was pretty much the same for Shila. She, too, fit the quota requirements. She was Romanian and a woman, both of which the Russian government thought would make them look good in the eyes of the world. Shila was only 30 years old, and this was her maiden voyage into space and on the ISS.

The co-commander was a female astronaut from the United States, a 51-year-old Air Force colonel named Teresa Reed. Unlike her Russian counterparts, Teresa did have a family back home—a husband and twin 20-year-old daughters—at least until a few nights ago when ED14 came crashing into the U.S.A.

Working alongside Teresa were Skip Taylor and Robert Powell. Both men were less than 40 years old and married, but neither had any children yet. All six members of the station had already completed eight months of their one-year tour in space. In a mere four months the astronauts were to have been replaced by a fresh team, yet today Teresa was concerned that there would never be any way for them to get back to earth at all, even if they could survive the dust cloud that they were just about to enter. All communication with earth had stopped 30 hours ago. There was no way to know how much damage the asteroid had done to their home planet, and they all feared the worst.

The space station came into view of the asteroid dust cloud at the terminator of the earth. The sight was spectacular. It was like a giant mushroom cloud from a nuclear blast, yet it extended 1,500 miles above the surface of the earth. "Here we go!" yelled Petra as he strapped into his command seat. Teresa was already in her seat trying to trim the thrusters to gain a little more altitude without launching the space station out into the deep blackness of space and completely away from the much needed earth's rotation.

The ship began to shake and rotate as if it were caught in a great sea of swells. The noise from outside the hull was frightening, much like a hailstorm in the middle of a tornado. The station was really taking a pounding.

Every team member sat perspiring and praying quietly. Soon the vibrations stopped and the defining noise came to an end. Teresa looked at Petra and blew out a sigh of relief. "I guess we made it," she said.

Petra nodded but did not speak.

"We've made it this time," said Samuel doubtfully.

"What do you mean?" Skip Taylor asked as he unfastened his belt.

All five of the space crewmembers looked to Samuel for an explanation. They had learned to trust in him over the last eight months. Each time the space station had an attack or a broken part, Samuel was the one who figured out a way to patch it up and keep things working.

"I mean," said Samuel softly, as he didn't want to worry his comrades more than they already were, "we have to make another pass in just a few hours. Even with our slowed rate of rotation thanks to our thrusters, we will see this cloud again. I calculate its dispersion rate at less than half of our rate of rotation which means we will see it at least twice more."

"Can we slow down any more?" Shila asked with a tremendous amount of fear in her voice.

"Perhaps," said Samuel, "but then we would use up all of our fuel, and we would never be able to correct again. Additionally, the increase in hull friction and structural stresses would be far too great for this big ship."

Robert Powell, the quiet member of the group, spoke up. "Samuel, we will not survive two more passes like the last one."

Samuel nodded, as did Teresa and Petra.

"Additionally," said Robert, "since it is unlikely that the world will ever be able to communicate with us, track us, or even come and get us out of this space station—" He paused. Samuel understood the point that he was making, and it aligned with Samuel Pearlman's personal ideas.

"What are you saying, Mr. Powell?" a frightened Shila asked.

"What he is saying," Petra said, "is that we have two choices. One, we can try to make it through the dust cloud two more times and, if we survive, we can wait for someone to come and get us out of here."

"If there is anyone left," interjected Skip.

"Or two," said Petra, "we can use our thrusters to point this station out into deep space."

"What good will it do to move out there?" said Shila as she pointed away from the earth.

"We have a couple of year's worth of oxygen, food, and water, if we conserve," said Samuel.

"Or we can end this all now," said Petra, "and go back through that cloud one more time."

"How do you know we won't make it?" Shila asked, nearly begging for a more suitable solution.

"Based on my calculations, we have about 30 minutes before we will not have enough fuel to break free of the earth's pull and move deeper into space. We need to decide now," said Samuel.

"This is crazy," said Shila with tears in her eyes. "If we go out there, we cannot come back!"

Teresa also had to fight back the urge to break down and cry. She knew she would never see or touch her family again. If they had survived the asteroid by some miracle, they would never see their mother again.

All eyes were on Petra. Finally there came a consenting number of head nods and, with a single turn of the switch, Petra launched the space station directly out away from the rotation they had been in for eight months. In fact, it was the rotation that the space station had been in for nearly a decade. The ISS groaned and shook as it struggled to pull away from earth's gravity. At last it was free and moving in a path that would take it very close to the moon in just a couple of days.

"Shut the thrusters off," Petra said to Teresa softly.

Teresa wiped the tears from her cheeks and flipped the two switches into the off position.

******

Tommy Glover was the first one to wake up. He was also the first one to realize that Martha and Harry, the ancient couple from Heaven who had helped and encouraged them, were nowhere to be found.

Tommy looked out of the window into what appeared to be an evening sky. He felt a little confused, but as a volcanologist, he had experienced some of this, though on a much smaller scale of course. The sky was a dark, burnt orange—a very frightening sight for sure. Tommy looked at his watch. It read 7:55 a.m.

"What time is it?" a soft voice from behind Tommy inquired.

He turned to see the beautiful, athletic Sara Allen with her dish blonde hair all askew, rubbing her pale blue eyes as she asked the question again.

"Later than you think," said Tommy.

Sara began to shift her head from side to side. "They're gone too," Tommy said softly.

"What's happening?" Sara asked with fear rising up in her voice.

Tommy moved to her side and embraced her tightly. "Remember the asteroid that was supposed to hit earth yesterday? Well, somehow we must have slept right through the impact."

"Do you think America was greatly damaged?" Sara asked.

Tommy nodded and spoke. "Yes, based on the size estimates, it must have been horribly damaged, so even if we could get out of here, we have no place to go."

"What should we do now? Martha and Henry didn't leave instructions," said Sara flatly.

"I'm not sure. Simon Koch will still be looking for us, and yet I know we need to do all we can to warn the world about Carlo Ventini's ID tags, but I don't know exactly where—or how—to start. In fact, I don't even know where we are. Northern Italy for sure, but how far north?"

"Well, let me make us some breakfast, and then maybe we can figure out what God wants us to do," said Sara with a smile.

But before Sara could take a step into the kitchen, the room flooded with a bright, soft light. Suddenly a large black angel appeared and stood in front of them. Fear filled their weary bodies.

"Blessings to you both," said the angel. "I am Philip. Be at peace. The Lord has sent me to give you instructions. Your path will be perilous and difficult, but the Lord is with you both. There are many who have not made their choice to follow after Jesus or—" said Philip as he paused briefly, "or the evil liar, Satan."

"What should we do?" a brave Sara asked.

Philip smiled kindly at the strong young lady. "You will need to pack up what you can carry and continue to head north."

"Where are we?" Tommy asked.

"You are at the basin to Europe. You are in Como, Italy, and from here you can reach as far west as France or east as far as the Baltic's."

"Which way should we go?" Sara asked.

"There are lost souls in every direction, but beware," said Philip. "Simon Koch will hunt for you night and day. Do not spend a single night in the same town you entered in the morning. Be like the wind, never knowing where it is coming from or where it is going."

"What can we do to help? What can we say that they will listen to?" Tommy asked with a heart full of compassion and sincerity for the lost.

"There are many like you out there witnessing today. Every continent has witnesses. There are also 144,000 Jewish witnesses who have been especially chosen by God to teach and proclaim the Word of the Lord. You will see some of these out there. They, too, have been working since the Rapture of the church. Beware! Others claim to be witnesses, but they are not. Soon you will be able to tell, but for now you will have to trust your own hearts and not your eyes nor your ears."

"What do we say to those who do not know about God? How will we know if they have taken the mark of the beast—the little, green ID tags?" Tommy asked.

"You will not know. Test everyone. Proclaim boldly the truth about the ID tags. Speak courageously against Simon and Carlo. Put your faith entirely in Jesus and cling to each other. God has united you as one. You are now husband and wife, and this will be throughout eternity." Philip beamed brightly as he observed Sara's response to being wed to Tommy. The angel reached out and touched both young people. Swiftly he was gone and the room was a drab color once again.

"Whoa! That was awesome," said Tommy enthusiastically. "So now we need to get packed up and ready to move out!"

Sara stood in amazement as she watched Tommy jump around. "Wait a minute, mister!"

Tommy stopped and stared at Sara with a confused and impatient look. Sara stood in the dining room with both hands on her hips. "Didn't you hear what he said?"

"Yes!" said Tommy. "We are going to be witnesses for God through Europe. Isn't that great?"

Sara was exasperated and speechless and just looked at Tommy.

He moved over to her and quickly kissed her cheek. "Come on, Wife! We need to get going!"

Sara looked up at Tommy and got a big smile and a wink from him. A grin spread across her pretty face. "Well, all right then—that's better!" she laughed out loud.

Chapter 2: Simon in Charge

Day 1267, January 1: Christopher Evans opened the hatch of his family's survival pod slowly. He had been in the pod for a week or so. It was hard to tell. He had lost track of time. Three steps up the stairs and Christopher's young, green eyes peered over the heavy metal door that looked very much like a submarine hatch.

Initially Chris felt confused. It looked like dusk with just a hint of orange sunlight, yet the light was coming out of the east and then simply disappearing into a thick, black cloud. The sight reminded Chris of the fires that he and his brothers and father had fought to no avail. *How long ago was that?* he wondered. He was 14 then, and now he was nearly 18 years old. The last three and a half years had rushed by.

The thought of his family was still very painful, but not nearly as much as it would have been for Chris had he actually seen Simon Koch torturing them to death. In fact, Chris was not even sure they were dead, although his heart felt the pain.

The young man stood and stretched skyward when suddenly a cool breeze blew across his handsome face. Instantly he felt a divine presence from Heaven. He had felt it before—the night an angel had come and taken him away from his parents, placing him gently in the survival pod.

"Is that you, God?" the shaky young man asked.

At once Philip appeared before Chris. "The Lord has sent me to guide you along your way, little one. Be at peace."

Chris looked up to Philip and whispered, "And my family?"

"They are in Heaven with God, child. Rejoice for them, for their sorrow and suffering is over." Philip smiled encouragingly at Christopher.

"Will I ever see them again?" Chris inquired through his tears.

"Of this I am sure," said Philip. "But now you have a duty before you which will require great courage. Be faithful to the Lord, and be wise and cautious. Evil is out in full force to destroy you."

"Where will I go? What will I do?" Chris asked.

"Head west to Brisbane and you will meet others like yourself. Join their cause and follow after them. Your testimony will be a great witness to those deceived by false religions.

"Christopher, do you believe in Christ completely, and do you love Him with all your heart?" Philip asked in all sincerity.

Chris paused for a brief moment. Finally he spoke. "I learned about Jesus by reading His Word in the Holy Bible. I know He died for me. I know He loves me and wants me to be with Him for eternity. Yes, I love Him. He is my King!"

Philips smiled as if he were a proud father. "This love will carry you through the worst of times and until the end of times. God is always with you, child. Now go!"

*****

Christopher Evans had been walking along a lone stretch of Highway 54 for hours. Not a single car had driven by in all that time. His mind drifted in and out of past adventures with his family—so many enjoyable times. Life on the farm had been good, and it had made Chris self sufficient and strong. Now with Jesus in his heart, he felt indestructible. Unsure—but indestructible nonetheless. However, at this moment Chris felt something else too—cold.

The sky continued to darken almost to the point that he considered stopping and pulling out the flashlight he had hidden away in his backpack along with food, water, and a change of clothing. As a kid from this part of Australia, it was not likely he had ever experienced cold weather below 30 degrees Fahrenheit, but now he was certain it was going to snow. Christopher had never seen snow up close.

Suddenly Christopher's own tall, lanky body cast a shadow on the highway in front of him. He turned quickly to see a vehicle approaching. He felt a sense of surprise mixed with fear and hope—fear that this would be other evil people like the ones who had taken his family away and hope that it might be one of the men Philip had spoken about.

Slowly the old truck came to a stop. Chris could barely make out the driver behind the wheel. He was certain it was a man, but that was all he could tell for sure. The vehicle was an old sheep truck used for ferrying small herds from one green pasture to another. *Certainly this is a farmer,* thought Chris. *He must be safe.*

The window of the passenger side rolled down as the driver leaned over. "Would you like a ride?" the stranger asked in a raspy, somewhat deep voice.

Chris was not in tune with his own instincts. He had not had to rely on them for his own survival to this point, so he could not accurately determine what he felt. *Is this fear?* he wondered. *Should I get in?*

Walking towards the truck Chris slipped his large pack off his back. The door pushed open before he even reached it. Again a sense of doubt filled his mind. He stopped and stared into the cab for a second. He could now more clearly see the outline of a balding, heavy-set man of about 50. "Come on, Son. I'm running late."

"No thanks, Mister. My dad will be here in just a few minutes."

The man slammed the cab door and hit the accelerator, squealing the truck tires as he sped away. The balding man wiped the perspiration from his forehead; a sense of disappointment combined with a sense of relief filled his twisted mind.

Two more hours went by as the numbing cold began to wear on Christopher. *Maybe a little food will help,* he thought. Chris pulled the heavy green pack off his tired, sore shoulders. Sitting down on the asphalt Chris fought against the hermetically sealed pouch of dried fruit. He had taken as much of this food out of the pod as he could carry. He had lived through the last three years or so, and he understood what hunger was. The world was starving to death, and maybe he would, as well, but for the next few weeks he had enough food to hold him over. If he could avoid the terrible plague that was running rampant through the larger cities across the globe, he would be okay.

With food in his stomach, Chris had a little more energy. Now if he could just overcome this numbing cold feeling. He took another shirt out of his pack and pulled it over the one he was wearing and put his light-weight coat back on. "I wish I had a parka and some gloves," said Chris aloud. Unfortunately for Chris, he never needed a heavy coat while living in Quilpie, so it was not something he even owned.

Just as Chris stood to leave he caught sight of a pair of headlights coming around the bend. They were heading west just like he was. *Maybe this will feel better than the last encounter did,* he thought. The car slowed as it passed by. The red glare of tail lights illuminated Chris where he stood. The driver-side door opened and out climbed a six-foot tall man of about 40 years of age. Chris was scared. He thought about running, but where would he go? It was a big, wide-open highway in the middle of flat prairie land.

The man stood next to his car. He seemed to sense that Chris was about to take flight. "It's okay, Son. Nobody is going to harm you. Would you like to get out of this cold weather and drive along with me?"

Chris pondered the question. He had to do something. There was no way he could walk all the way to Brisbane, especially in his half frozen condition. "My name is Christopher Evans."

"When in doubtful situations, always take the time to properly intro-duce yourself," was the advice Chris' father had given him. "It breaks the ice," he had said, "and it allows you to connect to the person to deter-mine if they mean you harm."

The man smiled at Chris. He thought the child's formality there in the middle of a deserted highway was amusing. "My name is Conner Crowley. Glad to meet you, Christopher."

"You can call me Chris. Where are you going?" the young boy asked with a little more confidence.

"Well, that is a bit of a mystery even to me," said Connor. "For some reason I felt like I needed to drive this road."

"How far?" asked Chris.

"Until it comes to an end, I guess. I really don't know. It's hard to explain," said Connor with embarrassment in his tone.

Chris waved his hand as if to say, *Hold that thought.* "We can talk as we drive. I am freezing."

******

Two hours later Chris was sound asleep leaning against the passenger door as Connor drove into an eerie sunset with no more than a red, semi-round glow at the base of the dark, dusty sky. Connor had learned a great deal about the last three or four years of Chris' life. He had heard the stories of his childhood back on the farm. He listened to Chris describe the terrible reality of learning that his church had deceived the Evans family into believing they would someday be gods. As a result they missed the Rapture and had to endure terrible times.

Chris told Connor about how the State had taken away his family, never to be seen again. The young man decided not to tell Connor about Philip and how he had been transported back to the survival pod or about the mission that he was soon to start in the name of Jesus. At the same time it was obvious to Connor that Christopher did not know what had actually happened to his family. He knew that Chris believed them to be in Heaven and, therefore, understood that they had somehow been killed, but Connor knew that Chris did not know how they had died. He was certain once he heard the names of Chris' family that they were the very people he had seen on television being tortured to the point that Connor had become nauseated as he watched in disbelief. He kept this knowledge to himself. He did not want to inflict additional sorrow and pain onto the brave, young man. *What would be the point in telling him?* he thought.

Connor Crowley had shared with Chris that he lived in Windorah. He told Chris his wife had died four years ago during childbirth. Both she and the baby died at home because Connor had been out on his ranch working and was not available when she abruptly went into a premature labor.

His wife, Cindy, had asked him to invest in a cellular phone, and he agreed to get one. Unfortunately it was not soon enough. For years now he spent his time alone on his ranch. Connor was self-supporting so he rarely traveled to town and often went months without speaking to a single person. Lately, however, he began to feel the world collapsing all around him. Finally, he decided to try to make sense of it all, and that is when he picked up his wife's old Bible and began to read about Jesus. After a few weeks of this he found himself talking to the Lord continuously. Then just this morning he heard a voice in his mind telling him it was time to move.

*****

Connor entered Brisbane and slowed as he pulled into the traffic. Chris began to stir. "We're here," Connor whispered just loud enough to wake the boy up.

Chris looked out of the window. He recognized Brisbane from the few times his father had brought him there to build a new church. Except today it wasn't the usual busy, sunny, coastal city. Today the traffic was slow and the sky was thick and black. The usual smell of salt water was gone, replaced by a metallic, acidic odor.

"Well, where should we go now?" Connor asked with a smile.

"I don't know, but I'm sure I'm supposed to be here. I was told to—" Chris caught himself and paused.

"Who told you to come here?" Connor asked inquisitively.

Chris sat silent for a few seconds and then decided to trust in Connor Crowley. "An angel," he whispered.

Connor looked at Chris suspiciously. "An angel?"

Chris told Connor the whole story about Philip and how he told him to go to Brisbane. "We will meet some people here," said the young man.

"What people? And what for?" asked Connor.

"Beats me, but it has something to do with witnessing to the people that do not know Jesus," said Chris boldly.

"Okay, then maybe that is why I felt the need to come here today, but what do we do now?" Connor asked with a small grin. Chris was glad he had met this man. Connor seemed kind and genuine. Loneliness was a terrible thing, and it was nice to have someone to go through this uncertain time with.

******

Dr. Raymond Hyder stood before Carlo Ventini shaking nearly uncontrollably. *This is not a man. He is a god,* thought Raymond. Simon stood beside Carlo as Dr. Hyder explained for the second time what the asteroid impact meant to the world. Simon was already bored with the topic. He just wanted Raymond to find some way to protect him so he could fulfill his life's dream as the leader of the world.

"In the end," said Raymond, "it is going to get very cold. All the plants will die as will most, if not all, animal life including the fish in the sea."

Raymond stood silently as Carlo evaluated the young scientist. Finally with an eerie smile Carlo spoke up. "I can see that you have a very good understanding of my planet. You will be useful to me. Simon, put Dr. Hyder on our staff."

"I've already done that, Your Highness," said Simon with a proud little grin. He was beginning to predict Carlo, and this made him feel even more like his equal instead of his employee.

"Excellent!" said Carlo.

"Dr. Hyder, you are dismissed. Mr. Koch and I have some matters of importance to discuss." Raymond nearly ran from the room, but first he felt compelled to bow before Carlo.

"Whoa!" said Raymond as soon as he had cleared the hall. *That guy is the most powerful man the world has ever known, but I'm not sure about him being a god. Gods don't need scientists to tell them how things work, do they?* Dr. Hyder mused.

Simon followed Carlo into a large executive room with a huge library at the far end and numerous televisions on the opposing wall. On another wall was a gigantic map of the world with multiple red flags protruding from it. Simon stepped closer to see what they were highlighting. It turned out that they were stuck carefully in the country of Russia.

"Come over here!" Carlo commanded.

Simon rushed to where Carlo stood looking down. "What is that?" Simon asked as he pointed to a scaled and very detailed model of what looked like a small city.

"This is Babylon, my new home," Carlo beamed. "Nebuchadnezzar wanted to possess it; Alexander the Great wanted to possess it; Hitler uncovered it after nearly 2,000 years of being buried under the sand. He, too, wanted to possess it. But none could. It is my destiny! My father has given it to me."

Simon looked back to the model. "What are those?" he asked as he pointed to the tall towers in the middle of the city.

"Let me give you a tour," Carlo grinned as if he were showing off his prize possession. Simon had never seen him act like this, and certainly he had never been this friendly to Simon, not even when he had his first look at the Agripod systems that Simon had built as part of Carlo's initial plan.

"These towers are called Ziggurats. They are used to house statues of Marduk who was the god of the Babylonians. Marduk works for my father, and he has spent his time on earth in this general region since the beginning of mankind. These temples, however, will be dedicated to me exclusively. Additionally, these gates with lions' heads and dragons are the Gates of Ishtar. They date back to King Nimrod and the original Tower of Babel."

"And that—what's that?" Simon pointed. He was fascinated with the history of this oldest of cities.

"That is the Hanging Garden of Babylon. Nebuchadnezzar had this built for one of his wives. The aqueduct system comes from the Euphrates and Tigris rivers, both of which run through Babylon about 25 miles apart, splitting the city into two unequal parts."

Simon found himself jealous that Satan had given such a remarkable place to Carlo while all he had was Vatican City and some old, useless castle. "When will it be done? Do you need anything from me?" Simon asked.

"No, I don't need anything. I am bringing in some slave labor from

Africa, and I will start building it next week. I am going there tomorrow to set my plans. It will take me about a year, and then I will move in. Until then I will live in Baghdad and in Rome, as necessary, but we need to make some changes."

Simon looked up attentively. "What changes?"

"I want every church and statue around the world torn down, every shrine of Buddha and every cross completely destroyed. I want statues of me in these places. I want special facilities built where people can come and worship me. This is your task. Don't fail me!" Carlo growled.

Now this was the Carlo that Simon knew and loved.

"Also it is time that you step up as leader of this world. It is not fitting for a god to be involved in politics." Simon's heart began to pound faster. He was about to get another promotion. "You can modernize that old Papal Castle and move your headquarters there, and I will transfer all responsibility and power to you. Your first act will be to destroy Russia's war capability."

Simon looked into Carlo's bright eyes and shuddered. Truly this man was a god. "Why do we want to destroy Russia?" he asked.

Carlo pointed to the two chairs in the middle of the room. Both men sat, facing one another. "Dr. Hyder did say that all satellites would be destroyed, did he not?"

Simon nodded. "Yes, I have confirmed that this has already happened."

"Good, then they will not see us coming," Carlo smiled.

"But why?" asked Simon.

"Do you know what the world will need most over the next few years?" Carlo asked as his eyes bore into Simon.

"Food, I guess," said Simon flatly.

"Well, you guessed wrong. They will need oil for fuel to keep warm. There will be a great need for oil to provide electricity, to provide heat, to protect our Agripods. Oil is the most important thing this world has to offer these people. They may have needed the fuel in the past for their cars, but this was not an absolute must. Now, however, they will have to have oil to survive. That is why I allowed the asteroid to hit earth."

Simon looked at Carlo in total surprise.

"Don't worry, Simon. You will survive. As long as you serve my needs, you will live on."

Simon smiled gladly.

"Now we need to control all the oil reserves of the world. This, along with the food from the Agripods, the antidote for the plaque, and all nuclear weapons, will put us in total control over the people of all nations. They will have no choice but to worship me and obey you." Carlo grinned at his own master plans. "Russia will go after the oil. They did not vote in support of the New World Organization. They did not vote in favor of eliminating NATO and the United Nations Organizations," said Carlo.

"But they haven't been able to stop any of our efforts. No country has," said Simon carefully.

"They do not worship me. They are disobedient!" Carlo roared.

Simon swallowed hard. Carlo frightened him greatly. This man had changed so much in just a few days. He seemed so powerful—not human at all anymore.

"Besides," said Carlo more calmly, "we need China to support our cause, and they are more likely to do this if we eliminate the threat of Russia."

"How do we do it?" Simon inquired.

Carlo stood and walked over to a large map. Simon followed. Carlo moved one of the red flags and read the name below. "Arzaqmas-16 is a nuclear design facility. Krasnoyarsk-26 is a plutonium factory, Sverdlovsk-44 is a uranium factory, and all these other places are either weapons facilities or uranium factories. We will destroy them all."

Simon started to get excited about the idea of launching some nuclear weapons of his own. "Now that the satellite protection system has been destroyed, I can attack all facilities at once and neutralize Russia. She will be weak and powerless," said Simon with an enthusiastic, evil grin.

Carlo turned on Simon. "You command the most powerful armies in the world. All of the NATO forces are at your disposal now that this organization has been eliminated. Every general in the world will report to you and your government, all except for the U.S.A. They have been so completely destroyed that all that remains is a small handful of leaders and military personnel. They will serve you, as well, but they may have to be persuaded. Today there is no one in charge of the United States' weapons of destruction. All government is at a local level in the states, and a few major cities are still operating. You need to take charge of their country and their military—especially the nuclear side of it."

Simon grinned and nodded. "My pleasure!"

"Now as for the nuclear strike against these sites," said Carlo, "I do not want you to use excessive force. Use tactical missiles only. I want to prevent access to the Russian weapons. I do not want to detonate them or cause any more damage than necessary. I want the people of Russia to feel liberated so they can worship me freely."

Simon remembered the last time he disobeyed Carlo. It was in Australia. He so enjoyed torturing the Evans family that he lost sight of the audience. His image was forever damaged, and Carlo was furious. He would not repeat this mistake. *Moderation and self-control,* he warned himself silently.

Suddenly the room began to shake violently and a large, bright silhouette appeared. "Father," said Carlo as he fell to his knees. Simon followed suit awkwardly.

"Rise," said Satan. "We have much work to do. There are many Christians witnessing and in hiding around the world. You need to find them and destroy them. We need to prepare for the coming battle with Christ. I need to assume control over this world. It is my planet, and these people belong to me!" Satan roared causing the room to reverberate.

"Tell me where they are, Your Greatness, and I will go out and destroy them myself," said Simon boldly.

"Silence!" commanded Satan. "I do not know where these witnesses are today. Their God protects them, and I can no longer go into His presence to ask permission to test His people. You will have to seek these enemies out yourself."

Simon was surprised by Satan's lack of omniscience. It seemed that he was not as all knowing and powerful as God himself, and that worried Simon greatly. *And what is this asking God permission junk?* Simon won-

dered. *And what did he say about us fighting a war against Christ?* Everything
was closing in on Simon. He was getting confused. Carlo had somehow
changed and was truly more god-like than ever before. Satan seemed less
powerful and definitely not omnipotent, yet Satan was the source of
Simon's powers that enabled him to perform spectacular signs and won-
ders. Simon was now the most powerful man on earth besides Carlo, and
it seemed that Carlo was no longer a man. All of this caused him even
further confusion. *If Carlo is not a man and Satan is not a man, and if they are
both powerful, but within limits, then what will happen if and when we fight a war
against Christ?* Simon would be the only mortal among them. Suddenly he
felt vulnerable.

"Can we defeat Christ?" Simon asked cautiously.

Carlo looked at Simon disapprovingly. "He must be defeated!" Satan
demanded. "We need to eliminate everyone that is against us. All of those
who have taken my mark will serve me for eternity. We have to get to
those who have not made their choice yet, and the only way we can
prevent them from choosing Christ is if we kill all Christian witnesses on
earth."

"Father, we will rule this world, and the people will bow down before
us. We will find those uncommitted to us, and we will help them choose.
Your will be done!" said Carlo loudly.

"Soon I will bring you some help. Apollyon will be free and with him
will come an army of helpers. After that others beyond the Euphrates
will be turned loose to help our cause. Now if you are going to attack
Russia, do it quickly, because you have more troubles coming your way
and very soon!"

The room shook as Satan departed, leaving behind a great stench
that infiltrated Simon's nostrils. "What trouble?" Simon asked aloud in a
very worried voice. "And who are Apollyon and his army?"

"Apollyon is one of my father's head angels. He has been locked away
in the Abyss for eons, but soon he will be released with an entire army of
angels," Carlo smiled.

"That's a good thing, right?" Simon asked uncertainly. "What troubles
are coming next?"

"My father will tell us when it is time for us to know. Now go! You have a lot to accomplish and quickly." Carlo walked out of the room leaving Simon standing alone.

He doesn't know much more than I do, Simon thought. *Okay, I need to get organized. I will call in my generals, renovate and move into my new castle, assign my Special Forces to find these horrid Christians, and then make plans to gain control over the United States military and all their weapons. Then I will go find Peter Bastoni and the rest of those nasty scientists myself. But first I think I will nuke the pants off Russia.* At this last thought Simon smiled and shook off the fear and confusion he felt by the weight of so many new responsibilities.

*****

Tommy walked a few steps ahead of Sara. The wind had been blowing hard for the last two hours, and he felt nearly frozen to death. He was beginning to believe that the huge pack he was carrying was a poor choice on his part. Finally he lost his step and stumbled to the ground headfirst. Sara dropped her pack and ran to where Tommy lay. She helped to remove his pack and rolled him onto his side. The bridge of Tommy's nose was cut and bleeding.

"Are you okay? You're bleeding!" Sara cried.

Tommy said nothing. About that time it began to snow—not just the usual small flakes to start with, but huge gray flakes. Within a minute it was nearly impossible to see more than five feet from where Tommy lay.

"Dear God!" said Sara. "What now?"

Tommy reached up to Sara's cheek. "We will be okay. We just need to get out of this cold and rethink our plan a little."

Sara smiled weakly through her tears and helped Tommy to his feet. "Let's see if we can get back to the train station where we got off when we came here. Maybe we can find an empty car to hide in."

The two staggered blindly though the snow and wind trying desperately to hold each other up. If they separated in this weather, they would never find each other again, and they would surely freeze to death in no time.

Finally Tommy led Sara out of the dense forest and into a clear-cut area. Tommy did not know he had done this because the snow was so blinding. Another step forward and Tommy and Sara both nearly tripped over something underfoot.

"What is that?" Sara inquired.

Tommy bent his sore and tired back and reached out to touch the obstacle on the ground. His frozen hand quickly understood the shape beneath. "It is a track—a train track!" said Tommy with enthusiasm.

"Let's follow along. It has to lead to shelter somewhere somehow," Tommy said hopefully.

Sara knew they would not last much longer, so she began to pray to God to help them and to deliver them from this horribly cold place. Ten minutes down the track Sara began to wobble and to stumble. "I can't go—" Sara cried out as she fell onto the snow-covered tracks. Tommy sat down next to her. He didn't have the strength to lift her up. All he could do was to hold her soft, yet frozen little hand.

"I am sorry. This is all my fault," said Tommy.

Before Sara could respond, she and Tommy both heard a familiar voice from behind. "Nobody is to blame for this." The voice was scratchy and high pitched, but what a pleasant sound it was to Sara and Tommy.

"That's right!" said a deeper yet just as recognizable voice. "The weather is the result of a massive asteroid that hit the United States a few days ago."

Tommy turned to see Martha and Harry standing beside the track holding hands as if they were two love-struck children—the oldest looking, love-struck children they had ever seen for sure. Martha and Harry both wore heavy parkas with hoods and large leather gloves. "Hello, Tommy. Hello, Sara. God has been kind enough to let us come back just for a moment to help and encourage you."

Harry stepped forward and reached down to Sara and helped her to her feet. His strength was enormous and all the more peculiar considering that he looked like a 100-year-old man which, of course, he was and then some.

"Follow us," said Martha enthusiastically.

Her pace was nearly too much for Sara and Tommy, but finally both old people stopped and pointed to the north. "There," said Harry, "do you see that amber light?"

Tommy could barely make out a faint, golden glow some 75 to 100 yards away. "Yes, I see it."

"That's the next train leaving, and it is going to Switzerland. That's as good a place to start as any," Martha smiled.

Harry took his coat off and handed it to Tommy. Martha did the same for Sara. Additionally they both handed over their huge, tan leather gloves. "Follow the light. We will be back to help you when we can," said Martha as she and Harry turned and walked out into the deep snow and out of sight.

Ten minutes later Tommy had lifted Sara into a boxcar full of wooden pallets and bales of straw. They sat back regaining their strength as the train began its slow climb over the Italian Alps and into Switzerland. Sara took a look at Tommy's face and smiled. Next she began to dig around in her pack until she came out with a little first aid kit she had taken from the cottage. Sara knelt over Tommy and patched up his wounded nose. "If you are lucky, you won't get any black eyes from this," Sara spoke gently. After bandaging Tommy's nose, she leaned in and kissed him lovingly on the lips. She could tell Tommy was depressed and embarrassed by his inability to protect and lead her. Though his intentions were good, he simply had no experience in any of this. He needed to get stronger and become wiser.

"I nearly got us killed today," said Tommy angrily.

"It is not your fault. Who can control the weather?" said Sara reassuringly.

"No! I have to be more careful. We are going to encounter many awful things like this every day from here on, and there are many evil people out there who will hurt or kill us if they catch us, not to mention Simon Koch. We have to learn how to eat off the land and hide out when necessary. We need to learn to tell the good from the bad. I don't know how long things will be this way, but—"

Sara interrupted. "Three and a half years."

Sara knew that Tommy was not too terribly versed in the Bible and had never attended a church as a child, so he did not know the greater details of John's Revelation. "After the people disappeared in the Rapture, we entered what the Bible calls the Seven Years of Tribulation, and it has been three and a half years since then. So while we were in the cottage, it is likely that Carlo Ventini desecrated the rebuilt temple in Jerusalem. From this time on, God's wrath will fall on the earth.

So you see, my sweet husband, that none of this is your fault. It wasn't until the Rapture that I finally gave my heart to Jesus, just like you and probably millions of others did. Now there are many who are lost, and they need our help before it is too late."

"What will happen in three and a half years?" Tommy asked.

"It will be a tremendous and glorious day when Christ returns and defeats Satan, Carlo, and Simon. If we live to see it, we will enter into 1,000 years of peace. We will live our lives in the actual presence of Jesus." Both Sara and Tommy beamed at this thought. "Keep this goal in your mind every day, Tommy, and if God is willing, we will be married into the millennium, and if God is not willing, He will take us to Heaven to be with Him. Either way we cannot lose."

Sara's words encouraged Tommy to the point that he actually smiled. "I am hungry," laughed Tommy.

"Me too! In fact, you may think I'm crazy, but I could swear I smell corned beef."

"So do I!"

"I wonder," said Tommy aloud as he reached into the deep pocket of his parka. His fingertips felt paper. Quickly he pulled out a large package wrapped in dark brown paper. Tommy opened the package revealing a deep pile of red corned beef between two large pieces of Jewish rye bread. Sara reached into her own pocket to see if she, too, had a sandwich, which she did. In the other pocket Sara and Tommy found two small glass containers of orange juice.

"Thank you, Martha and Harry," said Tommy with a mouthful of sandwich. The corned beef was slightly salty and delightful as he swallowed each bite.

"How long do you think it will take to get to Switzerland?" Sara inquired between bites of her own sandwich.

"I think it will take about four hours, but if we want to ride the train into Zurich—provided it will go that far—then we have another four hours further. So maybe we can hold out here for a total of eight hours."

Sara smiled. "Okay, then we have time to sleep. I will make us a bed out of some of that straw." Sara pointed to a mount of broken bales of straw at the far end of the boxcar.

Tommy swallowed hard. "Is this our honeymoon?"

Sara set her sandwich down and kissed Tommy softly. "It is if you want it to be," she blushed.

******

Connor Crowley drove down to the waterfront and parked his car. "We will be out of gas in a few minutes, and I cannot buy anymore."

Chris stared at Connor. "You did not take the ID tag?"

"No, something about it seemed wrong to me. Besides, I didn't need it living on the farm. Why didn't you take it?"

Chris looked at the 40-year-old man. He was amazed at how childlike Connor was in many ways. Chris began to feel like Connor was kind of a big brother to him. "These ID tags come from Carlo Ventini, and he is the Antichrist. If you take one of his ID tags, you will not be able to go to Heaven. You will be condemned to Hell forever."

Connor studied Chris very intently. "How do you know this? Did that angel tell you?"

"No, my mother and father read about it in the Bible, and they understood what Carlo was really doing. Later Simon Koch started printing articles asking people to help by turning those in who had not taken the ID tags. He called them traitors. You see, they are forcing this mark on everyone. It is a way to identify those who belong to Satan."

"Well, we had better tell people about this before it is too late," said Connor with an irritated look on his face. For as long as he could remember he hated bullies and the way they made weaker people do things against their will. How evil and cruel they were. He now had no tolerance for this behavior at all.

Connor and Chris walked down towards the beach. The water looked ominous. There was already a black and gray covering across the surface of the sea. Even the froth was gray. Both men stood there as the wind cut through them like a knife. "How will we get started, and where should we go?" Chris asked out loud.

Connor put his arm over Chris' shoulder and walked him towards the car. "Let's drive until we run out of gas. Maybe God will lead us to someone who can help."

Chapter 3: Sickness
in the Camp

Day 1320, March: Calvin stood just outside the mine entrance right next to the old sign that read: *Colton Mine—No Trespassing.* "Tomorrow," said Calvin before his crowd of Christian soldiers, "we will leave this place in groups of three. Time is short, and if our small groups are going to make a difference, we will have to start right now. Every moment we wait is another moment a person can be deceived by Satan and lost forever!"

The plans had been carefully laid out. Every group would take a sector, one group of three people per state. This seemed so inconsequential in the grand scheme of things. Each state was so big and in many cases so far away that it would be nearly impossible to get there. But after numerous debates on the value of staying together, they finally decided that every voice would be necessary and that people in each state needed to hear the truth from a believer. "The Word will spread, and our chances of getting caught are reduced if we break up. At least this way some of us may escape the Antichrist long enough to get the message out," said Calvin.

Supplies were given out based on the distance that a group would have to travel, but expenses would be a real problem. There would be no way to pay for anything. This was going to require a great deal of creativity and good fortune on the part of each disciple.

Getting to the East Coast and across the Pacific to Hawaii, let alone into Alaska, was to be a huge feat, but Calvin's group had placed their faith completely in God, and if it was His Will, then they would reach their respective goals.

Calvin allowed groups to be self-forming until he got down to the few that had no preferences. At this point he made the decisions for them. Two days earlier each group had drawn from a hat to determine which state they would shoot for. The understanding was the same for each person. All were to witness along the way toward their goal, and if the Lord allowed each to make it all the way, they would share the truth of God and the deception of Carlo Ventini with the people of the state that they were assigned. Cory drew a state for his partners, Calvin Fraser and Leasa Moore. Ironically he drew Alaska. This was the state that Calvin had lived in when he was serving in the Air Force and where he was when Mount Denali erupted, killing his partner and eventually landing him in Leavenworth for years on the charge of involuntary manslaughter.

As Calvin stood at the mine entrance, he thought through his plan one more time. *We will work our way through California and Oregon into Washington. Then somehow we need to get through Canada and the Yukon until we make it to Alaska. Why, God?* Calvin wondered. *Why back to Alaska?* It was going to be a 4,000-mile trek, and it was going to be cold and very dangerous. Calvin doubted that he and his faithful team would ever make it all the way to Alaska, but they had to try.

The next morning Leasa woke to an agonizing and choking cough. She found it hard to breathe and terribly painful to swallow. She was not alone. Within an hour every member of the 150 people in the mine were coughing terribly. Cory ran from person to person trying to administer water and provide comfort wherever possible. It was useless. The whole group was suffering horribly, and soon they would begin to die.

"Cory," Leasa whispered. Her eyes were nearly swollen shut from so much painful coughing. Cory noticed a small spot of blood on Leasa's blouse as he came closer. He lifted her head and stroked her curly, black hair. She may have been a prostitute and a drug addict in the past, but that was not how Cory ever saw her. To him she was a young, beautiful black woman with the kindest, gentlest spirit he had ever known.

"I think I am dying," Leasa moaned.

Cory turned his own head to bark out a painful cough of his own. *I think we are all dying,* he thought. "You will be okay. God will help us," Cory smiled weakly. He was so concerned for Leasa. Of all the people in the mine, she seemed for some reason to look the worst. Maybe her previous lifestyle had worn down her body's ability to resist even a little bit.

"Are you sure?" Leasa whispered as she closed her swollen eyes, too weak to even hold them open.

Calvin approached Cory. He was weak and unsteady as he walked by. "We are not going to make it without the antidote. This must be the plague that has been killing everyone. I don't know how it managed to take two months to get here. I guess it is airborne."

Cory nodded without looking up to Calvin. He gently placed Leasa's burning head back down on her blanket. "I will go get help."

"Where will you go? Who will help us?" Calvin inquired.

Cory felt disappointment over the last statement. Calvin was his leader, but all of a sudden it seemed he lacked the faith necessary to stand against this plague. "God will help us," said Cory boldly as he stood and towered a solid foot above Calvin.

"Yes, you are right," said Calvin as he ducked his head in shame for doubting the greatness of God.

"I will be back as soon as I can. Keep a close eye on her," said Cory as he looked down to Leasa with a heart full of love and concern for this precious girl.

******

The walk from Las Vegas to the mine had taken the group over nine hours—not bad for a 30-mile walk—but for Cory this was going to be an unacceptable amount of time. He began to jog through the desert, and what a difficult task this was! The desert floor looked like a minefield with small to large holes everywhere including areas that were burned black where the intense heat of the tektites had bored their way into the ground, in some cases more than 10 feet deep. If Cory fell in one of those holes, he would surely break a leg or maybe even his neck. In any case, he would die alone, unable to climb out. But the holes in the desert floor were only a portion of Cory's problems. The tightness in his chest was excruciating, and the temperature in the desert had dropped off so much that it now approached the low teens. This only zapped more strength out of the poor man's body, but Cory was determined, and with a silent prayer he asked God to strengthen his sick body and help him find the antidote before it was too late.

Cory entered the city of Las Vegas just after 10:30 a.m., a little over four hours after he had left the mine. All the while the plague inside his body ate at his lungs with ferocious tenacity.

He had formed a plan while on the run. The only logical place to find an antidote was at the local hospital. Not every hospital would have the medicine, thanks to Simon who had tried to limit its availability to only those deadly infested regions of the world. This, of course, allowed him to come into the community as if he were their savior with antidote in hand.

From the direction Cory entered into town, the closest medical facility would be Mountain View Hospital. He had never been to this facility, so he moved cautiously as he entered through the emergency room's automated doors. A registration clerk at the front desk looked up at Cory. The woman was all of 20 years old, sitting up prim and proper. "Can I help you, Sir?" the young lady inquired as if she were completely bored to death with her job. "Are you here to see a patient?"

Cory started to cough uncontrollably before he could answer the young lady's question. The woman stood and backed up quickly, "Mister, are you sick?"

"Do you have the antidote here?" Cory asked in a whisper.

The receptionist looked into Cory's red eyes and began to scream out, "He's got it! He's got the plague! Oh, my God, now I am going to get it and die!"

People began to run down the halls away from Cory while holding their hands over their mouths. One man dressed in army green scrubs stood in the middle of the emergency room floor. "Mister, we don't have any antidote here at all. Maybe another hospital—I don't know—but you need to leave here before we all get sick."

Cory turned to leave. "Good luck! I hope you find help," said the doctor as Cory passed through the sliding doors.

Time was running short. Cory could feel his chest filling with fluid. He speculated that if he felt this bad, as big as he was, then Leasa was really going to be in big trouble by now. There was another hospital that Cory knew about—Sunrise Hospital—and it was a really big place, so maybe they would have some medicine for Cory and his friends.

******

Back at the Colton Mine things did not look or sound good for Calvin's group of followers. He wandered from person to person trying to comfort them. He prayed with them. He gave them cool water to drink, and he encouraged them by saying that Cory was probably on his way back by now. He wasn't even sure Cory had made it to Las Vegas yet or if he ever would, but the people needed to hear something positive.

Calvin's lungs were filling with fluid, too, and soon he became too weak to attend to the others. He staggered over to where Leasa lay unconscious. Calvin knelt down next to her and began to cry out to the Lord. "Please, God, You are the only one who can help us. Lord, don't let us die this way. We have so much we need to do for You."

Calvin lay down next to Leasa and closed his eyes. His breathing became terribly labored as he drifted into unconsciousness.

******

Thirty minutes later Cory found himself walking through the parking lot of the Sunrise Hospital. He was nearly delirious from exhaustion and lack of oxygen as the plague destroyed his lung capacity a little more as each moment passed. Quickly a dark blue Jeep rounded the corner into the parking lot, nearly hitting Cory as he stumbled into the vehicle's path. The man parked the car in a slot reserved for doctors and sat staring at Cory as he stumbled forward, determined to find the cure. Cory was across the parking lot and up to the sidewalk before the driver of the Jeep caught up to him.

"Hey, Mister, are you all right?"

Cory stopped and turned on the man. His massive frame and bright red eyes frightened the young doctor. "I need the antidote," Cory mumbled.

"Who are you? Where did you come from?" the young man inquired.

"Cory Parker and I came from out there." Cory pointed towards the northern desert.

"How long have you been sick?"

Cory's eyes bore down on the man. "Are you a doctor? Can you help us?"

"Yes, I am a doctor, and what do you mean *us*? Are there others?"

"In the mine," Cory whispered.

The young man did not understand completely, but he knew Cory needed immediate help or he would soon die. He also knew he was exposed and would catch the virus soon as well. "I received a shipment of the antidote last night. It is heavily guarded and only given out to people recommended by hospital management." The young doctor obviously had bad feelings about this hospital policy, but there was nothing he could do about it.

"How many people have the virus?" the doctor asked as he led Cory in through the hospital's side door.

"What is your name?" Cory asked as he coughed horribly.

"Jerry Little."

"There are 150 people counting myself. They are all hidden in the Colton Mine about 30 miles north of here."

Jerry smiled as he remembered playing around that mine as a teenager. He could still remember how angry his father had been at him when he found out that Jerry had snuck into the mine to explore. Jerry's dad was a physician, as well, and a very practical man. He saw most of Jerry's hobbies and recreation as dangerous and unfruitful.

Cory knew it was unwise to tell this man about his hideout, but if he were to die soon, how else would anyone know where to go to help Leasa and the rest of the group?

"Mr. Parker, why are you and the others hiding in that old mine?"

Jerry led Cory into a small office down a narrow hall. "Try to keep your coughing down or someone will hear you."

Cory nodded. "We are hiding out because—" Cory paused and looked deep into the face of the young, redheaded doctor who was probably no more than 25 or 26 years old. Jerry felt nervous as Cory stared him down. Suddenly he was frighteningly aware that Cory was a monster of a man and, by the look in his swollen eyes, he was a man capable of doing whatever was necessary to protect the people he cared about. Jerry swallowed hard and considered running from the room. Cory grasped Jerry's bony wrist tightly. Jerry looked at Cory and held his breath. "Do you have an ID tag inside of you?" Cory asked.

Jerry almost laughed. "No! I mean, not yet. I mean—why?"

Dr. Little did not tell Cory that this was going to be his last week on the job because he did not take the ID tag as requested by the hospital staff. In fact, as of January 1 it was a law that every person worldwide had to have the insertion completed. The only reason Jerry had not been dismissed right away or turned in to the authorities was because of his father's relationships with many of the hospital staff members. Additionally doctors were so scarce now that the hospital could hardly afford to lose Jerry, even if he was only a second year resident.

"Why do you ask?" Jerry inquired.

Cory squeezed a little tighter on Jerry's wrist until the hand began to turn blue.

"No! I don't have an ID tag, and I don't want one, but what choice do I have?"

Cory released the pressure off Jerry's wrist, but the pain from the powerful grip lingered. "We are in the mine because we are Christians. God sent us out there, and He is sending us across the United States, but first we need some medicine."

Jerry nodded and smiled at Cory. "Well, Mister, I am not a Christian. I was never raised that way, but I don't like the crap I have seen Carlo Ventini and Simon Koch doing either, so what can I do to help you?"

"We need to get to the medicine. Where is it?"

"I can take you to it, but there will be a guard watching over it."

"Lead the way," Cory said as he coughed loudly.

Jerry held his finger over his mouth reminding Cory to control the cough. This was a little like asking a fire not to smoke.

*****

Jerry and Cory stood silently next to a few other hospital employees as the elevator climbed to the fourth floor. All the while Cory was in anguish as he tried to hold his cough in. The nurses made way as Cory and Jerry stepped off. Cory could feel the stares on his back as the elevator closed once again. Zigzagging their way down the long hall, Jerry finally stopped outside a set of locked glass doors with heavy dark curtains. The glass was labeled *Quarantine Area.*

"This is where we bring people with contagious diseases. The medicine we need is in the far room on the right." Jerry pointed through the edge of the glass and down the hall. "There will be one guard sitting just inside the door."

Cory looked around the room and then tried to open the glass door. "It will not open without someone from inside pushing the release button. The only other way in there is a key that goes right here. It is used in case of fire. We have drills once in a while so I've seen it used," said Jerry as he pointed to a key lock on the near wall.

Cory began to scan the room from where he stood. The burning in his chest was nearly unbearable. He had to do something right now or he and his friends would all die and very soon. Cory's eyes spotted a red-handled fire alarm. He thought it over quickly.

"Can you get in by picking up that phone and calling the desk?"

Jerry looked at the phone on the wall. "Yes, that's how I always go in."

"Okay, then you call and go in. I'll wait about 30 seconds and then I will pull this alarm. Hide behind something, and when everyone clears out of the room and the doors shut, you can open them and let me in."

"Where will you be when everyone runs out of the room?" Jerry asked.

Good point, Cory thought. "What is in that room?" Cory inquired as he pointed to a dark brown door 20 feet back down the hall.

"That's a janitor's closet, but it is locked."

Cory took five large steps and was soon standing in front of the closet. He turned the large metal handle and, in fact, the door was locked tightly. Cory looked both ways briefly and then with one massive blow of his shoulder he rammed the door and it swung open as the latch shattered. Cory stepped in and hid himself. This was a lucky thing for him because the noise did get a response from one of the nurses in the quarantine room. An older lady stuck her face up to the window in time to see Jerry walking towards the glass doors. The lady opened the door for Jerry and asked what the loud noise was. "Oh, somebody down the hall rammed a bed into the wall while they were moving it. Clumsy," said Jerry as he shook his head. The glass doors and curtains closed behind him.

"Hey, Jerry," said one of the younger nurses. "What are you doing here?"

"Hiding from my dad."

Everyone in the room laughed at this joke. They all knew Jerry well enough to know he and his father often sat on opposite sides of the fence.

Jerry walked towards the restroom, and the instant he reached the door a red light started flashing overhead and a siren began to blare out. Standard protocol for this hospital was to prep and move the patients to a safer place if time permitted, but in the quarantine area this protocol did not apply. Every nurse in the room ran out of the glass doors and down the hall to the stairwell just like they had been trained. Jerry poked his head out to see the four women running down the hall. Everyone in the hospital was a bit nervous that another asteroid would hit America and that this time maybe it would be in their backyard.

Jerry saw the guard poke his head out. He had hoped the man would leave with the nurses, but now it was too late because Cory was walking directly towards the guard, and the look on his face said this guard was in trouble. Jerry quickly looked around until he found a rechargeable battery pack. Reaching out, he grabbed the heavy but small object with both hands.

"What are you doing here, Mister?" the startled man asked as he struggled to pull out his revolver.

Cory was about to tear the guard's head off and get himself shot in the attempt when suddenly Jerry stood behind the guard and lowered a battery pack firmly on the back of the man's skull. The guard crashed to the ground face first, dropping his gun as he fell.

"Sorry," said Jerry as he lowered the battery pack, but he knew this was the best thing for the guard. Cory would have killed him, and in turn he would have shot Cory.

Both men entered the dimly lit room. "Where is the antidote?" Cory asked in a panic as he stumbled back against the frame of the door.

Jerry grabbed Cory's huge arm and led him over to a chair. "Sit down and I'll give you a shot, and then we can take the rest of this—"

"We need to go now!" said Cory.

"We're not going anywhere until I give you a shot. Now sit down!" Jerry yelled. He was really starting to feel the stress of this entire situation. Dr. Little rolled up Cory's sleeve and injected a large amount of the pink fluid into his vein. Next he gave himself a shot. "I will get it next, so this should prevent that."

Cory looked at the plastic box of small, pink vials of medicine.

"How many people will this cure?"

"About 500 maybe."

Cory stood to grab the medicine, but he was still very weak. "It will be hours before the virus in your body is completely dead and until then you will be sick and weak."

Jerry looked into Cory's concerned eyes. He understood this man had others that he loved and was very worried about. Jerry grabbed a large box of syringes and the plastic container of antidote. Then he paused and pulled one small bottle out and sat it on the table. Next he filled a syringe and walked over to the unconscious guard and injected the medicine in his arm. "Okay, let's go!" said Jerry as he helped Cory out of the chair.

Cory looked back to the single bottle of antidote Jerry had left behind for the nursing staff. Hopefully they would understand and inoculate themselves against the virus that was now floating around in the room.

Jerry and Cory were lucky enough to avoid seeing another person as they exited the hospital. All of the employees had gathered on the other side of the building for a roll call and to wait for the fire department to issue the all clear. Jerry helped Cory into the passenger seat of his Jeep and handed him the antidote to hold onto. "Okay, Colton Mine here we come," said Jerry as he backed his vehicle out of the parking lot.

The sky was a sinister black with streaks of orange. There was absolutely no wind so the gray ash just stood suspended in mid-air all around. As Jerry drove off, the ash that had accumulated on his hood blew across the windshield, forcing him to turn on his wipers. A fire truck sped by Cory and Jerry as they drove out of the parking lot heading north towards the mine. Cory prayed that he would not be too late to save Leasa, Calvin, and the others.

******

Chris Evans and Connor Crowley had run out of gas just as they suspected they would. Since then they had wandered up and down the streets of Brisbane not knowing what to do or where to go. They slept in alleyways and lived off the food that Christopher had packed and whatever else they could find.

They were both downhearted, afraid that they had misread God's intentions. Maybe they had done something wrong. They really didn't know for sure. All they did know was that much time had gone by and they had not seen a single person witnessing to others about Jesus.

It was late at night around 11:00 p.m. when Connor was stirred from his sleep by the sounds of cheering. As he sat forward in his sleeping bag, he turned his ear to listen more carefully. The roar of the crowd was coming closer. *What was it?* he wondered.

Connor woke Chris from a dead sleep. He had been so exhausted after walking the streets 16 hours every day. "What is it?" Chris asked.

"I don't know, but it's coming this way!" said Connor.

The two of them stuffed their supplies and sleeping bags into a corner of the alley and walked out onto the street just in time to see a crowd of at least 50 people parading down the street. In the front there were eight men pulling a trailer. In the middle of the trailer stood a wooden cross that was at least seven feet tall, and nailed directly onto the cross was a young man of maybe 20 years of age. His clothing had been completely stripped from his body. He had obviously been beaten numerous times. The nails in his hands dripped with blood, but his feet were not nailed to the cross at all. Instead they were left hanging free. The man was supported exclusively by the nails in his hands and by a single piece of rope tied around his chest and over the cross bar. He was not heavy, but just the same it wouldn't be long before the nails ripped completely through his hands. It was too much weight for such a weak structure to support for any real length of time.

The crowd was cheering, singing, and mocking the man as they pushed the trailer further down the street. Chris stepped forward. He was ready to go to the aid of this poor man despite the fact that he was outnumbered 50 to 1. "No, Chris! We cannot help him—at least not yet. Let's follow along and see where they take him."

The two men stepped into the crowd and walked along as the procession headed toward the very beach that they had stopped at months ago when they first came to town. The air around smelled bad, and it was terribly cold. The scene felt like something from the age of Spanish Inquisition, or at least that was how Connor imagined it might have been.

It would have been a dark, cold night with the putrid smell of death all around as masses of ignorant people came along and performed monstrous cruelties to the Jewish people from their own community. Now over 500 years later things had not changed one bit. Anger welled up in Connor's heart as he walked along.

The procession stopped after pulling the trailer about 10 feet down the sandy path. "Okay, start gathering all the wood and paper you can find. It's time to have a barbecue," said one man. The crowd cheered and laughed as they ran off in every direction to find anything that would burn.

Connor and Chris stood back in horror. "What are we going to do? They are going to burn this man to death," said Chris with a heart full of fear for the poor man.

Connor looked up to the man on the cross. His body was so terribly bruised and bloody, yet the man was alert and looking around. Finally he spotted Chris and Connor and stared into their eyes. Both men began to weep as they observed the tears flowing down the beaten man's face. The man on the cross shook his head as if to say, *Do not weep for me.* Connor looked deeply into the young man's dark eyes. He was obviously not from Australia. In fact, he appeared to be from the Middle East. Connor's eyes told the man how sorry he felt for him. He nodded back at Connor just as the crowd returned with armloads of wood and paper.

Chris began to pray for God to help. *Why can't You at least send an angel or something? They are going to burn him to death. Please, Lord, help us,* Christopher pleaded silently.

******

Tommy and Sara walked along the tracks quietly as they held hands. The only sounds that could be heard were the crunching sounds their feet made as they walked across the frozen ground. For months now they had wandered through the small towns outside of Zurich. They had met people along the way, and some were kind enough to share food with them. Some even offered a place to sleep for the night, but Sara reminded Tommy of Philip's warning against spending the night in any town where they had spent the day, so Tommy graciously declined the offers.

It had quit snowing weeks earlier, but the ground was piled with the black snow. It was a very odd sight to say the least. The ash from the asteroid had so infiltrated the air around the world that it even clung to the ice crystals as they formed into snow. The dust didn't just cling to the wet snow but was actually embedded into the structure itself, giving the snow a very odd, acrylic, black finish.

Sara and Tommy were lucky enough that first day to catch a train that went all the way to Zurich, but unfortunately the snowstorm had been so bad that it caused the train to stop 320 miles south of the city. For the better part of two months Sara and Tommy trudged along in the frigid weather determined to get to Zurich. Neither of them had much of an idea as to what would happen when they got there, but they felt compelled to move in that direction just the same. Still the going was slow. All of their food supplies were gone, so daily they had to find enough to live on.

"I am hungry," Sara grumbled. The steam of her warm breath rolled out of her mouth as she spoke.

"Me too!" said Tommy as he tried to remember the last time they had eaten a real meal. It was the evening before. They had come into a lovely little town next to a small frozen lake some 40 miles south of Zurich. At first Tommy hadn't even noticed the lake with all the black snow covering the surface. To him it was just a little slice of valley. As they approached, however, they caught sight of an elderly man with a gas operated hand-held augur. He was drilling his way through the ice down to the freezing water below.

Tommy watched the man cautiously as he put the augur aside and picked up a small fishing pole. Within a minute the man lifted a large fish out of the hole in the ice. From the distance it looked like a trout, but he couldn't really tell from that far away.

Sara and Tommy made the decision to talk to the man. Each day as they walked along, they met people, but sometimes they decided it would be best not to talk to the stranger and draw unnecessary attention. Other times they felt compelled to speak. This was the process they used as they traveled north. It was also the way they continued to find food and shelter. So far they had not encountered a single bad person. In fact, every person they met to date had been a Christian. Each of them expressed concerns about Carlo and Simon, and all were anxiously awaiting the return of Christ. This would not always be the case, Tommy knew, but while it lasted, he was grateful.

Broaching the subject of Jesus was scary at first, but quickly Tommy figured out a trick that would help him out. He figured that a real Christian would never under any circumstance profess Carlo to be god, and all he had to do was ask the question in such a way that he did not look like a follower of Carlo and at the same time he did not sound like a Christian. *Middle ground,* he told himself, until he was sure it was safe. He understood the flaw in his logic was that there would be no value in witnessing to Christians, so sooner or later he would not be able to stand on this imaginary middle ground. Very soon he would have to stand on Jesus and the truth even at the expense of incurring the anger and wrath of others.

Sara held Tommy's hand as they walked carefully down a small slope towards the lake. The toughest part about meeting strangers in Switzerland was figuring out what language to speak. Many of the Swiss spoke English along with Italian, French, and German. Unfortunately for Tommy, he only spoke English and a little Spanish. However, Sara spoke French quite well.

The old man stared at Tommy and Sara as they walked towards him. The look on his face showed his fear and apprehension. He, like so many others in the world, did not trust strangers. One never knew when someone would drop by and kill just for food or simply come along and leave the plague behind. This was a common theme among all people.

The man who had been kneeling over the small hole in the lake stood and turned towards Tommy. He was an intelligent, handsome man probably in his early sixties. "Was ist los?" the man inquired.

"Do you speak English?" Tommy asked gently.

The man shook his head indicating he did not speak English, at least not well enough to converse in.

"Parlez vous francais?" asked Sara.

"Oui," said the old man.

Sara smiled as she explained that she and Tommy were American tourists who had come over on vacation but had been stranded during the snowstorm. She further explained that they were on their way to Zurich to meet some friends. The man listened carefully. He was judging every word Sara said to determine if she and Tommy were safe or not. Finally he spoke up, but this time it was in English.

"Your French is very good."

"I thought you didn't speak English," said Tommy suspiciously.

"Yes, well, I lied. Kind of the same way she lied about being a tourist," said the old man as he pointed towards Sara and winked.

"Are you two hungry?" the man asked as he lifted his stringer of fish. There were two nice ones, and they were trout after all.

"Yes," said Sara before Tommy could open his mouth.

"Come in then and we'll see what you are all about." The old man turned and walked carefully down an old, but well used trail that led directly back to a small, brown house nearly covered in black snow.

The man didn't speak a word as he prepared the trout for the skillet. Sara and Tommy sat side by side on the comfortable, old sofa. A fire blazed in the fireplace, lighting the room while giving off wonderful warmth that the two travelers enjoyed immensely. This cottage was the kind of place people spent a lot of money to rent for a winter vacation.

Finally the senior man spoke. His English was nearly perfect—too perfect for a native—and Sara knew this fact. "So why are you here?" the man inquired.

"What is your name?" Tommy asked. The conversation had not started off the way he had expected. He was afraid that he had already missed his opportunity to determine if this man was a Christian or one of Carlo's followers. There was no middle ground with this person.

"My name is Hans Mueller. But everyone calls me Mueller. What are your names?"

Tommy thought hard on the question. He was beginning to feel himself losing control of he whole conversation. *Should I lie?* he wondered. "My name is Tommy,and this is Sara."

Mueller nodded. "Dr. Sara Allen and Tommy Glover."

Sara and Tommy looked into Mueller's face as great concern filled their eyes. "How do you know that?" Tommy asked. He grabbed Sara's hand and was once again ready to take flight if necessary.

Mueller pointed to a newspaper on the table. Like all newspapers around the world, this paper was full of information given to Simon's media puppets—information that could be published or broadcast around the world upon his request. "The paper states you are evil scientists who are partially accountable for the plague and the underground scientist movement, as well as responsible for tampering with Carlo Ventini's ID tags."

Sara and Tommy stood to leave when the man spoke more sternly. "Stop. We haven't eaten our fish yet. Besides, I'd like to talk to you about Chimborazo."

Tommy froze in his tracks. *How does he know about Mount Chimborazo?* he wondered.

What is Chimborazo?" a confused Sara asked.

"It was a huge mountain in Ecuador," said Tommy without taking his eyes off Mueller.

"What do you mean *was* a mountain?" Sara inquired.

"It exploded over four years ago. What do you want?" Tommy asked as he looked into the older man's eyes.

"I want to help if I can," said Mueller. "See, I am a retired physicist myself, and I take it personally when that weasel, Simon Koch, accuses us scientists of being evil."

Sara told herself that she knew this man was not a typical Swiss native. *I'll bet he studied in the U.S.A. as well,* she thought.

"I pulled your name up on the Internet the day I got this paper, and I read all about your work in Ecuador. You helped to save thousands of people," Mueller said. "Once I read that, I knew the story in the paper had to be false."

Sara looked at Tommy and back to Mueller. The intense look on both men's faces told Sara that they were searching each other for truth. Neither man was naturally very trusting, if at all. This was going to be a matter of faith.

"We found out how the ID tags work," Tommy said cautiously, "and we fed this information to the world through our underground network. I don't know, but maybe we helped some people. It is possible that people avoided the ID tag after they read about the discovery."

Mueller smiled bright saying. "I am one of them. You saved my life. No! That's not true—you saved my eternity, if there is such a thing."

"Eternity is God's decision, not mine, but if I can help people see the deception and this gives them time to learn about Jesus, then maybe I have helped," said Tommy.

"So you are a Christian?" Sara asked.

"No," said Mueller. "I have not met God, but maybe it is time I do."

******

That was yesterday, and the full belly was nothing but a memory for Sara and Tommy. They had spent the night with Mueller and had an enjoyable evening of visiting with him. They shared their personal testimonies including their encounters with Martha, Harry, and Philip; the conversation Tommy had had with God many years ago when he and Tina, his sister, lived in the hotel in California; the science convention where Sara and Tommy first met Dr. Dedrick Bischof; and what had happened at the lab at UCLA. All of this finally led Mueller to the conclusion that he needed a personal relationship of his own with Christ.

Interestingly enough Tommy learned that Dr. Dedrick Bischof and Hans Mueller had attended UCLA and MIT together. It was a small world after all.

The morning before Tommy and Sara left Mueller had warned them that the paper had stated that Simon was offering a $1 million reward for each of them. "You will have to be very careful or someone will turn you in. I have heard rumors that Mr. Koch has a new Secret Police force, kind of a modern day S.S. right out of the pages of history. They will be looking for you and any other Christians they can find."

Tommy and Sara thanked Mueller for his kindness. The three of them prayed a little prayer to God that all three would be protected until Christ's return. "If you need help, contact me," said Mueller as he handed Tommy his phone number. "This hasn't worked all week. I guess it is because of the asteroid or maybe the destruction of the satellites or even the recent nuclear attack on Russia. I am not sure, but maybe if you need it, Lord willing, it will work."

******

Sara and Tommy continued to walk along hand in hand for the next few hours. They were hungry and cold. It was doubtful they would reach the outskirts of Zurich for another week. It was also unlikely that they would eat on this particular day. The piece of bread Mueller had given them to start their day was nothing but a fading memory now.

Stretched out before them was a wide-open valley between the huge mountains. The sounds of water could be heard from up ahead. Tommy knew they were soon going to cross over a river. Maybe this would be a good place to hide out for the night. Surely there would be a bridge ahead. Perhaps they could hide under the bridge away from the ugly black snow and chilly breeze. Besides, they both could use some water and rest.

"Are you ready to stop for the night?" Tommy asked.

"More than ready! But where do we stop?"

"Up there?" said Tommy as he pointed 50 yards ahead.

Sara looked at Tommy carefully. "Maybe you are delirious from lack of food," she smiled. "There is nothing up there but snow."

Tommy laughed. "Follow me, Wife, and see for yourself."

Tommy led Sara to the edge of the track and down a perilous little slope. Beneath the train track was a huge concrete wall, and below that there were four monstrous concrete pylons. It was the underside of a bridge, but from the top no one would have known it was there.

"How did you know this was a bridge?" Sara asked curiously.

"Special powers," Tommy laughed.

"Really!" said Sara. "Pray tell, what kind of special powers?"

"Big ears," grinned Tommy as he pointed to the stream below. "I heard the water, so I assumed there would be a bridge spanning it somehow."

Sara and Tommy broke through the icy waters of the stream and drank their fill. It was amazing how thirsty they were. They hadn't noticed it so much as they walked along in the cold weather, but once they stopped they both realized that they were dangerously dehydrated.

"We had better be more careful in the future to remember to stop for water along the way," said Tommy.

But Sara was not listening. She had found something in the water that was of greater interest. Sara turned towards Tommy and held up a large, gray shell.

"What is that?" Tommy inquired.

"Dinner!" smiled Sara.

As a small child she could still remember her father taking her on clam digs. She had learned to enjoy razor clams from the Pacific Ocean and even fresh water clams from some of the rivers and streams in California. "I wish we had some butter," she giggled.

Tommy and Sara knelt down and dug until they had five large clams apiece. "Thank you, Lord," said Tommy as he helped Sara to stand on the ice and move back to a drier place under the train tracks.

Immediately Tommy attempted to open one of his clams, but it was useless. The shell was locked tightly closed. "How are we ever going to eat these?" he asked out of frustration.

"Can we make a fire?" Sara asked. "I have a lighter, but what can we light?" she said as she looked around for something that would burn.

"I'll look down there for some branches. You look around here and see what you can find," said Tommy.

Five minutes later Tommy returned with a handful of dry pieces of tree branches. "These will work. Did you find anything?"

Sara smiled and held up a piece of cardboard. "I found this under there," she said as she pointed to where the bridge and the track came together. "I found this too." Sara held up an aluminum soda can.

"We can't burn that," said Tommy.

"I know that, silly. This is to cook the clams in!"

The clams tasted more like mud than clam, but they filled Tommy and Sara's stomachs, and more importantly they provided enough nutrition to keep them going for another day. The two weary travelers slept curled up together as the embers of their small fire slowly died out.

******

The line of people stretched for nearly a mile as they marched through the unusually cool, sandy desert. Above them the darkened sky had an amber glow sufficient enough to light their way. The crowd that wandered through the Judean desert looked like a scene from ancient history when Moses led the Israelites out of Egypt.

Only this time the people were not heading south to Mount Sinai. They were moving southeast to Ein Gedi, the lowest point on earth and some 400 meters below sea level. None, however, had any idea that was where they were headed.

The leader of this massive group of people was a tall, thin 22-year-old man named Elisha Kaufman, and at his side as usual was a beautiful, petite young girl, 20 years of age, Jasmine Hamar. Elisha had led these people out of Jerusalem at the same time Carlo Ventini was dedicating the new temple to himself by sacrificing Joseph Bastoni and Yvette Lewis. Elisha had barely gotten out of town as the incoming meteorites tore through the roof of the temple killing many inside including Pope Peter John.

Elisha had led the people for days until he reached Beersheba just north of the Negev. At this point, through inspiration from God, he broke his camp into more manageable groups, with one group leader for every 100 people excluding the groups that Ruth Jefferson and Peter Bastoni were leading. These groups were somewhat smaller than the rest.

Elisha formed a counsel of leaders that he met with daily to discuss the issues of the people. The whole scene was absurd to Elisha. All he wanted to do was take Jasmine, Peter, and Ruth out into the desert away from Simon and Carlo. He had no idea that he would somehow become a modern day Moses to the people of Israel, Jews and Muslims alike.

By the fourth day Elisha had led the people to the general location of the cave in which he and Jasmine had taken shelter during the terrible sandstorm. It was his hope that this group could occupy the cave, especially since there was a fresh water supply running through the middle of it. Unfortunately, however, Elisha could not find the opening to the cave. After the huge earthquake nearly four years earlier, the entrance had collapsed, and with the shifting sand, it appeared to be permanently buried.

Elisha met with his counsel to discuss the dilemma that he and the rest were in. "I can't find the cave. We've been out here for months, and we are running out of sources for water," said a discouraged Elisha.

Ruth Jefferson, the tall, black news reporter from Chicago, sat in the middle of the circle with Jasmine and 21 other men listening as the counsel tried to figure out how they would feed, shelter, and provide the all too necessary water rations for the 2,000 people camped all around them. Sitting next to Ruth was Dr. Peter Bastoni, the late Joseph Bastoni's older brother. He listened intently as Elisha tried to describe what the cave had looked like. Jasmine nodded in agreement as he described the size and general location of the cave.

"Okay, Elisha, I believe there was a cave, but what will that do for us today? We are going to need water and soon or we will die out here," said Ruth boldly. She was a confident woman of about 45 years of age who had been Miss Illinois as a younger woman. That was many years ago, but she was still very attractive and that had helped to open the doors for her journalism career. However, it was not Ruth's appearance that made her successful. She was a strong and brilliant woman. Ruth's only weakness was her need to test everything. She took nothing on faith. This had resulted in her walking away from a personal relationship with a God she could not see and was not fully convinced existed. Today, though, all Ruth had to rely on was faith. God would save her and the rest of this group or He wouldn't. In either case, she now knew for certain that she would soon be in Heaven with Jesus.

"Peter, how long can we survive without water?" Ruth inquired.

"Three or four days probably, but it depends on how active we are and on how hot it is," said Peter.

"Well, it is certainly not hot. Besides, I am sure God will give us water," said an irritated Jasmine. "He's given it to us every day for two months." She felt the need to come to Elisha's defense. "There was a cave here with a river running right through it, but if we can't find it, then we will just have to go somewhere else," said Jasmine as she folded her arms and looked towards Elisha.

******

It had been days since Elisha had given the orders to break camp. He had prayed for guidance from God, but none came, so Elisha made his own decision. *If we continue south, we will end up in the Negev,* he thought to himself, *and the Negev is nothing but the barest of deserts. If we go west, then we will end up in the Gaza Strip.* Elisha could not risk exposing all these people to the inhabitants of the Gaza. The only option he felt he had available was to head northeast towards Jordan.

After three days of marching, Elisha's group still had not stumbled across a single stream or functioning well. They had used up all of their water the first day after turning east. Elisha began to fear that he had made the wrong decision. It would not be long before the children among the group would die of dehydration and soon after that the elderly, and then he and the rest of the healthy adults would die. Sorrow filled Elisha's heart. He was too young for this burden.

Jasmine moved up next to Elisha and slipped her small hand into his and interlaced her fingers. "I've checked on the people," she said.

"How are they holding up?" a worrisome Elisha asked.

Jasmine detected the concern in Elisha's voice. She understood the burden on his shoulders. Neither of them had asked for this. They had been chosen many years ago, and since then they had gone through many terrible things side by side. Yet they remained faithful and obedient to God. "They are doing okay," said Jasmine. She knew this was not true, but Elisha needed the encouragement.

In fact, the 2,000 people were in dire straits and tempers were beginning to flair. There was a grumbling in the camp that Elisha was too young to lead people. "He is going to get us all killed," was the general statement heard throughout the camp.

As the evening approached and the little bit of amber light that had guided them disappeared, Elisha announced that it was time to stop for the night. The counsel members gathered around him to get their nightly instructions. Peter and Ruth stepped up next to Elisha to show their support while the other 19 men stood back with arms folded in a display of defiance. Jasmine saw this as an attack on Elisha and stepped up to chastise the men, but Elisha grabbed her arm gently and whispered that it was all right. "Let them vent."

Suddenly there was a rush of wind that blew among the small group.

A bright light began to glow in the center of the semicircle. "Be still and listen. I am the Lord, your God. Elisha has been chosen to lead you during this time of trouble. Do not make camp here tonight. You must continue east through the night."

All the men and women in the circle fell to the ground. Without looking up at the tawny glow, Elisha spoke, "God, we cannot go on without water. The children will die."

"None will die," said God gently. "These are My children, and I will meet their needs. Now leave this place and head for Ein Gedi next to the Dead Sea."

Instantly the air was calm again and the light was gone.

All the members of the counsel stood. Little Jasmine stepped forward towards the defiant men. "See, God has made Elisha your leader. Now you need to follow his decisions!"

The men all nodded compliantly as Jasmine stepped back over to Elisha and stood by his side. "Let's keep moving. Peter, can you look in on everyone and make sure that—"

"I'll take care of it, Elisha," Peter said and smiled.

Elisha headed back to the front of the line and began to walk with Jasmine by his side. "Why do you think God wants us to go to Ein Gedi?" Jasmine asked.

"I don't know for sure," said Elisha softly. Indeed Elisha had a vague memory of a story his grandfather had told him once about a place where there was a temple called the Chalcolithic Temple. This was an evil place where human sacrifices were made well before Christ walked the earth. It seemed that this was the same place that David and his men had hidden themselves away from Saul. And more excitingly, Elisha remembered, his grandfather had described fresh water springs pouring out of the rocks in the caves.

Jasmine gripped Elisha's hand once again. "What is all of this about? What are we doing?"

"I guess we are kind of like fugitives. We will have to hide from Simon and Carlo until Jesus comes back for us."

"How long will that be?" Jasmine asked.

"I don't know," said Elisha. "I guess it will be about three years from now."

"Can we really hide thousands of people for the next three years without getting caught? How will we survive?" Jasmine knew the answer even before she asked the question.

"God will have to do it all, that is for sure," said Elisha.

Jasmine and Elisha walked along silently through the nearly pitch-black night. There were no stars or moon to light their way, but thankfully there were enough flashlights in the camp to give at least enough light to keep them from wandering off into the wilderness.

Chapter 4: Then the Heavens Came Crashing Down

D ay 1321, March: Simon Koch sat in his leather chair behind his huge oak desk. He loved his new castle even though it needed extensive renovation to be livable. To one side of him standing at attention were four of his bodyguards. Standing next to Simon was a white haired man of nearly 60 years of age. His name was Oswald Heydrich. He was Simon's choice for leader of his new Special Secret Police force. Oswald was the illegitimate son of the late Reinhard Heydrich, an evil man who with the help of Heinrich Himmler and others managed to kill over 6 million Jews during WWII.

Simon had studied in great depth the subject of the *Final Solution* used by Hitler and his S.S. during the 1930's and 40's. He, too, was fascinated with a single ethnic society. Simon had read that secret police had been used as far back as ancient Greece and Rome. He now believed it was imperative to have his own private organization whose primary purpose was to collect and destroy any opposition to him or Carlo Ventini.

Oswald was an easy choice for Simon. He had met the man many years earlier and had taken a liking to him immediately. Oswald was a tall, neat person. Many of his mannerisms reminded Simon of himself. He was not well liked by the average person. He was smart and determined but angry and insecure. He brought meticulous order to everything he did in much the same way Simon had always done. He held grudges and disliked every person that he perceived as not having worked hard for what they had. Again this was much the same way Simon felt.

When the United World Organization was established three years ago,

Simon had the opportunity to give Oswald the job of Director of International Intelligence Operations, an entity very much like the CIA in the United States. Oswald Heydrich's job was to assess the behaviors of all the countries in the world to see if they were complying with Carlo and Simon's directives.

In other words, he supervised a group of spies. There was no real need for this agency any longer. The world was well within Simon's total control. Yet there were those individuals—the Christians, Jews, scientists, and other noncompliant people—who refused to take Carlo's ID tags. These people defied Simon, and this was something he just could not stand for.

Sitting quietly on the other side of the room was Dr. Raymond Hyder. He had been told by Simon to be available during his press conference. Raymond had moved into an apartment inside the World Headquarters as requested by Simon and Carlo. For the last month or so he had been studying the present conditions of the planet earth. Everything was tracking along just as he had predicted. Raymond concluded that the world would be a very cold place with the next few months. He further concluded that billions of people would die due to the cold and ensuing starvation. The only good news seemed to be a reduction in the number of people dying daily as a result of the plague. Raymond assumed that this was probably because it was too cold to go outside so people were inadvertently isolating themselves from others who carried the virus.

What really worried Dr. Hyder today was a nagging thought that there must be more trouble on the way. If one asteroid could make it to earth, then perhaps a piece of another one on the same collision course would, as well, but there was no way to track space to know for sure. The Jet Propulsion Laboratory in California was up and running again, but all of the ground-based equipment was nearly useless due to the dust cloud. It was also thought that all the space-based equipment had been destroyed by the dust and debris that by now had extended halfway to the moon. Without the ability to contact this equipment from the ground, it was impossible to assess its working condition.

Finally some of the phone lines had been restored in the World Headquarters and in other places around the world. This allowed Raymond the opportunity to call the facility in California to see if they had detected any other objects in space moving towards earth.

"We can't get a signal out of the Hubble. We are planning on sending another satellite up as soon as we feel it will be safe. With this satellite we can bounce a signal off the Hubble and redirect it to look our way, but there is so much space that this could take months to evaluate."

Raymond also learned that NASA had received a faint radio signal from the International Space Station. "Apparently they moved out of orbit to avoid the dust cloud. "Poor guys!" said the scientist from California. "We will never be able to put a shuttle in space again." Raymond understood that this meant those astronauts would drift around until they ran out of food, water, and air. *In reality,* Dr. Hyder mused, *they may very well live longer out in space than most people will on earth.*

One of Simon's security guards escorted a camera crew into the room followed by a blonde woman dressed in black. She was a lovely woman and in her late 30's. "Hello, Mr. Koch. I am Victoria Price." The woman extended her hand towards Simon. He stood and extended his own hand without taking his eyes off the woman's blouse. It was quite obvious that Victoria had very large breasts. Simon was a fan of large breasts.

"Mr. Koch, I have been assigned by the United World News Network as your personal news reporter," said Victoria with a charming little smile.

"I will have to remember to thank your management for their good choice," said Simon with an eerie smile of his own.

"Mr. Koch, are you ready for the interview?"

"Please, call me Simon."

The interview lasted five minutes with Simon explaining the reason he felt it necessary to liberate the Russian people with a nuclear strike on all of their weapon facilities.

"Is it true that these locations will burn for years?" Victoria asked.

Simon turned towards Dr. Hyder. "Well, let's ask our resident scientist," he suggested.

Raymond was not ready for this question. He was a physicist by degree, but all of his work had been in the field of natural disasters so he winged an answer as best he could. "With the cold weather and dust cover around the earth, it is likely that these facilities will burn uncontrolled for years. Of course, it depends on how much uranium and plutonium are in each location."

"Will this cause further damage to our planet?" Ms. Price inquired.

"It can't help, that's for sure, but I guess a controlled nuclear strike is better than a full scale multiple warhead detonation," said Dr. Hyder.

This last comment got an approving nod from Simon. Raymond blew a sigh of relief. In reality he figured the nuclear strike was the last thing this world needed. They were already in the midst of a nuclear winter. It was going to be a very long, difficult time for the Russian people.

Finally Simon proudly introduced Oswald Heydrich. "Oswald is the son of the late Reinhard Heydrich, a hero to the world falsely accused of genocide. The people now know that Reinhard had vision. He saw the danger in the Jewish religion. He knew they worshiped a false god and that they would be the cause of death and destruction until His Holiness, Carlo Ventini, took his rightful position as lord of this planet.

Oswald has been given the task to find all Christians, Jews, and those persons who have not taken the ID tags that were so generously given to them by the divine Carlo. We will rid the world of these evils, and we will establish a singular order where we can all live in peace and happiness with the love and protection of our god."

Once the interview was over Simon walked Victoria outside the castle and down the long, concrete walkway. The rest of the group followed while the camera crew was busy packing their gear away. In the yard there were many beautiful statues of angels that had been erected when the Papal castle was first build in 138 A.D. adorning the perfectly manicured landscape. "This place is incredible. What made you want to live here?" Victoria asked.

Simon turned and looked at the ancient building. The lights strung out around the courtyard gave the building a mythical look against the backdrop of the chilly and dark Roman sky. "This place was build for Saint Angelo before he died, and many rulers have used it over the centuries. Even Nicholas II occupied this castle back in 1277 A.D. It is not much of a place to live in right now, but I will fix it up."

"What about these nasty angels?" Victoria inquired as she pointed to one of the statues along the walkway.

"I am going to have them taken out and we will put up some statues of his Highness. And then we will redo the interior for me, but first—"

Simon was startled by a loud, booming voice. He looked up to see two men standing at the edge of the street directly underneath one of the streetlights that Simon had recently installed for security purposes.

"The Lord commands you to obey His laws!" said the medium-built man. He was dressed in a drab white robe made out of sackcloth with a braided sash around his waist. His hair was covered with a tan cloth and his beard was long and white as cotton, and to his right stood another man, slightly shorter than he. This man was also dressed in sackcloth and wore a long, white beard.

The camera crew quickly grabbed their equipment, turned towards the two men, and started to film the event as it unfolded. Of course, it was on a tape-delayed broadcast. Without satellites there would be no live broadcast, but Simon would correct this dilemma as well.

Raymond Hyder and Oswald Heydrich stood back and watched this amazing scene unfold. The shorter man began to speak. "Jesus lives, and He loves you. Do not receive the mark of the beast. Do not take Carlo Ventini's ID tags. He is the Devil incarnate. He is the foretold Antichrist, and this person is his prophet," the man said as he pointed a finger towards Simon.

Simon's anger was kindled, as was his fear of these men. "Shoot them!" he yelled to his bodyguards, but his men were frozen in their tracks.

"Shoot them!" Simon screamed out once again. At this request Oswald Heydrich pulled out his own revolver and fired multiple shots into the chests of both men, but neither man flinched. Finally Oswald's gun was fully discharged with no effect whatsoever. Raymond stood with his hands over his ears in disbelief as did the speechless news crew who caught all of this on camera.

The taller of the two men spoke up, "You will see God's wrath fall from the sky and burn upon the ground, and you will know Jesus is God."

Both men turned and walked away completely unscathed. Overhead Simon saw a flash of light as a glowing ball of fire flew through the wall of his precious castle.

He screamed out in anger, but before he could take a step back towards his castle, Victoria Price grabbed his arm. "We need to get under cover!" she yelled.

Simon and his bodyguards, including Oswald and Raymond, followed Victoria and her news crew to the two large trucks parked at the entrance. Simon entered the first truck with Victoria, Raymond, Oswald, one bodyguard, and two of the cameramen while the rest of his guards and the remaining news crew got into the second truck. "Who are those guys?" Victoria asked.

"I don't know," said an irate Simon.

The first truck sped away just a fraction of a second before a meteorite crashed into the second truck, exploding it upon impact. "Oh, my God!" said the driver of the first truck.

"Hey!" Victoria screamed. "We can't help them now, so move it! We need to find shelter."

Simon was impressed with this woman. She obviously had worked with the men who had just been killed yet she didn't bat an eye. Instead she was concerned for her own safety and Simon's. Instantly he felt more for her than just his usual sexual attraction.

******

Dr. Jerry Little and Cory Parker sped across the desert floor dodging the numerous craters that had been created months ago. Cory looked at his watch. It was past noon already. He had been gone for over six hours. *Lord, let them be okay,* thought Cory to himself. Suddenly the sky tore wide open as a large number of bright, glowing balls of fire streaked across the darkened sky.

"What are those?" Jerry asked.

Abruptly one of the orange balls of fire crashed into the ground just 50 yards away from his Jeep. The blast of the explosion shook the Jeep, nearly tipping it over. "Go faster!" Cory screamed over the sounds of other meteorites exploding all around them.

Jerry swerved and nearly drove into a deep hole in the ground created by one of the thousands of tektites. From behind another explosion lifted the rear of the Jeep. "Oh, my God!" yelled Jerry. "We are going to die!"

Another fireball came in from the right and smashed into the ground with tremendous force. The blast hit Cory in the chest and knocked the antidote out of his hands. The plastic box rattled on the floorboard, heading out of the Jeep since the vibration had caused the side door to pop open. Cory reached out quickly and grabbed the edge of the box just in time. Another bounce of the vehicle forced Cory into Jerry's lap, bringing the antidote back into the Jeep.

Right in front of them appeared another huge glowing rock. Both Cory and Jerry stared at it in total awe. "This one's going to be close!" Jerry screamed as he turned his steering wheel as hard as he could. The meteorite exploded right in front of them spraying the Jeep with molten pieces of rock and hot sand. The explosion, combined with the tight turn, caused the vehicle to flip over on its side, tossing Cory out onto the ground.

Jerry climbed out of the vehicle and ran toward Cory who was lying face down in the sand. Jerry feared the worst. By Cory's side was an empty box of antidote. Pink bottles lay spilled out everywhere yet none appeared to be broken. "God, let him be okay!" cried Jerry aloud. He knelt over Cory and carefully rolled him over while supporting his huge neck. Dr. Jerry Little looked into Cory's face. His nose was bleeding badly and was probably broken. "Cory!" Jerry yelled just as another explosion went off. "Cory, please be all right," said Jerry as he looked at the terrible scene unfolding around him. Why hadn't he minded his own business? He would still be at the hospital safe from all this. *I'd be safe maybe, but empty and dead inside for sure,* Jerry told himself.

Cory opened his eyes and looked at Jerry's concerned, freckled face. He almost had to laugh—this scene was absurd. Here he lay in the desert with Howdy Doody looking at him as hundreds of meteorites fell onto the already wrecked desert floor. Yet another memory flooded Cory's mind—a memory of a horrible time in life when he had served in Vietnam when explosions, fire, and death were all around him.

"Are you okay? Can you move?"

"I think so," said Cory as he leaned forward. Instantly he caught sight of the pink bottles of life-saving medicine. "Oh, no!" he said as he reached out for the plastic box.

"I think they are okay, but how are we going to get out of here? It is another 10 miles to the Colton Mine, and the Jeep is wrecked," said Jerry.

Cory stood and looked over to the Jeep as it lay on its side. This scene was déjà vu for him as well. There had been a time when he was trapped in a dangerous place. His military vehicle had rolled over, but that time shrapnel had gone through the engine's block, rendering it useless. Cory bent down, picked up each bottle of medicine, and carefully placed them back into the plastic box. Next he walked over to the injured Jeep. Cory set the box down with care, and then he put both of his powerful hands around the roll bar of the vehicle and pushed with all of his might.

Cory let out a scream as he dug his feet into the sand and lunged forward. The vehicle righted itself, bouncing from side to side as it did. Jerry was totally impressed with the big man's feat of strength. *He gets thrown out of a moving car while his body is infected with a deadly virus and still he can lift up my car. Whoa!* Dr. Little thought. *I'm glad he's on my side.*

Cory picked up his box and climbed into the driver's seat. "I'll drive if that's okay."

"Fine with me," said Jerry gratefully relieved of his responsibility as driver.

Cory drove with precision and care as he swerved to the left and then to the right as necessary to avoid the incoming missiles. Twenty minutes later Cory drove Jerry's Jeep right down into the near frozen stream below the mine. He parked and jumped out and ran toward the cliff where the cave was hidden. Jerry followed along with ease. He was always good at running and climbing since he was so thin and wiry.

Cory could hear coughs as soon as he entered into the cave. Quickly he made his way over to Leasa and Calvin who were both semiconscious and coughing up large quantities of blood. Cory handed Jerry the box and looked deep into his bright green eyes. "Please, help them!"

"I will do everything I can," Jerry whispered as he began to fill the syringes with medicine.

Leasa was the first one to receive an injection. Undoubtedly she was very close to death, maybe only moments away from the point of no return when the antidote would not be able to help her at all.

"There is a point," Jerry said, "when the lungs are just too damaged and full of blood." Jerry feared the worst for Leasa.

Cory knelt by Leasa's side and spoke gently to her, encouraging her to fight. "I came back just like I promised. Now you have to do your part. Fight this, Leasa. The medicine is in your veins so now it is up to you. Please don't leave me."

Leasa looked up through half-closed eyes into Cory's worried face and smiled. *She's going to make it,* he told himself.

******

Sara and Tommy jumped up at the sound of the first explosion. "What is that?" Sara screamed.

Tommy had no idea so he quickly climbed up to the tracks just in time to see three large balls of fire go hurtling across the sky. Again in the distance he heard another powerful explosion. Tommy turned to see Sara standing at his side. "They are meteorites, I think," he said.

"No, Tommy, they are God's wrath," said Sara as she grabbed his hand.

Tommy looked into Sara's eyes for more understanding. "The book of Revelation says that at the first trumpet God will call down fiery hail from the sky, and it will burn up a third of the dry land. This is the beginning of His judgment on mankind."

At that moment another fireball exploded 100 yards in front of Tommy and Sara. They both felt the blast and the heat wave. "We need to take cover before we get killed!" said Tommy.

The two spent the night huddled together under the bridge as large, glowing chunks of rock hammered the ground all around and below them.

******

Elisha had just reached the base of the first set of caves in Ein Gedi. The sound of rushing water was nearly more than he could stand. Like all the rest he was dehydrated to a very dangerous level. The thousands of people behind him filed in around the base of the cliffs. Had there been any light at all, the people would have seen some spectacular sights as cool and refreshing water poured from the face of the rocks. To the right they would have seen the steam rising off of a natural hot spring. They also would have noted two well-preserved, ancient buildings built from the fourth-millennial period B.C. This was what remained of the Chalcolithic Temple. They might also have caught sight of the Dead Sea as it stretched forth beyond where they stood.

The counsel leaders moved forward to Elisha to congratulate him on successfully bringing everyone to the safety of the caves and to the much-needed water. Peter stepped up next to Elisha and Jasmine. "Good job!" said Peter, but before Elisha could respond a blinding flash of light streaked through the night sky and crashed into the Dead Sea before them.

"What was that?" one of the leaders asked.

"Trouble," said Ruth as she moved in closer to Peter.

The next thing the camp witnessed was a massive, orange ball of fire crashing into the Chalcolithic Temple. The explosion disintegrated what was left of the ancient building instantly. The sky lit up again with multiple meteorites falling to earth at the same time. The blast of the simultaneous explosions knocked the thousands of people to the ground like a bowling ball hitting the headpin in just the right spot. The glow of the fiery rocks lit the area sufficiently for Elisha to survey the caves. "We need to move quickly!" he yelled out. "Into those caves!"

The people moved in near panic, stepping on one another along the way. Elisha grabbed Jasmine's hand to ensure that the crowd did not trample her. Peter did the same for Ruth as they pushed along behind the crowd. Another explosion came from above the cliff. Then suddenly a wall of rock tumbled down in front of the crowd. "To the right!" screamed Elisha. "Move to the right!"

The crowd shifted right and entered through the four major openings in front of them. Soon nearly all of Elisha's followers were in the caves except for the half dozen or so that had fallen or were pushed down. These still remained out in the open and in grave danger. Peter and Elisha ran out to help them. Jasmine looked at the other men tucked safely in the cave and shook her head in disgust as she, too, ran out to help with Ruth by her side. Two minutes later Peter was tending to the wounded as the barrage of meteorites continued to fall.

******

Christopher Evans stood crying as Connor Crowley wrapped his arm around the boy's shoulder. The crowd had collected enough wood and paper to make a huge fire. They placed wood all around the young man on the cross and began to sing and shout for joy as they lit the paper under the dry wood.

"God, he is going to die! Please help him," said Connor.

In an instant a huge meteorite crashed into the ocean a mere 50 yards in front of them, causing a massive explosion. The crowd turned to see what had just happened as another glowing ball came rushing in and exploded in the sand 30 feet to the right of them. The sand was turned to glass instantly and sent flying into the crowd, slicing them as it moved by. While all this was happening, the young man on the cross was trying desperately to hold his legs up above the fire that was now starting to blaze below him.

Another fiery meteorite smashed into the asphalt above the beach, sending a great shockwave into the crowd, and knocking every person on the beach to the ground while blowing most of the burning pieces of wood right off the trailer and onto the sand.

The crowd rose and ran off screaming as other pieces of molten rock came crashing in from every direction. Many crowd members were blown apart as they tried in vain to run away.

Connor and Chris ran to the trailer and climbed up. They kicked the last few pieces of burning wood onto the sand. Connor surveyed the man on the cross. *How are we going to get him down?* he wondered. The young man's hands had large spikes driven right through them, and there were no tools around to remove these nails. Chris was busy untying the rope around the man's chest as Connor considered the best way to approach this dilemma. When he realized what Chris was doing, he screamed out, "No! Don't untie that yet or else—" But it was too late. The rope was undone and the total weight of the boy was all of a sudden placed on the nails. Within a split second his body weight caused his flesh to fail, ripping the palms of his hands wide open, dropping him off the cross. The young man let out a cry of pain and fell to the floor of the trailer gripping both hands tightly.

Christopher quickly reached for the man. "I am sorry. I was just trying to—" he pleaded.

"Don't be sorry. You did what had to be done," said the man with a definite Middle Eastern accent.

Connor bent down next to the naked man who was shivering terribly from the cold night's air and from the shock of so much torture. He took his wool sweater off and put it on the man. "What is your name?" Connor inquired.

"Joshua Stein," the tortured man whispered.

"We need to get out of here," said Chris.

Connor nodded and looked up as another ball of fire flew by. "Let's get back to the alley, give Joshua some clothing, and fix up his wounds."

Chris and Connor helped Joshua to the sandy ground and supported him as they walked briskly back towards the alley. "Why were you on that cross?" Chris asked.

Joshua looked at Chris through the corner of his eyes. "Why did you help me?"

Chris studied Joshua closely for a few seconds. "I am a Christian."

Joshua nodded. "I know. I can tell."

"Are you a Christian too?" Connor inquired.

"I am Joshua Stein, one of the 144,000 witnesses chosen by God to preach throughout the world."

"Are you the one I was supposed to meet?" Chris asked just as they turned into the alleyway.

"Did God send you both here?" Joshua inquired as he climbed into a pair of Christopher's pants which were considerably long for Joshua.

Both men nodded.

"Then travel with me as I preach. Perhaps God has plans for both of you to help witness to the people of the South Pacific."

******

By morning it was all over, but the damage would never be fully appraised. Entire cities everywhere were in ruins, as were most of the major highways and airports of the world. There were fires out of control in virtually every part of the globe. The number of dead was in the millions.

While all of this was happening Carlo Ventini had been on a visit to Babylon to oversee the building of his new city. He was making arrangements for what would surely be the most spectacular sight the world had ever seen. As Carlo dined alone, Satan appeared, warning him to take shelter before the first meteorite hit. "God's feeble attempts will not stop us, my Son," said Satan as Carlo hurried to leave.

Chapter 5: The Mediterranean Sea is Dying

D ay 1322, March: Carlo stood on the balcony of his partially destroyed hotel surveying the damage to the site of his new Babylonian city while talking to Simon on the phone. "What did they look like?" Carlo inquired.

Simon had spent the night with Victoria in the basement of her news station. It was a terrific night. She was everything he had ever dreamed of—beautiful, sexy, smart, and ruthless. She was his queen. "They looked like—well, like Moses and Elijah, I guess."

"That's because they *are* Moses and Elijah," said Carlo.

The concept of Biblical characters showing up astounded Simon.

"What's the damage?" a very irritated Carlo asked.

"I don't know yet. I was stuck in a basement for the last 10 hours. All I know is that our OPEC contacts have reported massive oil fires in their refineries, and I have heard of many other fires throughout the world. None of the major cities have reported in yet. That is probably a bad sign," said Simon sarcastically.

"I want specifics! Get back to me as soon as you know something concrete," Carlo demanded as he hung up his phone. "I will build this city, and people will come here to worship in my presence. Nothing can stop me!" Carlo roared as he looked up towards the sky.

*****

Back in Rome Dr. Hyder made his third attempt to contact the Jet Propulsion Laboratory. Each time the phone was full of static, but he

finally got through. "What is the word? What happened?" Raymond asked
urgently. He was desperate. He knew Simon would soon come to his
office and demand an explanation that Raymond did not have.

"We cannot see out into space, so we just don't know. All I can say is
that we heard them coming. Our radar and sounding equipment spotted
them, but by that time, they were only an hour away from our atmosphere, and we did not know what they were."

"Well, what were they?" a more sympathetic Dr. Hyder inquired.

"Meteorites—tons of them ranging from just a few ounces to maybe
as much as 150 pounds."

"Do you hear any more of them coming?" Raymond was cautious.

"No! They were multiple targets with very small signatures, but we
do hear something else."

"What is it?" Dr. Hyder asked as he held his breath.

"We don't know. We are having a hard time bouncing our radar off it.
Maybe it is the space station coming back into orbit. We just cannot see
enough to know. The funny thing is that it seems to be in two separate
locations at any given time."

"Are there two of them? That doesn't sound like the International
Space Station," said a worried Dr. Hyder.

*****

Carlo Ventini sat in a beautiful golden chair perched atop an 18-inch
high platform centered in a great and mystical room at the Abbasid Palace in Baghdad. The Abbasid Caliphate people had built the palace in the
13th century directly alongside the Tigris River. There was a terrific bit
of history associated with this palace and its people.

The Islamic religion has its roots in this place with many harsh and
terrible laws passed to force the people of this region to declare the Ko-
ran as the only word of God. Failure to comply meant certain death which
was often the case. Nevertheless, the Abbasid Caliphates had been a
very advanced society and were the envy of Europe in those days. From
this very location came the Hippocratic Oath and some very advanced

medical science.

Astronomy was a heavily practiced science with al-Khwarizmi being the most significant contributor and the man from whom came the word, *algorithm*. Also various styles of writing (including calligraphy) and music came from this region, as did the world's first paper manufacturing. In 1258 it all came to an abrupt end when the army of Hulagu, grandson of Genghis Khan, raided the city and destroyed the Abbasid Caliphate people and their government, but they left the palace intact.

Kneeling before Carlo was the President of Zambia, and alongside him were representatives from the various tribes of that region including the Bemba, Ngoni, and the Lozi. Also present was the leader of West Africa, along with his tribesmen, and the South African leader, along with his Zulu tribesmen. To the right of Carlo, also kneeling, was the leader of the OPEC nations, the Prince of Saudi Arabia, and by his side was the leader and President of China and the advisor to the CPECC, the China Petroleum Engineering and Construction Corporation.

Carlo stood and smiled brightly. "Rise, my children, and listen to what I have to say."

The group stood slowly and looked up to Carlo cautiously. "My world is in a state of flux by my design. There has been too much evil, and I will not tolerate it any longer. I will continue to punish and weed out those guilty of worshiping false gods in my place. But," said Carlo with a charming smile for his audience, "for the sake of you and the rest of my followers, I will take a more active role in redesigning my world. We will rid the world of Christianity and all other religions. There is one god, and I am he. My Father has given me this planet to honor me."

Carlo stepped down from the podium and walked towards one of the frightened Zulu tribesmen. "You have been selected by me personally to rebuild my city. As a reward for your faithful work, you will eat three meals a day, and I will protect you from any illness."

Carlo walked over to where the Prince of Saudi Arabia and the President of China stood. Both men began to shake as Carlo stared them down. "I have allowed these natural disasters to test the faithfulness of my people. Only those selected by me will survive these disasters and those yet to come, but for the sake of all whom I have chosen, I will provide heat and shelter from the cold. We will begin to mass produce oil and distribute it to wherever my aide, Simon Koch, directs. This, along with food from my Agripods and the antidote for the virus, will provide what is sufficient for life."

Ventini walked back up to the podium and stretched out his hands. "People, I have great plans for you—a wonderful life serving and worshiping me. I will rebuild this world and turn it into a marvelous place to live." Carlo paused and then raised his voice. "I will not tolerate disobedience, and as long as there are those out there who resist me, you will all suffer. The sooner we rid the world of this menace, the better off all of you will be!"

The cameras had been following Carlo as he walked throughout the room. Now as he reseated himself in the extravagant golden chair the cameramen relaxed and locked their tripods into place. The room was completely silent.

Abruptly two white-bearded men appeared standing side by side on the podium. Carlo looked at the two men without flinching. It was as if he knew they were coming. Everyone else in the room let out a gasp of surprise. The cameramen zoomed in on the men—the same men that Simon had seen the night before in Rome. As soon as it was safe enough to put some more satellites into orbit, the entire world would see these recorded broadcasts and would fear and even hate these men.

"Obey the Lord your God. Do not follow after false gods like this man," said the taller of the two men, Moses, as he pointed to Carlo.

The shorter man, Elijah, turned towards the crowd and cameras saying, "The Lord your God is Love and Light and Life. Do not be deceived by Satan and his son or his prophet. They will be defeated and thrown into the *Lake of Fire*. Jesus is Lord."

Moses turned to the cameras and spoke boldly. "You will see the seas turn to blood and the islands wiped away. You will see the ships of the sea disappear, and you will taste the rivers as they turn bitter. When darkness comes, you will know God is God."

Both men walked off the podium and headed out through the main palace doors. As they went they heard Carlo screaming out their names. "Moses! Elijah! You are weak! You work for a weak God. My Father has given me this planet, and nothing can take it away from me. Nothing!"

******

The Catsa was just clearing the island of Malta on its way to the Strait of Gibraltar at just over 12 knots. It was fully loaded after leaving the shipping yard at Marseilles. A few hours more and the Catsa would be in the Atlantic and on its way to deliver its precious cargo of food supplies to Brazil. The people of South America were in terrible shape. Thousands died daily due to starvation and a massive outbreak of the plague. Simon had recently made a deal with the various governments of the continent to supply him with slave labor as needed to rebuild the many ruined cities around the world. This was in exchange for food and medicine.

The first task of this slave labor was to build massive crematory facilities to allow each country to rid itself of the hundreds of millions of dead bodies. Epidemics of cholera had already broken out in many countries, and the world could not afford another plague.

The ship's helmsman was sounding the depth of the Mediterranean floor. The last thing he wanted to do was run a shipload of Simon Koch's food onto a sandbar. The Mediterranean was a very old sea, perhaps the oldest sea, once called the Tethys Sea. However, when the continents squeezed together, the sea was greatly reduced, explaining the extremely high salt content of this water. The sea's depth at the Catsa's particular location was just over 500 feet, though on an average the Mediterranean Sea was approximately 5,000 feet deep with a couple of locations where the water was at nearly 17,000 feet.

This ancient sea had been crossed by some of the most famous people in earth's history—kings, prophets, Disciples of Christ, and warmongers alike. From Europe it had been a short trip to Turkey, Africa, or Asia Minor, and it was the quickest way to move around from Greece or Italy to Spain. At the sea's bottom was an incredible network of fault lines that fed Mount Vesuvious and Mount Etna hot gases. The Mediterranean Sea was the biggest of the many seas of the region including the Red Sea, the Black Sea, and the Caspian, all of which had been cut off from the Mediterranean Sea when the continents shifted. The Adriatic, Tyrrhenian, Aegean, and Ionian Seas were like the fingers of a hand and the Mediterranean was the Palm.

The Catsa continued on its course slowly. The visibility of the region had become very poor due to the constantly dusty sky. The ship's captain was afraid of running into another freighter on its way in or out of the Strait of Gibraltar. An incident of this type had just happened a week ago and caused a salvage team from Socomenia to come and tow the one remaining floating ship back into dry dock.

The captain sipped his coffee as he looked carefully out of the deck window. Suddenly the sky lit up brightly. The heat was incredible and painful. Within a fraction of a second the captain and every member of his crew were incinerated into fine powder as the 100,000-degree massive chunk of iron screamed by at over 40,000 miles per hour. The asteroid crashed into the deepest part of the Mediterranean Sea just below the Island of Rhodes with the explosive power of over 300 gigatons of TNT—just over 10 times the explosive power of every nuclear weapon of the world combined.

At once the asteroid buried itself some six miles into the earth. The water around the impact sight boiled off instantly forming a gas cloud of hot steam moving away from the epicenter at over 1,100 miles per hour. As the air blast approached the Island of Rhodes, it picked up sand and rocks along its path. The incredible and destructive gust of hot air hit the city of Lindos, home of the original Colossus and the Acropolis, also known as the city of the gods. Zeus and Apollo, to name a couple, were said to frequent this island. The blast of hot air moved along faster than the speed of sound, giving the air nearly the density of steel. The land was leveled, but not before the inhabitants were all degloved—a term for having their skin removed by the fast-moving hot air. Their bodies were ripped to shreds by the explosive power of the blast.

At the same time hundreds of cubic miles of superheated water vapor and molten rock spewed into the atmosphere at twice the speed of sound with sufficient velocity to eject the debris into outer space, adding to the already huge ring of dust and debris encircling the earth.

As the matter flew out of the ocean floor, a crater nearly 30 miles wide formed. As it did the surface of the sea came rushing in to fill the void left behind. Soon millions of metric tons of water began to build until it was hundreds of feet above sea level. In a 360-degree ring, the tsunami sped away at over 450 miles per hour gaining in size as it went along.

The entire complex of Greek islands was destroyed in a matter of minutes. The tidal waves moved along each of the adjoining seas of the Mediterranean, all except the Tyrrhenian Sea. Thanks to Sicily, Rome would be spared, but on the Adriatic side, Italy was leveled from Taranto to Fermo including Pescara and Carlo Ventini's mansion.

The tsunami approached Turkey at just a fraction under 900 feet tall moving at just under 400 miles per hour. The wall of water crashed upon the shoreline of the Aegean Sea after washing away all of the islands in that region including the island of Patmos. It rushed inland destroying everything in its path from Manisa to Gazipasa. Ironically this tidal wave destroyed the original site of the Church of Thyatira to the north and continued to destroy each of the original churches as it headed south including Sardis, Smyrna, Ephesus, Pergamum, and Laodicea. Although the tidal wave entered Turkey, it stopped just short of reaching the original site of the Church of Philadelphia.

To the east the tidal wave sped towards the shoreline of Asia Minor as it completely washed away the Island of Cyprus just below the base of the cliffs. Onward it went until it crashed into Beirut, Lebanon, and southward to Israel and Egypt. The wave was greatly reduced when it hit the western shores of Israel, but it still had sufficient power and mass to completely destroy the cities from Haifa down to the Gaza Strip although it did not reach Jerusalem. When the wave hit the port outside Alexandria, north of Cairo, it was met by the Nile River, the longest river on the planet at just over 4,000 miles long and the only river in the in the world to flow directly north. The 160-mile wide delta at Cairo reversed its flow sending a massive wall of water onto the largest city in Egypt. In short, the power of the tsunami sent the Nile River rushing backwards. With the flow reversed, heading south, the Nile soon ran into the first set of cataracts just below Aswan Dam. Pressure from the reserve waters of the Nile in this large reservoir combined with the massive wall of water building from the north was just too much for the old dam. Abruptly Aswan exploded and the millions of cubic feet of water raced out, reversing the flow of the Nile yet again. The water was redirected to Cairo which was still under water from the original tsunami. This would be the worst flood Egypt experienced since the time of Noah.

Finally to the west the wall of water raced out of the Mediterranean Sea through the Strait of Gibraltar, and the funnel effect caused the wall of water to slow to less than 300 miles per hour, but it also caused the tsunami to rise to nearly 2,100 feet. Every ship in the Mediterranean and its adjoining seas, except the northern Tyrrhenian Sea, was destroyed. The wall of water headed into the Atlantic sinking every ship in its path. The wave would decrease in power as it went along, but the coast of Newfoundland was not to be exempt from this disaster.

At the epicenter of the asteroid impact the water still boiled from the intense heat. Bubbling to the surface of the sea was a dark red material that began to spread across the surface of the water moving in all directions.

Later Dr. Raymond Hyder explained to Simon and Carlo that the change in color from a beautiful blue to a frightening blood red was the result of a chemical reaction. "The iridium released from the asteroid is a rare terrestrial element that, when combined with hydrochloric and nitric acid in the presence of massive amounts of iron ore, will create a redox reaction: this reaction oxidized the compound, turning it red. The sea will become polluted, and all sea life will probably die," said a terribly discouraged Dr. Hyder.

The impact of the asteroid also had an adverse effect on the fault line beneath the Mediterranean Sea. Massive pressure started to build, pushing hot magma and poisonous gas towards the closest low pressure area, Mount Etna and Mount Vesuvious. Both mountains exploded nearly simultaneously in a spectacular but deadly display of fire and smoke. Sicily had already been destroyed, and Naples was quickly covered with hot ash and toxic gases. Lava would soon flow from the 4,000 foot Mount Vesuvious killing everything in its path. Western Italy would not go unharmed after all.

Within hours the asteroid had destroyed nearly all of the original Greek empire and much of Italy, Spain, Northern Africa, and Turkey. Cairo was washed away forever, and the western shores of Israel were no more. Eons of fighting over this stretch of sand had been for nothing. Thousands of large ships were at the bottom of the ocean never to be seen again. The cities of the original churches described in the book of Revelation, excluding the Church of Philadelphia, were under many feet of water and debris. Over 300 million people were dead in an instant.

******

Carlo Ventini lay resting in his presidential suite in Baghdad. He had no knowledge of the asteroid that had recently smashed into the Mediterranean Sea. Had he not been sleeping so soundly, he might have felt the world shake slightly at his location. The word from Simon had not yet come, but it soon would.

Hundreds of miles away from Carlo in eastern Turkey north of Lake Van near Mount Ararat where Noah's Ark is likely to have landed, a river called the Murat bubbled forth. Flowing southwest it was met by the Karsu River forming the headwaters of the Euphrates River at Keban. The Euphrates flowed through the rugged Tarus Mountains that had on this very day protected Asia Minor's longest river, at just over 1,700 miles long, from the effects of the massive tidal wave coming in from the Mediterranean only 100 miles to the west.

Turkey relied heavily on the Euphrates for irrigation, drinking water, and hydroelectric power. Recently the Turkish government, at risk of war with Syria and Iraq, had begun to build dams for hydroelectric power and a more controlled irrigation management system. This massive dam project, called GAP, was the largest program of its type in the world. The goal was to build 22 dams throughout Turkey but to date only three were completed. The dams had so severely reduced water flow to their neighboring countries that the threats of nuclear or biological war were becoming all too real. Additionally Turkey attempted hydroelectric programs on the Tigris River that originates in Turkey as well, but their neighboring countries—especially Syria—became irate so Turkey's progress had been slowed considerably. These were desert countries, and the water from these rivers meant the difference between life and death. As it was the rainfall for this region had quickly disappeared, not that it was ever much to start with, but at least the accumulation of snow had always provided a summer runoff of water.

At the base of the Keban Dam the waters of the Euphrates were flowing at a controlled rate agreed upon by all neighboring countries when all of a sudden the sky split wide open and a massive ball of fire raced forward and rammed into the dam, exploding it immediately. The asteroid, nearly a quarter mile long and composed of nickel and iron, impacted the dam with the force of 50 gigatons TNT explosion. This region was barren except for a few small communities, and the blast of the explosion incinerated these towns almost instantly. The heat of the explosion vaporized as much as 5 million gallons of water while the rest of the river sped forth through the base of the Taurus canyons as a new, massive opening had just been created.

The shockwave fractured the very next dam in the series, the Karakaya Dam, but it held together until the colossal floodwaters of the Keban Dam arrived. This tremendous wall of water raced southwest until it reached the third completed dam of the GAP project, the Ataturk Dam. The shallow, slow-moving Euphrates suddenly was an incredibly deep, fast-moving inland tidal wave. The river began to wipe out every community along the ancient Mesopotamian route. These communities still had old canals used for irrigation, but now these canals simply provided easy access for the raging river. The historical sites of Nineveh and Eridu, as well as Nimrod, were washed away in the blink of an eye.

******

Carlo was nearly thrown from his bed as the shockwave smashed into his hotel. He ran to the window to see what had just happened, but to his uneducated eye things looked normal. He could not see, feel, or hear the hot rushing wind from the asteroid impact. Had he been a couple of hundred miles closer, he most definitely would have felt the blast of air and heat.

Carlo's room shook once again, but this time it was Satan. "You must leave now!'

"Father, what is it?" Carlo asked in panic.

"The second and third trumpets have been released. You must take your helicopter out of here immediately!"

"Father, why don't you just take me back to Rome?" he inquired.

"Not now. I have other things to do. No go!" Satan ordered as he disappeared from the room.

******

The Euphrates had gained considerable momentum as it left Turkey for Syria. The Syrians had complained a great deal lately about Turkey hogging all the water. They would never be able to say that again after today. The Euphrates raced down to the Revolution Dam, destroying it with total ease. From there the water finally caught up with the Tigris River as it flowed south. Above the Tharthar depression the rivers converged upon the Samarra Dam, Iraq's most important. After blowing it to pieces the Euphrates and Tigris Rivers, which were normally 25 miles apart at their closest point, were now one river as they swept Mesopotamia completely submerging the original sight of Babylon. As the waters continued to gain momentum, they covered the local lakes and streams until it was simply one large sea by the time it reached Baghdad. The Abbasid Palace, which had sat beside the Tigris River for the last 700 years, was washed away within a few seconds.

Finally this incredible ocean of raging water, along with the waters from nearby lakes and the Great and Little Zab rivers, formed a confluence as they reached the Shatt al Arab, the normal location where the Euphrates and Tigris rivers would come together. From here a great wall of muddy water, debris, and dead bodies raced out into the Persian Gulf and to the Strait of Hormuz. The entire Arabian Sea was a muddy brown color, but soon it would change to dark red just as the Mediterranean already had. The Strait of Hormuz was clogged with millions of tons of soil and debris. Undoubtedly this would only escalate the destruction of this gulf and all of its sea life.

******

The following evening Dr. Hyder was called into Carlo's chamber where he and Simon awaited a full report on what they could expect after the most recent disasters. As Raymond walked across the courtyard into the larger of the two buildings, he looked up at the fearsome Roman sky. It was an odd sight. Instead of being dark like Raymond would have expected, the sky had a weird luminescent quality very much like the northern lights he had seen once as a child on a family trip through Canada. Yet this luminescence set the entire night sky aglow, providing sufficient light to see by.

Dr. Hyder knocked once and swallowed hard as he entered the room. Simon greeted him with a sour look. Raymond diverted his eyes from Simon to Carlo who sat calmly by. "Come in, Dr. Hyder," said Carlo.

Raymond approached nervously.

"Have a seat," said Carlo as he pointed to the small sofa in the middle of the room.

"Well," said Simon almost immediately. "Tell us what happened."

Carlo waved his hand in front of Simon's face. Simon hated it when Carlo did this, especially now that he was the most powerful man the world had ever known besides Carlo himself.

"Dr. Hyder, why does the night sky look like that?" Carlo inquired softly.

You are supposed to be the god—you tell me, thought Raymond. "There must have been some minerals with luminescent properties in the last two asteroids. Perhaps that combined with the dust already orbiting our sky has formed something very much like a neon light. The light trapped in our stratosphere combined with the moon's light on the other side of the dust cloud is creating this very unusual effect. I am sure nothing like this has been seen since the creation of our planet. We have theorized that a similar effect could have existed when the surface of this planet was still cooling and the earth's atmosphere was thick with various gases such as neon, lithium, hydrogen, and oxygen."

"How long will this last?" an irritated Simon demanded. He still hated the fact that Dr. Hyder seemed much more knowledgeable than he.

"I suppose that this effect will only occur at night since the powerful sun would reduce the luminescent effect during the day. What I guess I am saying is that it will be much lighter during the night and probably more like night during the day. Additionally I would expect this effect to stay with us as long as this dust cloud circles the earth."

"And how long will that be?" Simon asked angrily.

"Well, frankly, Mr. Koch, I don't know. I would have predicted about two years for the first asteroid, but now with two others, the nuclear attack, and subsequent uranium and plutonium fires burning out of control in Russia, I just can't say."

"Well, what can you say?" Carlo asked with an annoyed look on his face. He was in an evil mood after hearing that his mansion in Pescara had been totally destroyed. This news, combined with the fact that his new building site for the city of Babylon was under many feet of water, made him less than happy.

Raymond swallowed hard. His mouth was so dry that his throat burned. "I can say that unless by some miracle this cloud burns off soon, our planet will be a frozen ball of ice. There will be very little water available, especially since the fresh water supplies on earth—at least the unfrozen ones—only account for less than a fraction of one percent of all the water available." Raymond looked into the confused face of Simon again. "Mr. Koch, the planet is three fourths salt water. The majority of the fresh water can only be found in frozen locations like the poles and mountaintops. Less than .000006 of one percent of the total water supply on this planet can be used for consumption, and this water is going to

freeze—not to mention the fact that the iridium dust from these asteroids has already poisoned much of it."

"What about the air?" Simon asked. "You said we need to do something or our air supply would be poisoned."

Raymond paused and scratched his head. There were nearly too many
effects to consider. "Mr. Koch, we need heat to survive, so we will have
to burn oil. It sounds like all the hydroelectric plants in the Middle East
have been destroyed, so they will have to burn oil, as well, which probably makes them less likely to want to part with any."

"You just let me worry about that!" Simon roared.

"Yes, Sir, I am sorry," said a panicked Raymond. "What I am trying to
say is that we need heat, because within the next few weeks this planet is
going to get very cold."

"How cold?" asked Carlo.

"Maybe minus 30 degrees Fahrenheit," said Dr. Hyder. "Additionally
all plants and animals will be dead within the next six months or so. We
will either starve to death, freeze to death, or die of dehydration. All of
these effects will kill us well before the air reaches a toxic level."

"All right, Dr. Hyder. Thank you for your comments. You are dismissed," said Carlo.

Raymond bowed low and hurried out of the room. *These guys are crazy,*
he thought. *What can anyone do to fix the world's problems? Time or some spectacular miracle is the only thing that will help, but we humans cannot survive until
then.*

As Dr. Hyder walked down the hall Victoria Price, escorted by two
of Simon's guards, met him. "Hello, Dr. Hyder," smiled Victoria seductively. Victoria scared Raymond. He was not sure why, but something
was very wrong with this woman. Oh, certainly she was beautiful, but
beneath all that she was evil. "Have you just come from seeing Simon?"

"Yes, he is with His Holiness."

"Good! I look forward to finally meeting Carlo Ventini."

Awkwardly Raymond nodded and walked past her. "Have a nice visit,
Miss Price."

Victoria was escorted into Carlo's chamber where Simon stood by his side. As soon as Simon saw her, his heart leapt for joy. Finally he had found the woman of his dreams, his equal in so many ways. Carlo stood as Victoria approached. "Well, who might you be?" Carlo asked with a handsome smile.

"This is Victoria Price, my personal news reporter."

Again Carlo waved a hand in front of Simon's face, embarrassing him greatly. "I am sure Miss Price can speak for herself."

Simon's anger and jealousy began to burn. He did not like the way Carlo was looking at Victoria. After all, he had found her first. "Yes, Your Holiness, I can speak. What Mr. Koch says is true. I am his personal news reporter, but I am at your disposal whenever and however you wish as well."

Carlo looked into Simon's face. He enjoyed the look of panic combined with the jealousy that he saw there. "Well, I will take that under consideration. However, for now, you will serve me well by reporting the news that Simon gives to you. I understand that we have footage of the two men who have appeared."

Victoria nodded.

"We hope to have at least three satellites in orbit within two months. As soon as they are working I want this footage broadcast, but first I'd like to work with you on some small edits of the footage," said Carlo.

He wanted the world to see these two prophets of God as evil. He planned to dub their voices and make changes to their words. But little did Carlo know, his film—although edited—would never be shown. Due to a mix-up at the news station the original, unedited copies would be shown instead.

Chapter 6: The Chase Begins

Day 1380, May: Jerry helped Cory with the last of the supplies as they strapped them into the back of his slightly damaged Jeep. Looking up Jerry was once again amazed at the nearly fluorescent night sky. Actually since the light was only seen during what would normally have been referred to as nighttime, Jerry and the rest of Calvin's group had adjusted their sleeping patterns to accommodate the luminescence. During what would have normally been considered daytime it was so dark that it was useless to try to function. Sleep seemed like the appropriate thing to do. The only problem was that there was much more darkness than light— nearly twice as much.

The temperature in the desert was very close to 20 degrees below zero, but since it had been some time since it had rained, it was a very dry cold. *What a ridiculous concept—dry cold,* thought Jerry, but he knew it was true.

Once as a child he had gone duck hunting with his father. As the two of them lay quietly in the blinds waiting for some poor, unsuspecting duck to foolishly fly by, it began to rain. Soon the wind blew in from the north, and quickly Jerry was frozen to the core. Within 30 minutes he and his father both suffered hypothermia. The temperature had not been any lower than the mid 40's, but moisture and cold wind together could be a lethal combination.

Back in the Colton Mine Calvin and the remaining handful of followers hugged tightly as they wished each other great success. After Jerry Little and Cory Parker returned with the antidote some two months back, people had begun to feel better and stronger each day. However, some— like Leasa Moore—required more time to recuperate. As teams became

strong enough they left the mine to pursue their ministry in whatever
state they had chosen.

In some ways Calvin knew it was a pipe dream, a hopeless cause that
any of these people could make a difference let alone reach their ultimate destinations, but then again Calvin had doubted God when he and
all the members of his team had contracted the plague. Yet God saved
them all. Calvin was learning not to question God or His plans regardless
of how small and trivial they might seem at the time. After all, what
could a carpenter from Nazareth do that would change the world forever?

Cory stepped up next to Calvin and Leasa. "The Jeep is loaded and
we have about six more hours of this weird light, so we had better go."

Calvin nodded. "God bless you all," he said as he walked out of the
mine that had brought them all much-needed shelter and safety. As Calvin
stepped outside into the eerie, seriously damaged desert he paused to
consider all the things that had happened to him over the last few years—
so much suffering and destruction. Life was forever changed. Jerry walked
over to him and stood silently. "Are you sure that you want to do this,
Jerry?" Calvin asked.

Over the past two months Jerry had learned to appreciate Calvin's
calling from God. He even began to feel the presence of God in his own
life, but Jerry was an analytical person and he would need more to be
convinced completely. Calvin had asked Jerry if he was ready to receive
Jesus into his heart. Jerry paused momentarily and then told Calvin that
he was sure that there was more to life than he understood, but because
he had so little understanding, he needed time to get to know God. Calvin
was satisfied that this was a genuine answer, so he decided to offer Jerry
the chance to follow them into the mission field. Jerry had to consider
this for a day or so before he decided that, if nothing else, he would be
useful in case they came across sick or injured people.

"Yes," said Jerry. "I am as sure as I can be. Besides, I can't go back to
work at the hospital. I didn't take the ID tag like I was supposed to, and
after being gone for months without saying a word to my father..." Jerry
trailed off.

Calvin smiled brightly. "Well, all right then. We have our very own doctor with us on this trip."

Cory very carefully escorted Leasa out of the mine and down to the Jeep. Since she had become ill, Cory had shown a remarkable quality as a caregiver. He spent nearly every spare moment by her side. Not only Leasa but others also received loving care from him. He fed them and carried them to their makeshift bathroom. Daily he broke through the ice and brought in fresh water and, occasionally, a couple of large native trout out of the stream below the mine.

Cory, of course, had the residue of his illness to overcome, but he did not let this stop him. During these last couple of months he also had grown much closer to Jerry Little. He had decided that this young man had a boldness and defiance that he admired, plus a kind and loving heart. He was glad that he did not kill Jerry when they first met in the hospital.

The big man lifted Leasa into the back seat of the vehicle and climbed into the driver's seat. "Okay, let's hit the road," said Cory with a smile.

Jerry now understood fully that Cory was never going to let him drive his own Jeep again so he climbed into the back with Leasa. Next Calvin assumed the co-pilot position beside Cory and latched the thin canvas door that Jerry and Cory had reattached. These doors would reduce the wind as they drove, but staying warm in this vehicle was always going to be a real problem.

Cory started the car and drove slowly across the small frozen stream and up the bank on the other side. Before he reached the top he switched on his headlights to help him navigate. The luminescent sky just did not provide a powerful enough light to help Cory make out the finer details around him as he drove. Once Cory cleared the crest of the ridge Calvin looked back towards the mine and whispered, "Thank you, God!"

"Alaska, here we come!" a frail Leasa laughed.

******

Oswald Heydrich studied the pictures closely as Simon sat back restlessly. Both men had the same desire in mind: to find and kill every per-

son that was against what Carlo and Simon had been building for the last
four years. Oswald shuffled the photographs and stopped at the picture
of Peter Bastoni. He studied the man carefully, noting Peter's dark eyes
and curly black hair.

"Who is he?" Oswald asked.

Simon was not paying any attention to Oswald. Instead he was contemplating his own life or, more precisely, his own mortality. All day Simon
had felt poorly, and all day he had felt an impending doom all around
him. Sure, some of it had to do with the fact that much of Europe had
been severely damaged by the most recent asteroid. Dr. Hyder had said
this monstrous pile of iron was no more than a mile wide. It was half the
size of the one that hit the United States, but for some reason it had done
considerably more damage to property. He had warned Simon that an
ocean impact asteroid was much more dangerous than a land impact one.
Simon now understood this very well.

Additionally Simon sensed the power of God and feared that he was
fighting a losing battle. His castle had been terribly damaged—not that it
wasn't already a wreck, but now it was nearly beyond repair. He would
have to move back to the World headquarters. The only consolation he
had was that Carlo's precious Babylon was also in ruins and still under
about 10 feet of water. What was really bothering Simon was the fact
that he was a man—a real flesh and blood man who could die and who
would eventually die. It seemed that Satan and, possibly Carlo, were not
human at all and could never die. *What about me?* Simon wondered.

Simon coughed hoarsely as Oswald repeated himself. "That is Peter
Bastoni. He is a doctor—the one who developed the antidote for the
plague. He and his brother caused us a lot of trouble," grumbled Simon
as he coughed again.

"Where is his brother?" Oswald asked.

"He is dead," grinned Simon. "I cut off his head."

The phone rang in Simon's office. "What is it?" he asked angrily.

"Hello, Simon. It's me, Victoria."

Simon's tone instantly changed. He had been seeing Victoria Price
nearly every day for months. This was much more than a crush. He was

in love. This might also have contributed to his feeling of vulnerability, but in Victoria's case he didn't care just as long as he could spend time with her.

"Are you okay?" Victoria inquired in a sweet, soft voice.

Simon coughed painfully. "I'm okay now that I hear your voice."

Oswald looked at Simon and rolled his eyes without Simon seeing him. Women were the worst things for a leader as far as he was concerned. *Just look at Mark Anthony,* thought Oswald. *That surely didn't turn out all that well for him.*

"I want to see you tonight," said Victoria in a seductive way.

"That would be great. I need another hour or so here at the World Headquarters and then I can be ready."

"Fine. I'll see you then. Bye," whispered Victoria.

Simon turned to see Oswald staring at him. Instantly he felt embarrassed and flushed. "Where were we?" Simon asked.

"What do you want me to do with these three people?" Oswald asked as he dropped the pictures of Peter Bastoni, Tommy Glover, and Sara Allen on the table.

"Catch them!" Simon commanded as he began to cough uncontrollably.

"I have our Special Police out in force around the world. I get daily reports from every district leader. In a weeks time they have found over 30,000 Christians, all of whom were in hiding in various places around the world. But if we are going to find them all, then we need to recruit more secret police. We haven't put anyone in the remote places like Iceland, the French Polynesian Islands, or Alaska. We can find all the Christians and these three here if I can get more support," said Oswald as he pointed to the pictures before Simon.

Simon really liked this guy, and he wondered why he had not considered developing his own private police force before. Then he remembered why—it was that imbecile Pope Peter John's responsibility to police the world for defiant religious fanatics. Simon hated the time wasted. Now he would have to hunt down millions of well-organized Christians.

"What did you do with the Christians that you caught?" Simon asked.

Oswald looked at his leader carefully before answering his question. A mistake here might cost him. He hoped he had done the right thing. "We never talked about what to do after we catch Christians, so I assumed you wanted them dead."

Simon stared into Oswald's nervous eyes. He appreciated the fact that he could intimidate such a rough and dangerous man. "So you killed them? All 30,000?"

"Yes," Oswald nodded.

"You killed over 30,000 Christians!" said Simon a second time with a smile. "Well, don't kill any more. We may be able to force these so-called Christians into accepting Carlo's ID tags. Let's find a place to put the people as we catch them. Then we will see which ones are willing to die for their faith."

Oswald smiled. "My father built a number of excellent facilities in Germany that we can use."

Simon laughed and then began to cough terribly.

"Are you okay?" Oswald inquired.

Simon waved his hand in front of Oswald much the same way Carlo always did to him. "I'm fine. So you want to reopen the concentration camps used during the war?"

Oswald smiled boldly. He could tell that Simon liked his plan. We can start with Dachau, the first camp build during the war. It's only 10 miles away from Munich, and if it is okay with you, I could set up my headquarters in Munich and monitor all concentration camps from there."

Simon liked the idea. He began to feel a little like Adolph Hitler, but he was sure he was a lot smarter than the *Little Corporal* had been. "Did your father build the first camp at Dachau?"

"No, not exactly. This camp was designed by Heinrich Himmler, the man my father worked for."

Simon began to think about his plans for Victoria tonight. "Okay, let's wrap this up," he said as he picked up the pictures and pointed. "This one is in Israel somewhere." Simon jabbed his finger at Peter's picture. "And these two," he paused to consider the day that he heard Tommy and Sara had escaped. Anger filled his sick body. "These two are here somewhere in Europe—hopefully dead after what happened in the Mediterranean two weeks ago."

******

Victoria was escorted into Simon's private chambers where he lay snoring horribly. Simon had given orders to allow her free access to his apartment.

This allowed her to sneak up on him even when he was asleep. This certainly was not something that Oswald would ever have approved of.

Victoria bent over Simon and whispered in his ear. Simon barely opened his bright red eyes and stared up at Victoria. He was too weak to speak or even to smile. Right away Victoria understood that Simon was deathly ill. She put her hand on his forehead and felt his fever just as Simon began to cough up blood. Victoria pulled back and gasped, "Oh, no! You have the plague!"

She considered running from the room to protect her own life, but just as quickly she realized it was too late. She was already infected. *In fact, this might just turn out in my favor,* thought Victoria as she knelt forward and began to caress Simon's forehead. "I will get a doctor for you, and then I will be right back to take care of you myself," said Victoria as she kissed Simon's sweaty bald forehead.

******

The light of the night sky had faded into total darkness as the morning approached. Cory drove silently while the rest of his crew slept peacefully. He had finally made it to Highway 80 after many hours on Route 95. His biggest problem had been the icy road conditions around Lake Tahoe, but now he had a much bigger issue—gas. He was almost out. As Cory approached Colfax in northern California, he saw the sign for Beale Air Force Base. *If I am going to find any gas, then this has to be the place,* thought Cory to himself. The question was whether or not he could make it another 15 miles.

Cory drove and prayed for the next 10 minutes until he finally caught sight of the intensely bright lighting around the perimeter of Beale. The Jeep began to sputter and lurch as it struggled to siphon the last ounce of precious fuel from the bottom of the tank.

Startled from a dead sleep, Jerry asked, "What is it?"

"We are out of gas," said Cory nonchalantly.

Cory turned around to see the worried look on Leasa's tired face. "How are you feeling?"

"Better," she smiled.

"What are we going to do?" Calvin, who was also awake by now, asked.

"I guess I'll go get some gas."

"I'll go with you," said Calvin.

"No! You need to stay here and take care of Leasa," said Cory. In reality Cory was just as protective of Calvin as he was of Leasa. He could not allow his leader to take any unnecessary risks, but over the course of the last few weeks Calvin had begun to feel like Cory was doing all the work. And it was really starting to bother him.

"I'll go," said Jerry.

"No, you won't!" said Calvin. "I'm going with Cory. You stay here and take care of Leasa. We'll be back soon."

Cory knew that Calvin meant business so there was nothing else to say. Both men climbed out of the car and cautiously followed the barbed wire fence. Cory and Calvin had both been in the military and, although Cory was a grunt—a foot soldier—and Calvin had been an officer and a pilot, both men understood how military bases were put together.

"There must be a motor pool somewhere in there if we can find a way in," said Calvin.

Cory did not hear what Calvin said. Something else had caught his attention. In the center of a wide-open area was a large building, obviously the headquarters for the base. In front of this gray building was a flagpole and on top of the pole was a royal blue flag that Cory could not identify. It was not a typical base flag and certainly not the American flag.

"What's the matter?" Calvin asked.

Cory pointed and whispered, "What is that flag?"

Calvin had excellent vision. He strained his eyes until he could read the lettering on the flag. Right in the center was a pentagram, and written in a semicircle around the symbol were the words: *United World Organization*. It was one of Carlo's flags. Just then a military police car rounded the corner and drove along the fence. Both men immediately dove to the ground and froze. The car stopped and two men got out. One man lit a cigarette and began to cough. The other man spoke to him in a language that Cory did not understand. Minutes went by until finally the man flicked his finished cigarette away, climbed back into the car, and drove off.

"What do you make of that?" Cory inquired.

"He was speaking Italian," said Calvin. "I guess Simon Koch has taken over the military bases in the United States and planted his own soldiers."

In fact, Simon had not only taken over the military in the U.S.A. but had done so in every country except for China and the Middle East. Carlo had forbidden Simon from assuming control over these armies, much to Simon's displeasure. He still had the issue of finding the President of the United States and his top advisors. He suspected they were all locked up in NORAD where the ultimate nuclear control was hidden away. Simon was going to have to find a way into this complex and soon, but for now he was content to assume control over every conventional military establishment in America.

Finally Cory found a place in the fence where a few of the links were rusted through. "This is where we can get in."

Calvin just looked at Cory suspiciously. "How can we squeeze through there?"

Cory grabbed the two separate pieces of fence and began to pull with all his might, which was considerable. Soon the fence started to pop and crack and the links began to fall to the ground. Cory dropped the fence and stood back. "Impressive," said Calvin as he walked through the newly created gap.

Once inside Cory and Calvin hid in the shadows created by the compound's lighting as they moved from building to building. Eventually they found themselves in a parking lot full of military trucks and moving equipment such as forklifts and bomb loaders.

"One of these must have a gas can or two full of fuel," said Calvin.

Both men began to climb from vehicle to vehicle. Each time they found a can of gas they brought it out to one central location and then went back for more. After a while they had more five-gallon cans of gas than they could carry.

"What's our plan?" Calvin asked.

"The Jeep's gas tank will take four of these, and maybe we can put a couple more in the back somewhere," said Cory.

"Then we need to make two trips," said Calvin as he picked up two of the heavy cans.

Cory smiled and grabbed four more cans, two in each hand.

Both men crept along silently with Calvin leading the way by about 40 feet. Calvin was nearly exhausted as he struggled to carry his heavy cans all the way back to the car. One hundred yards more and he would be back to the opening in the fence.

Suddenly Cory heard a sound from behind. Before he knew it two men—the same two men he had seen in the police car earlier—stepped up behind him with guns drawn. Calvin was completely unaware that this was even going on. He was so busy trying to muscle the gas to the fence that he was impervious to any distractions. Cory put his cans down and turned around. One of the guards ran past him to intercept Calvin. The other guard stepped in close to Cory as a broad smile stretched across his pasty face.

If the man had not been so happy with himself for capturing Cory, he would have noticed just how big Cory really was, and then he would have kept his distance. As it was he moved in just a little too close, and before he knew it Cory had kicked the gun right out of his hand. One more step forward and Cory clobbered the man so hard it was doubtful if he would ever wake up again.

Calvin was relieved to see the fence before him. Finally he would be able to set the gasoline down at least long enough to regain some strength.

"Hello," said the man with a heavy Italian accent.

Calvin turned in surprise just in time to see a nine-millimeter stuffed into his face. Calvin dropped his cans and froze where he stood. Through the corner of his eye he saw Cory creeping up on the unsuspecting man. As soon as Cory was within 10 feet he stepped on a frozen piece of ground. The crunch was loud enough to alert the armed military police officer. The man turned quickly to look behind him. As he did Calvin jumped for the gun and wrestled it out of the guard's hand. Just as quickly Cory stepped in and belted the man across his rugged jaw. The sound was like glass breaking. The look in the man's eyes was one of shock and pain as he crumpled to the ground unconscious.

"Thanks," said Calvin. "Now what do we do?"

"Grab your gas and let's go!" said Cory as he ran off in the opposite direction.

"Where are you going?" asked Calvin out of frustration as he picked up his two cans. He found them surprisingly lighter this time. The adrenaline rush from a gun in his face had sufficiently bathed his muscles and loaded them with power to spare.

Calvin caught sight of Cory running from the shadows with his hands full of large, olive drab colored cans. Two minutes later Jerry was helping Calvin store the two extra cans of gasoline in the back of the Jeep while Cory dumped the final five gallons of gas into the vehicle's tank.

"How far can we get with this gas?" Leasa inquired as Cory sped down the highway trying to get as far away from Beale Air Force Base as he could.

"We can probably make it to Oregon, but after that I'm not sure," said Jerry.

"Good job back there!" Calvin said to Cory as they drove along.

"You too!" answered Cory. This meant a lot to Calvin. He knew he had done a pretty good job himself, but to hear it from Cory was important. It seemed as time went by Calvin was changing or God was changing him. In either case he was becoming less of a man and more of a prophet. Soon he would have to rely on Cory for many things that he would normally have done for himself, including protecting him.

******

The stale smell of canned oxygen polluted Simon's nostrils as he lay semi-conscious in a hospital bed. Victoria sat by his side holding his hand. She was speaking softly to him, as she had been all the while he laid in a semi-coma. She knew that it was possible he would hear and remember what she said, and it was important to Victoria to score some points with Simon.

"From the first day I met you in your office at the Papal Castle, I knew that I loved you," Victoria whispered softly.

In fact, it was unlikely that Victoria had ever loved anyone. She had grown up in an orphanage in Romania. She learned her mother was most likely a prostitute and her father just as likely an American soldier. Apparently Victoria's mother gave birth to her in the back streets of Constanta, and within 12 hours Victoria had been dropped at the doorstep of the orphanage. From infancy to young adulthood she lived in this dark, lonely place. She was never adopted due to the fact that she was a blonde, blue-eyed child which was rare in Romania and frowned upon.

When Victoria turned 16, she snuck out of the orphanage never to be seen by them again. She traipsed across the coastline of the Black Sea and the Danube for months. She got odd jobs washing dishes and cooking, but the pay was so poor that eventually she took up prostitution.

Unlike her mother, however, she was determined not to make a career of it. Eventually she made enough money to take a few journalism courses. A couple of years later she received her big break and got a job at a local newspaper company in Romania.

During the energy crisis and subsequent fighting in Romania in the 1980's, Victoria Price developed a reputation as a brave and daring field reporter, the youngest in her profession. This new reputation combined with her terrific looks improved her career, but Victoria was never satisfied with her success or influence, and she never would or could be. She wanted wealth and power—absolute power like Simon's.

Simon began to stir as Victoria continued to speak niceties into his ear. Carlo entered the room and stood next to Victoria while looking down at Simon. "He will be okay in a day or so," Carlo said.

"I hope so," said Victoria convincingly.

"Did you get some of the antidote for yourself?"

"Yes, thank you, Your Highness."

Simon's private room was huge and well guarded. He would get the best of care because he was the world's leader, but also because Carlo Ventini, god of the planet, was bound to expect nothing less than the best for his prophet.

******

The steam rolled off of the hot spring as Jasmine sat back resting her tired head against the hard rock wall. For the last few months she and the other 2,000 members of Elisha's tribe had been living in the caves of Ein Gedi. Time had gone by very slowly for Jasmine. She was getting tired of having so many people around all the time, and in particular she was tired of them consuming all of Elisha's time. Jasmine looked up and smiled as Elisha climbed down the face of the rock and to the edge of the hot spring. "How is it?" he asked as he dipped a toe into the soothing water.

"Hot!" giggled Jasmine as she looked at the ridiculous shorts Elisha had borrowed. Probably no worse than the tee shirt and panties she wore. Besides, it didn't matter in the least, she was so grateful for this time alone with Elisha. She was unaware that he missed her constant companionship just as much as she did his. After all, they had been together night and day for nearly four years. It was Elisha who made arrangements with the counsel leaders to keep everyone out of the hot spring for an hour so he and Jasmine could relax.

Elisha nestled next to Jasmine and draped his long, thin arm around her shoulder. "I've missed you so much."

"What do you mean, you've missed me?" Jasmine asked, trying to act as if she hadn't a clue to what he was saying. "You see me every day— whenever you get around to it."

Elisha laughed out loud. "Oh! So that's how it is, huh?"

"Yeah! That's how it is," said Jasmine with a frown.

"It was a lot easier when it was just the two of us," said Elisha.

Jasmine nodded. "Yeah, I guess, but it wasn't bad when we lived with Benjamin and David either."

Both people sat back in the hot spring thinking about Benjamin Cohen and young David who for some reason never had a last name they knew of. Benjamin had been a godsend for Elisha and Jasmine. His food and shelter along with his love and guidance had really helped these two youngsters to grow up. David and Benjamin were sorely missed, but Elisha knew that Benjamin was in God's care now, although he had no idea what had become of David.

Elisha followed Jasmine's gaze up to the neon sky. The flicker of incandescent light was a primitive sight. Elisha felt as if he were sitting in the middle of a studio for the filming of a prehistoric movie.

"I miss the moon and the stars," said Jasmine.

This thoughtful, sensitive statement was atypical of Jasmine. Elisha knew that the young woman was growing up and, just as he was changing so very greatly, so was she. "I miss it too!" he said. "A little heat wouldn't be bad either."

Jasmine turned and looked into Elisha's tired, dark brown eyes. "What does God want us to do next? Sooner or later we are going to run out of food, and sooner or later somebody is going to find us and tell Simon Koch."

In fact, Elisha was aware that his camp could not survive another week without more food supplies. He had been praying and talking to God about this issue daily, but as of yet he had no answer as to what he should do.

"I don't know!" Elisha sighed, "But God will tell us eventually."

Jasmine nodded and kissed Elisha's cheek. "I know He will."

******

Jasmine and Elisha walked into the first set of caves where a warm amber glow met them. The fires were fully utilized to keep the caves livable and, after stepping out of a hot spring into the frozen desert,

Elisha and Jasmine were grateful for this heat. Besides, the fires allowed for at least moderate visibility throughout the caves. The problem now was that they were running out of wood as well. In fact, they were running out of everything except for water ironically.

Elisha tried not to think about these things. He knew God would provide. He had seen the proof of this over the last four years of his life. The issue for Elisha was the people's insistent demand for answers to every problem. They were not content with Elisha's answer that God would provide. They wanted to know when and how He would provide. However, at this very moment Elisha felt relaxed and hopeful that everything would work out.

Peter Bastoni and Ruth Jefferson met Elisha and Jasmine as they entered into the second set of caverns. This was where Jasmine and Elisha slept side by side, as always, even though Jasmine had reservations about this. Surely their relationship was platonic, but she was concerned for Elisha's image. Her concerns, however, were unwarranted because nobody ever complained. Perhaps they thought Elisha and Jasmine were husband and wife, or possibly they saw it appropriate for a leader like Elisha to have a woman at his side. In any case, a word was never spoken.

Peter smiled at the young couple. To him they were almost one person—inseparable. "How was the spa?" Peter inquired.

"Great!" Jasmine grinned.

"Maybe Ruth and I can try it out." Peter smiled at Ruth and winked.

Peter looked back to Elisha for a few seconds. The young man was only a child compared to his own 46 years of life, but Peter had developed a different opinion of Elisha as God's chosen leader. In fact, he felt he could not properly function or make decisions unless he received Elisha's blessing. "I—" said Peter as he looked over to Ruth.

Ruth nudged him encouragingly. "I mean—we—have something to ask you," said Peter as if he were a child confronting his parents to get their permission to go somewhere he was sure they would not like him to go. Elisha smiled at Peter and almost laughed, but he restrained himself. It was just that this little scene of the doctor confronting the child, instead of the other way around, was amusing to Elisha and even to Jasmine, if the truth were known.

"We want to leave," said Peter flatly.

Now Elisha was not smiling. This was a total surprise to him. "You can't leave! You are leaders. You have people counting on you. I am counting on you," said Elisha in a panic. He did not want to lose them. They were part of his strength and a big part of his courage.

"We know that, but hear us out first—please," said Ruth softly as she tried to calm Elisha.

Peter continued, "We feel like we can be of more use if we go back to Jerusalem."

"Use—in what way?" asked Jasmine.

"There are 2,000 people here," said Ruth, "and millions back in Jerusalem who need our help more than you two do."

Elisha was aware of this fact. He, too, wondered about all the people he left behind as they wandered through the desert. He always assumed God would send those people to him, but perhaps not. Maybe this idea of Peter's was a way to help others escape the city before Simon destroyed them.

"How will you survive? Where will you go?" Elisha asked.

"I feel compelled to go back to the city and start building a small laboratory where I can make antidote for the plague. It is only by God's grace that we are not sick today. Soon this plague will kill everyone or they will have to take the ID tag to allow them to receive the antidote. Maybe we can provide an option," said Peter compassionately.

"In reality all we are doing, even out here in the desert, is providing a choice to live freely instead of taking the ID tags or suffering the consequences of standing against the plans of Carlo Ventini. We all need to survive about three years without getting caught or killed. If we do, then Christ will return and take care of us for eternity," beamed Ruth.

"When will you leave?" Jasmine inquired.

"Tomorrow," said Peter.

"Simon will be looking for both of you," said Elisha.

Peter nodded. "If it is God's will, then we will be okay."

Elisha admired Peter's faith. He had grown in the Lord so much since Elisha had first met him. "May God bless you both," said Elisha as he reached for Peter to hug him.

******

"Do you think Elisha and Jasmine will still be in Ein Gedi if we come back later?" Ruth asked as she and Peter walked through the desert towards Jerusalem. They had another six hours of light left and then they would have to find a place to hide for the next 16 hours. At this rate it was going to take ten days to get to Jerusalem, but they only had about three days' supply of water and food. The other issue, of course, was the temperature in the desert. This made walking painfully slow and dangerous.

"I don't know. How far can 2,000 people go in the middle of this desert?" Peter asked.

"Well, Moses led millions out here for 40 years," said Ruth.

"Was that right here?" Peter asked excitedly. He liked the idea of being in the very spot where something of such historical significance might have taken place.

"No, this is the desert that Ishmael and Hagar wandered in and the desert that King David hid in, but Moses led his people from Egypt to Sinai."

Hours dragged on in silence for Ruth and Peter as they trotted along in the barren desert. "I am so cold and tired!" Ruth lamented.

"Me too! Let's see if we can find a place to stop for the day," said Peter.

A few minutes later Peter led Ruth towards a pile of massive rocks that sat low on the outer edge of an ancient looking valley. "Where are we?" Ruth inquired.

"I don't know," said Peter, "but I'll bet there is a cave in here somewhere."

Peter began to climb around the rocks as Ruth looked on. Soon he called out, "I've found one!"

Ruth just shrugged her shoulders as if to say, *Great! Now I can sleep with the bats and snakes for the next 16 frigid hours or so.*

******

It was another hard week in Ein Gedi. Elisha had just concluded his nightly meeting with his counsel members. Tempers were running hot this evening as they discussed the status of their provisions and what to do next. A tremendous amount of pressure was being placed on Elisha's young shoulders to come up with an answer.

"We will pray about it and see what God says," said Elisha.

"That's what you say every night, but God does not answer you," said one angry counsel member.

"In God's time!" blurted Jasmine out of anger.

The man snubbed Jasmine and walked away. "He's an idiot," said Jasmine as she turned to a worried Elisha.

Elisha broke out into laughter. "I love you, Jasmine."

Jasmine smiled at this and moved in next to him as they walked out of the first cave and over to the ruins of the Calcolithic Temple. "That meteorite sure did a job on this place," said Elisha as he stood looking at what was left of the evil temple.

"What do you really think God wants us to do next?" Jasmine asked as she took Elisha's hand.

"I don't know. I pray and pray, but I haven't heard a thing. Maybe I've done something wrong," said Elisha disappointedly.

"You haven't done anything wrong, but maybe the lack of faith of the others has made God angry."

Elisha had not considered this before. He knew that many if not all the people in the camp were murmuring and complaining constantly, but would this really anger God?

Jasmine and Elisha stood quietly for a few moments before Jasmine spoke up again. "I wonder how Ruth and Peter are doing."

"I don't know. They've been gone over a week, so they must be close to Jerusalem by now."

"If they can find enough unfrozen water and if the cold weather hasn't killed them," said Jasmine.

Elisha turned to Jasmine with a disapproving look. "Not you too!" he said.

"What do you mean?" Jasmine asked irritated.

"Have faith! God is in control and He will take care of Peter and Ruth and us, for that matter!"

Jasmine nodded and smiled. "You are right. Sorry! Besides, it doesn't seem that cold out here tonight for some reason.

******

Simon left the hospital with an escort of security police and Victoria by his side. It had been a miserable and painful few weeks, but at the same time it had been wonderful for Simon. He didn't have to worry about any of Carlo's daily requests, and he had Victoria there constantly to take care of him.

Oswald met Simon as he approached the limousine. "How are you feeling, Mr. Koch?" Oswald asked with a smile.

"Much better," said Simon as he turned to Victoria and smiled.

"I've given my driver instructions to take you to your apartment, or would you rather go to your office and catch up on what we have accomplished these last few weeks?" Oswald inquired.

Simon waved his hand. He was really starting to like this gesture of Carlo's as long as it was he who was doing the waving. "I am not going to either place. I will see you tomorrow. Come by my office."

Oswald was confused. "Where are you going? Do you want my security to follow you?"

Simon looked back to the many armed guards behind him. "Have four—no, make it six—follow my limo," he said as he climbed in behind Victoria. Oswald closed the door with a nod.

Victoria giggled like a schoolgirl as the car sped away. This, of course, was for Simon's benefit because there was nothing schoolgirlish about Victoria.

"Where are we going?" she asked as she nestled closer to Simon.

"I thought we would go to your house."

"My house!" said Victoria in a panic. "Why my house? We can't go there!"

"Why not?" smiled Simon.

Victoria didn't want Simon to see the plain small house that she had lived in for the last eight years. It was an embarrassment to her. "Well, because it's not clean. I mean, I have spent all my time with you, and I haven't had time to clean it up."

Simon patted Victoria's hand. "That doesn't matter. I want to see where you live."

Victoria sat back silently as the car drove through the dark, icy streets towards her little apartment. She had no idea that Simon knew where she lived and had even driven by it a couple of times. He knew she had little money and could not afford anything better, but he was about to change all of that forever.

Victoria unlocked her door slowly. She was terribly embarrassed. "It's not much," she said softly.

Simon entered into the narrow hallway behind Victoria. The first thing he noticed was a large oak coat rack with half a dozen different style coats hanging on it. Simon had suspected that Victoria put more emphasis on how she looked rather than how she lived.

Next they entered a tiny living room that was barely large enough for her couch and love seat. On the walls were pictures of flowers and a large picture of the Lichtenstein Castle in Germany. In fact, as Simon looked around the bare, small room he noted at least three different pictures of various castles but no pictures of family whatsoever.

"What's with the castles?"

Victoria was caught off guard by the question. She didn't want Simon to know that she had a preoccupation with royalty and medieval life. These castles were symbolic of her desire to live that fantasy. Coming out of an orphanage poor and hopeless Victoria had no idea what life had to offer. While attending journalism school she began to read about the wealth and power of royalty throughout the ages. She began to fanaticize about life as a wealthy and powerful queen.

"Oh, well, I like the architecture," said Victoria.

Simon smiled at Victoria. She was in her own home, but for some reason she was completely out of her element. She was vulnerable, and he knew it.

"Let's sit down," said Simon as he pointed to the small leather couch covered with unfolded clothing.

Victoria moved over and began to fold the clothes as quickly as she could. Simon stepped up and pushed the pile of laundry onto the floor. "Sit down!" he ordered.

Victoria sat down while holding an unfolded blouse in her hand. Simon sat next to her and took hold of her hand. "I don't like you living like this," he said as he pulled the blouse out of her hand and dropped it on the floor.

"I want you to have better things than this, and I don't want you to have to do any of these chores."

Victoria's heart began to pound. Was her dream of wealth and power about to come true? "I can't afford anything else!" Victoria lamented as she played up her situation for Simon's benefit.

"Well, I can," said Simon. "I am the most powerful man on this planet, and if I want something for myself or for you, all I have to do is demand it."

Victoria looked into Simon's lifeless, little eyes and smiled as she leaned in and kissed him tenderly. "I love you, Simon," Victoria whispered.

Simon's passion was unbridled as he began to kiss her lustfully. The two of them stayed in the apartment all afternoon. By the early evening Simon was hungry and wanted to go out for dinner. Victoria declined and asked if she could make him something instead.

"I don't like you cooking," said Simon agitatedly.

"Yes, well, if we go out, then we will just lose time we could be spending making love," said Victoria as she licked her lips and looked wantonly at Simon.

That was the final straw. Simon was hooked for life. He grabbed

Victoria's naked body and pulled her down to the floor. "I thought you were hungry," Victoria whispered seductively.

"I am," said Simon.

After another round Simon sat up and looked into Victoria's pale eyes. "I've decided that I want you to be my wife."

Victoria looked at Simon and began to cry. It was a fake, heartless cry, but it worked well enough on Simon. "I am not worthy to be your wife."

"I determine who is worthy!" said Simon in a roar.

"A leader like you should not be held to one woman."

Simon had not considered this before. He had no desire to be a monogamist. He just wanted to marry Victoria. As for other women—or boys—he would work that into his life as he saw fit. "I have made up my mind. I'll talk to Carlo and get his blessing. Then we will get married."

******

Ruth clung to Peter as they stumbled along in the dark. They could no longer afford to spend countless hours every day hidden away in the desert until the nighttime sky lit up. They were out of water and had not found a well or stream in over three days. Both were near exhaustion and it would not be long before they could not go on.

"Where are we?" Ruth inquired as she shivered from the cold and fatigue.

"I don't know. Maybe a day or two from Jerusalem," said Peter desperately.

In reality they were just outside of Hebron in the Judean desert south of Jerusalem, but with all this darkness they couldn't tell. It would be another five hours before the sun would have sufficiently charged the luminescent dust cloud enough to allow for the usual evening lighting.

"What's that?" Ruth asked as she noticed an orange glow about half a mile directly ahead of them.

"I'm not sure. I think it's a fire or something."

Both of them approached cautiously until they could finally make out a camp in the distance. They continued to walk in that direction slowly as they listened for signs of life. When they got within 50 yards, they heard the laughter of many. Something was going on in the center of the camp, but they were still too far away to see what it was.

Eventually Peter led Ruth to an area where three large tents had been put up. He peered out from behind one of the tents to see at least 100 men all dressed in green fatigues. They were sitting in a half circle facing the massive bonfire, drinking and laughing at something that was going on in front of them, but Peter could not make out what it was.

Suddenly one of the men got up and moved forward, revealing a young girl of maybe 15 being sexually assaulted by a half-naked man. The man moved aside as the next soldier moved in for his turn. The young girl stood and began to scream out for help, but the man slapped her face, knocking her to the ground. Peter looked around the camp and noticed that at the far edge was a fenced compound. The fence was at least 10 feet high and covered with barbed wire. Within the yard were a number of people standing and staring at the horrible event unfolding around the campfire.

"Let's go over there," said Peter as he led Ruth around the large tents.

"What was all that screaming about?" Ruth asked.

Peter didn't answer but continued to move towards the fence as quickly as he could.

When they reached the edge of the compound, Peter stopped and looked out towards the soldiers sitting around the fire. Another man stood and started arguing with the man who had slapped the young girl. The soldier bent down, tugged on the girl's lifeless arm, and then dropped it. Then looking at the man once again, he began to yell at him. Soon another soldier stood and began to walk toward the fenced compound.

Peter knew what he was coming for, and he felt helpless to do anything to stop him. Peter pulled Ruth to the ground and hid behind a small sand dune as the man approached the heavy, locked gate to the compound. From inside the men and women began to cry out. The soldier entered the compound and approached a teenage girl about 17 years of age. The girl began to cry as an elderly man, probably her father, stepped up to protect her. The soldier smiled at the man and lifted his rifle toward him, but the man did not budge an inch. The soldier cocked the gun and stuck the barrel of it in the man's chest, yet he still refused to move away from his daughter. Next the soldier swung the butt end of his rifle and hit the man solidly in the mouth, knocking him to the ground. He grabbed the young girl, dragged her out of the compound, and headed back to the campfire.

Peter stood quickly. "I don't think he locked the gate."

Ruth jumped up next to Peter. "What can we do? We can't help these people."

"We have to try!" Peter said in determination.

"But what about them?" asked Ruth as she pointing back to the campfire where the men were now cheering once again.

Peter crept along the sand dune close to the compound until he had no choice but to slide down towards the fence. Instantly many prisoners behind the gate saw him. One man spoke out in a dialect that Peter did not understand, although he knew it was Hebrew. He had heard Elisha speak it many times to members of his followers.

"Be quiet," Peter said softly as he crawled towards the heavy gate.

Ruth was only a few feet behind Peter when he finally reached the entrance. Looking up, he realized he was right. The man had put the lock back on the hasp, but did not push it closed. Undoubtedly the soldier thought that he might have to return for another victim and soon. Peter fumbled with the lock until it fell to the ground. Slowly he opened the gate about a foot or so and crawled in.

Blood oozed from the face of the man who had greeted Peter and Ruth. "Who are you?" he asked in English.

"We are Americans who have been hiding in the desert for the last few months. What are you doing out here?" Peter asked.

"We left Jerusalem a week ago when Simon Koch's soldiers came in looking for anyone who had not taken the ID tags and those who refused to bow down to Carlo Ventini."

"How did you end up here?" Ruth asked through the echoes of the young girl screaming in the background.

The man flinched as tears rolled down his face. "We walked from Jerusalem to Hebron and then out into the desert, but we did not move fast enough and they caught us."

"What are they planning to do with you?" Ruth inquired.

"They said we are going to be shipped to a concentration camp in Germany. My father was killed in one of those camps during WWII. It is happening all over again," said the man.

"No! It is not going to happen all over again if I can help it. We need to leave now!" said Peter.

The man shook his head. "There is nowhere to go and besides, there are 300 of us. How could we escape these men?"

"God will help us," said Peter. "Now get your things together." The wind began to blow up the sand as Peter spoke. The air was absolutely freezing. The temperature had stabilized at approximately 20 degrees below zero over the last few days, but now the chill factor would drastically reduce this. Peter stepped forward and placed his hand on the man's shoulder. "Don't let that young girl's suffering and death be for nothing. While they are distracted we can sneak away. It is so dark out there that they will have trouble finding all of us."

"Where will we go?" said the man with a hopeless look. "They will see our tracks in the sand, and by first light they will have helicopters looking for us."

"Probably," said Peter, "but we have to try."

"God will provide," said Ruth with compassion for this man.

Slowly each man, woman, and child crept out of the compound and over the small dune.

Once the group was gathered Peter began to lead them to safety as quickly as his exhausted body would allow. He had no idea where he was going, but he knew God would provide when the time came. The blowing sand was a nuisance and the chill factor was dangerously low, but the good news was that their tracks would be erased by the wind making it hard to track them at least until the fluorescing sky allowed for an air search party.

It was another 30 minutes before the young girl died and the soldiers realized their prisoners were missing. They broke camp 15 minutes later and headed out to find the prisoners but unintentionally went in the opposite direction. Simon and Oswald were going to be furious. Many soldiers would pay for this mistake with their lives.

At the first sign of the luminescent night sky, Peter stopped and looked out at the terrain. It was becoming rockier, more like Ein Gedi, but they were heading in the other direction. Peter wished he had a map. He also desperately needed a drink of water. In another few hours he was going to be too dehydrated to go on. "God help us," Peter whispered in a soft voice.

Ruth overhead Peter's prayer, and she whispered "Amen." Ruth moved in next to Peter and took his hand into hers. "You are a good man, Peter. I am proud to be out here with you."

He smiled at her and said, "You are a remarkable woman." To Peter, Ruth was regal and sophisticated yet a very natural woman—practical, tough, and definitely beautiful.

Out of the blue there was a bright glow in front of Peter and Ruth. Suddenly a large white man stood before them. "I am Barthemaus, an angel of our Living God. I am here to help you."

Peter and Ruth were afraid of the angel, but they did not fall to the ground as the other 300 people had. "You have been faithful and brave. God is pleased. Turn south," said the angel as he pointed in the direction he wanted Peter to go. "Tomorrow you will find a park in the Negev, and there you will find shelter and food for these people and for yourself."

"What about being spotted from the air? Three hundred people are a big target for a helicopter." Peter was reasoning with an angel. This he found bizarre yet amusing.

"There will be no air search. The sandstorm to the north will prevent this," said Barthemaus.

"Should we stay there with them?" Ruth asked.

"Only for a short while. Your paths are different. Peter understands this already," said Barthemaus as he looked to Dr. Bastoni. Peter could not help but see the beauty of this seven foot tall angel. He sensed his strength and his power.

The angel lifted his foot and stomped it on the ground with enough force to shake the desert floor. Instantly water began to gush forth. "Drink your fill and carry what you can. Tomorrow you will be in a different land, and God will provide. Stay long enough to gather your strength, and then leave these people in the park and continue your journey to Jerusalem."

Abruptly the angel disappeared leaving Peter and Ruth standing over a fountain of fresh water.

******

Elisha lay sleeping in the dark, cool cave. By his side, as usual, was the ever-faithful Jasmine. Suddenly the ground began to shake, and Elisha and Jasmine jumped up in fear. The room took on a foul smell and a red glow began to form in the center of the second cave.

"What is it?" a horrified Jasmine screamed.

Elisha was choking so badly on the rotten smell that he could not answer Jasmine's question. He, too, had no idea what was going on, but for sure it was frightening.

All of a sudden in the midst of the cave a large image appeared. All around people were terrified and frozen where they stood. A loud screeching noise like the call of a rutting bull elk reverberated through the caves.

"You cannot hide from me!" the voice roared. "I will destroy all of you!"

The caves shook so fiercely that the stalactites began to fall from the ceiling, injuring the people below. Screams rang out as the people ran from the falling debris and out of the caves.

"Who are you?" a frightened Elisha asked.

"I am the lord of this world!" said Satan as he pointed to Elisha. Suddenly Elisha felt himself lifted off his feet. He went hurling through the air and came crashing down against the wall of the cave. Jasmine screamed and ran towards Elisha, but before she could get to him Satan pointed a finger towards her and sent her careening into the wall, knocking her unconscious.

Elisha looked over to Jasmine as blood ran from the gash in his forehead. Jasmine's mouth and nose were bleeding. He feared the worst for her. His concern, along with his anger, began to consume him.

"You are not the lord of this world! Jesus is!" Elisha shouted over the noise of the shaking cave.

At this Satan became furious and moved towards Elisha. What could a child do against such evil? What could any mere human do to protect himself against Satan's attack?

Elisha began to pray loudly, "Jesus, You are my king and I love You and will serve only You. I will gladly die for You!"

"I was here in the beginning. I have known every member of your family since time began, and I have tested them all. I have made myself known to all of mankind, and like you, they are weak. Jesus does not want any of you!" said Satan with a laugh.

Elisha shook with fear as Satan moved closer. At this time Jasmine began to stir. Opening her eyes she witnessed Satan towering directly over a fearful Elisha as he called out to God.

"Jesus, help us!" Jasmine moaned.

Unexpectedly a rush of sweet smelling wind filled the cave and a beautiful bright light illuminated Jasmine and Elisha who were the only two remaining people in the caves. All the others had made it safely out into the cold desert where they stood by begging God for help.

Satan turned away from Elisha with a look of great concern on his face. Suddenly an angel appeared before Elisha and stood between him and Satan. This angel was not like Philip, the angel that Jasmine and Elisha had met before. This angel was so brilliantly lit that Elisha could not look directly at him. He could not make out the angel's face. All Jasmine and Elisha knew was that this heavenly being was truly more powerful than anything they had ever seen or felt other than God Himself. His wings filled the cave as his body towered some eight feet high.

"What are you doing here, Michael?" Satan asked. "It is not your time. This is my planet!"

"It was never your planet!" boomed a powerful yet soothing voice. "You have come back to the same cave you sent Saul to in order to capture King David. God knew you would come here. You are not allowed to harm these people. God has put a mark on their foreheads sealing them for eternity. Your time is short and you cannot have these children. Now be gone!"

"I am more powerful than you, Michael. I can destroy you!" said Satan.

"Not anymore," said Michael. "You may have delayed me in the past, but God forbids you to ever come into His presence again, and now the only power you have is what was created in you by God, all of which you have chosen to use for your own evil purposes. Now leave this place! I command you in the name of Jesus Christ, the King!"

The room shook terribly and again stalactites began to fall and explode on the hard rocky bottom. And Satan was gone.

Michael turned towards Jasmine and Elisha yet their eyes could not tolerate looking at his radiance. The Glory around him was just too strong for the human eye to endure.

"May the Lord heal your wounds," said Michael. Instantly Elisha and Jasmine felt their bodies being restored. Elisha wiped his hand across his forehead. There was no blood. He looked over to Jasmine whose face had been bloodied. She looked perfectly normal and as beautiful as before.

"Children, you must leave here. Satan will return. If he cannot have you, then he will want to kill you. He has little time to gather, and he does not want Christians in his way."

"Where should we go?" a worried Elisha asked.

"There is a route used in times of old from Arabia to the Mediterranean Sea. It is called the *Spice Route*. You will find shelter and water along the way. Follow it south, and then turn northeast once you leave the Negev."

"Elisha, stand before me," Michael commanded.

Elisha stood on unsure legs. Jasmine watched this as she remained seated against the wall.

"The Lord has chosen you as His leader to the people and not just these people in the caves, but all the people of His chosen land. You are their Moses. God is giving you powers to bring fresh water from rocks and to part the seas. He will go before you throughout the land, and He will feed His people. You are their leader until Christ comes back. There are many witnesses throughout the world, and God's two prophets are delivering His message and His wrath, but you have been given charge to lead His people as they hide in the desert. You are from the tribe of Levi, the tribe of Moses and Aaron, God's priest. Do not be weak in the flesh any longer. Do not doubt or fear because the Lord is with you."

As Michael departed Jasmine and Elisha walked out of the cave hand in hand as the others stood by. They were amazed that these two young-sters were even alive. They understood well enough that evil had come into their caves, and they were certain that Elisha and Jasmine were dead by now.

The people rushed in to see their leader and his companion. "How is it that you are not harmed?" said one of the counsel leaders.

"God has protected us," said Elisha. "Get the counsel members to-gether. We are leaving this place tonight."

******

Cory tried to shake the hypnotic sensation from his mind. He had been focusing on his driving so intently that his eyes began to cross. From the back seat Cory could hear Jerry snoring lightly. To his right Calvin sat quietly looking out into the darkness.

"How long until we get to Oregon?" Leasa asked.

The sound of her voice startled Cory out of his stupor. Cory looked down at his gas gauge. The needle was now below the red empty mark. "I figured we would have enough gas to make it to Ashland which is 40 miles from here, but now I am not sure if we will even make it across the border into Oregon before we run out."

Leasa leaned over and looked at the console. "Well, then I guess we will be walking to Oregon."

Cory saw the sign for Mount Shasta as he began to climb the initial grade into the Siskiyous.

"Are you hungry, Cory?" Leasa asked.

"No, I'm okay," said Cory, but that was a lie. He was starved. A big man like him needed a lot more food than the rest.

Five miles later Jerry's Jeep sputtered to a complete stop along the empty highway. "Well, this is as far as we can go, and there is no place out here to find gas," said Cory.

"Then we walk," said Calvin.

After pushing the Jeep into the brush all four members of Calvin's party loaded all they could onto their backs and began the long climb up the mountain pass. There were only a few hours of nightlight left in the sky, and Oregon was 35 miles away.

"Maybe we had better think about where we can hide out during the darkness," said Calvin.

"When I was a kid my parents took me to Lake Shasta. We stayed here for a week," said Jerry. He felt sadness fill his body as he thought about his mother who had long since died of an unsuspected aneurysm. Jerry didn't even want to think about his father and how he must have disappointed him greatly by now and probably worried him to death as well.

"There are boats there," said Leasa. "Houseboats!"

At this everyone turned towards Leasa and Jerry. "Did you stay in a houseboat, Jerry?" Calvin asked.

Jerry nodded.

Calvin looked at Cory and smiled. "The lake is frozen, so there must be a lot of—"

"Frozen houseboats stuck down there!" Cory grinned.

"Well, what are we waiting for?" cheered Leasa. "Let's go find one!"

Chapter 7: On the Ice

Day 1381, May: Cory held Leasa's hand as she climbed down the steep embankment. Below them spread out over many miles was a frozen lake. Calvin and Jerry led the way as they worked through the dried brush and down to the edge of the icy waters. The neon sky was just about gone, and soon they would not be able to see an inch in front of their faces.

"Over there!" said Calvin as he pointed towards a dim light to his left about a quarter mile out.

"What is that?" Leasa asked.

"It's a houseboat, but someone is living on it," said Jerry.

"How do you know that?" Leasa asked.

"The light," Cory whispered softly.

"Oh, yeah," said Leasa foolishly.

All four of them walked cautiously across the frozen lake. Cory in particular was afraid of this activity for two reasons. First he was large and heavy. If anyone were to break through the ice, it would be him, and secondly Cory had but one weakness and that was water. He couldn't swim a stroke.

When Calvin got within 15 feet of the large houseboat, he noticed that its pontoons were crushed like empty tin cans. The boat was wedged into the ice tightly. It was likely that it froze there quickly. Otherwise the fractured pontoons would not have kept the boat afloat. Jerry moved up next to Calvin. Together they listened for signs of life, but they heard nothing.

"What's the plan?" Cory whispered as he and Leasa stepped up next to Calvin.

"We knock," Calvin said brightly.

"Leasa, you stay back there with Jerry while Cory and I go and meet our new neighbors," said Calvin.

Calvin and Cory climbed up the side of the houseboat and walked quietly along the portside windows. The curtains were drawn tightly so they could not make out what was inside. "Where's the door on this thing?" Calvin inquired.

Just about that time Cory heard a familiar sound of a gun cocking. Slowly he turned around to see a very nervous young man pointing a shotgun directly at him.

"Who are you, and what do you want?" the frightened young man asked.

Calvin moved up next to Cory and smiled at the heavily armed man. "Mister, my name is Calvin Fraser, and this is Cory Parker, and we are here because we have nowhere else to go. If you want us to leave, we will. God will provide for us one way or another."

The man studied Calvin as closely as the dim light would allow. "Where did you come from?"

"A small mine in Nevada where we've been living for months," said Calvin.

"Why are you here?" said the man with a little more relaxed tone of voice.

"We are on our way to Alaska, but we ran out of gas back there a ways," said Calvin as he pointed in the direction from which they had come.

"I thought I heard a woman's voice earlier," said the young man.

"Yes!" nodded Calvin. "That's right. Wait right here." Calvin walked past the man and towards the back of the 35-foot boat. Soon he returned with Leasa and Jerry.

"This is Leasa Moore, and this is Jerry Little—Dr. Jerry Little." Calvin smiled.

"Are you a medical doctor?"

Jerry looked at the young man who was probably even younger than he was. "Yes, I am."

The man released the trigger on the gun and leaned it against the side of the boat. "My name is William Walker, but everyone calls me Billy."

"Well, all right, Billy. Glad to meet you," said Calvin as he extended his black hand to the young white man.

"Hey! Can we go inside? I'm freezing," Leasa asked.

"Yeah, sure, come on in," said Billy.

As soon as all five people entered the houseboat, Billy called out, "It's okay. You can come out now."

Soon a little girl of maybe three years of age wearing a thick, wooly pair of pink pajamas stepped forward. Next came a young woman carrying a small boy a little less than two years old. As soon as the lady handed the little boy over to Billy, it became obvious that this woman was pregnant—very pregnant.

"This is my wife, Peggy Walker, but everyone calls her Peggy Sue."

The woman smiled at the group. "Nice to meet you all," she said.

Calvin nearly laughed. The whole scene was terribly funny for some reason. Calvin made the introductions and soon everyone was comfortably seated. The boat was not much warmer inside than it was outside. There was a small propane heater in the middle of the room, but it was a big boat. Lanterns provided a soft, white light.

The group sat quietly for a moment before Jerry spoke up and asked, "How pregnant are you?"

"Extremely!" said Peggy Sue.

"We've been kind of worried," said Billy. "The baby is due any day, and there ain't no doctor around."

"We've been praying for help," said Peggy Sue.

"Are you Christians?" Leasa asked.

Billy laughed a silly little laugh. "That's why we are out here. We met some men last year, and they told us about Jesus and about this Carlo guy. They told us to hide and not to take that green tag. So we grabbed up the kids and hid out in the woods, but after the lake froze we walked out to this boat."

"We were living in a tent hidden in the woods, but it was really cold and there weren't much to eat. Once in a while Billy would shoot something, but lately the animals are all gone," said Peggy Sue.

Billy nodded in agreement. "I've done some ice fishing, and some-times I walk across the lake until I find a houseboat or a cabin on the shore, and I take what I can find. I hope God don't mind," said Billy sorrowfully.

"I'm sure God understands," said Calvin.

"So what's your story?" Billy asked with a foolish little smile.

Calvin recapped the last year and a half since getting out of prison. He felt it would be better not to mention Leavenworth to Billy and Peggy. Calvin told them about his encounters with angels and with God. Billy and Peggy Sue were awestruck by this testimony. All of a sudden they saw Calvin as a type of Peter the Apostle.

"Can we get you all some food?" Peggy Sue asked.

Calvin and the others felt extremely guilty at the idea of eating any of the food that could be used for the young children. "We are okay," said Calvin. "Besides, we brought some food with us."

"It's no problem," said Billy. "I've done a pretty good job of collect-ing things over the last few months."

Billy led the group to the back room where he had stashed all the bounty he had collected. As soon as he opened the door Leasa felt the chill. It was as cold in there as it was outside. "We keep this door closed so it don't ever warm up in here," said Billy.

Cory was amazed that this young guy had been so enterprising. The room was full of canned food, dried food, smoked fish, radios, portable TV's, kerosene, and a bunch of fishing tackle. "You can live off this for years," said Cory.

"What's that thing?" Leasa asked. She was looking at a small black box with a flashing blue light on its face.

"Oh, that! I took that off another houseboat about two miles up. It does a lot of things that I don't understand, but the one thing that it does that I can figure out is the temperature. It keeps a record of the tempera-ture every day. I can look at how warm it was last week or today if I push that red button on the side."

"Did you look at it today?" Calvin asked.

Billy thought for a second. "No, I don't think so."

Calvin picked the little box up and pressed the red button. The digital display lit up and began to scroll out numbers. They were readings taken throughout the day. At the end was a set of statistics which Calvin was sure Billy would never understand. The average of the temperature readings was minus 21 degrees with a range of three degrees. Calvin pushed the button again, and this time it showed the temperature results for the previous day. Calvin scrolled down to the summary. It read that the average temperature from this day was minus 24 degrees with a range of two degrees. Calvin was puzzled. He pushed the red button one more time, revealing the temperature readings from two days ago. This time the summary listed the average temperature at minus 26 degrees with a range of one degree. Looking back further Calvin noted that the summary data was nearly identical. Every day as far back as he went the temperature was minus 27 degrees with a range of a half of a degree or so.

Putting the black box down, Calvin thought to himself, *I will have to check that out tomorrow.*

"What's wrong?" Leasa asked.

Calvin smiled. "Nothing."

******

Calvin was the first one to wake to the noise of someone calling out in pain. He sat forward in his sleeping bag listening for the sound to repeat. Again a high-pitched moan echoed into the living room where he and the rest of his party lay sleeping. Suddenly Billy came running into the living room with a panic stricken look on his face. "What's the matter, Billy?" Calvin asked as he stood.

"Peggy Sue is sick! Something is wrong!" Billy cried.

"What's going on?" Leasa whispered as she struggled to wake up.

"I'm not sure," said Calvin as he bent down and began to shake Jerry.

Jerry was startled and jumped up quickly. "What's the matter?" he asked.

About that time another loud shrill could be heard coming from Billy's bedroom.

"Help her!" Billy pleaded.

Jerry ran into the bedroom with Billy and Calvin by his side. "It's too dark! I can't see anything."

"I'll get a lantern," said Billy as he rushed out.

"Peggy Sue," said Jerry. "What's the matter?"

"I don't know!" she moaned. "It's not like before. Something is wrong!"

Billy returned with the lantern and placed it on the bookshelf next to his anxious wife.

"Peggy, I need to examine you. Is that okay?" Jerry asked softly.

Peggy nodded as tears ran down her young cheeks. Jerry turned to see Cory standing next to Billy, Leasa, and Calvin. "I need you guys to leave."

They all turned to go when Jerry called back to Leasa. "But I need your help, Leasa."

"Me? I don't know anything about having a baby."

"Will you help me?" Jerry asked as Peggy Sue began to scream out in pain once again.

"Yes!" said Leasa nervously.

Five minutes later Jerry came back into the living room where Billy stood anxiously. "Billy, your wife is in labor but the baby is breech."

"What does that mean?" Billy asked as he began to sway back and forth.

Calvin took Billy's arm and led him down to the couch before he could pass out from fear.

Jerry looked into Billy's dim, brown eyes. "Billy, this baby is wedged inside of Peggy Sue very tightly. There is a danger here for the baby and the mother. If I were in a hospital, I would have called in an obstetrician by now."

"You are a doctor. You can fix her!" Billy pleaded.

"Billy, I am a second-year resident. I've only delivered three babies in my life and they were all normal deliveries. What your wife really needs is a surgeon."

There came another loud scream from the other room and quickly Leasa emerged. "Something is happening! I need you, Jerry—now!"

Jerry ran into the room in time to see Peggy nearly convulsing from the pain. When he went to examine her, he saw that she was hemorrhaging. "Oh, God, help me," said Jerry.

In the other room Cory and Calvin gathered around Billy and laid hands on him and began to call out to God. Billy cried and prayed as hard as he could as tears streamed down his face. Every time Peggy Sue creamed, Billy began to sob even harder. This young man loved his wife dearly, and it seemed that he was about to lose her and the baby.

Jerry called out commands to Peggy Sue, but she was in such pain she could not do much to help. Jerry had to lie nearly flat on his stomach between Peggy Sue's legs as he tried to turn the baby. Leasa held the lantern above his head. The sight of so much blood was making her very nauseated, but she maintained her post all the same.

Finally Jerry had the umbilical cord out of the way enough to turn the baby. Instantly the child's head moved down into the birthing canal where it stopped. Peggy Sue had suffered so much trauma and blood loss that her body naturally constricted, narrowing the canal with muscles tightly clamped in place. If Jerry had had a muscle relaxant or even a scalpel, he could have performed an episiotomy. He didn't even have any forceps to grasp the baby's skull. The situation was getting intolerable. Both baby and mother would die quickly if he did not do something. Finally Jerry managed to get his hand over the back of the baby's head. Then forcibly he pulled the child forward until he could feel the baby's shoulders. At this point, Jerry took two fingers and lodged them up under the baby's collarbone and, with as much force as he could muster, he pulled the bone towards himself. Leasa heard the loud snap as the bone broke into two pieces. As soon as Jerry pulled his hand back out the baby slid down the mother's birth canal and into his hands.

"You did it, Jerry!" said Leasa.

But the baby was not crying, and it was terribly purple. Jerry swiped the baby's mouth and hung the child upside down to drain the excess blood and fluid from its lungs, but still nothing. Finally Jerry put his moth over the little boy's nose and mouth and began to blow small puffs of air into the child. Soon the baby began to squall and cough. Jerry smiled, and

Leasa cried.

Jerry tied a piece of string around the umbilical cord and handed the baby to Leasa. "Put the baby on Peg's breast. The suckling will help to reduce the bleeding." Jerry went back to work to deliver the placenta and to stop Peggy Sue's bleeding with a uterus massage.

In the other room the men sat back impatiently. The noise of the screams had come and gone and the noise of a baby's cry had disappeared as well. They were all very worried men.

Finally, after about 30 minutes, Jerry and Leasa walked out carrying a small bundle. Billy stood and ran to Jerry. "How's Peggy Sue?"

"She's resting. She has lost a lot of blood, and she has some painful tears that will take time to heal, but she is going to be just fine."

Billy hugged Jerry tightly and cried.

"Meet your new son," said Leasa as she handed the small boy over to Billy.

******

A week had gone by and it was time to be moving on. Calvin and Cory had been working on the details of their trip. It was approximately 3,300 miles to Anchorage, and by foot that would take a lifetime if it could be done at all. But what choice did they have?

They checked all the houseboats they could find and in each case the frozen lake had crushed the gas tank allowing the precious fuel to leak out. They would have to rely on God to provide. *If we are meant to go to Alaska, then somehow we will get there,* Calvin thought.

Jerry sat back on the couch holding the little baby that had just recently been named after the doctor who delivered him into this horrid world. "It would be so much easier if we were all about this age," Jerry smiled.

"Well, let's have some supper," said Billy, "and then we can talk more about how you guys are going to get to Alaska."

"Sounds good to me," said Calvin. "What are we having?"

"Whatever you pick out of my warehouse I will cook up for you all,"

Billy grinned.

"Okay," said Calvin, "let me go see what I can find." Calvin entered the storeroom of the boat. It was still very cold in there. He mulled over the cans of food. Finally he found a few cans of spinach and some more cans of black-eyed peas and two cans of Spam. *This isn't exactly turnip greens and fried pork,* thought Calvin to himself, *but it's a close cousin.*

As Calvin turned to leave, the flickering blue light of the little black box caught his attention. He had forgotten all about the little temperature controller. Calvin set his food down, picked up the box, and pushed the red button. *Let's see what's been going on this week,* he thought.

He scrolled down the screen until he came to the summary. On this particular day it was only 14 degrees below zero on average, but the range was up to six degrees.

"Hum," said Calvin. He scrolled back to the previous day and then again to the day before that. Moving the readings forward, again it was clear that each day the temperature was a little warmer and the range was a little larger. "It's warming up," said Calvin aloud.

About that time Cory entered the room. "Having trouble picking out our feast?"

Calvin turned towards Cory. He held up the black box and smiled.

"What is it?" Cory grinned.

"It's warming up!" Calvin grinned.

"What?" Cory asked.

"Grab those cans and let's get out of this refrigerator. I will explain." Calvin set the black box down carefully. He didn't want to take it out of the room and affect the temperature reading. Just opening the door could confuse the results.

At the dinner table Calvin explained what he thought was happening to the weather. "I don't know why or how, but it is warming up for sure."

"What does that mean to us?" Billy asked.

"It means that soon you will be floating on a real lake again," said Jerry with a smile.

Calvin thought about this for a few seconds. "No, you won't."

"What do you mean?" asked Peggy Sue who was now out of bed and

~~moving around.~~

"Your boat has damaged pontoons. As soon as the lake thaws out, this boat will start to sink."

Peggy Sue looked to Billy for support. "Well, I guess we are gonna have to find another place to hide then. I'll start looking tomorrow. How long until the lake thaws out?"

Calvin had already done the math. "Assuming this warming effect does not stop and assuming it is a constant rate, which it won't be, but for the sake of my calculations, I'd say about 40 or 50 days from now this boat will sink."

Billy didn't understand most of what Calvin was saying, but he did understand the part about his boat sinking in 40 or 50 days. "I have a lot of stuff to move," said Billy aloud as he began to think about what he would need to do to protect his family.

"We will help you," said Cory with a smile.

"Too bad I don't know how to fly, or I'd just fly my way out of here," said Billy as he took another bite of the fried Spam.

Calvin dropped his fork and turned to the young man. "Billy, do you know where there is a plane?"

Billy nodded over a mouth full of food.

"Can you take us to it?" Calvin asked.

"Sure, but it is black as coal out there now."

"We can take lanterns. Do you think you can find it?" Calvin asked.

"Yeah, I think so."

"Jerry, you and Leasa stay here with Peggy and the kids. Cory and I will go with Billy."

Jerry looked at Calvin. "Can you fly a plane?"

Calvin nodded and smiled. "Yes, Jerry, I can."

Calvin and Cory walked alongside Billy for nearly an hour, but still there was no plane in sight. "I know it's here somewhere," said Billy.

"Tell us again how you found it," said Cory.

"I was walking along the edge of the lake and I came across a big wooden building. It was locked, but in the back was a window. So I broke it and climbed in. There was this little yellow plane just sitting there."

"And you are sure it is this way?" Calvin asked.

"I think so."

Thirty more minutes and Calvin was about to give up. It was just too dark even with the lanterns, and he knew they were all freezing to death.

"There it is!" said Billy.

There in front of them, just as Billy had described, was a large wooden shed. The men climbed around the back of the shed. Cory held the lantern high against the window as Calvin peered in, and before him was an old yellow plane sitting on a pair of pontoons.

"It's a Bellanca," said Calvin. "Probably a 1959 model—see the wooden wings."

Cory couldn't tell if the wings were wooden or metal so he just took Calvin's word for it.

"Let's get in there and see what we can do," said Calvin excitedly.

One by one all three men climbed into the old shed. It doesn't look like anyone has been here for years," said Cory.

"Except me," Billy laughed.

Calvin climbed into the cockpit and inspected the gauges. "Let's open the bonnet and have a look see."

Cory held the light up close as Calvin climbed around the engine compartment. "It's piston driven, but it is not the original motor."

"Will it run?" Cory inquired.

Calvin looked at him and smiled. "There is only one way to find out, but first we need to get these doors open or we will asphyxiate when we start this thing."

Cory looked around the shed until he found a tire iron. "I'll be back in a minute," said Cory as he climbed back through the window.

A moment later Calvin heard a loud splintering sound, and soon the large wooden doors began to open. "Okay, start her up!" said Cory.

Calvin climbed back into the cockpit and began to prime the motor. Next he set the choke and then he pushed the ignition button, but nothing happened. The fuel gauge read full. Assuming the gauge worked, there was no reason that the plane should not start. Then it occurred to Calvin like a bolt of lightning—*the battery!*

Calvin climbed back out of the cockpit. "We need a new battery."

"Well, I got lots of stuff back at the boat, but I ain't got no batteries," said Billy.

"Where can we get a battery?" Cory asked.

Suddenly a smile appeared across Cory's and Calvin's faces simultaneously. "Do you think it's still there?" Calvin asked.

"It should be. We pushed it into the brush," said Cory.

"What?" Billy asked.

"The Jeep!" said Cory.

"Let's get back to the boat. We can go after the battery as soon as the night sky comes up," said Calvin.

All three men walked out of the shop. "Sure looks small to me," said Cory as he took one last look at the plane before shutting the large wooden doors.

******

The following evening Jerry and Cory went back for the battery while Calvin and Billy went looking for a new home for Peggy Sue and the kids. Fifty yards up the bank of a small inlet sat a log cabin. How Billy never came across this place before, he had no idea. It was perfect for his family. There was plenty of firewood all around and the house seemed to be well built. Best of all it was hidden away from just about anyone. Even the tall trees protected it from the sky in case a plane should fly over.

Inside were a few supplies and plenty of towels and blankets. Billy would have to carry frozen water from the lake as usual, but the 50 yards wouldn't kill the young man.

"Okay," said Calvin, "this is your new home. We will help you carry all of your supplies from the boat before we leave. You will be safe here after we go."

Billy looked at Calvin, but said nothing. It was obvious to Calvin that the young man did not want them to leave. He had grown accustomed to having these other men around to help him protect his family. Calvin understood that Billy was not a well-educated man. All of this was very frightening to the poor guy. "God will take care of you, Billy. I think that is why He brought us to you just when you needed a doctor and help moving.

Billy nodded silently.

******

Cory and Jerry found the Jeep right where they stashed it. Cory popped the hood and Jerry fumbled around with the pliers Billy had given him, but he just could not get the battery loose from the car.

"What's the matter?"

"All thumbs," said Jerry. "I never could fix my own car. That's why I became a doctor," he laughed.

Cory took the pliers from Jerry and quickly removed the bolts holding the battery in place. An hour later they were back in the houseboat without ever seeing a single person.

The very next day, after moving Billy's family, it was time to say goodbye. Calvin stood next to Billy and put his hand on the young man's shoulder. "If we can't get this plane to start, then we are going to walk out of here—so either way this is goodbye." Calvin thought Billy might cry by the look on his face.

"Let's pray," said Calvin.

The group stood in a circle in front of the log cabin. Jerry held Little Jerry while Peggy Sue held Little Billy, and nestled next to her was the young Patty. Calvin's heart went out to them. This was not the time to have a family. "May the Lord bless you and keep you. I pray for protection over Billy Walker and his family. Lord, keep Your hand on them all. Amen."

Jerry handed the baby back to his father and smiled. As Jerry turned to leave, Peggy Sue leaned in and kissed him. "Thank you for saving me and the baby," she whispered.

Calvin and the group marched toward the wooden shed with battery in hand and heavy packs on their backs. Billy had loaded them down with extra food.

Once they reached the old shed, Calvin installed the battery and climbed back into the cockpit. *I hope this is a 12-volt system,* he thought silently. "Stand back!" Calvin pushed the ignition button and watched as the twin-bladed prop began to rotate. Large puffs of black smoke began to bellow out of the exhaust. "Come on!" said Calvin softly.

"Come on, baby!" Cory cheered.

Finally the plane's engine took hold and began to roar to life. Leasa jumped up and down as Jerry and Cory clapped their hands. Calvin thinned the choke until the plane started to idle on its own. He climbed out of the cockpit and walked over to Cory. "We need to push this thing down to the ice."

Cory nodded. "Leasa, climb in with Calvin. Jerry and I will give this plane a little push."

Both men took a wing and pushed. To Jerry the plane weighed a ton and was not going to budge, but then finally it moved forward. Jerry knew that his contribution to the forward motion was virtually unnecessary. Cory was doing all the work.

The men climbed into the small plane with Jerry in the back next to Leasa once again. Cory had to slouch down in his seat in order not to hit his head on the ceiling. This was not going to be a very comfortable ride, but it beat walking in the freezing weather.

Calvin gave the plane full throttle and one-quarter flaps as it skidded across the ice. Soon the plane was airborne. Calvin adjusted his altimeter and headed the plane to the north.

"How far can we go on this tank of gas?" Cory inquired.

"Good question!" said Calvin. "It always depends on speed and weight combined with head or tail winds. We are just going to have to wing it for a while until I can average our hourly fuel consumption."

Cory began to look around the compartment. He opened a small hatch in the front and pulled out a map. "What's this?" Cory asked.

"Open it," said Calvin.

It was a map of North America. "This might help some, especially if we have to ditch at some point," Calvin said.

"Ditch?" said Jerry as he looked at Leasa.

******

Five hours went by silently as the group sat back and enjoyed the plane's heater. They had not felt warmth like that for months. "Let me see the map one more time," said Calvin.

Calvin looked at his gas gauge and stared out into the night sky as he calculated how far they had traveled. "In about 30 minutes we will see a big frozen lake called Kluane Lake. I think this is as far as we can go."

"Are we going to crash?" Leasa asked.

Calvin smiled at the innocent question. "No, we are not going to crash."

Thirty minutes later Calvin circled the parameter of Kluane Lake. There were two distinct little communities on the west side of the lake. Calvin was not too enthused about landing the plane near people, although based on the number of homes he saw below him, there couldn't be too many people. Calvin chose the inlet furthest up which happened to be at the edge of Destruction Bay. His calculations had held true. Calvin landed the plane as best he could, but the ice made for a bumpy ride. Leasa let out a little gasp as the plane bounced around and leaped back into the air. Finally the plane coasted to a stop at the edge of the lake. "We're here!" smiled Calvin.

Chapter 8: Someone's Pregnant

Day 1435, July: Tommy held Sara's head as she bent forward once again. The smell of the vomit was nauseating, but Tommy didn't care. This was the third day in a row that Sara had been ill. It all started about a week ago while they had been working their way through the cantons of Switzerland. Tommy walked Sara over behind a large stack of wooden crates hidden in the alleyway behind an abandoned warehouse and sat down. "What's the matter with you?" Tommy asked softly.

Sara looked up to the luminescent night sky and sighed heavily. She had been thinking about this question for the last couple of days, but she didn't want to say anything to Tommy. Sara couldn't believe it could be true, but now she knew it was. "I am pregnant!" she moaned.

"Pregnant!" Tommy blurted. "That's not possible."

Sara looked at Tommy and frowned.

"Oh, yeah! I guess it is," said Tommy. "Well, what do we do now?"

"I guess we have a baby," Sara smiled weakly.

"When?"

Sara thought about it for a moment. "I'd say sometime in January or February."

"So we have seven months to get ready," said Tommy like an expectant father.

Sara had to laugh. "Get ready? It's not like we have a nursery to paint, you know."

Tommy was suddenly depressed. How could he be so careless as to bring a new baby into such an evil world?

"Well, look on the bright side," said Sara with tears in her eyes. "We will probably be caught and killed well before this poor baby is born."

Tommy held Sara as they both cried and mourned for their unborn child.

******

Back in the United World headquarters Raymond Hyder conferred with the scientists at the Jet Propulsion Laboratory once again. "Are you sure?" Raymond asked as he leaned back in his expensive leather chair. His office, kindly provided by Carlo and Simon, was extravagant—too much so for Raymond's taste. It was an elaborate prison as far as he was concerned, but what could he do about any of it? He was a puppet for these two crazy men and nothing would ever change that.

"Yes," said the man from the Jet Lab, "two whole degrees today alone."

"But how?" inquired Dr. Hyder. "It can't be possible!"

"We agree, but we also have noticed a change in the amount of light coming through during the day, as well, and a reduction in the luminescent quality of our night sky. Something is happening."

Raymond thanked the scientist and hung up the phone. He needed to ponder this new information for a while before he told Simon and Carlo. *How was it possible that after three asteroids and one massive nuclear strike against Russia the weather appeared to be warming up— maybe even to the point that the dust cloud was breaking down? This global cloud should be here for years,* Raymond told himself.

Everything had been as he had predicted right down to the subzero weather. This was a nuclear winter. In the last four months most of the plant life had already died, and soon all the trees would die. The oceans had fallen hundreds of feet as they froze, and the animals—at least those exposed to the elements—were all dead by now. People were freezing to death in places where oil was unavailable. *Perhaps,* thought Raymond, *there has been some kind of planetary shift. But how will I ever know that? he wondered. I can't see the stars or the sun.*

******

Sara and Tommy wandered along the streets of Zurich. The place was nearly empty. The temperature kept most people home—that and a fear of catching the plague. As Tommy rounded the corner, in full view of the local train station he spotted three teenagers taunting an elderly man. This was usually the way it started for Sara and Tommy. They would enter a town and wander aimlessly until they just happened to meet somebody. They had no real strategy or a specific target in mind. They would meet people and test them to see if they were followers of Carlo and Simon. If so, they would move along quickly, and if not, they would linger and share their testimony. On one occasion as Tommy and Sara worked their way through the cantons they were blessed to meet three Jewish witnesses, part of the 144,000.

These witnesses were powerful and convincing. Many followed after them and, as a result, small churches would start up in secretive places that so far Tommy and Sara had not been privileged to attend.

Tommy had shared his testimony with these three men. They were impressed with him and Sara. Their encounters with Simon, the work they did on the ID tags, and the underground scientific community they had established were an incredible help to the world, but most remarkable to these men was the fact that Tommy and Sara had had so much divine intervention from God, angels, and Martha and Harry.

Tommy had Sara stand next to the tracks—safely away—as he approached the three teenagers and the old man. "Good day!" said Tommy with a smile.

"Who are you, Mister?" asked one of the boys with a heavy German accent.

"I'm your friend," said Tommy.

"We don't need any friends," said another boldly.

"Has this man done something to offend you?" Tommy inquired.

"Yeah!" said one pimpled faced teenager, "He got born."

"This is a dirty Jew!" said another boy with a stupid grin on his young face.

"He is one of the reasons that Carlo Ventini, our god, has been punishing us," said another boy.

"But now, Mr. Koch has a plan for rats like this. His security leader, Mr. Heydrich has opened up the concentration camps in Germany, and soon all of these dirty pigs will go there to rot," said the pimply boy. Tommy was unaware until recently that the concentration camps had been reopened, but it made sense. There would have to be a place to send Jews and Christians unless they just wanted to kill them outright. If they did this, they would not be able to get any of them to take ID tags.

Tommy wondered whether a person who had an ID tag forced into his body would still go to Hell for eternity. *Perhaps even Carlo has rules to play by,* he thought.

"Well, it seems you boys have done a good thing in stopping this man."

The old man looked into Tommy's face, and fear filled his eyes. "I guess I will have to take him with me and turn him in."

"Wait a minute, Mister! Who are you, and what gives you the right to take him? We found him first."

"Well, then you can come with me," smiled Tommy, "but I hope you have some antidote with you, because there is a bad outbreak of the plague where we are going."

All three teenagers and the old man looked at Tommy in fear. "Hey, Mister, you take him in for us. We need to get home."

Tommy smiled and nodded as the boys ran off.

The old man looked at Tommy carefully. "You are American, no?" the old man asked.

"You come all the way to Switzerland to catch me?"

"I came all the way to Switzerland because Simon Koch brought me here," said Tommy as Sara walked up next to him. After seeing the boys run off she assumed it was safe to move.

The old man swallowed hard. "You work for Simon Koch?"

Tommy played it very cool as usual. "Is that a problem for you?" he asked.

"No!" the old man whispered as he looked down at his feet.

"What's your name?" Sara inquired.

"Joel," said the man.

"Joel what?" asked Tommy in an intimidating way.

Sara never liked it when Tommy acted this way, but she understood he had to be sure.

"Silverman."

"Well, Joel Silverman, who is your god?"

The old man looked up to Tommy. "There is only one God—Jehovah!"

Tommy smiled. "So you do not acknowledge Carlo Ventini as God?"

"I do not," said the man as he looked away from Tommy.

Tommy beamed at Sara. "Me either!"

The old man looked up to Tommy with a confused look on his face. "I thought you said that Simon Koch brought you here?"

"He did! In handcuffs, but we escaped," said Sara with a smile of her own.

Soon Tommy and Sara had fully introduced themselves to Joel. They shared their adventures of the last three years or so. The only detail they left out was their visit to Mueller's house as they walked toward Zurich. They explained to Joel that they had gone from town to town over the last few months witnessing and surviving off the love and support of other Christians. Tommy explained that their primary mission was to help people understand the dangers of the ID tags so that hopefully those who had not taken the mark of the beast would make a choice for Jesus.

******

Dr. Hyder sat in the living room of his lonely apartment brooding over his own uncertainty. He was to make his usual weekly presentation to Carlo and Simon as to the state of the world. Up until now he had been unfortunately accurate to the point that every miserable detail predicted by him had come to pass. *But now,* thought Raymond, *now I have big trouble.*

Raymond leaned back in the comfortable recliner and closed his eyes tightly. His head was pounding painfully from so many excruciating hours of studying. He had spent half the night in the basement of the Spaceguard

Foundation running simulations through the Teraflops computer, but he came up with nothing. There had to be a reason the earth was warming up. He had to find the explanation as to why this was happening, and he had to be able to predict what would happen next.

Raymond tried calculating various nutation effects, those effects where there are periodic variations in the inclination of the earth's axis caused by degrees of gravitational pull or, simply put, the earth's bend towards the sun due to gravitational pulls from the sun and other planets. All of these potential perturbations just seemed to add to the present Ice Age effect. *It should just get colder,* Raymond had told himself after reviewing the calculations for the third time. *What am I missing?* he wondered.

The phone in Dr. Hyder's apartment rang loudly, startling him back to reality. "Hello," said Raymond tentatively. He was afraid it would be Simon or maybe even Carlo himself.

Raymond breathed a sigh of relief as he recognized the voice on the phone as the senior scientist from the Jet Propulsion Lab. "I hope I haven't disturbed you too early this morning," said the man. "We've been working all evening to find some answers, and we finally have something."

Raymond sat up attentively. "I'm all ears. What is it?"

The phone signal began to break up as Raymond sat listening. "I can't hear you—say again."

Finally the static cleared up a bit. "This is part of the problem," said the man. "We are suffering from a magnetic storm, and we now know why."

Again the phone grew loud and full of static. Raymond waited patiently for the noise level to drop so he could continue the conversation. "What is it?" Raymond asked trying not to show his own anxiety.

"It all started with one of our technicians," said the man. "As we focused on what could cause the planet to begin to warm, he was busy listening into space trying to detect any further asteroid or NEO's. Suddenly he started hearing a low energy noise, and when he tried to plot its origin, he found that it was coming from a direction away from where we thought the sun was located or at least where we thought the sun should be. Simultaneously we got our first signal in months from the Ulysses spacecraft. It was obvious to us that there were at least some holes in the dust cloud allowing us to make intermittent radio contact. We thought Ulysses was destroyed, but lucky for us it was far enough out to miss the dust cloud."

Raymond began to sigh and fidget as he waited for the real details. "Okay, I'm with you. Continue, please!" interjected an impatient Dr. Hyder.

"Well," said the man, "when we pointed Ulysses' vision system towards the sun, it wasn't there. I mean it wasn't where we thought it should be."

"Why not? Where is it?" Raymond asked.

"It was in a completely different orbit than we expected! In fact, all of the planets are in a different orbit, and they're still moving toward some alignment that we are just now mapping out."

"How does this impact the earth's temperature or the breakdown of this dust cloud?"

"Our theory is complicated, but this is the short of it," said the man as he took a long breath.

Again as the phone grew noisy, Raymond thought he would die from anxiety as he waited for it to clear.

"That it's only going to get worse," said the scientist as the phone static quieted. "As you are aware, there are three basic layers to the atmosphere of the sun. The closest to the sun is the photosphere, above that is the chromosphere, and finally above that is the corona. Whenever the photosphere is agitated by some solar phenomenon, it reacts with a burst of energy. Temperatures rise above the normal 6,000 degrees Kelvin and this energy is absorbed into the chromosphere, raising its temperature from approximately 3,000 degrees Kelvin to as much as twice that. This again is transferred to the corona creating coronal holes and finally creating solar winds, huge quantities of electrons, and protons on a direct collision course with earth."

"What is causing this phenomenon?" Raymond asked. "Will it last long enough to burn through this dust cloud?"

"When we turned Ulysses we discovered an unusual culmination of the celestial massings. The conjunctions between Venus and Jupiter were separated by only 42 arc seconds where Venus occults Jupiter."

Raymond listened carefully. Astrophysics was not his specialty. He needed a simplified explanation. "What does this mean to me?" Raymond asked.

"I am sorry," said the man. "I am so used to talking this way around here that I forget not everyone is an astronomer. What this means is that the alignment between Venus and Jupiter is rare indeed. When we ran this through our planetarium program, we found that this conjunction with Jupiter has not happened this way since about 3 B.C. as referenced in the book of Matthew as he described the birth of Jesus Christ."

The Star of Bethlehem. Raymond felt a chill run down his neck. He swallowed hard and asked the man to continue.

"Dr. Hyder, we have found something here we just cannot fully comprehend. We got a single look by Ulysses before we lost our signal, and we have never regained contact with this or any other spacecraft to help us triangulate this phenomenon, but based on our calculations, we have nine planets—not eight, but nine including Pluto, which never comes into alignment with the other eight planets. All of these planets are heading into an orbit that has a substantial influence on the photosphere of the sun. We expect this solar storm to continue to bombard the earth, breaking this dust cloud up."

Raymond was stunned. What he was hearing meant that the earth would not die an icy death after all. "How long will it take to break up this cloud?" Raymond asked.

"Well, we thought you might ask that, so we ran a number of simulations on our Teraflops and—"

Raymond could hear the pause on the phone, but he could not hear any static. "What is it?"

"It will take a couple of months before it is gone completely, provided the solar storms last, but we have a bigger problem."

"What problem?" Raymond winced at the thought.

"We only got a brief glimpse, but if what we saw holds true, then all nine of these planets including the earth and sun will line up in such a way that Jupiter will hold the earth in very close rotation to the sun. And since the earth tilts as it rotates around the sun, it is likely that the moon will be blocked out as will part of the sun."

"What's bad about that?" Dr. Hyder inquired.

"Two things," said the scientist. "First we will be held very close to the sun so it will go from very cold to very hot quickly."

"How hot?" interrupted Raymond.

"Incredibly hot! Maybe 130 ambient and at the extreme over 150 degrees Fahrenheit."

"People will die!" said Raymond.

"Yes, they are freezing to death today, and in two or three months they will die from heat exhaustion. It's crazy!"

"And what was the second point?" asked Dr. Hyder nearly too scared to ask.

"After this alignment heats up the earth, it is going to move the planet into an orbit where the sun goes from being partially locked out by Jupiter to being entirely blocked out."

"So what you are saying is that we will have a partial alignment blocking some of the sun but still heating the crud out of the planet. It is a good thing that the sun is partially blocked anyway. And then you are saying the sun will be totally blocked out and it will get cold again."

"That's just about it, but it will not last as long as this dust cloud has, so it won't get as cold for sure, but it will be dark—very dark—with no luminescence to help out."

"What about tidal waves and earthquakes due to the planetary alignment?" Raymond asked cautiously.

"That's more myth and legend than anything," said the scientist. "People have always worried about this, but it is just not true. The influence on our tides due to planetary alignments, other than the moon's influence itself, are nearly nonexistent, and as for earthquakes there has been no correlation ever proven. The *Jupiter Effect* is all hype and little science."

"So these are the facts then? How confident are you in this?" Dr. Hyder needed reassurance before he met with Simon and Carlo.

"With only one brief look into space, we are not very confidant, but what else can we do? We have to explain these temperature changes." The phone began to break up slightly. "One other thing. When we plotted the course of all nine planets and the sun, we found that they actually formed a shape with the earth dead in the center."

"What shape?" Dr. Hyder asked.

The noise of the phone was starting to get bad again. "It is the shape of a cross."

"A cross!" said Raymond. At this the phone screamed out and went dead. The lights in Dr. Hyder's room began to flicker on and off until finally they calmed down again.

"Magnetism," said Raymond aloud as he grabbed his coat to leave for Carlo's chamber.

******

Simon entered Carlo's office with Victoria by his side. In the center of the room was the elaborate model of Babylon that Simon had seen once before. To the left Carlo sat back in his high chair with a passive look on his face as if he were deep in thought.

"Good morning, Your Excellency!" Simon smiled.

Carlo looked past Simon and directly to Victoria. His gaze frightened her greatly. "How are you feeling today, Simon?" Carlo inquired.

"Much better," Simon smiled. During the last couple of months Simon had completely healed from his bout with the plague.

"Good! We have a lot of things to discuss, but first there is someone I want you to meet."

Simon was not in the mood to have discussions about the state of the world. He had come this morning to get Carlo's permission for Victoria and him to get married. He had put this conversation off for too long already.

"Who is it?" Simon asked.

Carlo picked up his phone and asked to have Mr. Yin sent in. A moment later a middle-aged Chinese man came through the door and stood before Carlo as if he were a private in the military standing before the base commander.

"Mr. Yin, I'd like you to meet Simon Koch, the man I have entrusted with my world and my people."

The man turned to Simon and smiled. "Mr. Koch, it is my pleasure to meet you." Simon noted the man's heavy Asian accent.

"Who are you again?" Simon asked.

"My name is Whi Yin."

"Mr. Yin is the new president of China," said Carlo with a little grin.

"How can this be?" a confused Simon asked. "I just met with the Chinese President months ago before we nuked Russia."

"Yes, well, he is no longer capable of performing his role," said Carlo.

"Why not?" Simon did not like the fact that he was unaware of these massive changes.

Mr. Yin looked toward Simon and smiled.

"Unfortunately the previous president had an unhealthy agenda of his own," said Carlo.

"He's dead?" asked Simon.

"Yes!" answered Carlo.

Victoria stood by amazed that she was in the center of the room listening to the most powerful men in the world discuss the affairs of the largest country in the world, *and not just men,* she thought, *but a god too.*

"Why was I not informed?" an irritated Simon asked.

"You were ill at the time, Simon, so I thought I'd do you a favor and take care of it for you."

Simon looked into Carlo's eyes. Sometimes it was hard for him to remember that Carlo was the son of Satan and a god on this planet. All Simon knew at this moment was that Carlo had gone over his head, and he didn't like it.

"You can thank me later, Simon, but now we have some work to do. Victoria, you need to wait outside."

That was the final straw for Simon. He had come there this morning to share the happy news with Carlo, but now he found his own power being usurped and his fiancée dismissed before he could even ask Carlo for permission.

"No!" said Simon.

Carlo looked into Simon's eyes so intently that Simon's legs began to shake. "Did you say *no* to me?" Carlo roared.

Simon swallowed hard. Maybe he had gone a little too far. "Your Holiness, I came here this morning to ask your permission. Victoria and I want to get married."

Carlo raised his hand before Simon. "Victoria, come to me."

Simon looked at Victoria. She had a look of fear in her eyes. "Go to him," said Simon as he let loose of her hand.

Victoria moved slowly towards Carlo and when she was only five feet away she knelt and lowered her head. Carlo stood and walked over to her. With one hand he lifted her chin towards his face. "Do you want to marry Simon?"

"Yes!" Victoria whispered.

"Why?" Carlo asked.

Victoria was usually very sure of herself and capable of thinking quickly, but in the presence of Carlo she grew weak. "I love him," she said with a shaky and very unconvincing voice.

"Do you really! Why?" Carlo asked with a little smile on his face.

Simon felt very uneasy. He had no idea where Carlo was going with this line of questioning, and he didn't like seeing his queen bow before Carlo.

"Simon is a great man, kind and loving to me," Victoria said.

Carlo let out a laugh and turned towards Simon. "Is this right, Simon? Are you a kind and loving man?"

Simon hoped it was a rhetorical question because he had no intention of answering Carlo.

"Rise, Victoria," said Carlo. "Leave us. Simon and I will discuss your future after we conclude this more important meeting."

Victoria scooted by Simon in a hurry as she left the room.

Mr. Yin had watched the entire show and saw how Carlo treated the most powerful man in the world. His respect for the infamous Simon Koch was greatly reduced.

Carlo reseated himself. "Simon, Yin, come to me." Both men moved forward quickly. "I have a desire to control all of the oil in this world. Now how am I going to do that?" Carlo inquired.

"You wouldn't let me take control over the militaries in the Middle East," said Simon. "We would control all the oil refineries if I had military control. So now I guess I could stop food shipments from our Agripods or eliminate the antidote in those countries if you want. This might motivate Saudi Arabia, Kuwait, and Iran. As for Iraq, you already have their full support," said Simon.

Carlo looked to Whi Yin for his response. "I have the largest military in the world at my disposal. If you wish I could go into the Middle East with over 3 million troops and take captive the oil refineries," said Yin with a proud smile.

Simon's blood began to boil. *Where did this man come from? I am the most powerful man in the world, and I have the biggest army in the world, thought Simon to himself. In fact, China comes under my authority—including its military— and so does this weasel of a man. How dare he even consider attacking the Middle East without my consent.*

Carlo smiled at his prophet. He knew what Simon was thinking, and he liked the fact that Simon was not willing to share his power with anyone.

"Okay, Mr. Yin, I will take your recommendation into consideration. You go back to China and prepare your military. Simon will let you know if he wants your help or not."

At this Simon turned to Yin and leered at him defiantly as if to say, *See, I told you I am the most powerful man in the world, and you work for me for as long as I allow it.*

After Yin left Carlo led Simon back over to the model of Babylon. With his right hand Carlo touched the Ziggurat in the middle of the city. He so wanted this construction completed soon, but with the flooded Tigris and Euphrates, all of his efforts were delayed. Now, however, the rivers had receded and the mud was being removed. Soon construction would continue. As for the Tigris and Euphrates, things could not be any worse. The rivers had washed down millions of metric tons of dirt and debris into the waterways and out into the Persian Gulf. The natural flow of water had been permanently disrupted, all the dams were gone, and hydroelectric power was no more, but worse than all of this was the lack of fresh water throughout Turkey, Syria, Iran, and Iraq. What little water was left was muddy and unfit to drink, and all of it was frozen. Since it had not rained in months and probably would not any time soon, the rivers were dying.

"Who is that man?" Simon asked as he watched Carlo caressing his great city.

"Who? Whi Yin?"

"Yes," said Simon. "How come I wasn't involved in this? Why are you giving him any power and military control, and why didn't you let me take over the Middle East myself?"

Carlo turned on Simon with obvious displeasure. "There is much you do not know!" Carlo roared. "It is not the place of my prophet to start wars. We do not fight for control of the world. This is my planet. I do not have to go to war against man to possess it."

Simon swallowed hard as he listened to the enraged Carlo.

"You could not take over the Middle East without creating a world-wide nuclear war. It is best if we let China and those other countries fight it out. My father will give you powers when necessary to glorify me and to defuse this fight. We will need these soldiers again later when—" Carlo paused and Simon shivered at the thought. He understood that Carlo was talking about the *Return of Jesus* and the final battle that would be fought for total control over the world and the heavens.

"Where did Whi Yin come from?" Simon asked as he tried to divert Carlo.

"He is a man that my father has used before to capture and kill Christians throughout China. He is faithful to the cause and just crazy enough to go to war against the Middle East. The last president was unwilling to do this." Carlo turned on Simon and stared him down. "I will allow that these outbursts of yours come from having been ill these many months, but you must pay for saying *no* to me," he said.

Simon began to shake uncontrollably. He had really done it this time and now he would have to pay for his disobedience, but how?

"Do you really want to marry Victoria Price?" Carlo asked.

"Yes!" said Simon. "If you will allow it."

Carlo walked back up to his chair and sat down. "Bring her in."

Simon reentered the room with Victoria by his side. "Come forward both of you," said Carlo. "So you think you want to get married?" he laughed.

Neither Simon nor Victoria said a word. "As god of this planet I have the ability to make you man and wife if I choose, but first I will have to determine if Victoria is worthy to be the wife of my prophet. Simon, you bring Victoria by my chamber tonight and I will see just how worthy she is."

Simon was stunned by Carlo's request. In all the years that he had known Carlo he had never seen him with a woman. Why now, and why with his Victoria? His mind screamed out in hopeless jealousy.

Victoria just looked at Carlo and smiled slightly. She feared this man greatly, but then it wasn't every day that she got the chance to sleep with a god.

Suddenly there was a knock at the door. "That will be Dr. Hyder," said Carlo. "Victoria, you can leave now. I will see you tonight," he said with an eerie grin.

Victoria walked by Raymond as he entered the room. "Seems like we just keep meeting this way," said Victoria as she scurried past.

"Come in, Dr. Hyder!" said Carlo jovially. "What bad news do you have for us today?"

Raymond stepped up to an irate Simon and nodded politely. "Well, what do you have to say today?" Simon snapped.

Dr. Hyder hated these little sessions. These two men scared him to death. He swallowed hard as he spoke, "The planet is warming up."

Simon turned towards Dr. Hyder in disbelief. "What! How do you know that?" Simon asked suspiciously.

"It's true! The temperature yesterday alone rose two degrees. It is an uneven increase around the world so we did not detect it right away."

"How is this possible?" Carlo inquired.

"It's complicated," said Raymond.

Simon really hated this scientist. He hated the fact that everything was complicated and he didn't understand half of what Raymond said.

"Well, give us the simple version if you don't mind," Carlo smiled.

"The planets have moved and aligned in such a fashion that they are causing the sun to create strong solar winds. These winds are breaking down the dust cover around this planet. Some locations have broken down sooner than others and, thus, are warming up quicker."

"Will it clear up completely?" Simon asked.

"If the solar winds last long enough, probably. But there is more," said Raymond nervously.

"Why am I not surprised?" said Simon. He was instantly very depressed by the thought that Victoria would be in bed with Carlo by this evening and there was nothing he could do about it. As for this weather, there was nothing he could do about it either.

"Continue!" said Carlo.

"Our planet is part of this massive alignment, and we are going to be very close to the sun. Even though part of the sun will be blocked out by Jupiter, we will feel the effects of this close proximity."

"What does this mean?" Simon asked in an impatient roar.

Carlo looked at Simon and smiled. He loved the fact that his prophet was all bunched up. "Do not interrupt," said Carlo.

"The sun is normally 93 million miles away from earth, give or take a few hundred thousand miles, but soon we will be closer than we have ever been. The planet will heat up considerably."

"What will the effects be?" Carlo asked.

"First the sun will melt the rivers, lakes, and seas, and if this happens too quickly, then we will have massive flooding. Second and most importantly it is going to get very hot—maybe as much as 150 degrees in some places and not just for a few hours in the noonday sun but continuously 24 hours a day until this alignment and its effects have gone. What plants and trees have managed to survive the freezing weather will have to tolerate the heat next. If there are any animals left today, then they also will have to find shelter from the oven.

"How long will this last?" Simon inquired.

"It is going to come on quickly and last for maybe as much as six months, and then it will leave as quickly as it came," said Raymond.

"What about the polar icecaps?" Carlo asked.

"Good question! Today the seas have fallen dramatically because of the lack of rainfall and especially because they are frozen or nearly frozen anyway. After six months of 150 degree temperatures, the poles will start to melt heavily even though they are at the extremes of the planet and on a tilt with respect to the sun. They will heat up nonetheless."

"And this means what?" Simon asked.

"It means," sighed Raymond, "that the islands of the world may be swallowed up by the ocean—especially the Pacific Islands—but England, Greenland, and Iceland will see a great reduction in the size of their islands as well."

"When?" asked Simon.

"That's kind of hard to tell, but I'd say it will take two months to completely burn through the cloud and then another month for the planetary alignment to be at its worst, so I guess in about 90 days things are going to heat up considerably," explained Raymond.

"I thought you said it will come on quickly," a confused Simon snapped.

"Mr. Koch, the very day the planets align and the sun is in a near proximity to earth, the temperature on this planet will rise by at least 80 degrees. So if it has warmed up to say 50 degrees Fahrenheit by this time, then it will increase to 130 degrees in a single day. I think that's pretty quick."

"What will happen after that?" Carlo asked.

Why doesn't this supposed god answer his own questions? Raymond wondered. After all, this is his planet, isn't it?

"Two things for sure. First there will be a drought like never before. The damage to the rivers and lakes in North America due to the first asteroid combined with the effects of the third asteroid on the rivers in the Middle East has put the world's water supplies in jeopardy. The Mediterranean Sea has polluted all of the nearby seas in Europe and out into the Atlantic. The Persian Gulf is polluted and spreading into the Arabian

Sea. Soon all of these results will reach the Pacific Ocean, and before long all of the oceans of the world will be red with iridium and rotting sea life. The waters of the world are dying, and there will be no rain during this heat wave to slow this down."

"And the second thing?" inquired Carlo.

Raymond sighed and drew another deep breath. "There will be darkness like never before."

"What do you call that out there right now?" Simon snapped.

"Mr. Koch, that is a well-lit room compared to what is coming. At least there is a degree of luminescence, and the darkness we see in the day has some light waves penetrating through the dust even if you cannot recognize them as light. But when Jupiter occults the earth completely there will be no moon or stars or sun. You will experience the total blackness of empty space."

"How long will this last?" Carlo asked.

"Possibly three months or more," said Raymond. "In addition, it will get cold once again, but not as cold as now. The sun will still be close enough to add some heat by radiation, and the darkness will be short-lived compared to the dust we have dealt with all these months."

"All right, Dr. Hyder. Is that your entire report?" Carlo asked.

"Yes, it is," said Raymond.

"Dr. Hyder, you have been a great help to us. I hope that Mr. Koch has taken good care of you."

Raymond looked over to the brooding Simon. "Yes, I have a nice apartment. I am fine, thank you, Your Highness."

"Then you are dismissed," said Carlo.

Raymond bowed and turned to leave the room. He noticed the model of the city as he left. *I wonder what that's all about,* he thought to himself as he gratefully left Simon and Carlo behind.

Simon looked to Carlo for a clue as to how he felt about what Dr. Hyder had just said. "We have a lot of work to do, Simon. Oil is more important now than ever, and we are going to need water."

"Why is oil so important if it is going to warm up?" Simon asked.

"Power!" said Carlo. "We will need electricity. Hydroelectric plants will not get the job done. There are not enough nuclear power plants to meet our needs. We will need to convert oil into power so people can stay cool. We need to improve the output of every oil well and distribute this to refineries worldwide. I have some slave labor from Africa working on Babylon. We can export more of these and the ones you have in South America. They can be trained to build and operate these power plants for us. If necessary, we can use the criminals you have locked up in those little concentration camps of yours."

Simon was surprised that Carlo knew about Dachau and the other camps that Oswald was filling daily with Christians and other rebels. "I've been meaning to talk to you about these camps," said Simon carefully. "It was my idea to place everyone who has not taken an ID tag in these places."

Carlo smiled. He had abused Simon enough for now. "It is a good idea, Simon. One thing though."

"What's that?" Simon asked a little happier this time.

"Do not force the insertion of ID tags into these people. You can threaten them, starve them, and even kill them if you want to, but do not hold them down and insert an ID tag," said Carlo somberly.

"Why not?" asked Simon. He had just made arrangements to have numerous ID insertion machines moved into all of these locations. It was his plan to forcibly insert tags into everyone.

"It doesn't count unless they make the choice themselves. It has to be their will to receive a tag, but you can help them make this choice, I am sure."

"And as for the world's water needs, let's get to work on building water purification plants like the desalinization plants in the Middle East," said Carlo. "We have a great future ahead of us, Simon."

Both men smiled until Simon remembered that he only had another six hours before he would have to bring Victoria back and hand her over to Carlo.

******

Sara and Tommy followed Joel Silverman back to his small apartment. Joel held the door open to allow Sara into the pantry. Apparently Joel felt more comfortable entering his home from the rear. They followed him into the small dining room area. The whole apartment was probably no more than 700 square feet. The living room was only inches away from where Tommy sat at the dining table. On the far wall were a number of family pictures. Tommy assumed these were members of Joel's own family—perhaps his children and grandchildren. The furniture in the dimly lit room was terribly worn. Obviously Joel was not a wealthy man.

"Would you like something to drink or to eat? I have some cheese and a little apple butter and crackers."

Having vomited this morning, Sara was awfully hungry, but she felt badly about eating this poor man's food. "Are you sure you have enough for us?" Sara asked.

"I think so," said Joel. "I just wish we had some cold milk to go with the crackers."

Just the mention of a cold glass of milk made Tommy's mouth water. It had been months since he had tasted any dairy products, and it was likely he would never taste them again. In fact, nearly every unprotected animal around the world had died over the last few months, so dairy cattle were in scarce supply and only the wealthiest of people would ever be able to afford such a rare commodity as milk, butter, or ice cream, let alone any fresh meat.

"Tell me the rest of your story, Son," said Joel with a smile.

Tommy continued to share the details of his and Sara's last five months in Switzerland. They had met so many people and had witnessed in many places. So far they had been successful in leading people away from the ID tags and towards Jesus. They had helped many to come up with options for survival. "It is a joint effort," Tommy had told them. "Combine all of your resources and continue to move around as necessary. Jesus will help you, and He will be back soon for you who remain faithful." Tommy and Sara were an inspiration to these people.

"So you are convincing people not to take the ID tags? You are telling them that Jesus will return for them soon and they can survive without food and shelter until then?" Joel asked.

These remarks got Tommy's attention. "Are you surprised by this? Is there another option? You do agree that the ID tags are the mark of the beast, correct?"

Maybe I didn't test this man out thoroughly enough, *thought Tommy.*

"No! I agree with you completely," smiled Joel. "I just want to make sure I understand what your message has been. Tell me more about your life before you came to Europe. How did the two of you meet in the first place?"

Tommy and Sara shared their tribulations from the last four years or so as Joel sat back listening. Finally Tommy got to the part about Tina. Tears filled his eyes as he paused to compose himself.

"So she didn't agree with you. Did she hear the voice of God like you did?" Silverman asked.

"No!" said Tommy.

"What a pity," said Joel. "But now you two are here and working for the Lord and it sounds like you are making a difference, and certainly you have made a big difference in slowing down Carlo Ventini's ID tag program. I'll bet he is not happy with either of you."

"Tell us about yourself," said Sara.

"Me, well, I'm just an old man."

Sara smiled brightly and said, "I am sure you are a lot more than that. Tell us about your life, your family."

"I met my wife, Mary, at the university," he said with a smile. He began to elaborate on his 40-year marriage and the numerous children and grandchildren they had raised. "Mary got sick," said Joel softly. "We didn't have any money, and we refused to take the ID tags, so nobody would help her. It didn't help that I was Jewish."

"Was Mary Jewish?" Tommy inquired.

Joel appeared to be deep in thought. "I'm sorry. What did you ask?"

"It doesn't matter," said Tommy.

"How have you been surviving these last few years?" Sara asked.

Joel sighed and said, "It hasn't been easy. I'm nearly out of supplies."

"What about your children? Can't they help?" Tommy asked.

"They are all gone," said Joel softly. "They disappeared four years ago, and it has just been me and Mary since then."

Tommy was confused. "Is Mary alive?"

"No! She died, but to me she is here with me always."

Tommy and Sara spent the afternoon visiting with Joel. It was nice not to have to keep moving and certainly nice not to be out in the cold, but now it was time to leave. Tommy and Sara paid close attention to Philip's warning about spending the night in the same town where they had spent the day.

"Well, Mr. Silverman, it is time for us to go. There are a lot of people out there that need our help," Tommy smiled.

Joel looked into Tommy's eyes. He understood the determination of this young man. He knew Tommy would not stop until he had warned every person he could against Carlo and Simon.

Tommy looked over to Sara. It was obvious that she was not feeling well again. "Sara, are you okay?"

"No. Mr. Silverman, may I use your bathroom please?"

When Sara returned it was apparent she was still nauseated. *I don't know why they call this stuff morning sickness,* thought Tommy. *She is sick afternoon and evening too.*

"Sara, are you ready to go?" Tommy asked gently.

Sara looked at her husband and sighed. He understood she could not go on. Tommy paused and mulled his situation over closely. Finally he asked Joel if it would be okay if they stayed the night. Actually it was more like spend the day because the Europeans had adjusted their schedules to accommodate the night-lights as well.

"Absolutely!" said Joel. "I can make you a bed right here."

Hours had passed. Sara lay sleeping and softly snoring next to Tommy. Suddenly a cramping sensation in Sara's abdomen woke her up. The realization that she was about to vomit caused her to head to the bathroom. As she did so she heard a quiet voice from Joel's room. Sara held back the urge to vomit long enough to listen to Joel's conversation.

"They are both asleep, so I am sure they will not be going anywhere soon. Come by in a few hours."

Sara froze and nearly choked on the contents of her own stomach. She listened to Joel hang up the phone and then slowly inched her way back towards Tommy. Sara heard the door to Joel's room open, so quickly she lay down next to Tommy and pretended to be snoring. Joel poked his head around the corner. He could see the couple nestled together on the floor and he was content that they were not going anywhere.

Seconds later Sara stirred Tommy. He rolled over and began to speak, but Sara put her hand over his mouth to silence him. "It's a trap!" said Sara.

Tommy looked at her inquisitively. "I heard Mr. Silverman on the phone. He told someone we were here asleep. He said for them to come by in a few hours."

"We need to leave now!" Tommy whispered. *Why didn't I listen to Philip?* he wondered.

Tommy and Sara searched for their backpacks, but they were nowhere to be found. "He's taken our supplies and our coats!" said Sara. "We cannot survive out there without our coats."

Tommy hunted around the room looking for any tool that would help him fix his problem. He spotted the phone on the corner of the coffee table and an idea consumed his mind. Digging into his pocket he pulled out the carefully folded piece of paper. Tommy had held onto this since Mueller gave it to him months ago. He was grateful to see that the paper was still intact. *Why shouldn't it be?* Tommy thought, *it's not like we actually ever change our clothes or wash them.*

He walked quietly towards the phone while unfolding the number. The lighting in the room was not good enough to make out the penciled numbers. "I can't tell what this says," Tommy whispered out of frustration.

A speck of light from Joel's room suddenly lit the hallway toward the bathroom. Both Sara and Tommy fell to the floor and pretended to be asleep. Sara heard the bathroom door close behind Joel. "He's in the restroom," she said.

Tommy held the number up to his face. He could now read it due to the thin slice of light from Joel's bedroom. Tommy repeated the number over and over again in his mind. A few seconds later they both heard the toilet flush and soon Joel came walking out quietly. He peeked his head around the corner once again to observe Tommy and Sara pretending to sleep.

A minute later Tommy was dialing the phone.

As Sara sat forward waiting to hear Tommy speak, suddenly she realized she no longer felt sick. Perhaps the excitement and stress of the situation had cured her morning sickness—at least for the moment.

Every time Tommy dialed the number all he got was static. He began to worry. *What if I can't reach him?* Finally he heard the phone actually dial the number, and soon it began to ring.

"Hello?" said the familiar but groggy voice on the other end of the phone line.

"Mueller, it's me—Tommy," he said in a whisper.

"Are you in trouble?" Mueller asked.

"Yes, we are stuck in a house with someone, but we think he just turned us in."

"Can you get out of the house?" Mueller inquired.

"Yes, but he has our packs and, more importantly, our coats. We will freeze out there if we leave without them."

"Can you overpower him?

Tommy hadn't thought about that, but he was certain he could overpower an old man. "Yes, should I do that?"

"Where are you?" Mueller inquired.

"Four blocks north of the central train station in Zurich in a small gray apartment."

Abruptly Tommy and Sara heard a heavy click. They turned to see Joel standing at the edge of the hallway holding a loaded gun. "Hang up the phone!" Joel shouted.

On the other end of the phone Mueller could hear Joel yelling at Tommy. Then suddenly the line went dead.

"How could you?" Sara asked.

Joel looked at Sara with a sorrowful look on his face. It was obvious that he really didn't want to do this, but for some reason he was compelled. "I have my reasons," was all he could say.

"Mr. Silverman, let us go, please!" Tommy begged.

"I can't. They are coming for you."

"What? Who is coming for us?"

"Oswald Heydrich and his men. They are coming from Munich—Dachau actually."

"Who is Oswald whatever-you-said?" Sara inquired.

"He works for Simon Koch. He is his security officer in charge of the Christian round-up."

"Why, Mr. Silverman? Why?" Sara asked pleadingly.

"It's for Mary!"

"Mary?" said Tommy. "Mary is dead!"

"No!" said Joel as he shook his head. "She is in the hospital where they can take care of her."

"You sold out to Carlo," said Tommy.

"What about your children? Did they really go in the Rapture?" Sara asked.

"They went somewhere, but we didn't go and Mary was sick. Without the ID tag they would not help us, and Mary refused to take the tag so I had to…" Joel just trailed off.

******

Mueller grabbed his coat and keys and ran outside to his small wood shop. He propped the door open and walked inside. Before him was a large dusty canvas. He pulled the canvas back revealing the black hood of an old Mercedes. It had been years since he had driven this car. Mueller was tempted to pull it out when Sara and Tommy showed up, but for some reason he could not bring himself to do it.

This car had been Mueller's wife's favorite, and when she died, he put the car away in memory of her. Mueller pulled the canvas off completely and climbed into the old car. The smell of leather filled his nostrils. He could almost hear the laughter of his beloved wife as he sat back in the driver's seat. He put the key in the ignition and turned it, but there was nothing, not even a *click*. "The battery's dead," he said aloud.

Mueller popped the hood and stood over the engine looking down. *Somewhere in this garage I have a charger.*

******

Over two hours had passed as Sara and Tommy sat there at gunpoint. There was no hope. Joel had taken the ID tag and sold his soul to save his wife's life. Nothing Sara or Tommy said would change that.

"When will they be here?" Tommy inquired.

Joel looked at his watch. "In a little while."

"What will they do to us?" Sara asked.

Joel's eye twitched at this question. "I guess they will take you back to Dachau for starters."

"And then what?" Tommy asked

"I guess they will want you to take the ID tag."

"No, they won't! They will want to kill us for the work we've done encouraging others not to take the mark of the beast!" Sara lamented.

"Maybe so," said Joel, "but you brought this on yourself."

There was no point in talking to Joel about Jesus. His soul was lost. He had put more stock in surviving today than he did in an after life. Suddenly Sara felt sick. "I have to go to the bathroom," said Sara in a panic.

"Hold it!" said Joel.

"I can't!" said Sara as she stood with her hand clasped over her mouth. It was no use. Sara just simply could not wait. She quickly turned and ran towards the bathroom and, as she did, Joel stood to follow but then remembered Tommy.

"Leave her alone. She is sick," said Tommy.

"What's the matter with her?" an irritated Joel asked.

"Morning sickness," said Tommy flatly.

Joel looked Tommy hard in the face. He had six children of his own and a dozen grandchildren. "She's pregnant?"

"Not the best timing in the world, is it?" said Tommy.

This only made it harder for Joel. He didn't want to see these two kids killed, but he had to save his beautiful Mary. Little did he know that Mary had been dead for a week already. She had refused to take the ID tag in the hospital so Oswald had given the order to inject her with enough strychnine to kill her twice over.

Tommy tried as hard as he could to fix his gaze on Joel. This was a distraction technique, but Mr. Silverman didn't know that. Suddenly from behind Sara swung the heavy porcelain toilet lid down on Joel's back before he could see her coming. The force of the blow launched him forward. Tommy reached for the old man's gun, but before he could get a hold on it Joel fired the rifle hitting Tommy with the bullet. The velocity pushed Tommy back into the far wall, knocking him over the small end table where the phone had been sitting. Again Sara lifted the porcelain lid and with all of her strength she crashed the heavy object down on the back of Joel's skull, splitting his head open like a melon. Joel fell to the ground with a thud as blood poured from the back of the man's head.

Sara ran towards Tommy. "Oh, no! Dear God, help us!"

She lifted Tommy off the end table and sat him back on the couch. Blood was oozing from his left shoulder. "What do I do?" she cried.

"Look for some bandages—quickly. We need to get out of here," said Tommy. The pain in his shoulder was nearly enough to knock him unconscious.

Sara came back with a pile of gauze and tape along with a bath towel. She opened Tommy's shirt and inspected the wound and instantly felt nauseated again. "You're not going to puke on me, are you?" Tommy asked with a little laugh.

Sara leaned him forward and found a large exit wound in the middle of his shoulder blade. "It went all the way through," she said.

"That's probably good news," said Tommy. "Now try to stop the bleeding and patch me up so we can leave."

Five minutes later Sara was buttoning Tommy's shirt. "That's all I can do for now, but you need to go to the hospital." They both knew that would never happen.

Sara and Tommy heard Joel's groans as he lay there on the floor. They also heard the sound of ice breaking as a car pulled up outside Joel's house. "They're here!" Sara whispered.

Tommy stood and was lightheaded instantly. Sara propped him up with her shoulder. "How do we get out of here?"

"First we need to get our stuff," said Tommy. Sara led him into Joel's bedroom where they found their coats and packs. Tommy noticed a window behind Joel's bed. "Maybe we can go out through that," said Tommy.

A knock came from the other room as Sara dropped the last of the packs out of the window. "Go!" said Tommy as Sara hustled out of the window. Next Tommy climbed out. The pain of the climb and then the fall was nearly too much. He had to bite his tongue to keep from screaming.

Oswald and three of his Special Forces officers entered Joel's living room only to find the old man unconscious on the floor with his rifle lying at his side. The wall was splattered with blood, and there was a blood-soaked towel on the couch. "Check the house," said Oswald.

Thirty seconds later the men came back to report that it appeared as if Sara and Tommy had climbed out of the bedroom window. "They won't get far," said Oswald as he dropped the bloody towel.

"What do we do with this old man?" one of the men inquired of Oswald.

"Kill him!" said Oswald as he walked out of the house.

Tommy and Sara wandered aimlessly through the darkness as they headed in the direction of the train station. The bandages on Tommy's shoulder were soaked, and it would not be long before he passed out due to blood loss. Sara was cold, scared, and tired as she struggled to hold Tommy up. "God, please! We need your help!" Sara called up to Heaven.

Sara could hear the car coming before she even saw the headlights. "We need to get off the road now!"

Tommy was barely conscious so Sara wrapped her arms tightly around his waist and walked backwards towards a large metal power box next to the tracks. Once there she sat Tommy back against the box and huddled in close to him to try and keep him warm.

Oswald's car drove by slowly. "They are out here somewhere," said Oswald. The car continued by as Sara held her breath.

"God, what do I do now?" Sara pleaded.

As soon as Oswald cleared the block the area in front of Sara lit up brightly. "Be at peace, child. The Lord has heard your cry."

Philip appeared in the midst of the glow. "You need to go to Germany—to Linz. There are many there that need your help."

"Germany? But Tommy is hurt, and I think he is dying!"

"No, Child, he will not die. Now go back out on the street."

"But they are looking for us."

The glow disappeared leaving Sara holding Tommy in the darkness. "Come on, Tommy. We have to move."

Sara wrestled Tommy back out on the street just as another set of headlights appeared. "They've come back!" Sara shouted.

The car approached slowly and then stopped in front of Sara with its headlights shining directly on her and a limp Tommy. The door opened and out stepped a tall, mature looking man. "Sara?" Mueller said.

Sara recognized the voice at once. The perfect dialect was the thing she had noticed when she first met him. "Tommy's hurt badly."

Mueller ran towards Sara and helped her to get Tommy into the back of the Mercedes. She slid in next to him and cradled his clammy head in her lap. "How did you find us?"

"I don't know. I just sort of let the car do the driving," said Mueller. "Where to now?"

"Germany," said Sara.

"Germany! Why? Where?"

"Linz. God wants us to go to Linz, and I don't know why," Sara replied.

"Okay, I think I have enough gas to go that far, but first we need to get some help for Tommy," said Mueller as he turned the corner.

One street over Oswald drove slowly looking between the apartment buildings for any signs of life. Simon was not going to be happy about this. *Well, there will be other opportunities,* thought Oswald. He had converted many people in much the same way as the late Mr. Silverman.

Sooner or later someone would spot Sara and Tommy and maybe even Peter Bastoni.

******

Simon showed up at Carlo's chambers with Victoria. He had not said a single word to her, nor had she said anything to him. Simon knocked on Carlo's door.

A few seconds later Carlo opened his own door. This astonished Simon. Carlo never did anything for himself. He always had someone do his work for him. It would not surprise Simon if Carlo had people just to brush his teeth for him.

Carlo leered at Simon as he stood there. Simon tried to walk past him to bring Victoria into the room, but Carlo held his hand up. "I'll take it from here. Come by tomorrow and pick her up." Carlo slammed the door in Simon's pitiful face.

Simon turned to leave so full of anger and jealousy that he could not contain himself. About that time one of Carlo's chambermaids walked by with a handful of towels. "Come to me!" he demanded.

The woman rushed to Simon's side at once.

"You are coming back to my apartment with me. Let's go!" said Simon. The woman followed behind still carrying her load. "Leave the towels!" said an exasperated Simon.

Inside Carlo's chamber Victoria stood nervously. "So let's see why Simon wants to marry you," said Carlo as he walked towards Victoria. Carlo took her hand and headed towards his bedroom. Victoria smiled and walked alongside His Holiness.

Chapter 9: A Little Hope for the Islands

D ay 1500, October: Petra Sverdlov leaned back in his captain's chair gazing out into the empty blackness. No man had ever seen the space out here before. It was a lonely feeling. *How long had they been drifting along?* he wondered. It didn't really matter anymore. They all knew that it was just a matter of time before they ran out of water, food, or oxygen.

In the distance Petra could see a small constellation of stars. The light from these suns was nearly as old as time itself. It was unlikely that any of them even existed anymore. Petra was disturbed by a familiar voice. "I need you to look at this, Petra," said Samuel Pearlman.

Petra turned to see the little man holding a piece of paper containing a number of massive calculations. Samuel floated the paper to Petra who pulled it down to study it more closely. "What is this?" he inquired.

"It's a way home," said Samuel without any emotion.

"Home? Pearlman, we are on a space station hurtling out into space at 20,000 miles an hour, and here is the key part of this—" Petra said without a smile. "We are heading in the wrong direction!"

Samuel seemed nonplussed by Petra's statement. "This, too, will change."

"What will change?" Teresa Reed asked as she glided back into the cockpit of the ship.

"Our direction," said Samuel flatly.

"How so?" asked Teresa. "Have you found a way around the second law of thermodynamics, the irreversibility of certain processes? We are an object in motion, out of control, and there is nothing that can change that out here."

Petra smiled.

"We are not in a state of entropy. We are not changing from one state of heat or energy to another. We are simply changing orbit."

Samuel grabbed the piece of paper from Petra's hand and gave it to Teresa. "Maybe you can understand astronomy and astrophysics a little better than Comrade Sverdlov can."

Petra was no longer smiling.

Teresa studied the numbers. "Where did you get this? How can it be?"

Teresa went to the control panel and studied their present coordinates. "When was the last time these were updated?" She asked.

"Who cares where we are going? It doesn't matter anymore," said Petra.

Teresa studied Samuel hard. "What is doing this?"

"Doing what?" said Petra casually.

"Check the planetary grid and you will see what," said Samuel.

Teresa clicked on the radar mapping system and stood back waiting for it to complete the calculations. Three minutes later all nine planets and the sun were shown as big red dots in the middle of the space grid. "We went by the moon nearly a year ago," Teresa whispered.

"Well, we are coming back towards it now," said Pearlman.

It was true the space station had passed by the moon but not close enough to get into its orbit. There was too much risk of damage from the dust cloud, so they had had to pass it by the first time. This, of course, launched them into deep space forever—or so they thought. But now they found themselves in a complicated conjunction of planetary alignments of an order of magnitude that only Samuel was intelligent enough to sort out.

"The gravitational pull on the ISS is turning us back towards earth. We are going to go by the moon again, and we can capture its orbit this time if we want to. We have just enough thruster fuel left to get into an orbit," said Samuel.

"What difference does it make? Who wants to just circle the moon for the next year or two until we run out of air and die?" Petra asked rhetorically.

"If it gets me closer to home—even if it is just to look at it—then I am all for it," Teresa said softly.

"Me too!" said Samuel.

"How long until we get there?" asked Teresa. It was as if she were going to see her husband and twin daughters again after a year and a half away from them.

"About three months, but there is something else," said Samuel.

Petra and Teresa looked at the brilliant man closely. "What? Are we going to burn up and die or something?" Petra asked with a bored little smirk.

Samuel just looked at Petra.

"What? Did I get lucky and guess right?" Petra asked.

"What is it?" Teresa inquired.

"The sun will be particularly close to earth by the time we get there."

"Have you calculated the temperature and gravitational effects on the station?" Teresa asked.

Samuel reached into his pocket and pulled out another wadded up piece of paper full of radiation and magnetic calculations. He handed it to Teresa. She looked at it, then back to him. "Do Skip, Bob, or Shila know?"

"Nobody knows."

"Good!" Teresa whispered. "Let's leave it that way."

Petra glared at the wrinkled piece of paper. He almost wanted to know what it said, but then he changed his mind.

******

Christopher Evans woke to a terrible sloshing motion. His stomach nearly came up as he sat forward. *What is happening?* he wondered. Chris climbed the steep little ladder and popped his head out for a look. Instantly a painful, bright light greeted his eyes. Chris let out a yell and covered his face with his hand as the boat tossed him into the cabin door smartly.

"Here, take these and put them on," said Joshua Stein as he bent forward to help Chris up the ladder and onto the deck. Chris felt the sunglasses being applied to his face and slowly he opened his eyes. Although the glare was greatly reduced, it was still painful.

"That's the sun!" said Chris.

"Yes, it is," said Joshua. "At least a piece of it anyway."

The sky was full of very small holes where light was escaping and rushing towards the earth. It looked a little like a showerhead with strands of water coming out of distinct, little, precise holes. Over the course of the last few months the planet had begun to warm—slowly at first—but over time things started to feel a little more normal, although things by no means looked normal. The sky was still black by day and luminescent by night, but there was a more subtle transition than in the past—kind of a gray point. However, today the sun had actually broken through some of the dust clouds, and from this point on there would be light during the day and little or no luminescence by night except at the extremes—the poles—where the sun had not been capable yet of burning through the clouds.

For the last three weeks since the icy Pacific started to break up and melt, Christopher, Joshua, and Connor had been making the rounds to various islands. This was an extremely dangerous effort. The water in the South Pacific had frozen just like every ocean had, yet here at the equator the ice was very thin because the ocean had much more heat to lose than other parts of the globe. Now the pathways were wide open, but large chunks of ice were everywhere, making it very dangerous and stressful to navigate.

The three men had started their island witnessing in New Caledonia 10 days earlier. Most recently they had been chased out of Fiji in a hurry with no time to gas up. Their next stop would be Papua, New Guinea, but it was still a long way off and anything could happen.

The boat Joshua piloted was a 32-foot cabin cruiser. It had been his uncle's boat, but after a meteorite crashed through Joshua's uncle's home and killed him, he had taken possession of the boat and made it his home. The cabin cruiser sat in dry dock for years, but Joshua hoped one day to move out to the sea.

Joshua would sleep on the boat by day and go out and preach by night throughout Brisbane. After his near crucifixion he moved Connor and Christopher into his home. They hid out there as much as possible, but they still went throughout the Australian coastline and preached boldly—or at least Joshua and Christopher did.

Connor, on the other hand, was just not very well equipped by nature to preach. He just accompanied these two young men and helped out however he could. They traveled by foot up and down the coastline from Newcastle to Rock Hampton. Things were getting bad in Australia. The people's hearts were changing dramatically. They accused the two witnesses they had seen on television, Moses and Elijah, of being the reason for their misery. They did not want to hear about Jesus. After all, what practical use did any of that have for them today? It was enough just to struggle through life hoping to have sufficient food for tomorrow and grateful they did not have the plague yet. The people set their hopes on the men in Rome to fix their planet and to protect them from any further troubles.

Things had gotten increasingly bad after a television interview with Simon Koch, as presented by his fiancée, Victoria Price. In this interview Simon promised that he was about to warm up the planet and return the daylight. "We will purify our waters and genetically engineer new and better animals and plant life. And soon our Agripod products and the virus antidote will not have to be moved by small air shipments. We will be able to ship via the ocean ways directly to each community in much larger quantities.

There will be feasting and happiness for all. Things will get better, but our benevolent god, Carlo, is still unhappy with the support we are getting on our ID tags and with the constant diabolical efforts of these Christian and Jewish fanatics. This must stop now, or there will be even greater punishment.

The people of the world took this message to heart. They believed Simon had powers, because many of the people had seen them. They also believed Carlo would punish them further if they did not comply with his wishes. Now they believed that all Simon and Carlo requested was justified and reasonable.

"Those of you alive today are here because our Holiness believes you are worthy to live on his planet. Do not disappoint him like many of others have. You are his chosen children. Let's rid the world of these menacing rebels. I have developed a Special Police force to aid in this, and certainly by now most of you have seen or met members of this force. Please give them your total cooperation and we will rid the world of evil quickly. Then we can live in total harmony and happiness." Simon smiled as he closed his public address.

******

Daily fewer and fewer people came to know the Lord, but Joshua knew this was to be expected. His work in Australia was nearly done. He was just biding his time until he could move out to the distant islands scattered throughout the Pacific. Finally that day came. The ice was breaking up and it was now time for them to leave.

The Jewish network that Joshua was a part of was strong and well organized. From it he obtained enough food, gas, and water to make an extended trip, and he also got the help he needed in getting his uncle's boat moved from dry dock and placed carefully into the harbor at Brisbane.

New Caledonia was a fresh harvest for Joshua, Chris, and Conner. These native French Polynesian people were much less influenced by Simon than the Aussies had been. Many of them received Jesus as their savior, and within days these three people had helped to lead thousands to Christ. But just as in every case, sooner or later those that served Carlo faithfully would intervene, sending Joshua and the rest running for their lives.

After narrowly escaping the government officials in New Caledonia, Joshua steered his boat towards Vanuatu where they were also successful in leading many to Christ. It seemed that Simon had not given these islands much attention, and for some reason many had not taken the ID tags. It also seemed that they had not suffered the effects of the plague or starvation like the rest of the world.

After leaving Vanuatu, Joshua headed for Fiji. This is when the seas began to grow turbulent. As the ocean thawed it began to swell and this created some very dangerous waters to navigate through. Connor was extremely grateful to set foot on Fiji. He was not much of a sailor, and after three days straight of seasickness, he was exhausted.

Quickly Joshua and Christopher realized that Fiji was going to be more difficult than the other islands had been. For some reason this island had suffered greatly from the plague, probably because it was a favorite vacationing spot. Many tourists brought the plague with them—not that there were all that many tourists nowadays, but still the rich found a way to entertain themselves. Fiji was also Joshua's first encounter with Simon's Special Police force.

They entered the city on foot, and for once they were not cold. The surface of the earth was beginning to bask in the sun's near proximity. The temperature was up to 50 degrees even though it was still dark and cloudy. As usual, Joshua led Christopher and Connor to an area where large numbers of people could be found. Then he would stand and begin to sing loudly until he drew a crowd. Connor was always fascinated by the young man's courage. It wasn't likely that Connor would ever step up to strangers and start singing. It didn't help that he had a terrible voice which his wife used to make fun of when they had first started dating many years back.

Joshua sang his heart out until there were nearly 100 people standing by. He finished his song and turned to the crowd. "Jesus loves you," he smiled. Not a sound could be heard from the crowd as Joshua continued to speak about the end of time prophecy and of the mercy and grace of God. When the time came for Joshua to offer a prayer for those who wanted to accept Christ, none came forward.

"People, do you understand you are making a choice to live for Satan and to suffer an eternity in Hell? This planet is dying and nothing can stop that. God's word says that these islands will be wiped from the surface of the earth. This is coming very soon."

Finally a little native girl stepped forward, dragging her mother by the hand. "I want my mommy and me to go to Heaven with Jesus. Will you pray for us?"

Connor's heart was broken for this little girl. She alone still possessed the ability to discern good from evil and had the courage to do something about it. Joshua prayed for the child and her mother and then kissed the dark haired little girl on the cheek. "Bad people will try to put a little green tag under your skin, but don't let them."

"How can we stop them?" the mother asked.

"Just say no!" said Christopher.

"What will they do to us?"

Joshua looked at the young women intently. "They may kill you both. It is the price you will have to pay to be with Jesus for eternity."

The woman swallowed hard and nodded in agreement as she and her daughter walked off.

Later in another part of town outside an abandoned temple Christopher stood on a pile of broken bricks preaching the Word from the book of Hebrews 1:3 "'The Son is the radiance of God's glory...'" said Christopher. "We are made in God's image, but we have not been made to be gods. We have been created to worship the one true God. We have been redeemed and cleansed by the blood of Christ which was shed for our sins."

The crowd around Chris grew ugly and they began to accuse him of all kinds of evils. "Carlo Ventini is god. We were created to worship him and him alone. Jesus is not real. We have never seen Him. Nothing that was ever said in that church behind you was real, and nothing you say here today is real. You are the reason we are suffering."

"This church may have deceived you, but I am speaking the truth. Jesus lives, and He will come back for you." At this the people picked up bricks and threatened to throw them at Chris.

Connor stepped up to Chris and took him by the hand. The three of them ran behind the broken down temple and circled the small town. As they reentered the city on their way back to the boat, they caught a glimpse of a larger crowd marching along behind seven uniformed men. All seven men had blue jackets with the same white insignia—pentagrams with the inscription of the United World Organization circling the symbol.

Joshua caught sight of the little native girl and her mother among the crowd. One of the policemen turned and grabbed the mother and pulled her out in front of the crowd.

"Oh, no!" said Joshua.

The woman began to cry as the man dragged her out by the hair. "What have you done?" the man in blue asked.

The woman did not say a word, so the man slapped her hard across the face. "Did you pray with those evil Christians?"

The man raised his hand once again to strike the woman. "Yes!" the young lady cried, "I prayed for Jesus to come into my heart."

The man's hand came down hard. "Are you willing to die for this Jesus?"

The woman rose up with blood running down her nose. She looked the man directly in his hateful eyes. "Better to die now than later."

The policeman had no idea what the young woman meant by the statement, but he was more than willing to oblige her. He pulled his weapon from his side and pointed it towards the lady's head. Suddenly a shout came from the crowd. The officer turned to see a man holding a small child. "This is her daughter. She said the prayer too."

The little girl looked terrified, and Joshua's heart broke for her. "Bring her to me," said the man. The woman looked into her daughter's eyes as she was handed over to the officer. The young mother's eyes told her child how sorry she was that this had happened.

"Is this your mother?" the officer asked.

The little girl nodded and began to whimper.

"Did you say a prayer with those bad men?" the officer asked.

Again the girl nodded.

"Do you want to take it back? Do you want to change your mind, little girl?" the man asked.

The child looked into the man's cruel eyes. "No!"

The officer was stunned by the boldness of the child. It never ceased to amaze him that nearly every time he encountered new converts he could not dissuade them from their sworn allegiance to Christ even with the use of brutal force.

"Little girl, if you do not take back your prayer, then I will shoot your mommy."

The child looked at her mother and smiled. "We will be with Jesus pretty soon, Mommy."

The mother smiled at her child and said, "That's right, Sweetheart, very soon."

Connor and Chris stood side by side hidden from the crowd as they watched this incredible exchange between mother and daughter. They had only been saved for a few hours, yet they now had the courage to face death. Tears filled Connor's eyes and ran down his cheeks.

"Which one do you want me to kill first?" the officer asked as he looked at the crowd.

"The girl!" they all shouted.

"Okay, lady—one last chance to save your life and the life of your daughter. What's it going to be?" The woman looked at the policeman carefully as if she were making a mental image of someone she never wanted to forget. The man was short and Polynesian just like she was. How was it possible that someone from her own island could do this to her and her baby girl?

"To die for Christ is to live forever!" she smiled.

The man grew so angry at her defiance that he put his gun to her head and said, "Then live forever, lady."

Just before the man could pull his trigger another officer in blue came around the corner and yelled out a command. The man lowered his gun as an angry look plastered his face. The older officer stepped up to the woman. "So you have accepted Christ. Let's see how long this lasts in a concentration camp in Europe. Lock them up," said the man as he turned to the officer who still had his gun drawn. "Now go find those Christian witnesses!" the man shouted.

This was Joshua's cue—it was time to run. Connor led the pack as they skirted the city and made their way down to the waterfront where they had moored their boat. Chris jumped on deck and began to untie the ropes. "Stop!" said Joshua. "We need gas."

Both Connor and Chris looked at Joshua. He had to be kidding. There was no way they could go hunting around for gas with the men in blue right on their tails. "Better to run out of gas out there than to get caught here!" said Connor as he tossed off another line.

Joshua nodded. "Let's get out of here!"

******

Jasmine helped Elisha pull in the net. It was nearly bursting due to the weight of the shrimp. It felt so good to be doing something productive. Now that the weather was beginning to change and to warm, Jasmine felt almost like her life was new and somehow better. She was so grateful to leave Ein Gedi, even though she missed the hot springs.

Elisha had led his people to Avdat National Park in the Negev. The march through the desert had taken five days, yet they were uneventful days and for that Elisha was eternally grateful. As soon as they entered the Negev it became apparent that the city had been abandoned or, more precisely, that all the living people were gone.

He was unaware that most of the community had run out into the desert heading in all directions including Avdat Park to try to avoid the certain death of the plague that was running its course unabated throughout the city. The only thing Elisha was sure of was that there were a number of dead people everywhere. This is when he decided to skirt the remainder of the city which inevitably led him to Avdat.

Elisha had never seen this place before, but like all good Jews he had heard the stories about David Ben Gurion, the country's first prime minister and the founder of this national park. The park was perfect for Elisha's people. There were a number of deep caves and caverns throughout and ample food and water from the neighborhood.

Interestingly enough Negev was a farming community right in the middle of an extremely dry and normally very hot desert, but this was no ordinary farming community. The areas main crops were shrimp and cactus along with various types of algae used for food and medicine, and there were huge irrigated ponds throughout the region full of salty water and shrimp.

Upon arriving at the park Elisha was surprised to find out it was already occupied by a number of people. Soon after he met with one of the leaders of the group and listened to his story. He was stunned to find out that many of these people had been saved by Peter and Ruth and then led to this park as they escaped Oswald's soldiers. Elisha was disappointed, however, to find out that Peter and Ruth had left the camp two days earlier.

Elisha sat on the ground with Jasmine sorting shrimp into baskets and throwing the smaller ones back for another day. The shrimp had survived being nearly frozen, but they would not survive Elisha's growing population of over 3,000 hungry people.

"I like it here!" said Jasmine.

Elisha smiled at his faithful companion. He knew Jasmine was happy here and he was glad, but he knew this feeling would come to an end soon. "Me too!" smiled Elisha.

"How long can we stay?" Jasmine asked.

Elisha considered the question for a while. He knew there were more people in need of his help—probably hundreds of thousands out there looking for someone to help them, someone to lead them. "For a little while anyway," he smiled.

"I wonder if Peter and Ruth made it to Jerusalem," said Jasmine.

"I hope so!" said Elisha.

******

Peter and Ruth had been in Jerusalem for quite some time. They had slept on the streets and in between buildings trying to stay out of sight as much as possible. Neither person had a clue as to what would come next. They had marched into town without being seen, or at least nobody cared about them if they were seen. It seemed that everyone was celebrating the warm weather. Finally the cold would be gone and life would get back to normal.

"Okay, Peter, we're here. Now what?" asked Ruth with a beautiful smile on her face.

Peter laughed. "I guess I didn't think that far into the future, but I am sure God has a plan for us somehow."

Ruth put her hand on Peter's woolly cheek and rubbed it softly. "I am sure He does. How about you and I take a walk through this city and see if we can find a little water and maybe some food? I'm starved!"

"Me too!" said Peter.

Ruth led Peter over to a fountain where they both bent down to get a drink of water, but to their displeasure the fountain was dry all except for a small amount of green, slimy water in the bottom of the concrete basin.

What Ruth and Peter did not know was that water in the Middle East was becoming an extremely rare commodity. Israel was more fortunate than most because the Jordan River did not rely on the Euphrates, but it did rely on rain and snow run-off. After the recent thaw the Jordan was nothing but a small stream, and much of this was being redirected into farming communities in an effort to replant as quickly as possible.

The primary source of drinking water now came from Israel's desalinization plants. However, the Mediterranean was a mess, and this was having a disastrous effect on the water purification plants. They spent more time replacing filters and clearing clogged pipes than they did making pure water. All of the original equipment had been completely washed away by the tidal wave and now they were trying to rebuild each coastal city as they took direction from Simon Koch who required them to install three times as many water purification plants as before.

"Strike one," said Ruth.

"Well, there has to be water somewhere," said Peter as he led Ruth away from the fountain.

The two wandered on for another hour or so until they came to the temple. Nearly a year ago they had run from Carlo and Simon. It was here that Peter's brother, Joseph, lost his life. Peter stood silently as he relived that terrible moment in his life. He missed Joseph and Yvette very much. *If Joe were here, he'd tell me what to do next,* thought Peter. He may have been the older brother, but Joseph was much better equipped to handle life on the run that he was. Ruth interlaced her fingers in Peter's. "It looks like they are repairing the place."

Peter looked up to see a massive crane lowering a large concrete wall. The temple had suffered greatly from the barrage of tektites, but Carlo would have it rebuilt in no time, and now it would officially be his temple. Carlo knew that the Jews would never see it this way. They had been conditioned over thousands of years to see any temple in Jerusalem as a holy place to God alone. It would be hard, if not impossible, to get very many of these people to worship him in this place, and that angered him greatly. He had no love for Jews. The sooner Simon got rid of them, the better, as far as he was concerned.

Ruth and Peter walked along hand in hand past the temple. When they rounded the corner they began to hear a lot of shouting and yelling. Slowly they walked up to a large crowd of people who were obviously upset by something or someone. "Listen to me," said a youthful voice from within the circle of people. "You have to understand the signs of the times. All of this was predicted by Jesus and his prophets thousands of years ago. Don't turn your back on Him once again. You will not get another chance!"

Peter looked at Ruth and grinned. "I know that voice," he said. Slowly Peter worked his way into the center of the group, and lo and behold there standing on a park bench was young David. Peter had grown particularly fond of this brave teenager, and he hadn't seen David since the day of the temple dedication. The boy was taller than he remembered but just as courageous.

"You'd better leave here now!'" said one elderly man.

"Mister, they are rebuilding our temple and they're planning to put statues of Carlo inside. Doesn't that bother you at all? Can't you see that he is evil? Can't you see that—" David paused and looked at Peter in surprise. "Can't you see that God is angry and this is why we are suffering?"

"We are suffering because of people like you," said one woman.

Peter waved to David inconspicuously. David nodded and spoke one more time. "People! Jesus is real. He came to us once and we rejected

Him. Since then we have been suffering the abuse of the world. Do not reject Him again. There will be no hope for you this time."

David stepped down from the bench and walked through the crowd past Peter as if he hadn't even seen him. Peter turned to watch the young man walk across the parking lot. As soon as the crowd began to break up Peter and Ruth headed off after David. As they rounded the corner, they saw him standing there against the wall of the temple.

"Hi, Peter! Hi, Ruth!" said David with a bright smile.

"David, it is so good to see you! We were worried that you might have died when Benjamin—" Peter dropped off.

David smiled at Peter. "It's okay. Benjamin is in Heaven. Now what are you two doing here?"

Peter spent the next 15 minutes updating David on the events of the last year. "After months in Ein Gedi, Ruth and I ended up in Avdat Park living in caves for a short time," he said.

David followed along. He was impressed with Peter's story. "And what about Elisha and Jasmine? Where are they now?"

"Probably still in Ein Gedi taking care of all those people," said Ruth.

"So Elisha is their leader—kind of a Moses or something?" said David.

"Exactly!" replied Ruth.

"Where are you living?" Peter inquired.

"With Daniel Cohen, Benjamin's son."

"His wife, Jill, let you stay there?" Ruth asked in surprise.

"After Benjamin got killed I was put into a hospital for a few days because I got kind of beat up," David frowned. "But after three days Daniel Cohen came and picked me up. Apparently he paid all the hospital bills and told them I was his son. When I got back to his house, Jill was gone. I asked him what happened to her. He said that when he took his father back to be buried beside his mother, he told Jill that he was going to bring me home after my stay in the hospital. She disagreed and said it was either me or her, so I guess he chose me."

"But David," said Ruth, "Daniel has the mark of the beast."

David nodded. "Yes, I know that, but he took it without any understanding of what he was doing."

Ruth looked at Peter and then David. "I don't know the rules—" Ruth paused, "God's rules behind the mark—but if he took it willingly making the choice to serve the power to be, then he has chosen against Jesus."

"This may be true. All I know is that I can trust Daniel, and he has helped me out."

"What are you doing out here today?" Ruth asked.

"The same as every day—I'm witnessing to the people."

"What about Simon Koch and the soldiers we saw in the desert? Aren't you afraid of getting caught?" Peter inquired.

"Yes, and every day it gets harder, but what can I do about that?"

"What does Daniel have to say about your witnessing?" Ruth inquired.

"He sees it as dangerous and useless, but he does not try to stop me."

"Where are you two staying?" David inquired.

"Nowhere!" said Ruth flatly.

"Come home with me," said David.

Peter was hesitant. "Look, David, we are here because God wanted us to come here. I think it has something to do with us putting together a lab where I can make an antidote for the virus. It is for sure that Simon is never going to send any of the medicine here, and soon the people will be infected and dying by the thousands."

"Come home with me and we can talk to Daniel about this. Maybe he will have some ideas."

Ruth looked at Peter. She felt the same way he did about Daniel, but what choice did they have?

David entered into the house first. "Daniel!" he called out. There was no answer. "Come on in, guys. I guess Daniel is out for a while."

Peter and Ruth walked into the familiar, old house. Everything was still in its place as best Peter could remember.

"Are you hungry?" David asked.

"Yes," said Ruth without waiting for Peter to respond.

Daniel and David did not have much food but at least they had some. Daniel had the ability to buy supplies since he had the ID tag implanted in his right hand. David made sandwiches for all three of them while

Peter explained what he needed to build a small lab. "The most important thing is to find the right chemicals and to be able to distill them until they form a composition that can be injected into a human."

"You know," said David. "Daniel works for a chemical company here in Jerusalem. Maybe he can help you out."

"David," said Ruth, "doesn't it worry you that Daniel is not a believer?"

David had tried to deny this reality many times. All he wanted to know was that Daniel cared about him. He had never had a home of his own, and although this situation was by no means permanent, David didn't want to lose Daniel so he just simply ignored the fact that Daniel had taken the mark of the beast. "Daniel is not serving Carlo. He just made a mistake and took the mark without the facts."

"David, he isn't serving Jesus either, and he never will," said Ruth.

"Maybe not, but he does take care of me, and he is Benjamin's son."

Peter nodded. He understood that David had feelings for Daniel as a son does for a father and nothing could change that—just as he still had loving memories for his ex-wife, Melissa, but there was nothing he could do for her either. She, too, died horribly without ever knowing the truth.

Ruth heard the front door shut, and she grew nervous as she waited for Daniel to enter the room.

"David?" Daniel called out.

"I'm in the kitchen," said David. Daniel walked into the room and was surprised to see Peter and Ruth sitting there at his table.

"What are you two doing here?" Daniel asked in an unfriendly manner.

"They're here to help," said David.

"To help with what?"

"We came to build a lab to make antidote for the plague," said Peter softly.

"Why?" Daniel asked.

"Because Simon Koch is never going to send any medicine here, and soon there will be an outbreak and everyone will die." Ruth spoke succinctly.

Daniel looked at Peter. "Can you really make medicine?"

"If I have the right equipment and chemicals, I think I can make something that will work."

"Where will you make this antidote?" Peter looked into Daniel's narrowed eyes. "Oh, no! Not here!"

"Daniel, this is the only place we have," said David. "We also need your help getting some supplies to make it work."

Daniel sat at the table. "Why do you think Simon would hold back the antidote from the Jewish people?"

"Because you are God's chosen people," said Ruth.

"But Simon is Jewish," said Daniel.

"Not anymore," said Ruth.

Ruth wondered if Daniel ever pondered the mistake he had made in taking the mark or if he even understood what he had done.

"Give me a list of supplies, and I will see what I can do," said Daniel.

Peter smiled and took another bite of his sandwich, but Ruth sat quietly by. She was not nearly as trusting as Peter and David.

******

Joshua pumped the accelerator a few times and turned the key. It was hopeless. They were out of gas in the middle of the South Pacific. Joshua stood and surveyed the situation. All around him was a wall of water mixed with large and small pieces of ice. Above him small slices of sunlight raced to the earth's surface. In the distance was a small speck of land, but it was at least 20 miles off. Joshua was not sure what island he was looking at, but it didn't really matter. He could never get there now.

Connor climbed up into the cockpit with Joshua and put his arm around the young man's shoulder. "We will have to see what God has in mind for us now," Connor smiled.

"Well, we may as well have some lunch," said Joshua. "Chris, break out the poles and let's see what we can catch today."

Every day they fished for their food. This was not an easy task. For some reason the ocean just didn't seem to have much in the way of fish to catch. Yesterday they fished for three hours and all they caught was a moray eel. Needless to say, this was not the best meal they had ever eaten.

Chris baited the large hooks with the leftover pieces of eel and dropped the lines into the water. "Okay, let's see how it goes today."

Connor and Joshua moved in next to Chris and sat down on the wooden deck on the bow of the boat. "What are we going to do?" Chris asked.

"I don't know," Joshua sighed.

It was an interesting situation. Chris and Connor were aware that Joshua was a special witness for God, 1 of 144,000 called by Him. They assumed that this assignment would come with more power and protection, but so far they had seen Joshua nearly crucified, chased out of every town they had come into, and now stranded in the middle of the South Pacific.

"You are God's chosen witness," said Chris. "There must be an answer and a way out of this."

"Chris, you and Connor are chosen witnesses, too, and even Paul the apostle suffered greatly as he went out and witnessed for Christ. In fact, he was shipwrecked many times, stoned, and imprisoned. Why should we be any different?"

Connor did not know all this until now and somehow it helped. "Okay, then we will wait on God and see what happens next."

Suddenly Christopher's pole bent down into the water. "Whoa! I got something big."

"Put your pole in the holder, Chris, before you lose the fish," said Connor.

Chris slid the huge deep sea pole into the metal holder anchored on the front of the boat and moved his hands up to the reel. "The drag is too tight! He's going to break the line!" Chris cried out. He tried to adjust the reel, but the knob would not budge. All of a sudden Chris felt the forward momentum as the boat began to be pulled along by the fish.

"What is going on here?" Connor asked.

"The fish is pulling us!" said Joshua with a broad smile.

"What kind of fish can pull a 30-foot boat?" Connor asked.

"A big one!" laughed Chris.

An hour went by and the boat was still being dragged towards the shoreline of the not-too-distant island. "I can't believe this is happening," said Connor.

"Why?" Chris asked. "Don't you believe God can do anything? Didn't He have a great fish swallow Jonah and vomit him up on dry land?"

"Yeah, I guess, but I thought those were just tales to help illustrate some point—not for real! But this fish is even swimming around all the ice as we go."

"It is real," said Joshua. "It's all real!" he laughed.

"What island is that?" Chris inquired as he pointed to the small wooded island not so far off.

"I don't know, but I don't think it's New Guinea," answered Joshua.

Thirty minutes later Joshua's boat was within half a mile of the small, heavily wooded island when suddenly there was a loud popping sound.

"What was that?" Connor asked.

Chris began to reel in the line on his pole. "He broke it!" said Chris.

"So long, good and faithful fish," Joshua laughed.

"What now?" Chris asked.

"It looks to me like we are drifting in towards that inlet over there," said Connor as he pointed to a beautiful, little sandy cove a little less than half a mile ahead of them.

The water around the island was the most terrific blue with just a few small whitecaps breaking against the sandy shores—one of the few bodies of water that had not turned red yet.

Joshua headed up to the pilothouse. "I've got maps up here."

A few minutes later Joshua and Connor were poring over the large map. 'So if we left Fiji three days ago traveling at maybe 15 knots, then we must have run out of gas just about here," said Joshua.

Connor traced his finger over the map. Then the fish or whatever that thing was must have pulled us to about here." Connor tapped the map directly on top of a very small island called Woodlark.

"Do you really think so?" Joshua asked, "Because if it is Woodlark, then I know this island."

Chris and Connor looked inquisitively at Joshua. "Well, does it look familiar to you?" Chris asked.

Joshua squinted against the sun's glare. "I'm not sure. When I was a kid my uncle brought me to an island called Muyuw—or at least that's what the natives called it—but my uncle called it Woodlark."

"Was it a nice place?" Chris asked.

"Were the people friendly?" Connor asked.

All of a sudden Joshua wished he had paid closer attention the last time he came to this island. "I don't know, guys. I can't even tell if it's the same place or not."

Well, we're going to find out soon!" said Chris as he pointed to the small inlet that Joshua's boat was now drifting to.

The cove was narrow and deep enough. Along the edges were large fallen trees that were some kind of hardwood, but Chris didn't know what type. Suddenly the boat came to a loud, abrupt stop. The inertia sent all three men flying towards the rail at the bow of the boat. "We're here!" Connor yelled as he grabbed the rail to avoid falling into the freezing water.

What Connor said was not exactly true. Yes, they were in the cove, but it was another hundred yards to the closest shore and a 100-yard swim in water that had only recently started to thaw was not a safe thing to attempt.

"How are we going to get over there?" Chris inquired.

At this Joshua only smiled and climbed down into the bowels of the boat. Quickly he emerged with a bright yellow inflatable rubber raft. "Stand back," said Joshua as he tossed the raft into the cold water while still holding onto the lanyard. Instantly the raft grew to a size large enough to accommodate all three men.

Connor was the first person in the raft and the first person out of it as well. He knew he'd never make a good sailor, and he didn't care. All he wanted was to feel the solid ground under his feet. Thirty minutes later all three men had traipsed through the forest and out onto a sandy, well-traveled access road. "Do you think this is the island you and your uncle visited?" Connor asked.

"I'll know as soon as I see the town."

"How come?" asked Chris.

"I remember a lot of fresh vegetables everywhere, piles of big yellow yams, and the loud noise of birds."

"Well, I don't hear any birds," said Chris, "and I doubt there will be any vegetables after all the cold, cloudy weather we've had."

"You're probably right, but the other thing I remember was an old but very large Methodist church in the center of the town. It was built in the late 1800's, but it was well kept."

"Do you think we will run into more of those soldiers here?" Connor asked.

"I don't know! Maybe, but if we're lucky, Simon hasn't gotten to Woodlark yet."

******

Daniel Cohen and Peter Bastoni had united their efforts. The entire back half of Daniel's house was full of lab equipment that Daniel had pilfered and given to Peter to make the antidote.

Peter grabbed another piece of copper tubing and stretched it as far as he could. "I wish this stuff was already pre-curled," said Peter with a grunt. The stress Peter felt as he tried to carefully coil each piece of tubing caused him anxiety. He knew how hard and dangerous it was for Daniel to get these supplies for him. So far Peter had completely destroyed two long pieces of copper tubing, and if he ruined just one more piece, he would not be able to complete his distillery.

"Let me try something," said Daniel as he left the room. He had been watching Peter closely, and although he was sure Peter knew how to make the antidote, he doubted that Peter would have the skills to build the equipment he needed. Daniel returned with an acetylene torch in hand. "Maybe we can soften this stuff up some as we bend it."

"Good idea!" exclaimed Peter.

The two men worked all afternoon and into the evening. Finally the lab was complete, running from one end of the hallway all the way into the guest room and onto the roof in the back of the house.

"Okay, now explain to me how this thing is going to work," Daniel said.

"Well, here goes!" said Peter. "First we fill the condenser on the roof with sterile water."

"Where are you going to get that?" Daniel asked.

"We can boil tap water and it should be okay. Then we need to add the sulfur to the kettle, and finally we need to add the naphthalene tablets to this pressure cooker. Light a match and heat the water and sulfur. Eventually they will migrate to the pressure cooker through this tube."

"This stuff is going to stink up the neighborhood," said Daniel.

Peter nodded. "Unfortunately yes. So we should only run it at night."

Daniel looked deeply into Peter's eyes. He could tell that Peter had gone through many trials in his life. He was getting hard and tough. Daniel respected this warrior. "Okay, we'll run it at night."

About that time Ruth and David came through the front door. "Peter?" Ruth called loudly.

"In here!" he replied.

Ruth entered the new laboratory and smiled at Peter. "It looks like a great big Erector Set."

"That's pretty much what it is," said Peter.

"Will it work?" David asked.

"As soon as Daniel gets me some naphthalene we will be in business!"

"Look at this," said Ruth as she held up the daily newspaper.

Peter read the article. It included a quote from Simon Koch: "'I am disappointed to have to inform all of you living in the Middle East that we, His Holiness and I, have been monitoring your daily oil production, and we are very dissatisfied with this effort. As you are no doubt aware, our world is in great need of this oil to provide electricity. Your unwillingness to support our cause has brought about Carlo's anger. There will be no more antidote given to any country whose oil output is not doubled in the next 30 days. Additionally we cannot guarantee that some other oil-deprived country will not retaliate against you and simply take the oil necessary to survive."'

"This is a bunch of lies!" said Daniel angrily. "We refined more oil last month than we ever have before."

"I wonder what country he is talking about," Ruth said rhetorically.

"Well, then it is a good thing we have built this lab," said Daniel.

Just the fact that Daniel was talking this way bothered Ruth greatly. He was a lost soul and nothing could change that, and now he acted as if he were on the same side of the issue as she was, but that could not be the case.

******

Christopher enjoyed the warmth of the sun as he, Joshua, and Connor walked along the sandy road. *What a beautiful place,* he thought. The forest surrounding the island was dense and full of color—from lime green to dark olive. The ice had not killed all of this vegetation. The only thing missing was any sign of indigenous life.

As the three men walked toward the center of the island, they had not seen a single bird nor any small reptiles or animals. It was as if the entire island was deserted.

Thirty minutes later Connor was the first one to hear the sound of singing. "What is that?" Connor asked.

"It sounds like music to me," said Joshua.

About that time all three men observed a handful of children running across the sandy road. The children either did not notice the men or they simply didn't care, because none of them stopped to look. "How old do you think those kids are?" Chris asked.

"They can't be any more than three or four years old," said Connor.

"Then their parents cannot be far—" Chris never got to finish his sentence, because at the same time a small group of women walked out onto the road. All three men stopped and stared at the women. Simultaneously the natives stopped and stared back.

"What do we do now?" Connor asked.

Joshua began to wave his hand and smile brightly.

"Do you know them?" Chris asked.

"No," Joshua continued to smile, "but better to seem friendly than to scare them away." Slowly the men walked towards the women who by now had gathered their young children together.

As the men approached one of the women placed a couple of her fingers in her mouth and sounded the loudest whistle Chris had ever heard. In fact, the noise was so loud and unexpected that all three men froze in their tracks.

All of a sudden a large number of men came running towards the women from out of the woods, all of them carrying big sticks.

"Okay, now what?" said Connor.

"Keep smiling and walk forward slowly," said Joshua.

The three men eased their way towards the natives. Chris' hands were shaking at the mere sight of so many men all wearing angry looks on their faces while carrying large pieces of wood. Finally when Joshua was within 10 feet of the group one of the men held up his stick and spoke out in a dialect that neither Joshua nor the others could even begin to comprehend.

"I think we are in big trouble," said Connor. "I hope they aren't the kind of natives that eat people or something."

"Eat people!" Chris said. *Do they still have cannibals in the world?* he wondered.

"We come in peace," said Joshua as calmly as he could. He'd already been nearly crucified once, and he hoped to avoid it again if possible. We come in the name of the Lord," he smiled.

Suddenly a deep voice could be heard from a distance. The group of natives parted to allow a very large man to step forward. "John 3:16," said the man.

Joshua looked into the dark eyes of the man and repeated the phrase, "John 3:16."

"No!" said the man. "You say."

"I think he wants you to quote John 3:16," said Connor.

"'For God so loved the world that He gave His only begotten Son that whosoever believeth in Him should not perish, but have everlasting life,'" smiled Joshua as genuinely as he could.

For a moment there was total silence and then abruptly the large man extended his arms and spoke. "Welcome to Muyuw." The natives lowered their sticks, moved towards the three men, and began to shake their hands enthusiastically.

"My name is Joshua."

Each man and woman introduced themselves, yet it was unlikely that Chris, Connor, or Joshua would ever be able to repeat any of the names. Finally the large man spoke up and said, "I am Tilu Muywata, but you can call me Ezra." Joshua had to laugh. *How did the man get the name Ezra? And how did he learn to speak English? He didn't exactly look like an Ezra at all. However, it surely was an easier name than Tilu Muywata.*

******

Simon walked into the center of NORAD in the heart of Cheyenne Mountain as easily as a person could walk into a laundromat. The previous day he had orchestrated the takeover of all United States military regional centers at Tyndall Air Force Base in Florida, Griffin Air Force Base in New York, McChord Air Force Base in Washington, and finally March Air Force Base in California. Along the way he collected the necessary military personnel to allow him to open NORAD without any resistance.

All of this was easily done since Simon had already taken control over the majority of the United States military forces nearly a year earlier. If it were not for his recent illness and his preoccupation with Victoria, he would have taken care of this necessary task long ago. It would have been easy since the U.S.A. was in such disarray after the first asteroid hit in the heart of the country.

As expected the President of the United States, his wife, and the Joint Chiefs of Staff were all safely tucked away in the mountain. Simon had located the Vice President, Speaker of the House, and Secretary of State earlier that week. All of them cooperated fully. This was an unfortunate surprise for Simon. He had really been looking forward to torturing these men, but today things were starting to look more favorable. It was unlikely that this President would cooperate and hand over the keys to the nuclear arsenal of the United States of America.

Simon entered the main control center with an entourage of armed soldiers. This was the pinnacle of his career to this point. The sense of power and ultimate control he felt was euphoric. He only wished he had brought Victoria with him so she could see how utterly powerful her man was.

Simon walked past a host of generals and admirals and stepped up to a gray-headed man who was wearing an extremely nervous look on his face. The President was surrounded by a number of very worried Secret Service men and one extremely frightened First Lady, all of whom knew they were in big trouble.

"Mr. President," Simon smiled, "it's been too long. How are you feeling today?"

The President swallowed hard but remained silent.

"I believe you have some very important codes that I need," Simon grinned.

"I will give you nothing!" said the President.

"Really!" smiled Simon. "Well, let's just see about that, shall we?" Simon turned his head and nodded to a number of armed men who pointed their rifles at the members of the Joint Chiefs. Each of the generals looked to the President and then to the men with guns. "Are you sure you don't want to change your answer?" Simon asked.

The President said nothing which was exactly what Simon wanted to hear. "Kill them!" Simon ordered. The noise in the room was deafening as smoke filled the air. All four generals fell to the ground dead. Two of the secret service men tried to pull their revolvers, but both men were blown to pieces instantly. The First Lady screamed hysterically at what had just happened before her eyes. The President stared in disbelief at the lifeless evil face of Simon Koch. "Now!" beamed Simon as he looked down at the dead men. "Have you reconsidered?"

It really didn't matter to Simon. He could get the codes through other means or simply reprogram every weapon in the United States arsenal, but it was a matter of principle for him, and as far as he was concerned, he was the principal—the most powerful man in the world.

"You can go back to Hell where you came from!" said the President. "Jesus protects those He loves. We will dwell with Him for eternity."

Simon laughed until tears filled his eyes. "Kill him! Kill them all!"

Five minutes later Simon walked out of NORAD and into a crowd of news reporters he had arranged for this occasion. "Mr. Koch," said one of the reporters "was the President in there? Is he okay?"

"Yes and no," said Simon with a smile.

"What do you mean, Sir?" the reporter inquired.

"Yes, the President and his military staff were all cowering in this fortress. None of them had the courage to come out and help their own people, and none of them believed in His Holiness, Carlo Ventini. They were planning a surprise attack on the world, but I have put a stop to that forever. From now on all nuclear weapons are in my control and are totally unnecessary. We are creating a world of love and peace for all." Simon smiled at his closing statement. Oh, how he wished Victoria was here to see this. His only consolation was that this was being broadcast live around the world. Now that new satellites had been put into orbit, Simon and Carlo could easily reach into the homes of nearly every person in the world—at least those homes with electricity.

As Simon stood basking in his new glory, Moses and Elijah appeared at his side. Simon drew back in surprise and fear. "Woe unto the world!" said Moses. "You have not obeyed the Lord. You have turned your back on the one true God to follow and worship the beast."

Simon grew angry and turned towards Moses. "Carlo Ventini is god, and I am his prophet. There is no other god. You are liars!"

Elijah turned towards Simon and glared into his scared eyes. Simon shook with fear. Turning towards the cameras Elijah spoke forcefully, "The Lord Jesus Christ loves you and wants you to return to Him. Do not follow after this man or any other. Repent and kneel before the King of Heaven and earth. Jehovah is a God of mercy and forgiveness."

Moses pointed toward the sky. "Because you have mocked God and have hardened your hearts, you will suffer terribly at the hand of Satan.

For months you will be tormented by his demons. You will beg for death to mercifully spare you from this pain and torment, but death will not come," he said.

"Shut the cameras off!" Simon yelled, but it was too late. The message was out and the world had heard it clearly. Simon turned towards Moses and Elijah just as they disappeared. Terror struck his heart. *What torment can they be talking about?* he wondered.

******

Deep beneath the ocean floor in the center of the Kuril Trench off the continent of Asia the water began to bubble and churn. At the entrance of the abyss was a large shaft that would have normally vented gas to the surface of the sea if it had not been sealed up thousands of years ago. There beside the shaft stood two large and wondrous angels. They were deep beneath the surface of the ocean, yet they stood as if they were on dry land.

One of the angels pointed a large, golden rod towards the sealed shaft and suddenly a bright bolt of lightning leapt out of the rod and exploded in front of the shaft. Instantly the shaft split into two sections creating a large hole. Black, murky water and millions of large bubbles began to bellow out of the new opening. Soon a small, atrocious looking creature came forth. His head was disproportionately large compared to his hideous body. Behind him it appeared as if there were millions of similar creatures packed densely into the abyss, all of them evil looking—almost insect-like, with razor sharp teeth, claw-like hands, hairy manes around their necks, and large wings on their backs. Without opening his mouth one of the angels spoke to the creature saying, "Apollyon, you have months to torment, but you are commanded not to kill any human."

Apollyon turned to the multitudes standing behind him and roared like a lion. Nearly instantaneously all the creatures flew out of the abyss at an unbelievable speed. On the surface of the ocean smoke began to bellow forth as if a volcano were erupting. The smoke and stench filled the sky and were carried to the four corners of the earth, a sign that evil had been turned loose on mankind.

******

Daniel entered his home carrying two large boxes full of very smelly chemicals. For the last few weeks he had been supplying Peter with the necessary components to make the antidote. Daily Ruth and David would take the medicine into the city and the surrounding countryside. They gave the people the instructions Peter had given them along with the small, pink vials of antidote and a good supply of syringes, complements of the local hospitals from which David had stolen crates of them.

Daniel walked into the bedroom where Peter was working away as usual filling bottles with medicine and monitoring his distillery. "Are David and Ruth still out?" asked Daniel as he set the heavy boxes on the floor.

"Yeah, I am starting to worry. They have been gone all day."

"Well, we'll just wait a little longer," said Daniel.

Peter could not help but like Benjamin's son. He had such a kind and generous heart. Peter found that he had to continually remind himself that this man's fate was sealed and it was only a matter of time before they would have to part company. Peter's heart grew heavy as he considered his new friend's fate. "Are you hungry?" Peter asked. "I made a stew out of whatever I could find in your cupboards."

Daniel laughed, "I hope you didn't throw any of this stinky stuff into the pot."

Peter chuckled. "No, but it might taste better if I had. I'm not much of a cook. My brother won all the awards for that particular skill."

Peter grew solemn as he thought about Joseph. Daniel understood Peter's thoughts. Although he had never met Joseph or Yvette, he was aware of their fate. In fact, he saw the whole thing on the television set in the hospital waiting room where he had taken David that very day.

Daniel sat at the empty table as Peter ladled the stew into a bowl and set it before him. "Smells good to me," he smiled.

"You'd better reserve your comments until after you've tasted it,"

Peter grinned.

Abruptly the small house began to shake. "Are we having an earthquake?" yelled Peter. A thought occurred to him that perhaps his lab equipment had exploded under the pressure. Peter looked towards Daniel just in time to see him clutch his throat and fall back, knocking the bowl of stew onto the floor.

"Daniel!" Peter shouted. "Are you choking?"

Daniel rolled around on the floor in obvious pain. Peter was a doctor and had seen many things, but this was something new and very frightening. Finally Daniel leaned up and grabbed the corner of the table, pulling his body into a sitting position. Across his face was an agonizing look of pain. "What is it? What's wrong?" Peter asked.

Daniel stood and stared at Peter for a few seconds and then walked out of the room and into his own bedroom. Peter stood in the center of the kitchen amazed at what he had just seen. What Peter didn't know was that all around the world scenes just like this one were unfolding as the unsaved and the damned were being possessed by the evil creatures from the abyss. This torment was to become commonplace in Daniel Cohen's home, and there was nothing anyone could do about it.

******

Ruth and David traveled the five miles to Bethlehem and stood in the small town square not four blocks from where her station manager, Scott Turner, had given his life to save hers. The memory of that day still haunted Ruth, but she knew Scott was in Heaven with Joseph and Yvette and soon she would be there too.

David had successfully witnessed to the people and although many of them had already taken the ID tags or were still undecided, they listened all the same because they had heard about the young boy and black lady working their way through Israel handing out lifesaving antidote.

Today things were proceeding as usual—a few mockers, an occasional threat, a few new converts, but nothing out of the ordinary, until a fierce wind blew past Ruth and David and into the gathered crowd. Suddenly people began to fall to the ground writhing in pain and screaming out.

"What is it?" David yelled as he reached out for the safety of Ruth's hand.

"I don't know!" said Ruth. She stepped back out of the way of a young woman who was rolling towards her while screaming in pain.

Ruth gripped David's hand tightly. "We need to leave now!"

"What about the antidote? We haven't handed any out yet," said David.

"Leave some for them and let's go!"

David set a case of pink bottles and a large box of needles on the bench in front of him and left the wild scene as quickly as he and Ruth could run off.

The next few hours for David and Ruth were a nightmare right out of a storybook. No matter where they went the scenes around each community were the same. People were screaming out in pain, rolling on the ground, or crashing their cars into buildings or other cars. Death would have been deliverance from such torment, but death would not come. Each person seemed to be prevented from harming themselves—at least to a lethal degree.

Finally after numerous detours Ruth and David found their way back to Daniel's home. As the entered the house Peter met them. Ruth gave Peter a big hug and began to cry. "What is it, Ruth? Where have you guys been?"

Ruth and David told Peter the whole story, and when they were through, Peter looked towards Ruth, "Is this in the Bible? I mean, do you understand what is going on?"

Ruth had given this a lot of thought. "Yes, Peter, I think it is one of the first of three woes."

"What do you mean?" Peter asked.

"The people continue to mock God and turn their backs on Him, and as a result He is giving them over to their own desires. He had opened the abyss and turned Apollyon and the imprisoned demons loose."

"Who is Apollyon?" Peter inquired.

"He was a very powerful and evil demon working for Satan. God locked him and millions like him into an abyss somewhere on this planet. They were to be released only in the end of times and then only to torment the unsaved or the followers of Satan."

At this last comment David began to look around the room for Daniel. Fear covered his face, "Where is Daniel?"

Peter put his hand on David's shoulder and looked into his young, brown eyes. "He locked himself in his bedroom."

"Did he? I mean, did a demon—" David cried.

"Yes," said Peter softly, "it was awful, but I think he is somewhat better now. We should leave him alone for a while though."

David sat on the arm of the sofa and began to sob. Ruth put her arms around him to comfort him as best she could, but what could she or anyone say? The man was destined for eternal separation from God, and there was nothing—absolutely nothing—anyone could do.

******

The space station had reached the moon as predicted by Samuel Pearlman. All six members of the ISS team stood weightlessly in the main control cabin as they stared out at the gray moon's cratered surface. None of them ever expected to see this satellite again, and none of them really knew what to think about this situation.

"Well, we have just enough fuel to break into the moon's orbit if we want," said Samuel.

"And what will that buy us?" Petra asked harshly.

Shila Torpof, the Romanian astronaut on her maiden voyage, spoke up. "Maybe if we stay in the moon's orbit, they will send someone after us. At least we won't go wandering out into that black nothingness anymore."

"I agree," said Skip Taylor.

Teresa Reed and Bob Powell nodded in agreement.

"Okay!" said Petra, "but I still don't see any point."

Samuel looked at Teresa intently. "Tell them."

"Tell us what?" Bob asked.

Petra sat in his command chair and kicked his feet up defiantly. "Yeah, tell them what is coming next!"

Samuel reached into his pocket and pulled out a yellow piece of paper and unfolded it carefully. "We got back here to the moon because we rode the effects of these gravitational pulls from this massive planetary alignment, but this alignment has other repercussions."

"Like what?" Skip asked as Petra sighed heavily.

"Just tell them, Comrade!" said Petra with frustration.

"We are going to have an issue with the proximity of the sun," said Samuel flatly.

Bob Powell took the paper from Pearlman's hand and studied the numbers carefully. Slowly he looked up to Teresa. "How long have you known this?"

"A few months," said Teresa.

"Why didn't you tell us?" Bob asked.

"I didn't want to worry you until we knew for sure that we were going to make it back to the moon," Teresa apologized.

"Are we going to burn up?" Shila asked as she began to whimper.

"It's quite possible," said Samuel softly.

"More like it is going to happen for sure," said Petra.

Shila began to cry uncontrollably. Bob put his hand on her shoulder. "God will help us!" he said.

"He'll have to!" said Petra in a low grumble.

Skip Taylor took the paper from Bob's hand and studied it closely. "No, this is wrong!"

Every head in the room turned to look at Skip.

"What do you mean?" asked Pearlman.

"You haven't accounted for the effects of Jupiter on the moon."

Pearlman took the paper back from Skip and stared at it intently as if he were doing mathematical calculations in his head which, of course, was exactly what he was doing. "You're right! I calculated this based on an earth locality."

"Does that mean we won't burn up?" Shila cried.

"It's going to be close," said Pearlman, "but I think we can hide from most of the direct sun rays and Jupiter will shield us from much of the radiation. We may just survive it after all," Samuel smiled.

"Then what are we waiting for?" said Teresa. "Let's put this thing into orbit around the moon, and in an hour we will get a glimpse of the earth and maybe even be able to contact NASA if they still exist."

******

Victoria climbed out of bed quietly so as not to wake Simon. She was grateful that the disgusting little pervert was finally asleep. The things she had to endure in her life in order to be successful were sometimes nearly unacceptable, but,in the case of Simon it was all worth it. She would soon be his wife and that would make her the most powerful woman in the world.

Yes, Simon was a pathetic little toad, and since his return from NORAD his libido was even greater than before, but he was her stepladder to fame and fortune. *Besides, who knows,* she thought, *maybe I will get another chance to sleep with Carlo, and maybe this time he will take me away from Simon forever.* If the truth were known, Victoria was in love with Carlo. One night of passion with him was all it took, not to mention he was a god and if she could get him interested in her, then she could be the wife of a god. She could be a goddess. For now, however, she was content to use Simon to fulfill her desires for greatness.

Victoria took a step into the kitchen of Simon's apartment just as the room began to shake. Suddenly an invisible force came crashing into her chest, knocking her to the floor. The pain was excruciating causing Victoria to scream out for help. Simon came running in from the bedroom in time to see Victoria contorted on the floor wearing nothing but a nearly transparent nightgown. "What's the matter?" shouted Simon over the loud shrill of Victoria's screams of agony. Abruptly as Simon bent down towards her a loud rush of air swooshed by his head, knocking him back against the stove, and banging his left shoulder hard enough to break the glass in the center of the range. Terror filled Simon's mind as he remembered what Moses had said just 24 hours ago. *Torment for months,* he thought as he screamed out in pain.

As Simon reached up for the phone, agony constricted his body making it nearly impossible to dial the number, but at last the phone began to ring. Eventually a servant picked up the line, "Let me speak to His Holiness!" Simon cried out.

"Who is this?" the annoyed servant asked. "It's three in the morning!"

Simon felt an excruciating pain flow through his veins. Lying in front of him Victoria continued to scream out in torment. "It's Simon Koch! Get Carlo now!" he yelled into the phone.

Moments later Carlo picked up the phone and in a very irritated voice asked, "What is it, Simon?"

In the background Carlo could hear Victoria screaming. With a loud moan Simon spoke up, "Help me, Carlo!"

"What is it, Simon? What's going on?" Carlo said casually.

"It's the plague that Moses talked about. We are being tortured to death!" Simon cried.

"Okay, Simon, I will be over soon," said Carlo as he hung up the phone. Carlo knew about this demonic attack. He had seen it in his own office and among his servants, but he seemed to have immunity from it. *How pathetic Simon truly is,* thought Carlo. *How human!*

Thirty minutes later Carlo entered Simon's house without an escort because all of his employees were suffering just as Simon and Victoria were. Carlo could hear the screams from the kitchen. "Simon!" Carlo shouted.

"Over here!" Simon cried.

Carlo stood in the center of the kitchen looking down at the half-naked Victoria and the whimpering Simon. "Well, isn't this pathetic?" Carlo said. "Don't you even have the power to command these demons to leave? After all, don't they work for my Father? Stand up!" Carlo commanded.

Both Victoria and Simon struggled to their feet. "Father," prayed Carlo softly. "Father, please come to me!"

Soon the room began to shake uncontrollably and the lights began to flicker. Smoke filled the kitchen along with the pungent smell of rotten flesh. Before Carlo was a silhouette of Satan. The mere sight of him scared Victoria so much that she passed out and dropped to the floor with a thud. "What is it, my Son?" Satan asked.

"Father, Simon has a visitor tormenting him."

Satan laughed out in a hideous and frightening way. "Yes, Apollyon is loose again."

Simon doubled over in pain.

"Demons, be gone!" said Satan.

Immediately there was a rush of air. Then Simon felt a release and the pain was gone. Simon looked down to check on Victoria. She, too, had stopped twitching and moaning.

"Thank you, Father," said Carlo.

"I am pleased with you, my Son, but there is more that must be done. There are Christians and Jews around the world still in hiding. They must be found and converted so they will worship me. Time is short. Simon, you have done well so far, but there is much more to do. Fill your camps and eliminate those that do not cooperate, especially those that are out witnessing throughout the world."

The room shook as Satan departed. Simon and Carlo both turned to look at Victoria as she lay unconscious on the floor. "You're a lucky man, Simon," said Carlo with a grin that reminded Simon that Carlo had taken his woman away—at least for a night. Simon vowed that this would never happen again.

******

Chris and Connor stood side by side at the front steps of a large Methodist church located smack in the center of the tiny island community. They watched as Joshua told his vivid tale to the natives. A handful of children sat in a small circle around Joshua's feet, listening intently. It was unlikely that they understood a single word of English, but the mood and voice inflection seemed to tell them a story all their own.

Then Joshua pointed to Chris and Connor saying, "They saved my life as I hung there nailed to a burning cross." Joshua held up his hands for the natives to see the nail scars. Many of the women let out gasps of shock and disbelief. Finally quietly Joshua told the natives of Woodlark the story of the little girl and her mother back on the island of Fiji. He described the security forces and how harshly the mother and little girl had been treated.

"Where are they now?" Ezra inquired.

"Who?" asked Joshua, "The little girl and her mother, or the security police?"

Joshua studied the old man closely. He had learned that Ezra was the chief of this island, an extraordinary man who had come to know the Lord on his own after the Rapture. The story went that most of the island's people disappeared late one night. The next morning those that remained gathered around Ezra for an answer. "Well," said Ezra, who had been taught about Jesus by the island missionaries like most of the community, "it is obvious to me that Jesus has come back and taken our families and friends. We must repent and serve Him and then He will come back for us too!"

Joshua was encouraged by this man's story and by his unswerving faith. He had missed the boat once, but he would not miss it a second time.

"Both," said Ezra.

"The head guard said something about taking them to a concentration camp in Europe. I'm not really sure," said Joshua. "As for the security police, they are on Fiji and it is only a matter of time before they come this way."

The chief flinched at the thought. "We will let God handle that. Right now we have work to do."

Ezra stood and looked at Christopher and Connor closely and then at Joshua. "God has chosen you three as ministers to the islands. I can see God in you. My island is your island. You can come and go from here as you please. We will provide food and shelter and whatever else you need."

Chris smiled at the large chief. His enthusiastic nature warmed Chris' heart. "We need gas for our boat," he said.

Connor shuddered at the thought of getting back into that boat, but he understood the need to travel to the other islands in search of the unsaved.

"We have gas!" Ezra beamed. "But tonight you stay with us and we will have a feast, and tomorrow you can go to the next island," he said, assuming that would be New Guinea.

Bright and early the next morning Joshua, Chris, and Connor were escorted by the entire village down to the cove where they had moored their boat. From the edge of the beach Chris could see that the boat had been loaded with provisions graciously given to them by the natives. The boat was also full of gas and ready to go.

Joshua turned towards Ezra and extended his hand. "Thank you for your kindness. May God protect you until Christ returns."

"This is your home now. You three come back as often as you need to, and we will help you all we can. May God go with you, and may your harvest be plentiful."

"Amen!" said Connor as he helped Chris into the small rubber raft.

Twenty minutes later Joshua pointed the boat northwest on a direct course with Papua, New Guinea. "Jesus, help us to spread Your Word before it is too late," Joshua whispered as he stood quietly behind the helm of his cabin cruiser.

Chapter 10: The Wedding

Day 1645, February: Raymond Hyder gathered up all his material. He had 20 minutes before he would have to present the current state of the planet to Carlo and Simon. Lately Dr. Hyder had found it nearly impossible to concentrate on anything. He had suffered greatly from the tormenting demons just like the majority of the world had. At one point Raymond even tried to jump out of his apartment window. It was a 40-foot drop and he was nearly certain that the fall would kill him, ending his suffering. But no matter how hard he tried to let go of the windowsill, he just could not. Something prevented it—something outside of his control.

This morning Raymond awoke to an empty but pain free feeling for the first time in many months. His tormentor had left during the night. Raymond's fear now was that this unseen monster would come back.

Over the last year or so Raymond had spent many days simply sitting around his lonely apartment trying to understand what had happed to his life and to his world.

He felt enormous guilt over his participation in the newscast from the United States where he had told the American citizens that they would be safe from harm when ED14, the massive asteroid, hit the earth. Nearly 80 million people had died that day and throughout the next week from its effects. Dr. Hyder felt a terrible burden for all of those people even though he realized he could not have prevented the asteroid and he understood that there just wasn't enough time to warn the people. They had received less than 10 days notice that the asteroid was approaching the earth and even less time than that to determine how big it would be and where it would hit.

Now as Raymond mulled over the events of the last year, the nuclear winter, the plague, starvation, the blackness of the sky, and finally the intolerable heat and suffering, life seemed incomprehensible. So many people were dead or missing—and now this demonic torment which had lasted for many months. *What was the point to life?*

Dr. Hyder was not even sure why he continued to give Carlo and Simon updates. He detested both men and held them accountable for much of the misery in the world, but what option did he have?

He had pondered God—or the existence of a real God—but until now he could not imagine such a being existed, especially one that would allow all this misery. Now, however, Raymond was beginning to understand that maybe mankind had made its own choice and turned its back on the one true God. As a result they were suffering for their own disobedience. The concept was difficult for him. "God, if You do exist, please reveal Yourself and tell me what to do," said Raymond out of desperation just as he closed his apartment door.

As he walked towards the main office of the United World headquarters building, the sweltering heat was just too much. It actually hurt to be outside. Raymond could feel his skin blister as if he were being burned from a hot stove or a coal of fire. He was grateful to enter the dark, air conditioned hall of Carlo's office. One flight of stairs later and Dr. Hyder was standing in front of the large, brown door that led into Carlo's chamber. At the door two scary-looking security guards met him.

"What is your business?" the taller of the two guards asked gruffly.

"I am Dr. Hyder, and I am supposed to give His Holiness a weather briefing."

"Well, I hope it is good news," said the smaller of the two guards.

Raymond put on a fake smile for the occasion. "Can't get much worse," he said.

One of the guards opened the door for Dr. Hyder, allowing him to walk into the chamber. At the far end seated at a long narrow table were Carlo, Simon, and Oswald. Simon looked up at Raymond and said, "We'll be with you in a few minutes. Take a seat."

Dr. Hyder took the closest seat next to the door and sat quickly. Simon was never friendly to him, but today he noted that Simon seemed to have a shorter temper than usual. As he sat there listening in on the conversation, it was obvious that they were all deeply into a subject of some grave interest.

"Okay, Oswald, give me a status from these three camps," said Simon as he pointed to three of the concentration camps on the map in front of him.

"First Dachau," said Oswald. "We have been successful in converting as much as 30 percent of inhabitants."

"Thirty percent?" roared Carlo. "Last month you said it was 50 percent!"

Oswald swallowed hard. "Yes, it was 50 percent, Your Holiness, but something has happened. After these many months of torment our converts have dropped off. Frankly, we could not torture them any more than they were already being tortured by whatever it was that attacked all of us."

Carlo nodded. Apollyon, or Abaddon in Hebrew, did his job so well that it worked against Carlo and his plans for total world control. "Continue," said Carlo more softly.

"Auschwitz is also down to approximately 30 percent for tag insertion, but I expect this to return to normal now that the tormenting seems to be over. Mauthausen in Linz has also seen a reduction in ID tags as well as—" Oswald paused for a second—he knew Simon was not going to like the next report. "As well as an increase in the number of escapes."

"What do you mean an increase? Do we *normally* see prisoners escaping?" Simon asked angrily.

"Well, no! This is the first time we've seen it."

"How many and how long has this been going on?" Simon inquired.

Raymond sat quietly, trying as hard as possible to listen in on the conversation. He had heard rumors about concentration camps, but until now they were just rumors.

"At last count maybe 300 or so," said Oswald.

"Three hundred!" screamed Simon. "How long has this been going on?"

"Maybe three months. It all started with a rumor that the tormenting we were all suffering was not happening to the Christians. An additional rumor was that if a person confessed Jesus Christ as Lord, the pain and suffering would stop for them also.

Simon cringed at the mention of the name of Jesus. He knew how much Carlo hated this name.

"What does this have to do with people escaping?" Carlo asked angrily.

Oswald drew a deep breath and continued. "Well, shortly after these rumors emerged, there was another rumor that there was an American scientist who was spreading information about our ID tags. He was telling everyone that if they took the tag, they would be sent to Hell. Furthermore, if they tried to take the tag out of their body, it would kill them. He also told them that the ID tag was a way of locating them no matter where they were in the world."

Simon grew impatient with Oswald. "So what does this have to do with people escaping?"

"Apparently this man got to some of my guards. It seems that not all my people had taken the ID tags either. Well, once they heard that the tormenting would go away if they accepted Christ as their savior and after hearing that they would go to Hell if they accepted the ID tag—"

Simon roared and slapped his hand down on the table. "Your own security helped these people escape! Your own people don't even have ID tags?"

Oswald was panicking, and Raymond was astounded by what he was hearing. *All this time I sat back in torment, and I could have asked Jesus to come into my heart and the pain would have been gone,* thought Raymond.

Carlo held up his hand to calm Simon. All this did was annoy Simon even more. "Where are these guards now?" Carlo inquired.

"We don't know, but it is a safe bet they are still in Germany somewhere. We'll find them," said Oswald as perspiration ran down his red face.

"And the rest of your guards—how do we know they have taken the ID tag?" Carlo asked.

"I have had every one of them re-injected just to be safe. This is happening as we speak."

"And what about the Christians who escaped and the American who is leading all this?" asked Simon angrily.

Oswald swallowed hard. "We don't have any leads on the ones who escaped, but we do think we have identified the American responsible."

Simon looked up at Oswald. "Tommy Glover!"

Oswald nodded. "That's right! He and Dr. Sara Allen have been sighted in a number of locations throughout Germany. We will find them soon."

"Not soon enough!" Simon roared. Oh, how he wanted to kill both Tommy and Sara.

After Oswald left with his tail tucked away it was Raymond's turn. His mind was spinning from all the information he had overheard. It seemed that the power of Jesus was real and did help. It also seemed that the Christians were giving these three men fits of rage. Apparently there was a fellow American stirring up trouble for Simon and Carlo. Raymond wanted to meet this man and shake his hand.

"Well, are you just going to sit there, or are you going to give us some more of your usual bad news?" Simon screeched.

"Calm down, Simon!" Carlo ordered. "Dr. Hyder, what do you have for us today?"

"I spoke with my contacts at the Jet Propulsion Laboratory today. It looks like Jupiter is moving as predicted and will eclipse the earth very soon."

"What does that mean?" a frustrated Simon asked. He was lucky to understand every fourth word that came out of Raymond's mouth.

"Today as of 45 minutes ago it was 138 degrees here in Rome and 162 degrees in Cairo. The temperature at the North Pole is 93 degrees and at the South Pole 87 degrees. Every river in the world has suffered greatly. It has not rained on this planet in over a year. The oceans were terribly damaged by the asteroids, and now that we have a drought of such magnitude, there is no fresh water coming into the seas and oceans and all snow pack is gone. Not to mention the oceans are dying even though they are rising at a dangerous rate."

"What do you mean rising at a dangerous rate?" Simon inquired.

"The poles are melting at least enough to raise the water level of the Pacific nearly 18 inches so far and the Atlantic over 30 inches.

"Then this should be adding good fresh water to the oceans," said Simon.

"No, the ice is melting from the top down, and the top is covered with millions of metric tons of ash and dust from the last three asteroids. The melted water is only making things worse. As for the islands of the Pacific and Atlantic, they are in real danger of being totally submerged in the next few months."

"Any good news?" asked Carlo.

"Like I started to say, Jupiter is about to eclipse the earth. This will block out the sun and the temperatures will come down greatly, but only for a short time. During this time it will be darker than you can imagine."

"How long and when?" Carlo inquired.

"I'd say within two weeks the sun will be completely blocked, and the darkness will last for a month or so."

Simon considered this closely. He was supposed to get married in two weeks. Carlo, on the other hand, had a bigger issue. He was making plans with Whi Yin and the Chinese military behind Simon's back. He wanted to own and control every inch of the Middle East and Asia Minor, especially all of the oil nations, and China was his instrument for getting this accomplished. However, his plans were for an invasion within the month. He would have to reconsider this.

"Anything else?" asked Carlo softly.

Raymond paused for a second. "No, I guess that is it. Oh, we did make contact with the International Space Station."

"Really!" said Carlo. "You mean they were not destroyed with all the satellites?"

"No! I guess they moved out into space far enough to avoid the debris."

"Where are they now?" Simon asked.

"Orbiting the moon."

"How long can they do that?" Simon inquired.

"I am not sure, but I heard something about them having less than a year's worth of oxygen and food."

"Can we take any supplies to them or bring them back to earth?" Simon pondered how this might make him look if he were to go out and rescue astronauts.

"I don't know. NASA is not operational, and I am not even sure if we have a working space shuttle and a crew available."

"Well, find out and get back to me next week!" Simon commanded.

******

Back in Avdat National Park it was a stifling, deadly 164 degrees. If it were not for the natural air conditioning flowing through the caves, Elisha, Jasmine, and the thousands of people hidden out in the desert of the Negev would have died, but God continued to provide for their needs. Water bubbled up from a crevice between two enormous rocks deep within the first set of caves. This water was ice cold and refreshing to the body. Although the shrimp ponds had dried up, Elisha's people still managed to survive off of the smoked shrimp they had put back over the last few months. Additionally they harvested fresh mushrooms from the cave's floor every morning. It was as if some mysterious person planted them each night. Mushroom and shrimp stew kept the people healthy and well nourished.

Elisha had finished his nightly counsel meeting and was just sitting down to a light supper with Jasmine. He was annoyed this evening— almost apprehensive. It could have been the sweltering heat or the claustrophobia he felt after being closed up in the caves for many months, but Jasmine understood Elisha. She knew it was none of those things. She knew he had a burden in his soul for the lost Israelis. He felt the need to go in search of others that might be in hiding or wandering out in this insufferable and lethal heat while trying to escape Simon's Special Security force.

"Are you okay?" Jasmine asked as she handed Elisha a bowl of mushroom stew.

Elisha looked at Jasmine and set his bowl down at his side. He reached in and pulled his faithful little companion into his arms. "I love you," said Elisha as he hugged Jasmine tightly.

Jasmine nestled her face into Elisha's chest, "I love you too!"

Elisha gently pushed Jasmine away from his chest and stared into her pretty face. "I can't stay here anymore."

Jasmine looked into her man's deep, brown eyes. She was anxious. Everything in life was frightening, but as long as she had Elisha she had hope. Of course, her faith in Jesus was always there, but she and Elisha were a team. They were soul mates and were meant to be together. "I know," Jasmine whispered. "But if you spent 10 minutes out in this heat, you would die."

Elisha nodded in agreement. This was, in essence, his frustration. He knew he needed to leave and go in pursuit of others, but how could he? Death awaited anyone who stepped outside for more than a few minutes. Unknown to Elisha millions had already died because of the heat throughout the world, and soon millions more would die from the drought too. Even with the desalinization plants installed at Simon's request, water was in critically short supply.

"I know," Elisha sighed.

Jasmine pulled Elisha towards her and placed his head in her lap. Oh, how she admired this young man. He had grown up so much since the day they met in the back of the military van after being arrested. Elisha was an instrument of God, and she understood this very well. She, too, was an instrument. She was his companion and, in many ways, his strength. Jasmine leaned back against the hard, rocky wall of their little private cell. "God will make a way when the time is right." Jasmine stroked Elisha's dark hair until they both fell asleep.

Sometime late in the evening they were both disturbed from their sleep by a softly spoken word. Elisha opened his eyes to see two very old men standing before him. The taller of the two men smiled at Elisha. Jasmine opened her eyes and let out a little sound of surprise.

"Hush, Child," said Elijah.

"Rise up, Elisha!" said Moses as he reached out a hand to help the young man to his feet.

Elisha stood on shaky legs, staring at the two men. "Who are you?"

The smaller of the two men smiled at Elisha and Jasmine and said, "I am Elijah and this is Moses."

"Moses!" Jasmine whispered.

Elijah smiled at Jasmine once again. "Stand before us, Child," he said.

Jasmine stood next to Elisha and reached out for his hand. She was frightened, but even more than that, she was impressed. These two men were so important to the Jewish faith, and although she had grown up a Muslim, she still had many of the same views on prophets as did the average Jew.

"Elisha, God has commanded that you go to Jerusalem and escort out of the city all of the Jews and Muslims that want to follow after Christ. Take them to Mount Carmel. There you will find caves for shelter and God will provide for your needs," said Elijah.

"Beware!" said Moses, "The Antichrist and false prophet will be looking for you. They want to destroy the nation of Israel and God's people. You are His chosen leader now, and Satan will be looking to kill you. Be strong and obedient and God will be with you."

"How can we travel in this heat?" Jasmine asked bravely.

Elijah's bright eyes looked deeply into the young girl's face. "You are a faithful companion for Elisha, and the Lord is pleased. In God's eyes, you are now Elisha's wife. May God bless your marriage."

Jasmine smiled happily.

"God is going to hide the sun and the stars for weeks. It will be darker than it was in the beginning of time. The temperature will start to drop even before the total eclipse of the sun. By this time next week you will be able to go to Jerusalem through the desert of Beersheba without dying from the heat, and during that time there will still be enough light to navigate by, but time is short," said Moses. "You must not delay."

"The Antichrist is amassing an army to overthrow every oil producing nation, and God is about to give the Archangel, Michael, the keys to release four evil Angels of Death bound beyond the Euphrates River.

You must be swift because destruction is coming to mankind like never before," Moses sighed.

Jasmine was greatly alarmed by Moses' description of future events. "Be courageous, Child," said Elijah. "The victory is ours. Nothing can ever change that."

Elijah placed Elisha's hand into Jasmine's. "Let your love for Jesus and each other unite your every effort, and know God is with you always."

Instantly both men disappeared before the young couple's eyes. "Whoa!" said Jasmine.

"Yeah, I'd say. Well, I guess we are going to Jerusalem after all," Elisha said excitedly.

"Yes, but not for a week." Jasmine wrapped her arms around Elisha, kissed him passionately, and then whispered, "We're married!"

******

The little yellow plane skimmed over the Kivalina River for the second time. The trees around this river were sparse and sickly looking. The only real issue was finding a place with enough water to land the plane. Calvin studied the terrain closely. "I think that spot right there will work."

"I hope you're right," said Cory.

"Me too!" echoed Jerry as he held Leasa's hand for comfort—more his than hers.

The little plane jumped and skipped across the shallow water and skidded to a hard stop by the rocky shore of the river. "We're here!" Calvin laughed.

"And where is here again?" Leasa asked.

"Point Hope," said Calvin as he stepped out of the plane.

This was the fourth such stop throughout Alaska in the last year and certainly the most remote of the places they had gone to other than maybe Destruction Bay in the Yukon. This, of course, was the first place they landed after leaving Shasta Lake.

Originally it was Calvin's plan to hike out of Destruction Bay and on to the Alaskan Highway where he hoped his small group could catch a ride with some passerby heading for Anchorage.

It was lucky for Calvin and his crew that God had other plans, for as soon as they landed their plane on the ice covered Kluane Lake, they were met by a very old Aleut Indian named Klak. He was running his dogs and sled along the edge of the lake when he stopped to watch the plane land. It had been ages since anyone flew across this lake, so the man was sure that this was an important visit. Being curious and brave the old man drove his dog sled right out to where the plane had stopped. Cory was the first one to spot the man and dogsled heading towards the plane with the help of a luminescent sky to navigate by.

"What have we got here?" said Cory.

"What is it?" Jerry asked.

"It looks like an Eskimo to me," replied Cory.

"No!" said Calvin. "We are still too far south for that." But he had to admit the man approaching looked like he was on a whale hunt.

"Are you sure we didn't fly all the way into Alaska?" Leasa suggested.

Calvin laughed. "I'm pretty sure."

The man steered his dogs up to the side of the plane while Calvin and the rest sat by in wonder. As the man approached the plane's door on Calvin's side, he pulled back the hood of his parka and smiled wide, revealing the two teeth that still remained in his mouth. Cory let out a hearty laugh. "One thing's for sure—he's not planning on eating us."

Cory and Calvin opened their doors and climbed out to greet the man. As Cory walked around the plane, the dogs began to growl and snarl at him. "Down!" the man shouted and instantly all six dogs seated themselves quietly.

"Hello," said Calvin with a smile.

"I am Klak. You have come a long way, right?"

"That's right, we have. My name is Calvin, this is Cory, and those two over there are Leasa and Jerry," Calvin pointed towards the couple as they climbed out of the aircraft.

"Why are you here?" Klak inquired.

"We ran out of gas," said Calvin.

"Where were you going?" Klak smiled.

Cory had to turn his head so Klak would not see him laughing at his toothless grin.

"We are on our way to Alaska," said Calvin.

"Alaska is a big place. Where were you planning to go?"

Calvin hadn't really considered this question until now. All he knew was that he needed to go to Alaska. He looked at the man closely. He could tell he was a native Alaskan from some tribe—Aleut or Inuit. He wasn't sure. He also knew the man was well past 60 years of age. What he could not tell was whether or not the man had an ID tag and whether he was a follower of Carlo. "We were planning on going to Anchorage," said Calvin unconvincingly.

"Are you hungry?" Klak asked.

Every eye turned to Calvin. It was obvious that his troops were starving. The question was whether or not he could afford to take the risk. After all, he didn't know this man, but he had to do something. They couldn't just stand there on that frozen lake all night. "How far away is your home?"

Klak smiled and pointed at the base of the tree line. "Just past that stand of trees over there."

"What about our plane? We can't just leave it out here in the middle of this lake," Calvin suggested.

Five minutes later Calvin and his team marched alongside Klak and his dogs as they pulled Calvin's small, wooden plane across the ice.

"Why do you want to go to Alaska?" Klak asked.

Calvin couldn't stand not knowing Klak's position on God. He wanted to know if this man had taken the mark of the beast. He could not confide in him until he knew for sure that the man was safe. "How do you buy food out here?"

Klak stared at Calvin. He understood that his question was being avoided. He, too, was not sure what to think about this situation. "I trade for food—like always."

Calvin mulled this over. There still weren't any facts on the table that would help him to understand this man. Then unexpectedly Leasa called out from where she sat in Klak's dog sled as Cory pushed her along. "Are you a Christian?"

Immediately the Alaskan native stopped the dogs, turned towards Leasa, and then looked at the others briefly. "When I was a boy missionaries came to Yukutat where I lived. They told my parents about a man named Jesus. I did not understand who this man was. We Indians had our own gods to worship. Later that year there was a terrible outbreak of smallpox. Many in my village began to die, especially the young children. My sister died," said Klak softly, "and I, too, got the smallpox. My parents called in the local missionaries and had them pray for me. They were hoping that the missionaries' God was more powerful than ours, and they not only accepted prayer, but also the much-needed medical help. Two weeks later the smallpox was gone. Seventy-five people had died, but I was still alive. After this my family went to the white man's church, but when I grew up and went out on my own, I walked away from Jesus and lived my own life. I drank and got into much trouble, but one day I was sitting in my cabin when my wife, who was a Christian woman, disappeared before my eyes. I knew at that point that Jesus had come and taken her to Heaven. I decided then that I was going to live my life for God the way my wife had. So now I live alone, and I trade for food and supplies, but I have not taken the ID tag because I think it is the mark of the Devil."

Calvin looked at Klak, smiled, and said, "We are going to Alaska to witness to the unsaved about Christ before it is too late."

"I thought so," Klak nodded.

******

Leasa sat beside the fireplace warming her tired body. Cory moved in next to her and placed his big arm around her waist. "How are you feeling?" he whispered.

"I'm getting better every day," she beamed brightly.

Cory gave Leasa a light squeeze. She rested her head on his massive chest and the two of them stared into the fire silently. There would be very little time for rest, and they both knew it.

Jerry admired all the Indian artifacts decorating the walls of Klak's cabin. Many animal skins lined the walls along with pieces of hand carved ivory. In the middle of the room was a large barrel full of animal furs, and the smell coming from it was putrid. Sitting next to the barrel was a flat piece of wood and some oddly shaped knives. "What is all this for?" Jerry inquired.

Klak walked over and picked up a small fox hide. "This is how I survive. I trade furs for food and gas for my generator. In the last year nearly all the animals in the woods have disappeared. These are hides from last year. I am soaking them so I can tan them and trade for some more food. This will be my last trade, I guess."

"How will you survive?" Leasa asked.

"I can fish, but even this is getting harder. I guess God will have to provide."

******

Back on the banks of the Kivalina River nearly a year had passed since the day Calvin and his team had met Klak, and it had been a year since Klak had died from a heart attack. He died in his sleep peacefully, and it would be months before anyone discovered his body. Thankfully, the day before Klak died he provided Calvin with enough gas to fill his plane and, although this was not aviation fuel, Calvin knew it would work for low altitude flight.

Today the weather was much different than the day Calvin landed in Anchorage on their first Alaskan stop. On that day it was minus 60 degrees. Calvin and his team had found it nearly impossible to witness, and in fact, there were so few people on the streets that Calvin made the decision to leave Anchorage and fly to Seward. *At least it should be warmer down south,* he had reasoned.

Calvin's team had a lot of success in Seward. They met various people that housed and fed them. Over time they helped to start a new church, but eventually Calvin received an impression from God that it was time to move on. With the help of some of the new converts Calvin acquired more fuel for his plane and flew on to his next location.

The third stop was Kodiak Island. There was a harvest to be had there, as well, so Calvin's team set up camp for many months. It was surprisingly easy to find people who had not taken the mark, and it seemed that few in the community had a bias against Christians. "Perhaps they don't watch TV or read the newspaper and maybe they haven't heard all of Simon Koch's lies," said Jerry during a conversation he had with Cory on this very subject.

In any case, resistance was low and success was high. From Kodiak Calvin flew his team to Bethel and again things went well for them. By this time the weather had improved greatly and temperatures approached the mid 80's. This was an increase of 140 degrees over the temperature they had experienced in Anchorage months earlier.

After a couple of months in Bethel Calvin decided it was time to go back to Anchorage. He knew the big city would not be the pleasant experience they had seen so far. The community would most certainly reject their testimony, and there was a chance of violence or even arrest.

One evening as Calvin and his team lay sleeping on the floor of a friendly neighbor's house a rushing wind invaded the home. Next a soft, bright light filled the room. Leasa was the first one to wake. "Somebody is here," she said softly as her voice trembled.

Cory lifted up his head in time to see Barthemaus standing before them. "Peace be with you." At this all four people sat forward.

"You have done well. God is pleased!"

"However, you cannot go to Anchorage. It is too late. The Antichrist has taken over that community and everything that has anything to do with oil. He has brought in slave labor to work on the north slopes of Prudhoe Bay, and he has established a headquarters in Anchorage for Simon Koch and his Special Security force."

"Where should we go?" Calvin asked softly.

Barthemaus smiled at Calvin. "You have done well, Calvin Fraser. It is time to go to Point Hope. There are many who need to hear the truth."

"And after that?" asked Cory.

"For some of you there is another assignment, but this is not the time."

Suddenly the room grew dim and quiet. Everyone kept Barthemaus' last statement in their mind. They did not fully understand the meaning, but they knew that somehow their team was going to be broken up. They had grown so close over the last year or so. Nobody liked the idea that somehow this was going to come to an end.

******

Calvin climbed up the ravine and looked back at his plane sitting on a bed of rocks. *Soon,* he thought, *it is going to be hard to find any water to land on.* Jerry climbed up next to Calvin as Cory helped Leasa up the hill. Down in the valley there were a number of small houses and a few larger buildings scattered about. "Point Hope, I presume," said Jerry with a smile.

"I hope so!" Calvin laughed. He, too, was nervous. Somehow his team was about to change, but how and when he did not know.

******

Tommy sat close to the air conditioner because the heat was intolerable. It seemed simply amazing to him that just seven or eight months ago he and Sara were nearly frozen to death as they traveled from town to town throughout Switzerland. Now, however, he would have gladly traded this 130-degree weather for the 20 below zero stuff they had lived through.

Sara waddled into the room carrying a glass of ice water. "Just imagine," she said, "if we lived out in the desert where there was no water. We wouldn't last an hour."

Tommy smiled at his pregnant wife and slid over to make room for her and her enormous stomach to sit down. "How long did Mueller say he was going to be gone?" Sara asked in between sips of water.

"About an hour—he should be back anytime," said Tommy. Mueller had really been a godsend for Tommy and Sara. He had not only come to their rescue in Zurich after Tommy had been shot, but he had taken them to Germany and found a friend of his—a medical doctor—to patch Tommy up. Now they were living in Mueller's sister's house in Linz, Germany. This was conveniently located near Mauthausen where Tommy and Sara had been witnessing for months. Mueller's sister had disappeared four and a half years earlier like so many others. He had visited this place from time to time. He even considered renting it out to someone, but for some reason he never did. That had turned out to be a very good thing for all three of them.

The first month or so Tommy and Sara rarely left the house. Neither of them really had any idea why God wanted them in Germany. In addition, Tommy was still weak after being shot and nearly killed. Eventually, however, they began to comb the neighborhood until they discovered the truth about Mauthausen and heard the stories of the atrocities that were going on there.

"Apparently," said a shopkeeper to Sara early one morning, "they are starving and beating these people to get them to take the ID tags. I've even heard that they have burned some of these people to death. Others are being sent out to different parts of the world as slave labor."

When Tommy heard about all of this from Sara, he knew it was a clear message from God. He needed to find a way to minister to those who were being held under tight security. Tommy talked this over with Mueller. "There has to be a way of getting into that place without getting caught," said Tommy.

Mueller thought about it for a while and then responded. "If only we could convert some of the guards, then we would have a chance, but how?"

All three of them set up a stakeout beside Mauthausen. For weeks they watched the guards come in and go out of the camp on a daily basis. They had the routine down and now it was time to form a workable plan. Mueller was the first to come up with an idea. "I will follow one of these guards home and see if I can make contact with him."

Sara looked at the elderly man suspiciously. "Are you crazy? What happens if he figures out that you are a Christian?"

"How's he going to do that? I look the same as anyone else. Besides,

I speak German and neither of you do," Mueller smiled. If the truth were
known, he, too, was scared, but if he could just test the water a little to
see if these guards were all evil, maybe—just maybe—he'd find a good
one in the bunch.

The next day Mueller and Tommy followed one of the guards as he
left the compound. This particular guard was Sara's choice. She had noted
the sad look on the man's face every time he walked out of Mauthausen.
"He's your best bet," she said one morning. Today, however, Sara had
been left behind in their small house. Tommy was not willing to risk his
pregnant wife. There were just too many unknowns. This guard could be
as evil as ever, and if that turned out to be the case, then Tommy wanted
to be sure Sara was safe.

He and Mueller went over the plan one more time. "Okay, I will get
out and follow him up to his house while you circle the block. If he turns
out to be working for Simon after all, then I will run and you need to pick
me up," said Mueller with nervous excitement.

"What if he has a gun or something?" Tommy asked. This whole idea
was harebrained at best. But how else were they supposed to be able to
get into the prison without actually getting arrested. Besides, Tommy
knew that in his case if he were to be arrested, he would never be sent to
that camp. He would be sent directly to Simon and killed for sure.

"I will just have to play it by ear," said Mueller. Tommy had really
grown to love this old man. He was like a father to Tommy, and since he
never had a father, this was an experience he treasured.

Tommy pulled in alongside a small delivery truck and watched as the
guard walked up a small flight of stairs into an old apartment building.
"Here we go!" said Mueller as he opened the car door to get out.

Tommy reached over and grabbed his hand. "Be careful!"

The old man smiled and climbed out quickly. He followed the same
path the guard took and soon found himself standing in a corridor where
there were two different apartments side by side. Now he had to choose
which door to knock on. "God, it is in your hands," Mueller whispered as
he turned to the left and knocked on apartment door 106. A few seconds
later a tall, thin man around 23 years of age came to the door. The man

was wearing a tee shirt instead of a uniform, but Mueller could tell by his uniform trousers that this was, in fact, the guard he had followed.

"Can I help you?" said the young man in German.

"Do you have something to eat?" Mueller asked. He was not sure why he said that, but in fact, he had not planned what he was going to say in the first place.

The young guard looked at Mueller suspiciously at first, but suddenly compassion filled his eyes. "What is your name?"

"They call me Mueller."

"Come in, Mueller," said the young man kindly.

So far so good, thought Mueller to himself.

When Mueller got inside the door he was surprised to see an old woman sitting on a couch clutching a two-year-old child. "This is my mother, Gretchen, and this," said the young man as he lifted up the little child, "is Lisa, my sister's daughter." Mueller looked around the room expecting to see a young mother somewhere. "My sister died last year."

Mueller nodded. So many people had died over the last four and a half years. Who could keep count any more?

"What is your name?" Mueller asked softly.

"Jon."

"We don't have much food either, but have a seat and I'll see what I can make for you," said the young man.

Mueller sat next to Gretchen and tickled little Lisa's chin. The poor child was so thin. How unfortunate to be born into such a horrid and dying world.

Outside sitting in the car Tommy began to squirm. All this was taking too much time. *What if he has been captured and he needs me?* Tommy worried.

Back in the apartment Mueller sat back slurping on a small bowl of cabbage soup. On a small plate beside him was a scrap of bread. These people were very kind to share what little they had with a complete stranger. He hoped they had not taken the mark of the beast and sealed their fate.

"What do you do for a living?" Mueller asked casually.

Jon looked at him carefully. He could tell that there was something different about Mueller. He was obviously an intelligent, well-educated man—not a man to need a handout from anyone. "I work in security."

"Really! Where?" smiled Mueller.

Jon was starting to feel uncomfortable around the old man. "Where did you say you were from?" Jon asked suspiciously.

"I didn't say," said Mueller. "Switzerland."

"You are a long way from home," said Gretchen in a screechy voice. She, too, was getting suspicious.

Out of the blue there was a knock at the door and both Jon and Mueller jumped in surprise. At once they made eye contact with each other. This confirmed for both of them that each was as nervous as a cat. Jon went to the door and opened it slowly. Standing just on the other side was Tommy. He had selected the right apartment as well.

Mueller nodded his head. "May as well let him in too."

Jon turned to Mueller and said, "What is going on here?"

Gretchen grabbed Lisa and held her tight as the scene unfolded.

"Jon, this man is an American. His name is Tommy, and he and I have been watching you come and go from Mauthausen for the last couple of weeks."

Jon turned toward Mueller and then to Tommy. "I don't understand. Who do you work for? What do you want?"

"We work for Jesus," said Mueller in his Swiss German dialect.

Jon looked deep into the elderly man's face. "Jesus!"

"Jon, have you taken the ID tag?" Mueller asked plainly. Tommy didn't understand a word, but he knew he was in the middle of a very dramatic scene.

"No!"

Mueller beamed brightly. "Me either!"

From that day on Tommy and Sara worked with Jon to establish a network within the camp. Eventually they converted six guards who helped to sneak the couple in and out of the camp unnoticed. The timing was terrific because shortly after they met the torture of the demons started to plague men. It was an awesome time to show the power of God. Many people made a commitment to or strengthened their existing relationships with God. Those that were saved by confessing Jesus as their personal savior did not suffer from the torturing demons. This was proof enough for thousands within the camp.

Eventually things in Mauthausen began to get too complicated and a division grew between those Jews who would not confess Jesus as their savior and those who would. Before long there was great concern that someone would tell the bad guards what was going on. Something had to be done and soon! This was when Mueller and Tommy planned a great escape for many of the prisoners. They decided to do it in small increments so that no one would be wise to it.

Whenever it was time to take a daily count of the prisoners, Jon made sure that he or one of the other Christian guards did the counting. This way weeks could go by before it became obvious that many were missing. Eventually Jon began to hear whispers from some of the evil guards that the prisoners were talking about people escaping. It was at this point that Mueller decided to plan one large, final breakout.

Soon an effort between all six guards and Tommy and Mueller was in place. One evening over 150 Christians and all six guards disappeared. This nearly doubled the number that had already escaped over the last few weeks. Mueller had made arrangements with some of his friendly connections in Zurich. All of the people were ferried out by car and relocated within Switzerland.

Since that day a few weeks ago Tommy and Sara had not left their apartment. Only Mueller, who had not entered the camp, could go out in public without risk of being noticed. There were large wanted posters for Tommy and Sara as well as a long list of names of those who escaped, including those of the guards who helped out. Jon's name was on the list, but Oswald would never find him. Mueller had sent Jon, Gretchen, and Lisa to his home in the most rural part of Switzerland. Jon and his family would be safe there until Christ's return.

This afternoon as Sara and Tommy sat waiting for Mueller to return, there was a sense that their time in Linz was coming to an end. Tommy felt good about what they had accomplished, but it was only a drop in a bucket. There were literally tens of thousands of people imprisoned in Mauthausen and the other concentration camps.

Tommy helped to increase the courage of the prisoners so they would not break down and accept the ID tags. Still he was only able to help 300 people escape. Then again how many had he and Sara led to the Lord through their witness while in the camp? Tommy knew he had to stop thinking in terms of freedom and safety for today and start thinking in terms of freedom and safety for eternity in Heaven.

Tommy looked over towards his wife who was fidgeting in her seat. "What's the matter?" he asked.

"Just a little indigestion, I guess. When is Mueller coming home? Where did he go anyway?" Sara sighed.

"He didn't say where he was going, only that he needed an hour or two," said Tommy.

"How long ago was that?" Sara asked with a souring look on her face.

"Are you okay?" Tommy was getting worried.

About that time he heard Mueller's old Mercedes pull into the driveway. "There he is now," Tommy said as he stood to greet Mueller when he came in.

A few second later Mueller came through the front door breathing heavily. The side of his face was bleeding from a deep cut. "Pack your things. We need to leave now!" said Mueller.

"What is it? What happened to you?" asked Sara.

"They are coming for us," said Mueller.

"Who?" Tommy asked in a panic. "What happened?"

"A couple of old friends of mine live here in Linz. I have avoided them until now because I know they are not Christians. They are true Darwinists, but I decided this morning to go see them. We need food and gas for the car. I also thought one of them might be able to give me some information on this new Special Police force. I figured we needed to know something about our enemies before we drive out of here to our next location. My first visit seemed fine," said Mueller as Sara wiped the blood away from his face with a clean towel.

"You need stitches," said Sara as she held the towel to his brow.

"Yes, I know. Anyway, what I was saying is that the first visit went well. I got some gas and a trunk full of food, but when I went to my other friend's house, he was waiting for me. Apparently after my first stop my old college buddy had called my other friend and told him to expect me. I was led into the house and into the living room where I was offered a drink. Shortly after that another man whom I have never seen before entered the room and asked me why I wasn't purchasing my own food and gas. He also asked me what I was doing in Germany."

Tommy looked into Mueller's worried face. "What did you tell him?"

"I told him I was out of work and money, therefore I could not scan my ID tag for food or gas. He asked me what I knew about the recent escapes in Mauthausen. I told him I didn't know anything. Then he inquired about you and Sara. Again I played dumb, but he said there was proof that you had been in Switzerland many months ago and apparently had left the country about the same time I did. After this I said I didn't know anything and that I needed to leave. As I headed for the door, the man grabbed my arm. I fought my way loose, but then my old friend tried to grab me. I knocked him to the ground and he hit his head hard on a table. I think it broke his neck. The other man attacked me again and we wrestled. I got away, but they will track us to my sister's house very soon."

"What are we going to do now?" Sara cried as she sat back down on the couch holding her stomach.

"Are you okay?" Tommy could feel things getting out of control in a hurry.

"I don't know," said Sara, "but I'm going to have to be, because we need to leave now!"

Mueller walked past Tommy and into the kitchen. Quickly he returned with a set of car keys. "These belong to my sister's car. It is parked in the shop on the side of the house. I charged the battery just the other day, and it is full of gas. Let's load the food into the trunk and we can use that car to get away."

Tommy nodded in agreement.

Five minutes later they were all packed and ready to go. Sara was in obvious pain and discomfort, and Tommy was frightened. His world was coming unglued quickly. Suddenly they heard the sound of a car approaching. Mueller looked to Tommy and threw him the keys to his sister's car. "Go out the back. I'll drive off and distract them."

Tommy looked into Mueller's bright, old eyes. He loved this man dearly. "We can all go through the back. They won't catch us!" Tommy pleaded.

"Son," said Mueller softly, "do as you are told. We have no time—they will catch us all. You have greater work to do." Mueller smiled at Sara and Tommy.

Tommy stepped up and hugged the man tightly as Sara kissed his cheek. "I love you both. Now go! I'll meet up with you in Munich somewhere around Dachau, I am sure."

Sara and Tommy ran out the back and down the alleyway to the car while Mueller raced out of the driveway in his Mercedes. Soon two white cars sped past the house in full pursuit of the black Mercedes. Mueller gave them a run for their money. For the next 20 minutes he headed them north to the Czech Republic towards Prague and in the opposite direction of Tommy and Sara. Eventually Mueller's luck ran out. A barricade of police cars and special force vehicles surrounded him. Mueller was dragged from his car and beaten severely, but this could not dampen the joy he felt over helping Sara and Tommy escape once more.

Six hours later deep into the night Tommy pulled the car off the road into a wooded area just outside of Munich and parked. Sara had been moaning for the last couple of hours. The pain was intense and Tommy knew she was about to delivery the baby. Fear filled his body as he turned towards Sara who was now crying aloud.

"I feel like I am dying!" Sara cried.

"No! No, you are not going to die. God will help us!"

Sara suddenly let out a scream of pain. "God, help me, please!" she moaned.

Tommy laid Sara down in the front seat and held her head in his lap as she moaned and screamed out in pain. "Please, Lord, help us!" Tommy begged.

Abruptly there was a disturbing knock at the driver's side window.

This startled the young man who turned to see Martha and Harry standing there smiling. "Thank you, Jesus!" Tommy whispered as he opened the door to the stifling and unbearable heat.

"Hello, Son," said Martha in her usual crackly voice.

"It looks like you are about to become a father," said Harry as he patted Tommy on the back. "You come with me and leave this to Martha. She has delivered more babies than any stork I know."

Tommy looked at Sara who was rocking and crying. "It's okay, I'll take care of her," said Martha as she pulled Tommy from the car with the strength of a weight lifter.

"Come and sit over here with me, Boy," said Harry as Tommy stood beside the car.

Tommy walked towards Harry until he heard Sara scream out his name in pain. Again he turned to run back to the car when Harry spoke up more sternly, "Tommy! Come over here and sit down beside me now! Everything is going to be all right."

Tommy sat next to Harry and moaned every time he heard his sweet Sara scream out. "Birth is a time when God takes a woman to death's doorstep, Son. This is a result of sin in the Garden of Eden. In fact, it was because of that sin between Adam and Eve that the world is where it is today, and until Christ comes back to reclaim the world it will remain at death's doorstep. Do you understand me, Tommy?"

The young man nodded, although he wasn't sure what he understood anymore. He was horribly hot and terribly worried for Sara and the baby.

"You two did a brave thing back in that concentration camp, but there is more for you to do. You will have to be willing to lay down your life and the life of your family in order to save those who are lost. Can you do that, Tommy?" Harry asked as he placed his large, ancient looking hand on Tommy's back.

"I don't know," said Tommy.

"You are tired and scared right now, but you have already shown your bravery," Harry smiled encouragingly.

Tommy thought about Mueller. Was he dead or alive? *"No! I have not been brave, but I have seen bravery," said Tommy.*

The old man smiled as Sara screamed out again. "You are referring to Mueller," said Harry.

Tommy looked up in surprise. "You know Mueller?"

"We know of him. We have seen his work since he met you and Sara. Be joyful, Son. You led him to a right relationship with Jesus."

Tommy smiled for a brief second and then turned serious. "Is he still alive?"

"Yes, Child, for now at least," said Harry softly.

Suddenly Tommy heard a cry, but it wasn't Sara's usual cry. This was much smaller than that. The door to the car opened and Martha stepped out holding a little bundle. "Come closer, Papa."

Tommy ran towards Martha. As he approached he noticed that his newborn child was wrapped in a shimmering little cloth. The stars and the moonlight reflecting off this heavenly cloth gave off a glorious shimmer. It was as if something supernatural were happening. In fact, the mere presence of Martha and Harry was supernatural in itself. God had taken the time to have these two come here to delivery his baby.

Tommy moved in close to Martha and pulled back the cloth from the baby's face. "What is it?" Tommy asked.

"A baby!" Martha grinned.

Harry laughed out loud. "Good one, Martha."

Tommy was still pretty stressed out, but these two old people were undoubtedly the funniest and strangest people he had ever known. He could not help but laugh out loud as well.

"It's a little boy!" said Martha.

"How is Sara?" Tommy asked.

"She is resting for a while. I need some water and fresh towels."

"I think we have some jugs of water in the trunk, and I have a couple of clean tee shirts you can use as towels," said Tommy happily.

"All right, Son, as long as you don't want those shirts back," she said with a smile.

******

Carlo stood in the center of an incredible garden below an elaborate palace. For as far as the eye could see there were huge, flowering vines hanging over large masonry fixtures. The grass in the inner courtyard was a deep jade green color. Next to the palace was a fountain chiseled from solid marble. In the center was a large gargoyle figure holding a kid goat. Along both sides of the palace, snaking through the entire garden, was a complex aqueduct system that fed water to all the plants and trees. The outer court stretched for a mile in every direction. Again there were flowers and hanging plants as well as numerous fountains. Babylon was complete, all except for the formal ceremony planned for next week. The culmination of this ceremony would be the wedding of Victoria Price and Simon Koch.

Carlo turned and headed back towards the palace. He was pleased with the work that his numerous slaves had accomplished. He was also grateful that somehow in the middle of this expansive heat wave his gardens were flourishing. It probably had something to do with the fact that he had detoured nearly all the usable drinking water from the Tigris to his new city. Tomorrow Carlo would tour the other portions of Babylon including a new ziggurat built for the people of Babylon to worship him. The only problem he had was that there were no citizens in Babylon since the city had lain in ruins for centuries. Carlo had a plan, however— he would import his own citizens. There would be a governmental system very similar to that of the early roman civilization, and he would rule the world from this one central location.

Back in the palace Carlo wandered through the massive halls into a cathedral room at the center of the palace. Again he marveled at the architecture. Along each wall were extravagant paintings and handcrafted gold ornaments. Persian rugs covered the jade floor, and the masterpiece of the entire palace was a hand painted ceiling nearly the size of a football field. This painting depicted Carlo in the center of a heaven-like setting where masses of people of all nations and tribes bearing gifts knelt before him in somber worship. There were hand painted figures of creatures never seen before by men along with numerous gargoyles and evil looking demons.

Carlo walked the long, circular staircase up to a master suite that was the size of three presidential suites like those often used by important men of wealth and power. Carlo entered the master bedroom and looked at the spectacular bed in the middle of the room. It was twice the size of a king bed with a huge mahogany headboard with hand crafted designs throughout. Carlo took a long look at the bed and then smiled an eerie grin.

Throughout the palace and courtyard were many well-dressed slaves trained to provide for his every need; however, he preferred to be alone most of the time, so he kept his servants at a comfortable distance. Now, though, he did have a need, and he was forming a plan to get what he wanted.

******

Simon picked up the phone from his office in Rome. "Hello?"

"Simon, I want you to go to China and see Whi Yin," said Carlo.

"What? Why?" Simon asked suspiciously.

"I have been working with Whi Yin to develop his army and to prepare for an invasion into the Middle East, but now I want him to hold off for a while."

Simon was fuming mad. How dare Carlo make arrangements behind his back? To go to China now when he was supposed to be in Babylon in just a few days for his wedding to Victoria was absurd.

"I am getting married in just a few days," said Simon.

"Yes, Simon, that is why I am here—to plan your wedding for you so that it will be remarkable," said Carlo soothingly.

Simon knew that this statement was a lie. Carlo was in Babylon because he was obsessed with his little city. "I'll go to China after my wedding."

"You'll go now!" Carlo roared.

Simon swallowed hard. *How is it that I ever liked this man?* he wondered.

"I will make arrangements to fly Victoria out here today so she can get ready while you go and see Whi Yin."

Simon's mouth fell open. So this is what he wants, he thought. *He wants to have Victoria again before we get married.* "I can take Victoria to China with me. We will meet you in Babylon when I get things taken care of with Whi Yin."

"No, Simon. Your inability to prevent these Christians from witnessing to those who have not taken the ID tags has cost me many souls. You must be taught a lesson. I will bring Victoria out here to me and, shall we say, get her ready for your wedding."

Tears filled Simon's eyes as rage shook his lumpy, little body. "What do you want me to do in China?"

"Darkness is coming according to Dr. Hyder and in just a few days. I think we had better postpone this war for a while," said Carlo.

"How long?" snapped Simon.

Carlo was smiling on the phone. He understood Simon's jealousy and he found it amazing that this man actually loved Victoria. Obviously she was a whore, but Simon just didn't seem to understand that. "I have not decided. Tell him at least three or four months from now. We will have to think this over."

There would be nothing to think over if I had been given control of these nations, thought Simon. As it was Simon hated the fact that there were functioning governments that existed in the world. There should be only one government, and Simon believed he was the chosen leader. "I'll leave this afternoon," said Simon somberly.

"Cheer up, Simon. After all, you will be a married man in just a few days."

Carlo hung up the phone laughing.

Simon dialed Victoria's number. Actually she was staying in his apartment so one of his servants answered the phone. "Get Victoria now!" commanded Simon.

Victoria spoke softly into the phone—all for Simon's benefit, of course. "Hello, Sweetheart."

"You have to go to Babylon," said Simon holding back his desire to cry.

"Of course, Sweetheart—we both do in just a couple of days!" she said.

"No! I mean you have to go today. Now!" said Simon flatly.

"Why? I don't understand," said Victoria with worry in her tone.

"Carlo wants you."

Victoria's heart leapt for joy. "Wants me for what?" she said cautiously as if she were worried instead of elated.

"He is mad at me for not getting rid of all the crazy Christians by now, so he is punishing me by sending you to him again!" Simon lamented.

Victoria's joy could nearly be heard over the phone. "Honey, it will be okay," she said, "after we are married, he will never do this again, I am sure."

Simon wasn't sure at all. He was beginning to think he could do a much better job of running the world than Carlo could and he wouldn't have to endure Carlo sleeping with his woman.

"Besides," said Victoria, "he is not half the man you are, and whenever he tries anything he gets no participation from me."

"Really?" asked Simon hopefully. "Half the man I am?"

"Less than half the man, Sweetheart—honestly! It will be okay. Soon we will be husband and wife forever."

After Victoria hung up the phone she nearly danced across the floor. "Pack my things!" she yelled out to one of the servant girls Simon had hired just for her. "I am going to Babylon!"

******

Simon entered Tiananmen Square with his usual escort of soldiers. He expected to meet Whi Yin there and drive to his summer palace located on Lake Kunming which was now merely a dry lakebed. To Simon's dismay Whi Yin was nowhere to be found. Instead he had sent his escorts and one government official to meet him and to bring him to the palace. Simon fumed as he drove through the streets of Beijing. "Who does this guy think he is, Mao Zedong?" Simon vowed that as soon as this war of Carlo's was over he was going to have Whi Yin killed.

Simon entered into Whi Yin's palace, and it was extraordinary. In fact, it made his headquarters at Vatican City look like a dump. The usual oriental gardens surrounded the palace which offset the beautiful architecture of the Chinese people. *Maybe after I kill this guy I'll make this place my winter headquarters,* Simon thought with a grin.

"Mr. Koch," said Whi Yin as he entered into the reception room of the palace, "so good to see you again."

Simon was in no mood for pleasantries. By now Victoria would be in the arms of Carlo Ventini in his precious palace while he was stuck there dealing with this little pest of a man. "The war is off," said Simon flatly.

"What do you mean?" said Yin with a surprised look on his face.

"I mean we have decided to wait for a while," said Simon forcefully.

"Well, I will have to confirm this with His Holiness, of course," said Yin.

"You'll do what I tell you when I tell you!" Simon ordered.

Whi Yin took a step back. He knew he was pushing Simon to the edge, but he figured he had the largest army in the world and nuclear weapons of his own, and now that he had taken control over Taiwan, he had the technical capabilities for total world domination. All he needed to do was to secure the Middle East for Carlo and maybe wipe out Israel as a favor to His Holiness, and he would certainly become Simon's equal if not his superior.

"When does the Divine Carlo want me to capture these oil fields?" Yin asked more softly.

"When I tell you to!" Simon leered at Yin closely. He really disliked the man intensely. "Maybe four or five months."

"That will be great. This will give me more time to train our Peoples Liberation Army in some of the newer technologies we have acquired," said Yin with a smile.

"What technology?" Simon asked suspiciously.

Whi Yin spent the better part of the day showing Simon his military capabilities. It was obvious to him that Yin was showing off for his benefit. Simon allowed this. He figured if this man was stupid enough to show him every capability he had, then Simon would be glad to listen and learn. *Besides,* thought Simon, *you never know when you may need this information.* In addition this activity occupied Simon's mind so he didn't have to think about what Victoria and Carlo were doing at that very moment.

******

Back in Babylon Carlo walked Victoria through his prize garden. The view was spectacular as the sun drifted over the desert and out of sight. "So are you ready for your wedding?" Carlo asked flatly.

"Yes, I think so, Your Holiness," said Victoria softly.

She didn't really want to talk about Simon. It spoiled her mood. "How is it that all these plants are alive with this terrible heat?" Victoria asked as she wiped the sweat from her brow. She had only been outside for a few minutes, but the pain from the heat was nearly unbearable.

"I am the god of life, and I bring life to this garden," said Carlo boldly. "Let's go in before you burn up."

Once they entered the palace Carlo ordered a chambermaid to take Victoria upstairs and give her a soothing, cool bath. "I have ordered our dinner for 8:00 tonight, and after that we can have dessert and drinks upstairs in the master bedroom."

Victoria could not hide her delight and beamed brightly as she followed the servant upstairs.

******

Two days later Simon showed up at the palace in Babylon. It was a torturous two days for him—maybe even worse than when he was tormented by Apollyon's demonic forces. Once Simon entered into Carlo's palace, jealousy consumed his body. He had a strong desire to kill something. Simon stood in the center of the palace just below the marvelous painting of Carlo being worshiped. If he could have spat on the painting, he would have.

As he looked ahead he saw Victoria coming down the circular staircase with Carlo walking beside her. Simon had to choke back the tears he felt welling up. He wanted to scream, but instead he merely stood there shaking from anger and jealousy.

Victoria smiled, walked up to Simon, and wrapped her arms around his plump little body and kissed him firmly. "I missed you so much!" Victoria said with all the enthusiasm she could muster.

Simon stood rigid and did not hug Victoria in return but instead pushed her away and looked at Carlo. "I did what you said. The war is postponed."

"Nice job, Simon," Carlo grinned. "Well, now I guess it is time you and Victoria to get married, and I am sure Victoria will prove herself a worthy wife for you."

Simon clinched his fists in rage. "Yeah, well, I'm not sure there is going to be a wedding."

Victoria looked at Simon with legitimate fear. She loved Carlo, but she needed Simon. She knew it was unrealistic to think Carlo would ever take a wife. It was enough to believe that he would always treat her well and that once in a while she could sleep with him, but without Simon she was nothing—powerless and penniless.

"Don't be ridiculous, Simon. All the arrangements have already been made, and I am certain it will prove to be the best wedding the world has ever seen," said Carlo with a grin.

Victoria took Simon's hand and placed it on her breast. Then leaning in close to his ear, she whispered, "He is not half the man you are, Sweetheart. I love only you!" Then she tenderly kissed Simon's fat, sweaty neck.

Simon looked into her lovely face. Victoria was the only woman he had ever really loved. "Okay, I guess we will get married tomorrow," said Simon somberly. Then he looked to Carlo, grabbed Victoria's hand, and walked off.

Carlo was angered by the gesture and considered punishing Simon for this show of power and disobedience but then decided he would save that for a later time.

******

There was an eerie sky the afternoon of the wedding. The sun was blood red with a large black shadow covering part of its surface. The desire was to have an outdoor wedding in the new hanging gardens, but it was just too hot—nearly 120 degrees—so the wedding was moved into the cathedral room with the banquet in the adjoining room. There were guests from every part of the globe, men and women who worked for Carlo and Simon in positions of authority and power. Additionally there was news coverage from each country. All eyes would be watching as Carlo performed the marriage of Victoria Price to Simon Koch, the President of the United World Federation.

Simon waited nervously as Victoria walked down the aisle escorted by Oswald Heydrich, his number one aide and security leader. Simon was still angry at Oswald for the poor results in his concentration camps and for the escape of the 300 Christians. Mostly, however, Simon was angry at the fact that Tommy Glover and Sara Allen were still on the loose and undoubtedly causing trouble for him somewhere in the world. Still, Oswald was Simon's closest companion and the only one he would trust to escort Victoria.

Victoria stepped up next to Simon as Oswald moved to his right side. Carlo stood before them wearing a flowing white and royal blue robe with a golden sash around his waist and a golden collar set with precious gems around his neck.

Carlo looked to the camera and smiled brightly. "As god of this planet I reserve the right to marry whomever I choose, and today it gives me great pleasure to join together Simon Koch and Victoria Price. I give these two the right and privilege to live on this planet and in my sight as man and wife. Only I have the authority to create this union, and only I have the authority to separate them if I choose," said Carlo as he looked Simon directly in the eyes. "I now pronounce you husband and wife," said Carlo loudly.

Simon lifted Victoria's veil and kissed her firmly on the lips. "Now you belong to me!"

Unexpectedly there was a shout throughout the room. Simon recognized the voice immediately and turned around to see Moses and Elijah walking towards the podium where Carlo stood with a very displeased look on his face. At a hand wave request from Oswald, two security guards ran towards the heavenly prophets. As soon as both guards touched the robes of the two men they fell over dead at their feet. Elijah and Moses stepped over their bodies and continued towards Simon and Carlo.

"You mock God with your words and actions. You are disobedient and black hearted," said Moses as he turned toward the crowd and cameras.

"God is loving and forgiving. Repent and turn back to Him! Do not follow after this pretend god. He will be thrown into the pit of Hell where he came from, and this false prophet will be thrown in with him, locked up for eternity," said Elijah.

Victoria was annoyed that these two men had interrupted her beautiful wedding. "Kill them, Simon!" she shouted.

Simon looked at these men in total fear. He saw the two guards die by a mere touch of their robes, he had seen their plagues come true, and now they were saying that he was going to be locked up in Hell with Carlo forever.

Moses looked up. "Today you will see the sun disappear from the sky, and you will know darkness like the darkness of your own hearts."

"This is not a plague from your God. We know an eclipse is coming, and we know it will last for weeks!" Carlo roared. "Come to me again, and I will destroy you both!"

Suddenly the room grew pitch black, as did the entire world as the planet Jupiter occulted the sun's light completely. Screams of fear rang out throughout Carlo's palace as the people found themselves in complete darkness.

Chapter 11: Captured

D ay 1669, March: David lit a second candle, but it gave hardly enough light to see across the living room of Daniel's house. The sky had been pitch black for over two weeks now, and to make matters worse there just wasn't enough electricity in Jerusalem to handle the community's needs. The whole city—all except the crucial places like the hospitals and military bases—was facing a total blackout. This was pretty much the same situation throughout the world. The electricity demands had been incredibly high throughout the heat wave as people used fans and air conditioning to stay cool. This excessive demand along with the severe water shortage had simply broken the back of the power companies. Once again this was another reason why Carlo wanted to take charge of all oil fields and refineries.

David looked across the room to where Daniel sat quietly. The poor man had suffered terribly for the last five months. It had broken his will to live and nothing David did seemed to help. He had grown so fond of Daniel, but the reality that Benjamin's son was doomed to Hell really began to set in as David observed the demonic activity going on inside of Daniel's body. The young man rarely spoke to Daniel, but now that the demon was gone David was hopeful that they could reestablish their relationship. But for some reason it seemed that Daniel was unwilling to draw close to him.

Now that the world was in total darkness everyone including Peter and Ruth was going nuts. They tried to stay occupied by running the lab, but they were now out of supplies and had no way to get any more—at least until it became light outside again. Luckily they still had ample quantities of antidote ready to hand out, but now there was nobody to give it to. Every person was locked up in their home, and this was how it was going to be for at least another week.

Peter slouched on the couch as Ruth napped with her head reclining on his broad shoulder. "Well, isn't this the pits?" said Peter with half a laugh.

Daniel stood and began to pace the floor as David watched him closely. "So you need more sulfur and what else?" asked Daniel.

"What are you thinking?" Peter asked.

"I think I will go to work and get some supplies so that we can build ahead a little. This darkness won't last forever."

"Daniel, it is pitch black out there. You couldn't walk one foot without running into something," said Peter.

"Well, we have to try. Besides, this is the best time to get the supplies without getting caught."

"I'll go with you," said David smiling.

"No, you had better stay here," said Daniel.

Peter made a list for Daniel and handed it to him. "Be careful."

"I will."

Ruth woke in time to see Daniel close the door behind him. "Where in the world is he going?" Ruth asked as David walked past her into the kitchen.

"He is going to work to get some more supplies."

Ruth looked at Peter inquisitively. "Is he crazy? No one can go out in this darkness."

"Well, he just did," said Peter.

While Ruth and Peter were discussing the idiotic nature of what Daniel was trying to do, David snuck out the back door. He stumbled over the trashcan as he worked his way to the street. He had a total sense of disorientation. There wasn't a speck of light to be found. His eyes would never adjust to this darkness. David reached down towards the trash he had just dumped over and felt around. His fingers touched a piece of material. This was an old towel that Peter had used to clean his lab. David could smell the chemicals on the cloth. All he needed was a stick and he could build himself a torch. "The broom," said David aloud. He knew that he had left the broom just outside the back door to the kitchen. Slowly he felt around until he found the wooden handle. David placed the old broom handle under one of his feet and stomped on it. The dowel broke neatly into two pieces. David selected the longer of the two pieces and wrapped his towel around the end carefully. Fishing into his pocket he found the matches he had used to light the candle. David struck the match and instantly the chemically soaked towel ignited into a bright light.

The young man walked down the driveway where Daniel's car was usually parked. He knew that since Daniel was driving his car he would get to the factory long before him, but if he cut across some of the yards in the neighborhood, he could shorten his time greatly. David figured he had roughly 10 minutes of torch life before he was stuck in total darkness again. He never even considered the risk he was taking. With this kind of darkness he could get lost and wander around for days without finding anyone to help him. In fact, he could get lost and fall into something that would hurt or even kill him.

David jogged along as fast as he could dodging obstacles along the way. His torch began to glow dim just as he approached Daniel's factory. To David's surprise, the factory lights were on. *How was this possible?* he wondered. Power had been diverted to critical locations. *Perhaps they have a power generator,* he thought. As he approached the empty street he saw Daniel pull into the driveway of the nearly empty parking lot. "I hope he doesn't get mad at me," David whispered as he dropped his now dead torch.

David crossed the street just as Daniel entered into the front office. From 50 yards away the young man observed another vehicle driving slowly through the parking lot. *Oh, no,* thought David. *Someone is going to catch Daniel for sure.* He continued to walk towards Daniel's car. It was so dark even with the lights coming from the building that David felt sure the two men in the car would not see him as he approached. One of the men got out of the small vehicle and walked towards the front of the building while the other man drove around to the side. "It's a trap!" said David aloud.

Unknown to David and Daniel, Oswald had been in Jerusalem since Simon's wedding. He was there to assess the condition of the Israelites and determine how large of a threat they might pose to Simon's efforts. Oswald was surprised to find that very few people had died because of the plague. It seemed that someone was supplying antidote. This angered him greatly. It was his job to infect every neighborhood with the virus and Simon's job to provide an antidote when things got really bad.

He had seeded the deadly virus in Israel twice now, but somehow these people had survived. Oswald was sure that Peter Bastoni was behind this, but how would he ever catch him? He considered that someone had to be helping Peter. Someone had to be supplying the necessary chemicals. Eventually this led him to Daniel's factory. For two weeks now he had placed Special Force agents around the building, but with the infernal darkness, no one was coming to work.

Daniel moved from room to room inside the cold, empty building. His arms were full of supplies, probably enough to manufacture another two weeks worth of medicine. From behind Daniel heard footsteps approaching. Quickly he made his way to the fire escape and quietly climbed down the steps and out the emergency exit. Just as Daniel turned to walk towards his car, a bright pair of headlights shone on him. "Freeze!" said a loud voice. Daniel dropped his supplies and began to run. Instantly the car sped forward cutting off his escape. The driver opened his door and fired a single gunshot into the air. Daniel stopped and lifted his hands high above his head. Then unexpectedly another car sped through the alleyway and rammed the security officer's car, knocking the guard into the open car door and injuring him badly.

David jumped out yelling, "Let's go!"

Daniel was surprised to see young David behind the wheel of his car, but he was grateful. Just as Daniel ran to the driver's side of his car, another gunshot could be heard, and the windshield of the car shattered. David was thrown back against the driver's seat from the force of the bullet as it entered into his chest. Daniel turned to see the second security guard running towards him with his gun out and ready. Daniel looked at David who was gasping for breath. "Are you okay?" he shouted. The young boy did not say a word as he was in shock.

Daniel and David were taken to the hospital where Oswald Heydrich met them. David lay on a table with his shirt cut away. In the center of his chest was a mass of torn tissue and a gaping hole. Even though Daniel was handcuffed, he still managed to hold David's hand. "Who are you working with?" Oswald asked sternly.

David looked into Daniel's worried eyes. "Don't tell him anything," he whispered.

Oswald looked at the impertinent young boy. "You are going to die unless he tells me who all these chemical supplies are for."

"Do you know Peter Bastoni?" asked Oswald as he looked into Daniel's eyes.

Daniel flinched at the mention of Peter.

"Look at that young boy. He is bleeding to death and unless you tell me where Peter is, I will let him lay there and die."

Daniel looked at David once again. David squeezed his hand tightly. "You have been a father to me. I love you. Please don't tell them. They work for Simon, and he works for the Devil."

Daniel looked down at the boy's tight grip on his hand. This was the very hand that he had voluntarily allowed an ID tag to be inserted into. *Why did I do such a foolish thing?* he wondered thinking back on this grave mistake.

"Not only will this boy die, but you will suffer and die too. Why would you want to protect Peter Bastoni? Don't you know he is the one who invented this plague in the first place?" said Oswald, not so convincingly. "I have checked your records, Daniel Cohen. You have taken the ID tag. What are you doing with these Christian fanatics?"

Daniel's head began to spin. What had happened to his life? First his father died and then his wife left. Then young David came into his life and into his heart, as did Peter and Ruth who were obviously good people. *But I took the ID tag,* he told himself. *I am not a Christian. I don't believe, and even if I did, it is too late now.*

David began to cough up blood. Daniel looked at the boy and then towards Oswald. "No!" David whispered under his dying breath. "You can't tell them."

"I have to," Daniel cried, "or else you will die."

"I will go to Heaven. It's okay!" David coughed. "Don't tell them anything."

Daniel looked at Oswald. "They are at my house."

"No!" David moaned.

Oswald nodded to two of his security guards who quickly left the hospital room. Then he turned and looked at David. "You are a tough little guy for sure. It is too bad that I have to kill you now." Oswald pulled out his own gun and pointed it towards David's head.

David looked at Daniel who was now crying uncontrollably. "I love you, Daniel!"

Oswald fired a shot and a bullet exploded into David's brain.

Daniel screamed out in rage and sorrow as he looked at what had become of the boy who had become like a son to him. Then next Oswald turned to Daniel. "You have been very helpful. Now I have a reward for you." Oswald pointed his gun at Daniel. "You will be in a better place real soon." Then he fired a bullet right between Daniel's eyes. Daniel's body hit the ground at the same time his spirit entered Hell for eternity.

*****

Back at Daniel's home Peter and Ruth had finally noticed David missing. They knew he must have followed after Daniel. "How will he ever find his way around?" Ruth asked like a worried mother. Both she and Peter had adopted David just as Daniel had.

Peter almost smiled through his worry. David was such a tough little customer. He could remember the first day he met the boy. David was trying to tackle Paul Laruso, the private investigator Pope Peter John had hired to track down Joseph. *What a brave young man,* Peter thought.

Abruptly the living room of Daniel's home lit up brightly. Instantly Peter recognized this as a visit from Heaven just like before. Peace and joy filled his heart. Philip stepped forward with a somber look on his face. "Peace be with you both," said Philip as he towered over Peter and

Ruth. "Be strong! David is dead."

"Oh, no!" Ruth cried out.

"What?" Peter said. "He just left here an hour ago—to follow Daniel we presumed."

"Yes," Philip said. "He was courageous until the end, but both he and Daniel are dead. David is in Heaven rejoicing in the presence of Jesus Christ, but Daniel—" Philip whispered.

Ruth and Peter nodded and mourned the loss of Daniel's soul.

"What happened to David?" Peter asked through his tears.

"There is no time for that," said Philip. "They are coming for you."

"What?" Ruth cried.

"What should we do?" Peter inquired.

"Nothing," said Philip. "Be strong and know God is with you. All things work for His glory."

Philip smiled and then suddenly disappeared just as the front door of Daniel's home came crashing open. In ran a half dozen armed Special Security men. Ruth and Peter hugged each other tightly as Oswald's agents brutally beat and cuffed them.

Thirty minutes later a bloody Peter and Ruth stood before Oswald and a dozen of his men. "Dr. Bastoni, good to see you at last. And you," said Oswald with an evil grin, "must be his faithful companion, Ruth Jefferson—all-American news reporter."

Peter and Ruth said nothing. It was quite possible they were going to die in just a few minutes, and they would not give Oswald the satisfaction of hearing them talk.

"Well, I have good news for both of you. Simon Koch, who is presently on his honeymoon vacation, has authorized me to take you both back to Europe. We have a beautiful concentration camp perfectly suited for the both of you. I am sure the people in this place will be glad to find out that you are the inventor of this plague that has killed millions." Oswald then turned to one of his senior specialists saying, "Escort them back to Rome and lock them up until Simon gets back."

Oswald had a little more work to do in Jerusalem and then it would be back to Europe for him as well. There was still the little matter of a couple of American scientists and 300 escaped prisoners to deal with.

******

Calvin and his team had been at Point Hope in a very northern region of Alaska for weeks. Initially the natives had been very leery of this small group of people, but after Jerry stepped up and provided an antidote for the plague that was ravaging their small community the people began to think of the team in a positive light.

Before long Calvin had witnessed to the whole community and converted each person who had not taken the ID tag. Since this place was so remote, very few had accepted Carlo's mark. When Calvin told the people what it meant to take these tags, they quickly rounded up every person who was known to have a tag inserted. They brought these individuals before Calvin and asked him what they should do with them. This was something he had not considered until now, so he turned to Cory for guidance. "We cannot let them go or else they will tell someone we are here," said Cory.

"What shall I do with them?" Calvin asked.

Cory looked deep into Calvin's eyes. He knew his friend was too gentle and kind to kill these people even though they were lost for all eternity and a real liability to the community. "Do they have a jail here?" Cory asked.

As it turned out there was not a jail in this small community. There had never been a need for one until now, so Calvin conferred with the city's leaders. "Can we build something that we can use to lock these people up?" Calvin asked.

The leaders of the community agreed that this was the best solution, but before they could finish the task, the sky turned dark. For the time being each person with an ID tag was under house arrest.

******

Cory entered into the home where he, Leasa, Jerry, and Calvin had been staying. He went directly to Leasa's room. Lately she had not been feeling very well, and he was concerned for her. Upon entering her bed-room Cory found Leasa nearly unconscious with perspiration covering her forehead. Cory tried to wake her up, but she just lay there moaning. Her breathing was labored and raspy so Cory left quickly to find Jerry.

A few minutes later Cory stood by as Jerry examined her. "I think she has pneumonia," said Dr. Little as he looked into Cory's worried eyes.

"Can you help her?"

"I'll try. I need to go to the clinic and get some antibiotics," said Jerry.

As Jerry left the room he ran into Calvin. "What's the matter?" Calvin asked, sensing Jerry's concern.

"It's Leasa. She is very sick," said Jerry somberly.

Calvin rushed into Leasa's room in time to see Cory kneeling beside her bed praying out loud. Calvin knelt beside Cory and joined with him in prayer on Leasa's behalf.

A few hours later Leasa began to stir. The medicine Jerry had given her was helping. Cory leaned in and held Leasa's small hand gently. "Leasa," he whispered.

Leasa opened her eyes and smiled up at Cory. Tears glistened down his face. He loved this young lady dearly.

"How are you feeling?" Cory asked softly.

"I'm not sure," Leasa whispered, "but I am glad you are here with me."

"I'll never leave you, Leasa," said Cory as he kissed her forehead tenderly.

Two days later Jerry walked into Calvin's counsel meeting just as it was ending. The sun had finally come back out after weeks of total dark-ness, and now it was time to finish building the jail. Jerry waited in the corner for Calvin to finish his business. Finally Calvin rose as the crowd dispersed. Jerry walked over to him with a very distraught look on his face. At once Calvin suspected Leasa had taken a turn for the worst.

"What is it Jerry? Is Leasa okay?"

"We need to talk," said Jerry quietly.

Twenty minutes later Jerry and Calvin walked into Leasa's room and found Cory reading to her. The big man was holding a Bible and reading a passage from the book of John. Leasa looked up and smiled to them. "I am feeling much better."

Calvin grasped Leasa's hand tightly. "That's good, Sweetheart."

Jerry stepped up and took a stethoscope out of his pocket and began to listen to Leasa's breathing. Then he checked her pulse and placed a thermometer in her mouth.

"She's getting better!" said Cory with a smile.

Both Calvin and Jerry looked at Cory in a way that made his heart sink.

Jerry pulled the thermometer out and recorded the reading. "Well, how is it?" Leasa asked with a little giggle.

Jerry looked to Calvin for support. They had already discussed this privately and agreed that Leasa should be told right away, but that didn't make it any easier. "Leasa, you have a specific kind of pneumonia called pneumocystis carinii pneumonia, referred to as PCP."

"Is that bad?" Leasa asked as Cory looked on.

"Leasa, it is an indication of some other, more dangerous problem," said Jerry compassionately.

"What is it?" Leasa asked as she reached for the comfort of Cory's hand.

"Based on your blood work, I have determined that you have AIDS," said Jerry flatly.

Cory felt a knife enter his heart as he listened to the diagnosis. It was all he could do to hold back the tears.

Leasa looked at Jerry and then to Calvin for confirmation. "AIDS! Am I going to die?"

The room was quiet enough to hear a pin drop. Leasa looked at Cory and then back to Jerry. "When do I get to go to Heaven, Jerry?"

Tears filled Cory's eyes as he looked up to Jerry for the answer. Jerry was also crying by this time. "I'd say five or six months if you stay here and rest—maybe a week if you try to get up and move around."

So there it was just as Barthemaus had said. Calvin's team was breaking up.

******

Calvin sat outside looking up at the moon. It was a hazy red color and there were no stars to be seen in the sky. So much time had gone by since that awful day he had climbed down from Mount Denali leaving his friend there to die alone.

Since then he had been a prisoner, a casino worker, the leader of a band of Christians living in a mine, and finally a witness to North America. He had met so many people over the years and had seen so much sorrow and destruction, including the destruction of his own planet.

Then there had been those positive moments, too, like when he met Billy Walker and his sweet wife, Peggy Sue. Many had come to the Lord, and he understood that this was truly all that mattered. But now with Leasa dying, Calvin felt tremendous sorrow.

Cory stepped up to where Calvin sat. "I need to talk to you," he said somberly.

"Have a seat."

Cory sat and looked up at the unrecognizable sky. "I have been with you for years," said Cory.

Calvin looked at his big friend and smiled.

"You are a prophet for God, and I am honored to be your friend."

Calvin knew where Cory was taking this conversation. He was a dedicated friend and a servant of the Lord. Calvin knew that his big friend would follow him to the ends of the earth if he asked him to, but what Cory wanted right now was to stay behind and care for Leasa until she died. This internal struggle was tearing Cory up inside.

"I am glad you are here," said Calvin. 'I wanted to discuss an idea I have."

Cory looked into Calvin's soft brown eyes. He had noted his friend's countenance changing over the years from that of an average looking black man into a righteous and beautiful man of God. "What idea?" Cory asked.

"Well, we have things pretty much complete here except for the jail and that will be done next week. All this community needs is someone to lead it for a while until the people mature in the Lord. I was thinking that this would be a good time for Jerry and me to fly over to Russia and see what work God has for us there. That is, if it is okay with you. I'd like you to stay here and lead these people and help them establish a godly community." Calvin smiled at Cory. "Besides, it would be nice to have you here to watch out for Leasa. Jerry can teach you what you need to know and give you the necessary medicine. We'd probably be gone for five or six months, and then we could come back for you and Leasa." Calvin caught himself in mid-sentence. He knew he would only be coming back for Cory.

Cory was grateful to Calvin for giving him this opportunity to stay with Leasa although he hated to see his friend go without him. Cory felt like Calvin's personal bodyguard, and he worried that something or someone would hurt his friend without him there to protect him.

Cory leaned into Calvin and hugged him tightly, nearly crushing his spine. "Please be careful!" said Cory.

Calvin nodded.

The next morning Calvin kissed Leasa Moore goodbye as tears streamed down his face. "I love you, Calvin!" said Leasa through her own tears and sobs. "I will see you in Heaven," she beamed.

Jerry hugged the young lady and kissed her forehead tenderly. "Cory has the medicine and instructions. You will not suffer."

"Thank you, Jerry. You are the nicest white guy I ever met," she smiled brightly.

Cory walked Jerry and Calvin to the plane which had been dragged back into the middle of the shallow river. It was fueled and full of provisions, including what remained of the antidote Jerry had brought with him. "Where will you go first?" Cory asked.

"We will let God decide that. I am just going to point it towards Russia and see what happens next," he answered.

Cory reached out and grabbed Jerry and Calvin and hugged them both tightly. "Take care of yourselves and come back for me, okay?

******

Oswald flew over the city of Jerusalem on his way back to Europe. He had replanted the plague in the heart of the city and he had added an additional security force to police the region for any Christian or Jewish activity that could be seen. His camps were full and he was considering building more, but he was still holding out hope that Simon would give the word to start killing many of these people who just simply refused to take the ID tags.

Slave labor accounted for some of these people, and he understood this was important to Carlo. He could not help the fact that he did not like the idea of using Christians and Jews for laborers. There was too much chance they would escape or worse yet actually witness to others around them, thereby spreading their ridiculous belief system to the world.

******

Below Oswald and unknown to him Elisha and Jasmine were marching towards Jerusalem. They had made arrangements with their counsel members in the Avdat Park to watch over the people. Elisha was not sure if he would ever be back, so he elected a leader over the group. The man he chose was the very man Peter had seen trying to prevent the security guard from taking his daughter out to be raped. This man had helped Peter lead the people through the desert. He was revered as a leader among all the men in the camp.

Elisha and Jasmine had said many tearful goodbyes. They felt sorrow, but they also felt a distinct force traveling with them as they walked through Beersheba on their way to Jerusalem.

Chapter 12: Concentration Camps

D ay 1800, August: Dr. Hyder entered Carlo's chamber once again. This time he had little to report. Looking across the room Raymond saw Simon sitting in Carlo's magnificent golden chair. Raymond knew that Carlo had moved his headquarters to Babylon months ago. He was amused to see Simon sitting up high as if he were the ruler of this planet.

"Dr Hyder, come in!" Simon grinned.

This unusually friendly greeting concerned Raymond. Simon had never been nice to him before, so something must be wrong.

"Well, what's the word of the day?" Simon laughed.

"Floods, I guess," Hyder said.

Simon leaned forward. "Really! Where?"

Raymond fidgeted around with his papers for a second. "Huge parts of Iceland and Greenland are under water. So are England and Ireland, but the worst is in the Pacific."

"Oh, how so?" asked Simon nonchalantly.

"The water level in the Pacific has risen nearly 30 feet since the heat wave."

Simon interrupted Hyder. "But the heat wave is over!"

"Yes, that is true, but the earth's climate has been greatly altered and the ice caps are still melting. I am afraid that within the next few weeks every island in the Pacific will be under many feet of water."

"Is that a fact? Then I guess we had better consider a rescue mission to remove all the islanders in the Pacific before they drown," Simon smiled.

This guy is acting weird, thought Raymond. Besides, many of island people had already drowned and the rest were heading for higher ground.

"What else can we expect?" Simon inquired.

"You can expect every sea and ocean to be dead within the next few months and the majority of rivers and lakes throughout the world to be dried up. You can also expect people to die for lack of water," said Raymond with a degree of intolerance in his voice.

Simon picked up on Raymond's annoyed tone. "Is there something that you want me to do?" Simon asked.

"I don't know what anyone can do," said Raymond somberly.

"I have desalinization plants running on all parts of the globe."

"They are not enough!" countered Raymond.

"Don't tell me what is enough!" Simon shouted. "Now how about the space station—did you ever figure something out for them?"

"We have had some very limited conversations with the station. The sun's radiation has made communicating difficult. We also think the ISS suffered greatly during the sun's close proximity. It is possible their radio equipment has been damaged. We have found a way to send up supplies and oxygen, but we cannot recover these astronauts."

"Why not?" asked Simon.

"All of the space shuttles have been damaged seriously from the meteor showers and there just isn't anyone to fix them or fly them for that matter."

"What's your plan?" Simon asked.

"We can use a satellite rocket and we can add a payload with the supplies they need. The only problem is that we cannot communicate this to them. They will have to spot the payload and try to capture it themselves."

"What are the chances for success?"

"Maybe 50 percent," answered Dr. Hyder.

"Good enough. Make it so!"

Raymond left the chamber in a somber and confused mood. His role in all this was coming to an end. The world was dying and there was not much left to report on. *What do I do with my life now?* Raymond wondered.

******

Simon leaned back in Carlo's chair. He liked the fact that Carlo had moved to Babylon. It was as if he didn't exist most of the time. Simon felt as if he alone ruled the world. Today, however, he did have one final task to perform for Carlo. He had been given direction to contact Whi Yin and initiate the war with the Middle East. Simon hated the little man from China, but he figured he would take care of him as soon as this small war ended.

Life was going just as Simon desired. He had his new bride, Victoria, all to himself with Carlo thousands of miles away. Oswald had caught Peter Bastoni and hand delivered him to Simon. Simon smiled as he remembered that morning. Oswald had led Peter and Ruth into this very office. He commanded Peter and Ruth to kneel before him. "So you are the brother of Joseph Bastoni," grinned Simon. "I certainly enjoyed chopping his head off. What fun that was! I saw you in the audience that day. What a wonderful time we had."

Peter looked at Simon with total disgust and hatred.

"Now, Dr. Bastoni, you have gone around the world saving lives with your own antidote. How commendable, but that was my job!" Simon roared. "And who might you be?" Simon asked as he looked to Ruth.

Ruth swallowed hard from fear but said nothing.

"Oh, yes, let me guess. You are that news reporter that helped Joseph Bastoni print all those lies about Carlo and me. What was that paper called? Oh, I remember. *Deacon's Horn,* right? Mr. Heydrich, what do you recommend we do with these two good citizens?" Simon asked with a broad smile.

Oswald grinned. "Death would be quick, but it wouldn't be that much fun. I have a better idea—I have a camp in Linz that is just perfect for these two. In addition, I have a great big furnace that could use some stoking."

Simon smiled. "You know, Mr. Heydrich, I think you have a great idea there. Let's send them to Germany for a while and then after they've had a chance to be fully appreciated by the people there, maybe they'd like to see the inside of that furnace you were talking about."

Simon looked at Peter intently. "Maybe—just maybe—Dr. Bastoni and his news reporter friend here would like to join us instead of going to that nasty old camp," smiled Simon.

"What do you say, Dr. Bastoni? Are you willing to serve His Holiness and me and denounce Jesus? That could go a long way to improving public opinions."

Peter looked at Ruth for confirmation. Death was surely coming their way, and it would most likely be a horrid and painful death. Ruth simply smiled at Peter in a very loving and gentle way. Peter turned to Simon and beaming brightly he said, "We will serve Christ for as long as we live."

Simon stood and roared like a lion. "Get them out of my sight! Throw them into prison where they can rot until I determine the best way to kill them."

Oswald moved quickly to escort Peter and Ruth from the room. "You will get what is coming to you now!" growled Oswald.

Simon reseated himself and leaned back in Carlo's chair. Now all he needed was Tommy and Sara, and he would be eternally happy. He knew Oswald had come very close to catching these two. Unfortunately all he came up with was an old man named Mueller who had helped them out. When questioned, Mueller was useless, so Simon had him thrown into the very concentration camp he had helped others escape from. Mueller was lucky that Simon had not tried to torture the truth out of him with regard to where the escaped Christians had gone. Simon had been so preoccupied with Victoria and Carlo in Babylon that he simply didn't give this much consideration.

Now as Simon leaned back he had one call to make, and that was to Whi Yin. Simon figured the call could wait until after lunch. He didn't want to spoil his date with Victoria, and he knew that talking to the Yin would put him in a very bad mood.

******

Joshua pulled into the cove at first light. The water was so deep around the island of Woodlark that less than a quarter mile of dry land still existed. Joshua was making his sixth trip to the island. Daily he and Chris ferried the Muyuwan people back to New Guinea. This was to be the last load.

Over the last six months or so Joshua, Chris, and Connor had worked throughout New Guinea and the surrounding islands. Occasionally they would run into trouble and had to make a fast getaway, but for the most part they had been very successful. However, lately it seemed that they had finally run out of people that had not taken the ID tags. Crowds became more and more dangerous and evil hearted.

As a matter of fact, just two weeks earlier Chris and Connor had gotten themselves into a situation in New Guinea that could have gotten them killed. They were witnessing in a small town outside Port Moresby when the crowd turned ugly and started throwing rocks at them. Chris had been stunned badly by a large rock and Connor had had to carry him at a dead run. The crowd only stopped because of the numerous military vehicles driving down the road towards them. What the locals did not know was that the Chinese military had moved into New Guinea as they prepared for a global war.

Chris, Connor, and Joshua spent the next couple of weeks in a small coastal town called Daru. This is where Joshua got the idea to build a small camp where he could transport all of the Muyuwan people. Joshua had known for quite some time that the islands were sinking. He knew he would have to do something to help and soon.

Daru was a part of New Guinea, and like all the islands, New Guinea was starting to lose ground to the ocean water. Daru, however, was close to Irian Jaya, Indonesia, and this region was higher than the rest of the island. Although Daru itself would undoubtedly sink, Joshua's goal was to move inland as soon as he got every person off Woodlark. There would be no need for his boat after this because there would be no islands left to visit. The people would either have fled or they would have drowned.

Chris jumped out of the boat and pulled the towline over to a large tree and tied it securely. Joshua prepared to jump into the water, but before he could do that, Ezra and the rest of the islanders came walking out of the woods carrying all they possessed on their backs.

"Hello, Joshua!" said Ezra with a big smile.

Chris walked over to the natives and received many hugs and pats on the back.

"Where is Connor?" Ezra inquired.

"He is back in Daru with the rest of your people," Chris smiled. "Connor is not much of a sailor."

Ezra's large stomach jiggled as he laughed.

Twenty minutes later Joshua had stowed all of the supplies and personal effects and was ready to go. Chris and Ezra finished pouring the last of the gas into the boat's fuel tank. Ezra turned and looked at his sinking island. This was all he knew—his entire world—and with tears in his eyes he said a final goodbye.

Back in Daru Connor organized all the people into small groups with individual leaders. "I want to make sure we have enough water and food for our journey, so fill every bottle and let's get a count on all our supplies," said Connor. This was more like what he liked to do. He was an organizer and was glad not to be back on the boat. Connor looked at his watch. In just a few more hours Joshua and Chris would be back. *We can leave tomorrow at first light,* he thought.

Suddenly there was a very loud noise. Connor turned to see an entire tank division moving in the direction of his outpost. Connor ran toward the center of the camp where 200 frightened natives greeted him. "Who are they?" one of the natives asked in a panic.

"I don't know! Grab your stuff. We need to leave now," he said.

The tank division stopped just short of Connor's camp. A number of Chinese military men came walking forward just as the group hurried into the brush and out of sight. One man stepped up and called out a number of commands. Apparently this was where he wanted to establish his base of operations. There was fresh water, which was rare just about anywhere in the world, and it was a great place to look out into the Coral Sea. From here he could load boats with supplies and soldiers as the warships came in from the Strait of Torres.

Connor crawled along on his stomach. He had to get to Joshua and Chris before they walked into a camp full of Whi Yin's soldiers. He had taken his people to a safe location five miles above Daru and had given them instructions to stay hidden away until he returned with their leader, Ezra, and his two friends, Joshua and Chris.

Connor cleared the camp, stood on his feet, and began to run toward the Fly River.

******

Chris walked along silently. He was grateful that he and Joshua had gotten everyone off Woodlark before it was covered with seawater, and he was also grateful that they had made the trip back without a single incident. God had really protected them this last year or so and had given them a sweet harvest of souls.

Chris was the first to spot Connor running toward them. "Something is wrong," he said. The young man ran out to meet Connor. "What's the matter?"

Connor was out of breath and unable to speak. Finally he said, "Soldiers!"

"Where?" asked Joshua.

"In our camp," said Connor.

"What about my people?" Ezra asked with a great deal of concern.

"They are okay. I've moved them up about five miles, but we need to be very careful as we go by the camp or else they'll catch us."

"Is there another way we can go?" Chris asked.

"No, the sea is to our left, and the Fly River is a huge gorge on our right. We have to go by the soldiers," said Connor.

Connor led the way as they approached the camp. With a wave of his hand he had every person get on their knees and begin to crawl. The camp was only 75 yards away, and there was still enough sunlight to spot them if they were not careful.

Chris moved to the rear to help the older people with their heavy loads of supplies and personal possessions. They really should have discarded these supplies and taken their losses, but for some reason the natives refused to part with all they had left from their lives on the island.

The group of 20 stretched out over an area of about 200 feet with Chris bringing up the rear. Slowly Connor led each member past the camp and into the woods.

Minutes later Chris was not more than 40 feet away from safety when a military Jeep came around the corner and spotted him. Chris jumped up to run as the Jeep approached. When Connor saw what was happening, he ran out to help. The soldier in the passenger side of the Jeep pointed his rifle at Chris and was just about to shoot when he saw Connor running towards his friend. Quickly the soldier turned his rifle on Connor and fired. With a thud Connor fell to the ground just as he reached Chris. The Jeep rounded the corner and stopped to back up. Chris grabbed Connor by the arm and tried to pull him to safety when suddenly Ezra and Joshua came running out from the woods and grabbed Connor. Quickly they headed back into the forest before the vehicle could turn around. The sun was just started to set, and the light near this part of the equator disappeared in a hurry. The soldiers stopped short of the wooded area and considered walking into the forest where the Jeep could not go, but after a brief discussion they decided it was not worth the effort. "Just a bunch of locals probably," said one soldier.

"Yeah, well, at least I shot one of them," the other soldier said proudly.

Ezra lifted all 200 pounds of Connor up on his shoulders and carried him deep into the woods. Finally after 20 minutes he stopped and laid Connor gently on the ground. Chris came over and knelt next to his injured friend. Connor smiled weakly at him and said, "I always thought that I would end up drowning or something. I never thought I would get shot."

Chris began to cry as he held Connor's hand. This man had come into his life when he had nobody else, and he had loved and cared for Chris for nearly two years. They had been through so much together and had become very close. Joshua joined Chris at Connor's side and opened his shirt to survey the damage. Connor had been shot in the stomach and the bullet had exited through his back. Bright red blood could be seen flowing freely from the wound. It formed a pool on the ground where Ezra had laid him. "Dear Lord!" said Joshua. "We need your help. Our dear friend has been hurt terribly."

A gentle wind began to cause the trees to sway and gradually a soft glow formed around the men. Ezra looked up to heaven in awe of the supernatural presence of God that he was now a witness to. Never before had he experienced the presence of the Lord in this way.

Connor began to smile as a sense of peace filled his body, and instantly the pain was gone. A voice spoke softly, "You three have served Me well. There is much more for you to do before My return, but Connor has fulfilled his destiny and is ready to come home to Me."

The trees grew calm as the glow diminished. Connor looked up at Chris and Joshua. "I love you two very much. Do not cry for me," he whispered. "I am going to Heaven, and soon I will come back with Jesus. Then I will see both of you again."

Chris cried out as Connor's hand went limp and his spirit left his body. Joshua pushed Connor's curly hair away from his face and kissed his cheek. "Goodbye, dear friend. We will meet again soon."

******

Oswald walked into Mauthausen with two security guards at his side. This was the day Peter and Ruth would pay for all the trouble they had caused. For months now they had been held prisoners in this camp. Oswald had spread a rumor that Peter was responsible for the plague and the death of millions. He expected the inmates to abuse him, but this was not the case. Instead Peter quickly became a revered leader—known as both the brother of Joseph, a man hated by Simon in a personal way, and a man who had saved many with the antidote he had helped to develop.

Oswald had been busy over these many months in search of Tommy and Sara and had not given Peter any attention. He was very displeased to find out that Peter was alive and well. He discussed this with Simon and they both agreed that throwing Peter and his faithful friend, Ruth, into a lit furnace was a reasonable punishment.

As Oswald rounded the corner he caught sight of Mueller. He had placed this man in the camp many months ago. The old fool was useless.

He had learned nothing about Tommy or Sara from him. He considered throwing Mueller into the furnace with Peter and Ruth. In fact, what he really wanted to do was kill all of these people. None of them were worth the effort that he and Simon went through, but Carlo had given instructions not to force ID tags into any prisoner and to be patient. "They will accept the ID tags on their own if we just give them a little time," said Carlo.

Oswald walked into the front office where Peter stood with a guard on each side of him. "Where is the other one?" Oswald roared.

"They are bringing her in now, Sir," said one of the guards.

Peter turned to see a frightened Ruth being escorted in. He had not seen her in a day or two. They were kept in different buildings and only saw each other on the days they were both allowed into the courtyard. Ruth moved up next to Peter and slid her hand into his. He smiled at her reassuringly. "It will be okay, Ruth. God will take care of us."

Oswald laughed and slapped Peter hard on the back. "Sure He will. Your God is dead, and soon you will be dead."

Peter and Ruth were escorted hand in hand past the main office and onto the furthest part of the camp. Mueller watched as Oswald walked along. He understood what was about to happen. He had seen the smoke coming from the chimney of the ominous building at the end of the row. This building had seen many broken hearts and much torment and death. Today it was going to see some more.

Oswald stopped at the entrance to the big, gray building. "Well, this is as far as I go. You two have a nice day," he said as he leered at Peter.

"And you enjoy Hell!" said Peter with a smile of his own. "Today we will be in Heaven with the Lord!"

"Yes, well, maybe, but not before you get a chance to feel the fires of Hell up close," said Oswald as he turned to leave.

Mueller watched Simon's right-hand man walk out of the camp as Peter and Ruth were escorted into the frightening building. Peter could feel Ruth shaking as they entered the large empty room. Along the walls on both sides were numerous incinerators. Peter knew well that these had been used thousands of times to kill the innocent or to cremate those that were already dead.

"Peter!" said Ruth with a quiver.

"It is all right, Ruth. God is with us."

"Peter, I want you to know that I love you, and I am glad I have been with you these last two years," said Ruth softly.

"I'm glad too," said Peter. "I love you too." Peter turned towards Ruth and kissed her tenderly on the lips.

"I'm scared!" said Ruth.

The guards opened the furnace, and it had a fiery orange glow. At once the heat from the fire nearly knocked Peter and Ruth to the ground. Ruth began to cry. "I'm scared! Jesus, give me strength."

The guards struggled to break Peter's grip off of Ruth. Eventually they were separated and one at a time their bodies were tightly wrapped in white sheets and their arms and legs were taped securely to their bodies. Then finally one at a time the guards hoisted the bodies up, threw them into the fire, and quickly closed the door.

For five minutes the guards stood around waiting for the cremation to be completed. "Time's up!" said one of the guards. "Turn the gas off, and let's clean this thing out."

A nearby guard turned the knob to *off* and another guard pulled the lever to open the door to the furnace. As the heavy door swung open, they were amazed to see Peter and Ruth holding hands standing next to another man. All three were dressed in white, and the looks on their faces were of victory and power. The strange man with them looked at the guards as fire danced from his eyes.

Instantly the guards ignited into flames. Soon the flames consumed the morbid old building, and the fire spread quickly to each of the buildings in the compound. Right before Mueller's eyes his prison was incinerated. The compound guards rounded up the prisoners and held them at gunpoint until Oswald could be notified that his concentration camp had burned to the ground.

The next day Oswald toured the burned out facility. As he walked towards the crematory where the fire started, he considered Peter's final comment, *"And you enjoy Hell."* Perhaps this camp had burned down by accident, but there was a rumor that Peter and Ruth were not consumed in the furnace but instead that Jesus had rescued them and burned the camp to the ground. Oswald tried to shake off the fear he felt.

The next day Mueller and thousands of others were sent to Dachau. The rest were redistributed to Auschwitz and other camps throughout Germany and the Czech Republic.

******

Elisha and Jasmine walked towards the temple hand in hand. They both seemed to have a sense of destiny as they approached the newly rebuilt building. It was as if their whole lives had been designed for just this moment. For months they looked to God to give them direction since entering town.

Originally they went to Bethlehem to Benjamin's deli and waited there patiently. Surprisingly the deli had not been touched or looted as one might have expected. In fact, the bodies of Scott Turner and Paul Laruso were still hidden in the freezer as Jasmine had found out the first time she opened the heavy, metal door.

Finally just two days before, Elisha and Jasmine received another visit from Moses and Elijah. "The time is coming," said Moses, "when there will be horrible death and destruction. There will be millions of soldiers fighting throughout the Middle East, and a third of mankind will die. You must go to the temple two days from now and escort God's elect to safety."

"Go to Mount Carmel as you have already been told," said Elijah. "God will protect you and give you the necessary power to overcome evil."

The streets were full as they arrived at the temple. Crowds of people pushed their way forward. Today was declared a holiday and many had come out for the festivities. Most of these people were faithful Jews and Muslims who had not followed after Carlo. They were anxious to see their temple reopened to the public. They still did not fully understand that this temple belonged to Carlo. To them it belonged to their God.

Jasmine stood beside Elisha looking into the crowd of tens of thousands. "I wonder if Peter and Ruth are here somewhere and maybe even little David."

The door to the temple opened and out walked a rabbi dressed in an ephod. Beside him was a Muslim holy man. "People," said the rabbi, "welcome to the temple of god—the temple of our god, Carlo Ventini!"

The crowd was quiet for a few seconds. Then suddenly they began to wail and moan loudly. Once again this pretend god, Carlo Ventini, had polluted their temple. The Muslim holy man lifted his hand to quiet the crowd, but they would not be consoled. The cameramen in front of the temple turned their cameras to the crowd. This was a live broadcast, and Simon was watching the dedication from his office in Rome. He cheered along as the crowd chanted curses against Carlo. Yes, it was his job to make sure Carlo was elevated to god of this planet. It was his job to rid the world of any opposition, and he knew Carlo was the rightful ruler of this world because he was Satan's son, but just for a moment it gave him great pleasure to see his leader mocked.

Suddenly the crowd grew silent as Carlo walked out the front door. The look on his face was one of anger. In a loud roar he said, "You will pay for your blasphemy and disobedience!" The crowd shrank back silently. As they did Elisha grabbed Jasmine's hand and pressed forward until he was no more than 15 feet from Carlo which put him at the edge of the stanchion where many armed guards stood.

"You are no god," said Elisha loudly. This caught Jasmine by surprise. She thought they were moving forward for a closer look, not for a personal conversation with the Antichrist.

Carlo looked at Elisha and pointed a finger at him. "Bring this blasphemer to me!"

Two security guards moved towards Elisha and grabbed him by the arm. Instantly they were thrown 10 feet into the air and their bodies ignited in flames. Jasmine looked at this horrible scene and then back to Elisha. "Did you do that?" she asked.

Elisha looked at his young wife and shrugged. "I don't know!"

The whole crowd saw this, as did the rest of the world that was watching their television sets. Simon sat forward and glared at the TV. The last time he had seen something like this was when he himself had ignited the man that shot Carlo in the head.

Carlo looked at Elisha, pointed to another security guard, and said, "Bring him to me now!"

The terrified guard walked slowly to Elisha and grabbed his arm. Again the guard went flying through the air and ignited on the ground. Suddenly before the camera crew and the world, Moses and Elijah appeared on the steps of the temple. Elisha's heart leapt for joy when he saw these two men.

Carlo, on the other hand, turned even sourer. "Shoot them!" he screamed.

Immediately numerous rifles were aimed directly at Moses and Elijah and discharged all their bullets, but none harmed either man. From his office Simon watched with his mouth wide open. "We are in big trouble!" he said aloud.

"You mock God and desecrate His holy temple. You deny His Son, Jesus Christ, as the one and only true God. You are a wicked people. This man is from Hell and back to Hell he will return," said Moses as he pointed towards Carlo who was defenseless against him.

"Turn from your evil ways and follow after Jesus. Leave here at once. Leave Jerusalem before Satan destroys you. Jesus wants you to repent and accept Him as the King of this world," said Elijah.

"Because you continue to mock God, a plague will come on you like never seen before. The angels of death will be released, and a third of the world will be consumed by war," spoke Moses with the power of God within him.

The people began to cry out as Moses spoke. "Help us! Save us!"

But suddenly before their eyes, just as they had appeared, Moses and Elijah were gone. Elisha and Jasmine turned and walked away from the temple knowing that the people had heard from the real God. The crowd parted as the two walked by, and immediately they began to follow them. Soon there were more than 10,000 men, women, and children following along behind Elisha and Jasmine as they headed north towards Mount

Carmel.

******

In an ancient part of the Euphrates River unseen by man since the time of Adam and Eve stood a massive and mighty angel with his wings outstretched in both directions. With a single hand he pointed a small golden rod towards the mouth of the river. Immediately the ground below the river split wide open, and the slimy, red water—or what was left of it—filled the fissure. The ground began to shake as a large monstrous creature appeared, and soon followed another and another until there were four hideous creatures standing before the Archangel, Michael.

All four of the evil, grotesque creatures began to stretch their webbed wings out to their sides. Their faces were dark and ruddy, and the skin of these creatures looked like that of a lizard. Their eyes were mere red dots in their faces, and their mouths were full of hideous, razor-sharp teeth. Their bodies were extremely large and powerful, although they looked horribly distorted. "At last!" said one of the monstrous angels.

"You have been given the authority from God to kill up to one third of all those who do not have the mark of God on their foreheads. You will not touch any of God's elect."

All four monstrous angels looked at Michael and grinned hideously.

"Your time is short, so be gone!" said Michael.

The angels of death sailed off with eerie and evil screams.

******

Whi Yin had given the orders to his generals. The war was on. They had many targets, the first of which was Saudi Arabia and all of the surrounding nations, excluding Iraq which was already under Carlo and Simon's control. Whi Yin had discussed his plans with Carlo numerous times, but each time Carlo sent him away to reconsider his approach. What Whi Yin really wanted to do was to use tactical nuclear weapons— those he had acquired from Taiwan—but Carlo had said absolutely not!

He did not want the oil field to be radioactive and useless for 10,000 years. He also would not allow for rocket launches from naval ships because he was afraid Whi Yin would destroy an oil field or start a fire that would take years to put out.

Eventually all Whi Yin was left with was an armed invasion supported by standard air defense, fighter jets. Still Yin's confidence was high. He knew that his generals had recruited and trained millions of soldiers. They could overwhelm any of the militaries of these Middle Eastern countries. What Whi Yin had not considered was the patriotism and desire of these nations to remain free of Simon's and Carlo's control. What Yin expected was a quick, weeklong campaign much like the Six Day War fought by the Israelis in June of 1967. In that brief campaign Israel defeated three nations: Egypt, Jordan, and Syria.

******

Sara wrapped her son, Philip, tightly in a soft, blue blanket. What a sweet child he was and so easy to care for. Sara had heard so much about the difficult first child, but this was not the case with little Philip. For nearly six months the child had brought her and Tommy much joy and a gentle distraction from the horrors of the present world. Sara tried not to think about what this poor child would never be able to experience in life. She knew his earthly life was going to be short, and if she and Tommy were caught, little Philip would have no one to care for him.

Sara looked at her watch again. She was beginning to worry. Tommy had been gone for too long already. Since moving to Munich six months ago they had moved from place to place trying to avoid Oswald's Special Police. Finally they had found a small Christian organization that had been willing to take them in as soon as they heard who they were. Tommy had shared with many in this group how he and Sara had actually been inside Mauthausen and how with the aid of Mueller they had helped hundreds to escape.

To this small group of Christians, Tommy and Sara were warriors. For the last six months, however, Sara had not gone out with Tommy to witness to anyone. He would not allow Sara to take any unnecessary risks. "Little Philip needs his mother," Tommy would say as a reminder whenever Sara complained that he was taking all the risks alone.

On this day in particular Sara was very concerned, because until now Tommy had been directed away from Dachau, the neighborhood concentration camp. The group of Christians he had been working with saw no chance of helping anyone unlucky enough to get thrown into this horrid place, so Tommy worked within the community witnessing wherever he could.

Finally, however, he had devised a plan that he thought might get him into the prison one day a week, and if it worked, Tommy would be able to bring comfort and words of encouragement to the prisoners.

Earlier that week Tommy had converted two individuals who were deliverymen for Dachau. Their job was to bring in supplies once a week. Tommy's plan was simple. He would take the place of one of the men, enter the camp, and check it out—nothing more. Then on the second visit he would know his way around well enough to sneak off and speak to the people for a few minutes. He hoped that if he did this every week, he would eventually help to lead those who had not made a choice for Jesus and encourage those who had. Today was Tommy's first day in the camp, and Sara was frightened greatly.

****

Tommy walked into Dachau wearing a pair of gray overalls with a German delivery truck logo on the back. On his shoulder he carried a crate full of vegetables, none of which would ever be seen by any of the prisoners. Tommy walked through the main compound and across the yard until he entered through the side door of the kitchen. Alongside him was one of the men he had converted earlier that week. He followed suit with everything this man did, being careful to blend in as if he had done this kind of work for years. He walked out of the kitchen and looked around inconspicuously as he moved back towards the delivery van. Crossing the yard his eyes caught sight of a prisoner who had his back to Tommy.

The man was tall and gray headed. From the back he looked somewhat familiar, but Tommy could not place the person. Finally the man turned around and to Tommy's delight it was Mueller. He wanted to shout for joy and to run to Mueller and hug him, but he didn't dare even stare. Mueller caught site of Tommy, and with one hand he made a small motion as if to say, *Don't look at me. Keep walking.*

Tommy reentered the kitchen with another crate. All in all he made 12 trips back and forth to the truck—approximately 30 minutes of work. This would be the amount of time he would have every week—that is, if both deliverymen accompanied him to the camp. *But how will I ever get away to blend in with all the other prisoners?* he wondered. In Mauthausen Jon had given him and Sara prison uniforms to wear. He could wear one of the Dachau uniforms under his overalls if he could just get his hands on one. Tommy reached into his pocket and pulled out a pen to mark off the inventory list. An idea struck him and he began to write in small letters on the corner of the paper. Quietly he tore the corner off and stuffed it in his pocket.

A few minutes later Tommy and the other deliveryman walked out of the kitchen and across the courtyard. As Tommy walked along, a soccer ball floated across in front of him. He picked the ball up right in front of one of the guards and turned to look in the direction it had come from. There stood Mueller and two young children. Tommy reached into his pocket and clutched the small piece of paper as he walked towards Mueller. Carefully he handed him the ball. Mueller felt the paper in his palm and closed his fist tightly. Tommy smiled, turned, and left the yard. Mueller had provided the opportunity that Tommy was hoping for when he wrote the note.

******

"Sara!" Tommy yelled, as he entered the small apartment that was being shared by six people. Sara ran forward at the sound of Tommy's voice.

"I'm here!" said Sara. "What is it?"

"Mueller!" shouted Tommy.

"What? Where?" asked Sara.

"He's in Dachau."

"How do you know that?" Sara asked.

Tommy kissed his wife smartly. "I saw him!" he grinned.

Throughout the next week Tommy worked his usual ministry through the streets of Munich, but his heart was not in it. The people were unreceptive and hard hearted. More often than not Tommy found himself on the run from the local police. He always had an escape route planned for each neighborhood, and many times he had used these routes. Today Tommy wanted to be in Dachau ministering to those in captivity, and especially he wanted to see Mueller. *This will all have to wait until tomorrow,* he told himself.

******

The next morning at first light Tommy and the two other deliverymen headed towards Dachau with a van load of supplies. Tommy's stomach growled nervously as they approached the camp. This had as much to do with terminal hunger as it did anxiety. A few minutes later all three men strolled across the yard carrying loads of fruits and vegetables straight from one of Simon's Agripods. One would think these prisoners were the best fed people in Germany. This would be true if it were not for the fact that the guards and office workers took all the food home for themselves as payment for working in this place. Undoubtedly Tommy would take some of this food home for Sara and Philip as well. He had already stashed some of the fruit under his seat.

Tommy dropped a heavy crate on the counter in the kitchen and then moved quickly to a near set of cupboards. There he found a uniform placed there neatly by Mueller.

Tommy looked around cautiously and then removed his overalls and climbed into the uniform. He stuffed the clothes into the cupboard and headed out of the kitchen without saying a word to his two companions. Casually he headed over to where he had spotted Mueller standing. The two men walked along trying not to draw any attention. "How are you, Mueller? When did you get here?"

"I was in Mauthausen, but it burned down so they shipped us here."

"I am so sorry you got caught," Tommy whispered.

"Hush now, that is not important. All things work for God's glory. I have been witnessing in here about what happened in Mauthausen and all that we did. Many have increased their faith or come to accept Jesus as Lord," Mueller smiled.

"I want to help," said Tommy.

"What did you have in mind?" Mueller inquired.

"I thought I could witness to these people, but it sounds like you are doing a fine job of that." Tommy paused for a second. "How about we break you out of this place?"

Mueller smiled. "I don't know, Son. There really isn't any place for me to go anymore, and besides, these people need me."

Tommy was a bit surprised by Mueller's attitude. The man had changed much over the last six months. "But there is more we could do. We could help many of these people escape."

"Where would they go?" Mueller asked. "Christ will be back soon."

"But I have heard rumors that Oswald and Simon are going to start killing people because the camps are too full," said Tommy with a serious look on his face.

Mueller had not heard this information before. He looked over to where a young mother and daughter sat side by side. He had met them the first day he arrived in this camp. The mother and daughter were from Fiji. They were very inspirational to Mueller and had changed his heart. He now cared much more for the people in this camp than he did for himself.

"I would like you to help those two escape, but as for me, I will stay here with these people and help them until the end comes," Mueller smiled. "Now how is Sara?" Mueller asked.

"Oh!" Tommy grinned. "She is fine, and we have a son."

Mueller patted Tommy's shoulder. "I am proud of you, Boy. You are a good man, and I'm glad you and Sara came into my life. I love you both very much!"

Tommy wanted to cry. He felt like he was about to say goodbye to Mueller for the last time. "Give me a plan for getting these two out of here, and I will make it happen."

"Next week when you come in, they will be ready. We will have them in the kitchen in a couple of those heavy, black trash bags. They are both very small, so you can carry them out as if they were garbage from the kitchen. Put them in the back of your vehicle and drive away. Simple as that! But then you will never be able to come back here again. Do you understand that, Son?" Mueller asked in a very serious tone.

Tommy nodded. He understood this was his last mission with Mueller, and he would not mess it up.

******

Simon walked into the temple in the heart of Jerusalem. It was a marvelous place full of gold and beautifully hand carved wood. The place had been restored to near perfection after the meteorites fell into it. Simon had been called back to the temple by Carlo to give an update on the status of the war which had already lasted months longer than Whi Yin had thought it would. Simon smiled at this fact. He knew the Chinese president had disappointed Carlo greatly. Not to mention the fact that the Saudi's had started fires in their own oil fields to confuse the Chinese soldiers and to make themselves less desirable for a hostile take over. The skies across the Middle East and Asia Minor were blackened with the residue of war and oil fires.

Simon walked to the center of the temple and noticed Carlo who sat looking out into space as if he were a million miles away. "Hello, Your Holiness."

Carlo turned and looked through Simon as though he were not even there. Suddenly the floor of the temple began to shake. The air filed with a putrid odor and Simon knew Satan was in the room. "Father!" said Carlo as he fell to the ground.

Simon turned and knelt before Satan as well. He was a bit surprised to see Carlo's Father here in this temple, but he was glad. Simon figured he had done so many good things around the world lately—especially his persecution of Christians—that he was sure to get some praise from Satan.

"Father, the people here mocked me. They did not worship me, and the two witnesses—"

"Silence, my Son!" said Satan with a roar. "Simon, the next time these two witnesses appear, you will have my power to kill them both."

Simon was elated with this news.

"Now!" roared Satan. "You have not been cooperative with my son. You have not taken care of this war. Already 100 million people have died. These are people that could be worshiping me right now, and still there are Christian witnesses throughout the world mocking me. This must stop!" Satan shouted as the room trembled. Simon fell on his face and begged Lucifer to forgive his failures.

"Enough! The world will divide. Those that are with us will worship, and those that are against us will die. No matter where they are, I want them dead," Satan commanded.

"Understood, Father. We will make sure this is taken care of right away," said Carlo.

Simon heard Satan to say that every Christian and Jew in the world would have to die. He needed to call Oswald and change their plans for the concentration camps right away. *The furnaces will be running hot for weeks.* Simon smiled at the thought.

******

Hours after Satan departed the temple Simon finished his briefing on the war effort. "We have not entered Israel, but we can if you want us to," said Simon.

"No! Not yet," said Carlo. "Whi Yin has failed me. Too many of my people are dying, and this war is no closer to being over." What Carlo did not understand was that four very viscous, demonic angels were making war on every front. Over 200 million soldiers had entered the war and over half were already dead, as were millions of civilians. These evil angels were keeping the battles going, confusing both sides, and preventing any army from surrendering. As a result the war would drag on until one third of all unsaved people had died. This number was not that far away since so many were already gone. They had died from starvation, heat, cold, war, and the plague.

"If you want," said Simon, "I will take over this army myself."

Carlo considered this carefully. He was tired of Whi Yin's failures, but he did not like the idea of his prophet making war. "Who else do we have?" Carlo asked.

"I have my ex-NATO commanders and a host of generals that could do a better job of fighting this war."

"Okay, Simon! Make it so," said Carlo.

"What about Yin?" Simon grinned optimistically.

Carlo waved his hand. "You decide."

At sunset Carlo and Simon went outside on the front steps of the temple for a news briefing. They had decided to tell the world that they would no longer tolerate any person who did not have an ID tag or had not sworn allegiance to Carlo.

This was not new information, but the way they said it was different. Clearly they were issuing a threat that all known Christians and Jews and every sympathizer would die very soon. Simon made the announcement that all concentration camps would be closed this week and all prisoners who had not accepted the ID tag would be eliminated at once.

"We have many blessings coming to us. His Holiness has assured me that the world will be improved immensely as soon as the Christians and unconverted Jews are eliminated, but as long as His Holiness is mocked and not worshiped, death and misery will come to the disobedient," said Simon.

Unexpectedly before Simon, Carlo, and the cameras, Moses and Elijah appeared dressed in sackcloth. Moses faced Carlo and pointed his finger at him saying, "You are an abomination to the Lord! Those that follow you will suffer the bowls of God's wrath that will be poured out from this time forward."

Elijah turned to the cameras. "The Lord wants you to repent before it is too late. The end is coming swiftly, and you will be lost for all eternity! Come back to Jesus and He will forgive you."

Simon could feel the power surging through his body. He stood and faced Moses and Elijah. Moses pointed to Simon. "Woe unto you! May the worm never die within your body."

Simon's anger was kindled. "I have had enough of you two!" And at this Simon lifted both hands and pointed them at Moses and Elijah. Instantly electricity extended from his palms hitting both prophets in their stomachs and knocking them to the ground. Quickly Simon moved his fat body over both men and pointed his palms at their chests. Fire flew from his hands nearly lifting Moses and Elijah off the concrete. Both men closed their eyes and shook momentarily, and then they were dead.

The world watched this from their television sets and cheered as Simon stepped back from the two prophets, revealing their dead bodies. "Throw them in the street!" Simon shouted. The sense of power flowing through his body had affected his mind. He felt euphoric and all-powerful. He had become a god himself. Carlo beamed! He was obviously satisfied with the job Simon had done.

Moses and Elijah were dragged into the street by two security guards. Their lifeless bodies lay before the temple, visible to the entire world through the cameras' lenses. "I declare a festival today and throughout the rest of the week," said Carlo with a smile. "The evil among us has been destroyed!"

At that very moment every non-believer in the world and those following Carlo experienced intense pain as their bodies broke out in large, bloody sores. Simon rubbed his forehead and wiped away a spot of blood that sat atop a grotesque sore. A bowl of God's wrath had been poured out on the people, never to be removed.

Regardless of the boils on Simon's body, he was determined to make one more stop before he returned to Victoria and his precious Vatican City. Whi Yin would not be glad to see Simon this time.

******

Elisha and Jasmine had crossed the Plains of Esdraelon on their way to Mount Carmel months earlier with people stretched out a mile behind them. They had made a short stop in Haifa for water and whatever food they could rustle up, but feeding over 10,000 people would definitely have to be an act of God. Elisha had been in Haifa as a child, but it looked greatly different back then. The tidal wave that came through the Mediterranean almost two years earlier had all but leveled the region.

Elisha led the people up the 1,800-foot grade to the holy place. Upon entering Carmel he gathered the people around him as he stood on a cliff just above the Turban Cave. "People!" said Elisha. "Today the Lord has delivered us from the evil one. He has commanded that I bring you here to the safety of these caves." Elisha extended his arms wide to reveal the region surrounding Mount Carmel. Although the water level of the Mediterranean Sea had increased greatly, it still fell short of burying the caves under the filthy waters. "Here is where we will live until God directs us to leave."

Jasmine climbed up next to Elisha and looked out at the mass of people. She slid her hand into Elisha's palm and stood there at his side, the wife of a prophet of God.

"Let us pray to the Lord for His blessing and for His protection to sustain us until the return of Jesus Christ," said Elisha.

Thousands of people knelt on the rocks and sand and began to pray loudly to Yahweh. Silently Elisha prayed that God would give him the guidance to handle such a large crowd of people.

******

Months had gone by since Elisha moved his people to Carmel and, on this particular morning Elisha and Jasmine exited El Wad, the largest of the many caves occupied by Elisha's people. Daily their routine included bathing in a nearby stream that had mysteriously appeared within days of taking up residence in the caves. After bathing Elisha and Jasmine would kneel facing the morning sun and pray to God for wisdom and strength for the day. After this they usually took a short stroll simply to be alone with each other. The crowded caves made it very difficult to have any quality private time.

Jasmine knelt beside Elisha as they prayed. Suddenly she began to hear a loud roar coming from above them. "What is that noise?" Jasmine asked.

Elisha was deep into fellowship with the Lord and had not noticed the noise initially. Now, however, he looked up towards the caves to see masses of people pouring out. There was a lot of emotion and confusion as they exited. "What is this all about?" said Elisha as he stood.

Almost immediately Elisha was overwhelmed by thousands of angry, crying people. "What is the matter?" he asked as the crowd began to push dozens of people forward to him. They were men and women of various ages, and all of them were trying to turn and run in the other direction. "Stop!" he yelled.

The crowd froze as Elisha closed the gap and began to walk towards the men and women that had been dragged out of the caves. When Elisha approached he noticed horrible, bloody sores covering the faces of these people. "What is this?" he asked.

Jasmine stood next to him. "Why do they have sores on their faces?"

"It is the mark of the Devil!" one man shouted.

Elisha turned and looked at the man. "How do you know this?" he asked.

"It is in the book of Revelation. It is the first bowl of God's wrath. These sores are on those who have taken the mark of the beast or have not yet accepted Christ as their savior."

"Is this true?" Elisha asked as he looked to the infected group. "Have you taken the ID tags?"

Many cried out, "No!"

"Then why do you have sores?" Jasmine asked suspiciously.

"Have you accepted Christ as your savior?" Elisha inquired.

"Yes!" they cried all except one young woman.

"How about you?" Elisha asked as he pointed towards the woman.

"No!" she moaned. "I have not asked Jesus into my life yet."

"Why not?" Jasmine asked sternly.

The young woman looked at Elisha and broke down. "I want to know Jesus. I want to love Him, but how? I was never taught that He was the Messiah. I never knew He was the Son of God until now."

"Why are you here then?" Jasmine inquired.

"Because Carlo defiled God's temple. He is evil."

Elisha looked at the young girl who could not have been more than a couple of years younger than Jasmine. "Do you want to make a commitment to Christ right now?" he asked.

"Yes, but how?" the girl cried.

"Do you now believe Jesus is the Son of God?" Elisha asked.

The young girl nodded carefully.

"Do you want to follow after Jesus, and are you willing to live for Him and declare Him as Lord of all?"

"Yes!" said the girl.

"Are you sorry for your sins, and do you want Jesus to forgive you and come into your heart?" Elisha asked softly.

"Yes! I am sorry," the young girl lamented.

Instantly her face cleared up and the sores were gone before the eyes of 10,000 witnesses. Elisha turned and looked at the rest of the people whose faces were still covered with sores. The looks in their eyes told the whole story. They were lost forever. "So you have not taken the mark of the beast and you serve Jesus?" said Elisha.

Again they nodded.

Elisha looked at Jasmine with tears in his eyes. He was faced with his toughest challenge ever, and there was no other solution. "Stone them!" Elisha commanded.

The crowd grabbed the sore infested people and began to drag them over to a deep ravine. The unsaved people cried out for mercy from Elisha. It broke his heart to hear their cries, but they were a danger to the camp, and their souls were lost forever. This thing had to be done. In groups of five the people were thrown into the pit-like ravine. Elisha stood at the edge and passed judgment loudly. "You have denied the only God and have taken the mark of the beast, and God's Word condemns you to Hell for eternity for those choices."

Thousands of rocks were hurled in as Jasmine and Elisha looked on. The scene was nauseating. Each time five were killed, five more were added to the pit until all had succumbed to the lethal blows of the heavy, sharp rocks. When it was all over, Elisha gave the order to bury the dead. Then he and Jasmine walked away from the pit and headed northwest towards the sea. Jasmine knew Elisha was in pain, and she understood the decision he had made was the hardest thing he had ever done and undoubtedly the most painful.

When they reached the sea Jasmine put her arms around Elisha and held him as he stared out at the murky water, hot tears streaming down his cheeks. "You did what God wanted. I know it is hard for you, but there are many who are lost."

Jasmine turned Elisha towards her. She stared at him for a few seconds. How could this be the same young man she had met in the back of a military van five years ago? God had reshaped him so greatly. She put her hands on Elisha's face gently. "Right now you feel the same way Jesus feels about those that are lost for all eternity. This is man hardening his heart and defying God. There is nothing you can do about that," she said forcefully. "Your job is to take care of His sheep."

Elisha looked down.

Jasmine pulled his face back up to hers. "Do you understand this, Husband?"

Elisha smiled at Jasmine through his tears. She was so tough and so beautiful at the same time. He knew she was right although he hoped he'd never have to do anything like this ever again. Elisha kissed his faithful wife tenderly and whispered, "What will our lives be like when we get to Heaven? Will you still be my best friend and advisor?"

******

Tommy heard all the bad news from Sara. His heart was grieved as she told him about the two witnesses being killed by Simon and the horrible news that Simon was going to close down the concentration camps. Hundreds of thousands of Christians and Jews who were being held against their will were sure to be killed by the end of this week. Tommy had to find a way to help. He was not supposed to deliver food for three more days, but that would be too late. He had to find another solution.

Tommy tried to convince the two deliverymen he had worked with to make a special run out to Dachau, but neither man was willing. They were very afraid after seeing Simon kill God's prophets. "You do not have the sores. God has protected you, so why are you so afraid?" Tommy asked.

"We have families to care for," said one of the men.

"Well, then at least give me your van and some food so I can go in myself and try to get some of the people out."

"They will catch you," said the other man.

"Maybe," he said, "but I have to try."

The next day Tommy prepared to go to Dachau with the delivery van and the small quantity of food the men had given him. He had no real plan and no way to contact Mueller. The woman and child from Fiji were not going to be hidden in the kitchen for two more days. He just could not wait. Tommy put on his prison uniform and covered it with his overalls as Sara stood by. "I am going with you, Tommy," said Sara.

Tommy looked into his wife's beautiful but worried, pale blue eyes. "No, Sara. You need to stay here and care for Philip."

Sara looked intense as she spoke. "I will not let you go without me and your son. We are a family. We will live and die as one family, and that is all there is to it."

Tommy nodded. He knew she was right. He was most likely going to be caught and killed, and that would leave Sara alone to fend for herself until the end of the seven year tribulation period. It was better for her to go with him and take the same chances.

The security guard at the entrance to the camp was surprised to see Tommy. "What are you doing here? You are not supposed to make a delivery for two more days."

"Change of plans, I guess," Tommy smiled. What German he had learned over the last year or so was barely enough to get him by. His face was covered with fake sores that Sara had applied to make him look as evil as all the rest. "Something about the food going bad if I didn't delivery it today. Maybe it is for one last supper for the prisoners," Tommy laughed.

The guards laughed. "Maybe so," he said as he pushed the button to open the gate.

Tommy handed the guard a small orange and smiled. "I won't be long," he said as he drove past. Tommy turned to see Sara huddled in the back of the van breastfeeding Philip to keep him quiet. *We are never going to get away with this*, he thought.

He opened one side door to the van while Sara hid behind the other. "Stay here and be very quiet," he whispered to her as he grabbed a crate of food.

"What are you going to do?" Sara asked with worry on her face.

"I have no idea!" he said as he shut the van door.

As he walked into the kitchen, Tommy could hear the screams of torture throughout the camp. Oswald was making one final attempt to convert as many as he could. He had three days to torture tens of thousands of people in this camp alone before he would have to start burning them.

Tommy's skin began to crawl at the horrible sound of misery and pain. Tears filled his eyes. He was just one man. What could he possibly do to help these people? He caught sight of Mueller just as he entered the courtyard. Mueller's face was terribly bruised and bloodied. Obviously he had gone through the torture himself. Tommy prayed that Mueller had been strong enough not to give in and receive the ID tag. He walked past the old man and into the kitchen. He set the food down and stood in the center of the room. "God, please help me. I don't know what to do."

"I do!" said a familiar voice from behind.

Tommy turned to see Mueller standing in the doorway. The sun was behind him making his body look almost transparent—kind of heavenly. Tommy ran to him and hugged him. Mueller patted Tommy's back. He, too had greatly missed his friend. "I knew you would come, Son."

"Where is Sara?" Mueller asked.

"She is in the van outside."

Mueller could read Tommy's concerned face. He nodded and said, "Then let's move fast." Mueller ran over to the huge gas stove and turned every knob to full.

"What are you doing?" Tommy asked.

"Creating a diversion." Mueller reached above the stove and grabbed a box of wooden matches. Instantly there was a loud whooshing sound as the gas ignited. Soon all the cupboards were on fire and quickly the flames raced to the ceiling.

"Okay, let's go!" Mueller said as he dropped the box of matches.

Quickly both men ran across the courtyard without being seen. From the corner of one of the crowded buildings they stood and watched as guards finally noticed the fire and began to scramble. "Okay, now what?" Tommy asked.

"Now we walk right out the front door," said Mueller.

Tommy thought the old man had lost his mind, but what choice did they have? Mueller opened the cabin door and shouted for the people to follow him. Again as they passed every building, Mueller gathered the people. Before long thousands were following him and Tommy to the front exit. Tommy rounded the corner as the armed guards were running towards the kitchen. They spotted the massive exodus and raised their guns, but before they could fire, they were attacked by hundreds of prisoners. Quickly they were disarmed and knocked unconscious if not killed outright. By Mueller were the young native woman and her daughter. He held the child's hand tightly for fear she would be trampled as the people rushed out of the prison. Tommy led Mueller over to the van where Sara and little Philip sat watching the scene. Suddenly from behind Tommy could hear the loud noise of rapid gunfire. The prisoners ran off in every direction screaming. Some would escape and find shelter, but most of them would be found and killed before the week was out.

Swiftly Mueller lifted the little girl into the cab of the van as he smiled at Sara. Then unexpectedly a bullet from the rapid fire behind him cut through his spine.

Mueller dropped the child on the seat and slid down the side of the van. Sara let out a scream, and Tommy turned to see his faithful friend—

his surrogate father—dying on the ground. He ran to Mueller as bullets pierced the side of his van narrowly missing Sara and Philip who were inside trying to help the mother and child from Fiji find a place to hide. "No!" said Mueller as he coughed up blood. "There is no time. I'm dead already. Go!"

Tommy's eyes burned as he looked at his dying friend. The scene was total chaos as people ran screaming in every direction. On the ground were numerous bodies as more guards quickly advanced. Mueller closed his eyes for the last time as he saw Tommy climb into the cab and speed away.

Five blocks later Tommy ditched the van and headed down an alleyway towards a neighborhood where he knew there would be safe homes that he could hide in. He could hear the sirens blaring throughout the streets as police and Special Forces hunted for the escaped prisoners. Tommy's first stop was a small house where he had met an elderly couple many months earlier as he and Sara struggled to survive on the streets with a brand new child. These two had sheltered them until they could get connected to the underground Christian network. Tommy tapped on the door lightly and soon an old, white haired man stepped out. "Tommy," he said with a frown as he noticed the sores on Tommy's face. Sara saw the man's concerned stare and quickly turned towards Tommy and wiped his face with her sleeve.

"Just makeup to fool the guards," she said.

"I'm glad to hear that," said the old man.

"Max, we need your help," Tommy said.

The old man's smile changed into a look of concern. "What is it, Tommy?"

Tommy stepped aside and revealed the woman and child from Fiji. "These two have just escaped from Dachau, and they need a place to stay."

Max smiled at the young woman and her daughter. "We will take care of them," he said as his wife stepped forward to the door.

"What is it, Dear?" she asked as she looked at the crowd outside her house.

"We are going to have a couple of visitors," Max grinned.

"Well, won't that be nice!" said the old woman.

"Tommy, how about you, Sara, and little Philip come inside also?" asked Max softly.

"Thank you, Max, but Sara and I need to get back to our own house. Please just take care of these two."

"You have my word," said Max as he ushered the two people into his home.

"God bless you both!" Sara said as she and Tommy moved away from the door. The young woman and her daughter smiled at them as the door closed, securing them in safety.

Forty-five minutes later Tommy and Sara were within two blocks of their home when abruptly they heard the squeal of tires. Tommy turned around just in time to see two vehicles approaching from both side streets. There was little chance he could escape, and with Sara and the baby there was no hope. The last thing Tommy wanted to do was run towards his safe house, endangering the others that were hiding and watching as this entire scene unfolded.

******

Oswald was the first to be notified that Tommy and Sara had been captured. By this time next week each camp would be empty and every prisoner executed. Now that Tommy was in custody, he could turn his attention back to the United States where he had heard rumors of small revivals breaking out. "Take them to the Federal Building in Rome so that when Simon gets back from China he can see what we have found. I will fly there myself today and take charge of them," said Oswald.

Chapter 13: The Celebration Ends

Day 1803, August: Raymond grabbed his papers and headed across the campus. He needed to get to Carlo's chamber. *No, strike that*, Hyder thought, *Simon's chamber.* He was to give his usual state of the world report which today consisted of droughts, droughts, and more droughts. The only good news he had to report was that the supplies for the International Space Station had been rocketed towards the moon. All had gone well. Now if the station could just manage to retrieve these supplies—provided they were not already dead for lack of oxygen or water. Without radio contact no one could be sure what was going on up there.

Upon entering Simon's chamber Raymond was surprised to see Oswald sitting in Simon's—*no, Carlo's*—big, golden chair. Kneeling before him was a young man and with him was a woman carrying a small, whimpering child.

"What can I do for you, Dr. Hyder?" Oswald inquired.

Raymond noted the grotesque sores all over Oswald's face and began to scratch the painful sore on his own forehead. "I have an appointment with Mister Koch."

"Yes, well, Mister Koch had some unexpected business in China." Oswald smiled. He knew that by now Simon would have killed Whi Yin which, in fact, he had—with the help of his security guards and semiautomatic weapons.

"Oh, sorry! I guess I will come back tomorrow," said Hyder.

"That will be fine," Oswald said patronizingly.

"By the way, I'd like you to meet some fellow Americans. Come closer," Oswald said as he waved to Raymond. "This is Tommy Glover and Sara

Allen. They are responsible for escapes in Mauthausen and Dachau. They are also the originators of the underground scientist network. They are the ones who have polluted the world with all those lies about the ID tags."

Raymond stepped up and looked at Tommy, Sara, and the little baby. His heart was heavy. The brave couple was surely in trouble now.

"I've just been explaining to Sara and Tommy what they can look forward to when Simon gets back. In particular, I am sure Simon will like Ms. Allen here. After all, she is a pretty thing."

Raymond felt sick to his stomach at the thought of Simon abusing this woman. "What are you going to do with them tonight?" Raymond asked.

Oswald licked his lips. "Well, I was thinking about locking this one away downstairs," said Oswald as he pointed to Tommy. Raymond had heard that there was a jail cell downstairs, but he had never toured the headquarters before. "And this one!" said Oswald as he grinned at Sara, "I think I will take her with me for the night." Obviously he had an attraction for Sara.

"That sounds like fun," said Raymond as he looked into the angry and frightened faces of Tommy and Sara.

Oswald was surprised to hear that the college professor liked his idea. He had thought of Raymond as an introverted bookworm and not as a man overly interested in pretty women. "My only concern, however," said Raymond casually, "would be how mad Simon will be when he hears that you slept with Sara before he gets his chance. But I am probably wrong. I am sure Simon is close to you and will understand fully," said Raymond nonchalantly.

Oswald's eyebrow rose at the thought of Simon getting mad at him. After all, he did suffer another breakout in one of his concentration camps. This time there were still more than 480 people unaccounted for. *Maybe Dr. Hyder has a good point*, thought Oswald.

A few hours later Raymond sat quietly in his room pondering Tommy and Sara. How heroic they had been to avoid Simon for so many years. And they didn't just avoid him—they also caused him a great deal of trouble. Raymond began to consider his own character. What had he done lately that had been noble? In fact, what had he ever done that was worthy in the sight of God?

Dr. Hyder looked at his complexion in the mirror. His face was covered with sores, and sorrow filled his mind. For how long now had he felt the tug on his heart? He knew all the evidence pointed to God—and not just God but God in the form of Jesus Christ, His one and only Son. Raymond began to cry, not only for himself but for the billions that were dead or lost. And he cried for the young man and his wife and child that he had met today in Simon's chamber. By tomorrow those two warriors would suffer and die a horrible and undoubtedly painful death.

"Jesus," Raymond moaned aloud. "Help me! Save me!"

Suddenly Raymond felt a surge of energy flow through his body. He began to shake uncontrollably. He held his hands up to his face and looked in the mirror. To his surprise the sores were completely gone. Dr. Hyder fell to his knees and cried uncontrollably as he thanked the Lord.

******

Sara leaned back against Tommy's chest as Philip lay sleeping across her lap. What an innocent babe—completely unaware that his parents were in the thralls of death. His world was the warm milk of his mother's breast and the sweet sound of a lullaby as he rocked in peace.

Sara kissed Tommy cheek. "Well, we did what we could."

Tommy nearly broke into tears as he considered Mueller lying in a pool of his own blood, and now his precious family who were under his protection were suddenly in a perilous situation. He couldn't think about it. His heart was too full of sorrow.

"Do you think Martha and Harry will come and help us?" Sara asked optimistically.

Tommy had considered this, but for some reason he did not feel they would help this time, and perhaps he would never see either of them again. "I don't know. Maybe," Tommy said.

"It's not dying I am afraid of," said Sara. "I know we are going to be with Jesus. It is the torture and abuse we are likely to face."

Tommy looked into Sara's wet, tired eyes. He knew the torture for Sara would be far worse than his own. She was undoubtedly going to be sexually abused and then tortured to death—maybe after he had already been killed which would leave her alone and could only make things worse.

A few minutes later Tommy heard the jiggle of a key in the lock of the door in front of him. As he stood up, he startled Sara who had just fallen asleep from exhaustion. Abruptly the door slid open while Tommy held his breath. He was sure it was Simon. The end had finally come.

Raymond stepped into the cell and stood there staring at Tommy. In his hand was a key that he had killed a security guard to get. "We have to go," whispered a very nervous Dr. Hyder.

"Go where? Who are you?" Tommy asked as Sara held Philip tight to her breast.

"My name is Dr. Raymond Hyder."

"An American?" asked Sara.

Raymond nodded. He felt ashamed that as an American he was working in Rome helping two of the most evil men in the world by giving them earthly predictions.

"Come on—I am going to help you escape," Hyder said nervously.

"Why?" Tommy asked suspiciously.

"Didn't you have sores on your face earlier?" Sara asked.

Raymond beamed "Yeah, isn't it great? I accepted Christ into my heart and look at me now."

Tommy and Sara followed Raymond upstairs and out of the door. Tommy was surprised to see two dead security guards along the way and one more just outside the front door. "Did you do this?" Tommy asked.

"Yeah, I hope Jesus doesn't mind. I am glad that it is Saturday or there would have been three times as many guards here. As it is they all disappear whenever Simon is out of town."

"How did you kill them?" Sara asked. "I don's see any wounds."

Raymond pulled out a large, handheld object. "With this!"

"What is it?" Tommy inquired.

"A hopped up stun-gun," said Hyder.

Raymond took Sara and Tommy directly to his car and stopped. "I've had this filled with gas. There are blankets, food, and water in the back."

"Aren't you going with us?" Tommy asked.

Raymond smiled. "No, I have more work to do. Besides, you'll have a better chance without me. I can run interference from this end for a while."

Sara kissed Raymond's cheek and Tommy shook his hand firmly. "God bless you!" said Tommy with a bright smile.

******

Raymond could hear Simon yelling at Oswald all the way down the hall as he approached the chamber for his meeting. His vest pocket was nearly bulging as he entered the chamber and stood before Simon.

Oswald was glad to see Hyder. It would be a diversion for Simon, but Raymond could tell by the hateful look in Simon's eyes that he was not glad to see him. Suddenly Simon got a surprised look on his face as he studied Hyder. Raymond began to squirm where he stood. Simon looked at Oswald. This was confusing for a few second until Oswald finally figured out what Simon had taken note of.

Although Raymond Hyder was a brilliant scientist, he was a poor makeup artist. The fake sores he had applied to his face were starting to run down his cheek. Oswald smiled brightly. He was off the hook. Some-one in Simon's own administration had betrayed him.

"So!" said Simon brightly. "What do you have for me today, Dr. Hyder?"

Raymond could tell that something was going on but he was not sure what. "We are out of water in nearly every country. All the great rivers have dried up."

"Well, by the time this war gets over, we won't need nearly so much water." Simon was referencing the fact that so many people were dying daily. Even he and Carlo had not expected such a loss of life. Carlo's kingdom was shrinking every time a rifle was fired or a bomb was dropped.

"What else?" Simon asked nonchalantly.

"Good news. We've put a rocket into space, and it is headed for the space station. They should see it any day now," Raymond put on a fake, unconvincing smile.

"That's great!" said Simon. "By the way, did you get a chance to meet our guests from America?" Simon asked.

"Yes, I did," Raymond said cautiously. "I met them two days ago—right here, in fact."

While Raymond was talking to Simon, Oswald was reaching into the back of his coat to locate his revolver.

"So tell me, Dr. Hyder," said Simon, "when and where did you get your ID tag?"

Raymond swallowed hard just as a little bit of his makeup dripped onto the end of his nose. Hyder went cross-eyed for a second to look at his melted disguise. All of a sudden he knew he was caught. The smile left Simon's face and was quickly replaced by a vicious look of rage. "Where are they?" Simon roared.

Raymond trembled as he reached into his pocket to pull out his altered stun gun. Just as he pointed the lethal weapon at Simon, Oswald fired a shot into Hyder's chest. Raymond's finger pulled the trigger as he fell backwards. The stun gun nearly took Simon's head off as the electricity flew by him and Oswald. If both men had not jumped out of the way as Dr. Hyder fell, they certainly would have been killed.

Simon stood over Raymond and looked down on his dying face. "Where are they?" Simon screamed. Dr. Raymond Hyder just smiled and closed his eyes for the last time.

******

The celebration continued around the world. For three days now Moses and Elijah lay dead in the street. Throughout the larger cities the streets were packed with evil people. Large television screens had been placed in numerous locations so the people could occasionally look up and see the prophets of God lying dead before Carlo's new temple in Jerusalem. All kinds of wickedness was to be had. Most were drunk or under the influence of drugs. Many had captured Christian witnesses and had tortured them to death for the sake of entertainment. In Rome alone 30 Christians had been captured and dipped in oil. They were raised up on long poles and ignited, used as human torches to light the night sky as the party raged on. Witchcraft and all sorts of sexual perversion were being practiced openly as the people from every part of the globe mocked Moses, Elijah, and the God that had sent them to earth. They would chant, "What kind of God do you serve that cannot protect you and save you from death?"

Simon lay nestled in Victoria's arms as he stretched out on the sofa watching the spectacle that was being reported live from around the world. He was most impressed with the human candles panning across his television set. *Serves them right,* he thought to himself.

The celebrating frenzy and live broadcast of people having sex in the middle of public streets was very arousing for Simon, much to Victoria's distress. She had been married for nearly half a year now and the novelty had worn off greatly. In fact, Victoria was bored to death. She had assumed that as the wife of the most powerful man on earth she would be attending all sorts of special functions where she would be exalted. Instead, however, she found herself locked away in Simon's apartment as if she were an expensive jewel only to be taken out and looked at once in a while. Additionally it had been months since Victoria had seen Carlo, and she desperately missed His Holiness. It was unlikely, however, that she would see him soon since Simon went out of his way to keep Carlo a safe distance from his beloved wife.

After killing Moses and Elijah, something in Simon had changed. He was still a man, but somehow he understood that he had defeated the true God. He had beaten Him by killing His two witnesses. Simon now had a new faith that there would be life after death and that he would always be powerful and important—immortal.

"Would you like something to eat?" Victoria asked casually. She was looking for any excuse to get off the couch and away from Simon. She was tired of looking at the two dead guys in the street, and she was afraid that the news coverage would pan to another orgy, exciting Simon all over again. She just couldn't t take one more sexual encounter with this disgusting toad of a man, at least not tonight.

"We have servants for that," said Simon. "If you are hungry, I will have them get you whatever you want," he smiled.

What Victoria wanted they could not get, and if Simon knew, he would kill her. "Sweetheart, I am fine. I was just worried about you," she said with a forced smile.

This gesture touched Simon's little, black heart and he began to kiss Victoria passionately. *What have I done now?* she wondered. Simon began to work himself into a sexual state once again.

******

Carlo walked through the lonely, empty temple. He had not slept well all night. Something was bothering him, but he was not sure what it was. Oh, he appreciated the celebration in his honor. It seemed the people were finally coming around, but somehow, there was a feeling in the air. Something bad was about to happen. Carlo wanted to go back to Babylon to his precious palace, but he could not leave Jerusalem until the festival in his honor was complete.

• Carlo walked out of the temple and onto the large marble platform just in front of the main entrance. From here he could see people still dancing and singing in the streets. He could see massive amounts of television equipment around Moses and Elijah. Carlo knew their lifeless bodies were being turned into trillions of tiny airwaves and sent out for all to see.

A cool breeze blew across Carlo's face, moving his perfect hair askew. He was grateful for the improvements in the weather lately. The cold was ancient history. The world or much of it had also survived the horrible heat wave. They had even survived the pitch-blackness that had come over the planet.

Carlo also considered that the people before him and around the world had survived the plague, starvation, asteroids, meteorites, drought, and now a raging war that even seemed to be out of his own control. *Maybe now,* thought Carlo, *maybe now that these two men are dead, I can begin to rebuild my planet so my people can worship me freely.*

Another cool breeze blew past Carlo. He looked up into the early morning sky to see just a hint of a dark red sun moving up from the east. Like a shadow sweeping across a sidewalk, Carlo watched the sun's rays panning across the crowds of people. Next these rays swept over the camera crews and finally they positioned themselves directly atop Moses and Elijah's corpses. Carlo had a sensation in the pit of his stomach as he strained to look at the lifeless bodies that now had a golden aura about them due to the intense sunray.

Suddenly the ground beneath Carlo's feet began to reverberate. In fact, the entire surface of the earth began to shake. People from every country looked at the televisions and large screens only to see the golden aura surrounding the two witnesses. The sight was frightening.

Simon himself looked up from where he lay beside an irritated Victoria. What he and the rest of the world observed was truly terrifying. The sunlight hovering over Moses and Elijah parted into two halves. A column of blinding, white light streamed down on their lifeless bodies. Then suddenly Moses began to stand, and soon after Elijah stood beside him. On their faces were determined looks of great power and awesome peace. Elijah and Moses looked directly at Carlo who simply stood there with his mouth open. "Your time is short!" said Moses. His voice somehow carried the distance to where Carlo stood. Additionally, all people received his message as it traveled the airwaves around the world.

Abruptly Moses and Elijah began to levitate as if they were in a great transparent elevator. They climbed through the sky as the cameras captured the event. Up they went until they were barely visible to the eye. Then miraculously the sky parted wide open and Moses and Elijah entered Heaven. Soon the sky closed itself off again as the people stood in awe and fear.

******

"What's that?" Teresa Reed asked as she pointed out into space.

Petra leaned in towards the thick glass of the cockpit of the space station. "I'm not sure," he said as he switched on his proximity radar.

Instantly a loud beep could be heard throughout the cockpit just as Bob Powell entered. "Are we going to run into something?" Bob asked.

"No," said Teresa, "but there is something out there."

Teresa picked up the microphone and began to page Samuel Pearlman to come to the bridge. A couple of minutes passed and then Samuel, Skip, and Shila entered the cockpit.

"What is it?" a worried Shila asked.

"Samuel, come look at this," said Teresa. "What do you make of it?"

Samuel studied the object and then turned to Teresa and smiled. "You know how I told you we had maybe two weeks worth of water and maybe a month's supply of oxygen?"

Teresa nodded.

"Well, unless I've missed my guess, I'd say our worries—at least for the time being—are over."

"A care package!" smiled Skip.

Bob Powell patted Samuel on the back. "I wonder who sent it. I'd like to shake his hand."

Capturing the payload was a nightmare for the space station. They only had two boosts of thruster left—all of maybe 10 seconds of available power. On their first attempt they overshot the payload as it went zipping by them at 17,000 miles per hour. "Okay, we missed that time," said Teresa, "but we have enough fuel for one more quick burn."

All eyes were instantly on Samuel. "We need your best guess, Samuel. When do we light this thing up, and for how long?" Teresa inquired.

Samuel sat down to a calculator and a piece of paper for nearly 15 minutes. If he failed to get this right, everyone would die within the next few weeks. Shila chewed at her fingernails as she watched the brilliant little man calculate equations that she could not even recognize.

"Okay," said Samuel, "here are the coordinates as best I can figure. As soon as we see the payload pass this point on the radar we will start counting, and when I tell you, we will burn for exactly four seconds. If we burn for three or five, we will miss the payload by a quarter mile and it will continue to pass by us as we sit here and die of dehydration or lack of air—whichever comes first."

"Well," said Petra, "I guess if we all die, it's your fault then."

Bob scowled at Petra. He had tolerated enough of this man's negativity. "If we die, it is God's will. Samuel has done all he can to keep us alive."

Suddenly the radar beeper went off again. "Mark!" Samuel shouted.

Instantly Teresa hit the timer on the console. "All right, now what?" she asked.

"We go out and get it," said Samuel.

Eventually Samuel gave the order to engage the thruster. After precisely four seconds the jet engine was turned off with less than three seconds of fuel remaining.

Skip and Bob operated the remote control arm as it extended into space. The first two attempts at grabbing the payload had failed miserably, and each time they missed Shila began to cry. Finally on their third attempt they got a tight hold on the massive object and pulled it towards their docking bag. Once inside all six astronauts began to climb around the frozen object. "There's nearly two year's worth of oxygen tanks on this thing," said Skip.

Teresa smiled. "Yeah, and enough packages of food to last for a long time—and frozen water too!"

Samuel was a bit more somber during the celebration. He realized that all of this was merely a temporary fix. They were still lost in space, and the mere fact that this payload was sent to them instead of a space shuttle said it all.

"What's this?" said Skip as he held up a VHS tape he had just removed from a small metal container.

"Looks like a message from our benefactor," said Teresa with a smile.

Chapter 14: Back to the United States

D ay 2100, May: Cory lumbered forward with a bunch of small white flowers. The sun was just coming up over the flatlands of Point Hope. He stopped and looked down. Softly he spoke, "It's spring time again, so I picked you some pretty flowers." He bent down and began to pull away the fireweed that had grown around Leasa's headstone. Gently he placed the handful of little white daisies at the base of the stone. The inscription read: *Here lies Leasa Moore's body.* Her heart and spirit are in Heaven with Jesus.

Cory wiped the tears away from his eyes and knelt before the headstone. With his eyes closed he drifted back to the last days of Leasa's life. The medicine Jerry had given to control the PCP was no longer working, and Leasa was very weak. Often she would become delirious as if she were talking to her father and mother. It was a very sad situation. Cory knew Leasa's past. He knew that she had run away from home as a teenager never to see her parents again. He knew that her drug habit and work as a prostitute had eventually led to her contracting HIV.

Cory stayed by Leasa's side night and day with virtually no sleep. Occasionally she would wake up and smile at him. When she was coherent she would ask Cory to read to her from the Bible. Just the sound of his voice reassured her that all would be well eventually, but it pained Leasa to see Cory grieving so much over her impending death.

"Tell me about Heaven," Leasa asked with a smile.

"I don't know much about Heaven," said Cory sadly.

"Then tell me what you think it will be like," said Leasa reassuringly.

Cory took a deep breath. "Well, first, I know Jesus will be there, and so will my grandmother." Leasa had heard Cory talk about the woman who had raised him from childhood. She knew he loved her dearly. "Next," said Cory, "I think we will get new clothes—nice and white. There is going to be a lot of good food to eat and no indigestion." He laughed.

Leasa looked up into Cory's dark and tired eyes. "Cory, do you think God has forgiven me for all the bad things I've done?"

Cory stared at the sweet young lady. As a tear rolled down his face, he leaned in and kissed Leasa softly. "I am sure of it!" he whispered.

Leasa smiled. "Me too! I asked Him to forgive me, and I know He has."

On the third day of Leasa's most recent bought with pneumonia, six months after Cory and Jerry had left, she awoke late in the evening with a choking cough. Cory was asleep on the floor by her side. Suddenly the choking sound caused him to get up in time to see Leasa gasping for air.

"I'm scared!" said Leasa.

Cory climbed into Leasa's bed and picked the young woman up and held her tightly in his arms. Through Cory's loud cries he told Leasa that he loved her more than any person he had ever known.

Leasa coughed out the words, "Cory, I love you with all my heart. I will see you in Heaven." She smiled weakly through her own tears as she closed her eyes for the last time.

Exactly six months to the day, just as Jerry had said, Leasa Moore left earth for an instantaneous trip to Heaven. Cory held her lifeless body for hours, crying.

Finally he got some towels and washcloths and cleaned Leasa up as best he could. He dressed her in a pretty outfit he had gotten from one of the women at Point Hope. The town council knew Leasa was deathly ill, so they took it upon themselves to select a gravesite. They even carved the headstone based on Cory's input. Leasa was buried the next day as hundreds looked on. Cory read from 2 Timothy 4:7 "'I have fought the good fight, I have finished the race, I have kept the faith.'"

Now as Cory knelt over Leasa's gravesite, his thoughts drifted to Calvin and Jerry. They were only supposed to be gone for five or six months, but more than a year had passed. Cory was worried that his friends were also dead. He felt so alone and useless there in Point Hope. "God, protect my friends and bring them back to me," he said softly.

******

Calvin stumbled forward as Jerry grabbed his arm. The exhaustion was simply more than he could endure. He and Jerry had been locked up in Kolyma, a Siberian gulag, for more than six months. This place was a death trap brought into existence by the Cheka government as far back as the early 1900's. Millions had lost their lives in this ungodly place. The temperatures in this part of Siberia often dropped to 90 below zero. Kolyma was located in the city of Magadan and was referred to as the Golden Ring because of the gold ore that was continuously dug out of the mines of this region. Of course, this gulag was nothing more than modern day slave labor. Often people were falsely accused and, as a punishment, they were sent to this or other remote places where they would live out their lives working under the worst of conditions for their Communist government.

Joseph Stalin was the master of this form of slave labor. While he controlled Kolyma and the other camps, he managed to build the White Sea Baltic Canal, the Moscow Volga Canal, and the Trans-Siberian Railroad. Subsequent to Stalin's demise the death camps began to close down. Kolyma closed in the mid-1950's only to be opened up again two years ago at Oswald's request.

Jerry and Calvin seated themselves on a large rock that had been dislodged from the ceiling of the mine. For nearly 20 hours they had been digging in this place trying to recover gold and silver for processing. One of Oswald's goals was to surprise Simon and Carlo with a vast fortune in gold and silver, perhaps even enough to build a treasure city for Carlo. Oswald understood his reward to be great if he could pull this off. Although he had killed all the Christians and Jews in the concentration camps strewn throughout Europe, he did not kill any of the laborers hidden away in Russia. He figured Simon would forgive him after he saw how much gold and silver he had amassed over the last couple of years.

Besides, it was not likely these people could ever be a threat to Simon or Carlo. In fact, they could never escape from such an ungodly place as Siberia.

Jerry looked into Calvin's tired eyes. He was worried about his friend. He knew Calvin could not endure much more. It wasn't so much the hard work and unlivable conditions that were killing Calvin—it was his inability to do the work God had requested.

When Jerry and Calvin left Point Hope, they had flown the shortest route across the Bering Sea and landed in the northeastern part of Russia called Holy Cross Bay, ironically enough. Calvin pulled his pontoon plane into an area where there were already many such planes parked. By all appearances they had been there for many months, maybe even years. To Calvin it seemed logical to hide his own plane among these. *Blend in, so to speak,* he thought.

The people of this predominantly Catholic community greeted Jerry and Calvin warmly. Many of these people had not taken Carlo's mark. Instead they continued to support each other's needs so that none of them needed to purchase goods with the use of an ID tag. The initial appraisal of this community was frightening to Jerry, because virtually all the people he saw had large sores covering their bodies just like those who served Carlo, but it turned out that these people were not serving Carlo. They had seen enough dictators and evil men to last a lifetime. The reason they had sores was because they had not accepted Christ as their personal savior. Oh, they understood God. The Catholics had preached in this region heavily, but during the high point of Communistic rule the Catholic churches throughout Russia had been exiled in favor of the government-controlled Church. A little religion went a long way for the leaders of the U.S.S.R.

So now it seemed that these people were lost. They understood or at least suspected that Carlo and Simon were not all they pretended to be. They were in search of answers and a way to survive this new world government and Simon's Special Forces that patrolled even this remote location.

Calvin and Jerry thanked the Good Lord for sending them to this place. The harvest was ripe and bountiful. The heart of this community was not black like so much of the world. Calvin and Jerry spent months working through Holy Cross and many of the neighboring communities. Those they ministered to continuously met their personal needs. Finally, however, it was time to move to the next location.

Calvin wanted another three-month harvest before he went back to Point Hope for Cory. Calvin missed his dear friend greatly, and just the thought of poor Leasa suffering and dying broke his heart. He had to remind himself over and over again that everything was a temporary state. Soon all would be in the presence of Jesus, and life forever would truly be wonderful—at least for the believer.

Graciously the community of Holy Cross fueled Calvin's plane and gave them an ample supply of water and food for their continuing journey. In return Jerry gave the leaders of the community numerous vials of antidote with instructions on how and when to administer it.

Moving inland to the west Calvin then flew the little yellow plant to Lake Baikal just on the outskirts of the city of Irkutsk.

Once again Calvin moored his plane in among the other pontoon planes. There was no way of knowing how long it would be before he would need the plane again, but he knew he could not get back to Alaska without it.

Irkutsk was not exactly the picnic that Holy Cross had been. This city had been ravaged by the plague, primarily because it was a hub for the Trans-Siberian Railroad and much traffic flowed through this region. Unfortunately for its citizens much of this traffic turned out to be infested people carrying the deadly virus across Russia as they went. The people of this city had numerous, painful sores all over their bodies, yet just like the people of Holy Cross, as soon as they accepted Jesus as Lord and Savior, their sores disappeared and God received the glory.

Calvin and Jerry found the work to be slow and dangerous in these local communities. Often they found themselves living on the streets without a single thing to eat. However, in one community where there was a terrible plague outbreak, Jerry made remarkable headway by administering his antidote to the locals. In fact, nearly every life was spared and nearly all accepted the message Calvin and Jerry delivered: "Repent and accept Christ, hide from Carlo, and do not take the ID tag under any circumstances."

Unfortunately many throughout Irkutsk and Lake Baikal had taken the mark of the beast which was evidence in the fact that their sores did not heal even after listening to Calvin preach. These situations were always tricky because those who did not have sores any longer instantly saw those that did as a real threat. The hearts of those with sores were reprobate. Those converted to followers of Christ wanted advice from Calvin as to what they should do about the black-hearted people who followed after Carlo and Simon.

Jerry looked at Calvin. He, too, wanted to hear this wisdom. Calvin squirmed as he thought through the question. "I guess that wherever possible we should give these evil people as much room as necessary. We need to run and hide until Jesus comes back. This world belongs to evil right now, and we cannot stop that. However," Calvin paused, "if you find yourself hidden away and evil still comes after you, or perhaps resides among you, then you may have to overpower them even unto death."

Calvin was very uncomfortable with his own answer. *Was this God talking or Calvin? Was it his military training showing through? Was this Godly counsel? Does God not say that we should not commit murder, but then if we are righteous before God, yet evil tries to kill us, should we not protect ourselves?* Calvin really didn't know the right answer, nor did he feel a leading from the Holy Spirit.

After three months in Irkutsk and the surrounding communities, it was time for Calvin to return for Cory. Jerry had given out all but a single bottle of remaining antidote. They had converted whom they could and left many new leaders behind to continue the good work. It was time to pay their respects to Leasa and to pick up their faithful friend, Cory. Lately Calvin had felt a burden to return to the United States—not to Alaska but to the lower 48 states.

******

Calvin and Jerry sat back in the warmth of the plane as they flew towards Alaska. The weather in the northeastern part of Russia was dry like the rest of the world, but today for some reason the winds were fierce. Calvin had planned on flying directly to Holy Cross Bay in hopes of getting some more plane fuel. However, the headwind he now faced caused him to reconsider. "We cannot make it to Holy Cross with this wind. We will have to put it on our tail and head south. I think we can make it to this place right here," said Calvin as he pointed on the map of Russia. "Vladivostok."

Two hours later Calvin landed his plane in the Golden Horn Bay right on the edge of an old military complex used during World War II as an outlook to prevent a Japanese invasion. This time there were no other planes to hide among. Instead Calvin drove around the bay until he found a small cove next to an abandoned warehouse. "Okay, we're here," said Calvin.

Jerry looked at Calvin and rolled his eyes. Neither man had the energy to go looking for gas, let alone take all the usual risks associated with meeting new people. "Fill it up, check the oil, and wash the window, please," said Jerry with a laugh. Both men were encouraged by Jerry's sense of humor and climbed out to start their next journey.

Vladivostok was also a community heavily influenced by the Catholic Church. The story was the same for this city. When the Communist government assumed total control over Russia they closed down all Catholic activity, yet after the fall of the U.S.S.R., Vladivostok once again became a community heavily influenced by the Catholic Church—at least until Carlo came on the scene and closed down every church around the world.

Both men entered the city on foot from the east. Like in most Russian cities, there were few black people. Calvin was a rarity and quickly drew attention. This time, however, the attention came from the goons in Simon's Special Security forces. Calvin and Jerry had just entered a small grocery store. Their mode of operation was the same as usual—mingle and watch until they spotted someone who looked friendly enough to strike up a conversation. This time it was Jerry who spotted a teenage girl. She was easy to notice, because unlike most people he had encountered, she did not have any noticeable sores on her face or hands and she was quite beautiful.

Jerry walked up to the woman and smiled. She smiled back and promptly asked Jerry a question in Russian. This was the other obstacle that he and Calvin had endured for many months—the language barrier. They had always been fortunate enough to meet people who could translate into English, but this just didn't seem to be the case this morning. While Jerry stood next to the young girl, Calvin noticed the storekeeper staring back and forth between Jerry and him. Instantly he felt uncomfortable. "Jerry, it's time to go!" said Calvin in a whisper.

"But she doesn't have any sores, so she must be a Christian," said Jerry.

As he spoke these words the young girl smiled brightly and repeated, "Christian—yes!"

Unfortunately she was not the only one to hear Jerry speak these words, for quickly the storekeeper was on the phone speaking Russian to someone. Calvin grabbed Jerry's bony arm and headed for the door. They had only walked half a block when two blue and white vehicles sped their way. From the street corner the young girl watched all of this unfold. The shopkeeper stepped outside, as well, to see how his phone call would play out.

Calvin and Jerry began to run when suddenly a third car raced down the center of the street and cut off the only remaining escape route. Calvin turned to run back towards the grocery store just in time to see the shopkeeper wrestling with the young girl. Calvin stopped dead in the street and held up his hand. Jerry looked at him in total surprise.

"What are you doing?" Jerry yelled.

Calvin continued to watch as the young girl struggled to free herself. Finally she kicked the shopkeeper firmly in his groin, dropping him to the ground. The girl looked at Calvin and then ran away. Calvin smiled and whispered, "May God protect you."

That had happened over six months ago, and now as Jerry and Calvin leaned against the large rock, everything seemed hopeless. They had been sent via train to Kolyma to work in Oswald's gold mine. Both had narrowly survived an incredibly cold but dry winter on no more than four hours of sleep per night and only one meal a day, and if ever they were caught resting as just now, they would lose that very precious meal.

Calvin began to cough. Jerry did not like the sound of it at all. "Are you okay?" he asked.

Calvin could not answer due to the continuous coughing. Soon he was spitting up blood. *That's not pneumonia,* thought Jerry. *It's the plague!*

Many had died in this camp from a plague that had originated in Russia—a plague that Simon had used to further his own reputation as a caring man. Each time a man came down with a cough like Calvin's, he was quickly taken out and shot in order to prevent the spread, although it was a remedy that was not working very well at all.

Jerry felt around in his coverall pocket. He slowly pulled out a small, partially full bottle of pink liquid. This medicine had been confiscated when they were hauled into the local jail in Vladivostok, but for some unexplained reason Jerry found this medicine back in his pants pocket the very morning they were shipped off to this gulag. It must have been due either to a Special Force officer with a conscience—which was unlikely—or an act of God.

Regardless, it was now time to use the remaining medicine. Jerry estimated that Calvin weighed 180 pounds maybe—which was approximately 20cc's of medicine. This was precisely how much of the precious pink fluid Jerry had left. He knew that he, too, would catch Calvin's disease, but there was not enough antidote for two. Quietly Jerry filled his syringe. He was signing his own death certificate, but it did not matter. His friend needed to continue for the sake of Christ's kingdom. Before Calvin could sit upright, Jerry aimed his needle at the base of Calvin's carotid artery and injected the healing drug.

"Ouch!" said Calvin as he reached for his neck. Jerry restrained his hand until all of the precious liquid could be forced into Calvin's body.

"What is that?" Calvin asked.

"Antidote—you have the plague," said Jerry softly.

"No wonder I feel so lousy," sighed Calvin as he looked around at the horror they were trapped in.

Jerry nodded. "It will take some time for this to work, so try not to cough and draw attention to yourself."

Calvin looked at Jerry. "How can I get the plague if I've already had it?"

"You are not immune to it. The medicine only cures you once per infection. It's like the flu. It can come back, and each time it needs to be treated."

"Then you had better take some medicine, too, because you must be infected," said Calvin.

"I must be," said Jerry as he held up the empty vial.

Calvin looked at the bottle and then back to Jerry. "You gave me the last of it?"

"Yes," said Jerry with a smile.

"But why? You are going to die!" Calvin cried.

"If it's God's will, but you have to continue your work, Calvin. Time is running out."

Abruptly the ground beneath Calvin and Jerry's feet began to sway and buckle. There was a deadly silence for a few seconds, and then suddenly a loud roar filled the mine. Men started running and screaming out in Russian. Jerry quickly understood the gist of their behavior. "It's a cave-in!" Jerry shouted as he pulled Calvin up from the large rock where he sat.

Both men ran forward and up the steep embankment. They were down beneath the earth some 1,100 feet. This was the layer that held the precious ore that Oswald so wanted. As the earth shook, the overhead lights went out and it was pitch-black. Soon the oxygen delivery system would not be able to overcome the dust even if it survived the falling debris. The prisoners were going to suffocate or be crushed under the weight of the mountain.

Miraculously, however, Jerry and Calvin continued to stumble forward. They managed to avoid the initial cave-in that had trapped hundreds of men, and they avoided the falling rocks, but since it was so dark neither of them knew how close they continued to come to the fatal blows.

Small specks of light began to shine into the cave as the two men approached the exit to within 50 yards. "We're going to make it!" said Jerry.

Twenty feet more and the whole side of the cave fell in towards Jerry as he let out a yell. Jerry was buried under a mountain of rubble. Calvin stopped to rescue his trapped friend when all of a sudden a bright light filled the cave. "Do not stop, Calvin. You must leave this place."

Calvin recognized the voice. It was the same one that had commanded him to leave his friend atop Mount Denali six years earlier. To this day Calvin hated himself for not trying to save his buddy. There was no way he was going to make the same mistake twice. "I won't!" said Calvin. "I won't leave my friend to die."

Even though Calvin realized that soon Jerry would die a painful, miserable death from the plague, still he would not leave his friend trapped without at least trying to save him.

"Calvin," said a soothing voice. "He is not there anymore."

Calvin began to cry. "I have to try. I have to!"

"Calvin!" said another voice.

"Jerry, is that you?" he asked.

"I love you, Calvin. Now leave this place and go back to Cory. I am safe forever."

"Thank you, Jerry—for everything!"

Calvin rushed out of the mine and into the bright sunlight. For a minute or so he could not see a thing. Finally he heard a train whistle bleating out. *The train,* thought Calvin, *maybe I can catch the train.*

Little did Calvin know, the Trans Siberian train was heading for the end of the track which happened to be at the edge of Golden Horn Bay in the city of Vladivostok. This was where all of Oswald's precious ore was delivered and processed into beautiful gold and silver bars.

So many of the guards were trapped in the mine and others running in various directions that nobody saw Calvin run across the open field and jump onto one of the large ore boxes. For the next 17 hours Calvin huddled in the corner of the boxcar and slept. The antidote was working to heal his diseased body, but only time and rest could heal his fatigue.

The inertia of the boxcar slowing down woke Calvin. Carefully he peered over the side of the boxcar. What he saw he immediately recognized as Vladivostok. "God," said Calvin, "thank You for bringing me back here safely, but God, I still need gas for my plane. Please help me!"

Calvin climbed down from the back of the boxcar and ran quickly into the surrounding woods. He could not show his face in town again or he would be captured for sure. Everyone would remember the one and only black man to enter their town in recent times. He walked slowly around the Golden Horn Bay. The sun was just starting to set. This probably would have been a beautiful sight in the past, but now the Bering Sea was just as polluted and dead as the rest of the oceans.

He had noted the same condition in the Artic Ocean during his first stop at Holy Cross Bay. Finally Calvin made his way to the cover where he had hidden his plane. From the backside he could see the old, gray warehouse. Another 50 feet and he would be able to see his plane, but still how was he ever going to fly away without any gas?

Calvin walked past the warehouse and down the steep slope towards the water. Panic filled his heart! His plane was gone. "Dear Lord, what now?" he called up to Heaven as he continued to walk towards the location where he had parked his plane.

As he approached his eyes caught sight of a small, white piece of paper. Calvin bent down and picked it up. It was neatly folded. Slowly Calvin opened the note. To his surprise it was written in English. "We heard of you from our friends in Holy Cross. We know you have been taken away to the gulag, but we are trusting God that you will return. When you do return, locate the sign on the front of the old building and turn it over. Wait and we will come."

Calvin looked up to the gray building, and to his surprise there was a large sign with a picture of Stalin in the center. Calvin climbed the bank and ran towards the sign. Quickly he lifted it from the hook that held it and turned it over. On the backside was the skeletal outline of a fish painted with bright red paint. Calvin laughed as he re-hung the sign.

Two very long, hungry days went by before someone finally came by.

Calvin was asleep inside the old warehouse when he was awakened by the sound of the large, squeaky door opening. From his own experience he knew this would be a great warning alarm in case anyone tried to sneak up on him. To Calvin's surprise the young Russian girl he had seen in the grocery store walked into the warehouse with two men. Calvin was nervous. Either these people were Christians, or he was about to get sent back to Kolyma which was more than he could bear. "Mister Fraser," said one the men as they approached.

Calvin stood but did not say anything.

"We are Believers. It is okay."

The young girl smiled at Calvin.

"I am Calvin Fraser."

******

Cory arranged the flowers and propped them up against Leasa's headstone. Just then he heard the noise of a plane. Quickly he looked up in time to see Calvin dip his wing and nose the plane down towards the near-empty riverbank.

Cory began to run towards Calvin's landing site as tears streamed down his cheeks. Calvin was hardly out of the cockpit before the big man grabbed him and hugged him nearly tight enough to break all his ribs. "I am so glad to see you!" said Cory as he looked into the cockpit, expecting to see Jerry.

"Jerry?" Cory asked.

"He's in Heaven," said Calvin. "Leasa?"

"She's in Heaven too," Cory whispered.

Both men hugged and cried as they walked up the bank and back towards Leasa's gravesite.

******

Simon read the latest field reports from his office in Rome. The shear magnitude of the numbers was hard to grasp—300 million people dead from a useless war that had lasted a year longer than anticipated. Simon knew that Carlo would call soon for the latest update. He would want to know how many oilfields had been captured. He would want to know how many people had died, and he certainly would want to know when it was going to be over.

Simon was at a loss to explain why this war was going the way it was. He had given clear directions to his generals, and twice now he had killed and replaced these leaders as they failed to carry out orders. The excuses were always the same. Things just didn't seem to play out as they ought to. What Simon did not understand was that there were four demons in charge of this war, and until they completed their desired task of killing one third of all unsaved mankind, they would not stop nor could even Satan himself stop them.

Simon's office phone rang loudly. He considered not picking it up, but he knew that he could not duck Carlo much longer. "This is Simon."

"Where have you been?" Carlo demanded.

"I've been right here!" said Simon.

The fact was that ever since Simon saw the two witnesses raised from the dead, he had developed a new sense of fear. His confidence was at an all time low. Lately he spent most of his time home with Victoria trying, he supposed, to live out the rest of his life enjoying what he truly loved before it was taken away from him. He could not stop this war nor could he catch all of the Christians who still plagued the world. *How can you fight against a force that is not afraid to die for their beliefs?* Simon wondered.

"I want you in Babylon tomorrow," Carlo growled, "and bring Victoria."

Simon's heart sank. *Not Victoria—not again!* screamed his aching mind.

******

Victoria could hardly contain herself during the plane ride to Babylon, although she played it down very well for Simon's benefit, of course. However, to Victoria this was a much-needed vacation away from her disgusting husband. He was spending far too much time with her. Meanwhile it had been nearly a year since she had seen Carlo in person.

Simon and Victoria were escorted to the garden area of Carlo's palace. Simon looked at all of the hanging plants. He had to admit it was an incredible spectacle, and he hated every bit of it.

"Simon!"

Simon turned to see Carlo walking down a garden path full of flowers and green shrubs. The irony was that the rest of the world was dry as an old bone and virtually all plant life had died over the last couple of years from cold, heat, or drought.

"Good to see you made it okay," said Carlo without taking his eyes off Victoria.

Simon understood the gesture Carlo was making, and he also understood that Victoria was returning the gesture. Hate filled his little black heart. If he could not possess Victoria alone, then he would have to contrive a way that nobody else could have her either.

"Victoria, go into the palace. Simon and I have important matters to discuss," said Carlo softly.

Victoria seemed legitimately disappointed to leave Carlo's side, but she was one to know her place—at least most of the time.

"Simon, walk with me!" Carlo commanded.

They walked past the numerous statues of Carlo. The sight of these marble statues made Simon sick and jealous. "My Father has explained to me why we are having so much trouble with this war."

Simon stopped and looked at Carlo intently. "What did he say?"

"It's complicated, Simon, but let's just say that four very powerful angels have deceived the world into killing itself."

Simon hated it when people used the word *complicated* as if he were a moron or something. This was one of the many things he had hated about scientists like Dr. Hyder. They always seemed to know and understand much more than Simon could grasp. "What do we do now?" Simon inquired.

The garden abruptly turned a hazy red color. Soon that usual putrid smell was back and Simon knew that Satan was about to appear. Carlo fell to his knees instantly. For a moment Simon considered standing but then unexpectedly the ground beneath his feet began to shake and he thought otherwise.

"It is time!" Satan declared. "Simon, go to Saudi Arabia today. Stand in the middle of the battlefield and declare the war over." Simon swallowed hard. Satan could not be serious. Stand in the middle of a battlefield where 300 million people had already died?

"I will be killed!" Simon whined.

"You will not be killed!" Satan growled. "I will give you power to display that will convince all to put their weapons down—at least for now."

Right, thought Simon, *just like you gave me power to kill the two witnesses. Well, they didn't stay dead! Besides, what do you mean—at least for now?*

"We have much to prepare for. Soon we will have to fight a great battle, but still there are Christians and Jews throughout the world. They have chosen against my son and me. They must be found and destroyed. There is one in particular, Elisha Kaufman. He has taken many from the nation of Israel out into the desert. He must be found and killed."

Five minutes later Simon was in Carlo's palace to say goodbye to Victoria. This was absolutely the lowest point in his life. Undoubtedly Carlo would be sleeping with his wife before the night was over, and it appeared to him that maybe Victoria liked the idea. Worse yet he was about to step foot onto a battlefield where he was likely to be blown to pieces and all for what—oil?

Victoria pretended to cry as Simon gave her the news, and then after a little reflection on the potential that Simon could really be killed, leaving her a powerless widow, she really did start to cry. Simon was almost moved by this display; however, Carlo was not.

*****

Seven hours later Simon's newly appointed general escorted him into the heart of the battlefield. Simon's hands were shaking and his heavy body was sweating profusely. All around were burned out tanks and destroyed bunkers. Dead bodies lay in piles as if they had been bulldozed to a specific location which, in fact, they had. There were pieces of steel all around, hardly recognizable as the bombers or fighter planes they used to be. Even Simon's general was frightened to be this close to the fighting. "Tell me again. Why are we driving into the heart of the battle?" the general asked nervously.

Simon put on a stern face and pretended not to be afraid. "Because I said so, that's why!"

******

Back in Carlo's palace Victoria enjoyed a hot oil bath and a frosty glass of champagne. She would certainly be dining with Carlo. Then after an exquisite dinner they would adjourn to Carlo's room for more champagne and dessert.

******

Simon's Jeep stopped squarely between three opposing forces. Mortar shells and rifle fire flew at thousands of miles per hour whizzing above Simon's head. "Okay, Satan, I'm here. Now what?"

Instantly Simon felt a strange sensation. His body actually start to inflate as if he were a flat tire that was finally getting a dose of air. Simon tilted his head and looked up at the sky. The feeling in his stomach was getting uncomfortable. He started to feel like he was about to explode.

Satan's prophet opened his mouth wide, and a stream of white and blue particles emerged. These were no ordinary dust particles, but highly charged sub-atomic particles. Soon these blue and white specks began to swirl as they left Simon's mouth. Sparks began to fly and the swirling turned into a huge tornado-like whirlwind.

The advancing forces from all sides witnessed this and ceased their gunfire. Soon the whirlwind turned into a gigantic blue cloud as it swept over each army. Once the soldiers became engulfed in the blue and white stream of light, they began to scream out in pain. Simon continued to stand with his mouth open until the last of the sub atomic particles were expelled from his lungs. By this time the entire battlefield was consumed and incapacitated in a blinding, blue swirl of fiery particles.

Next Simon began to speak, but not in an ordinary voice. In fact, he spoke in multiple languages simultaneously. His voice mysteriously carried to every soldier on the battlefield no matter how far away, and the message was the same: "The war is over. His Highness, Carlo Ventini, will not tolerate any more loss of life. Go home. If you pick up your weapons of destruction again without direction from me, you will be destroyed."

The war was over, and Simon had only one desire—get back to Carlo's palace as soon as possible. He had only been gone for eight hours, and in this time he had accomplished what no one had been able to do in over a year. He stopped the war and took possession of the oil fields of each nation.

When Simon got to the airport, he found out that his private plane was not there. Apparently Carlo was concerned that Simon's plane had gone too long without preventive maintenance. At least that was what Simon was told at the counter. He knew better. He knew that Carlo did not want him to get back to Babylon too quickly. Something had to be done to prevent his Victoria from becoming Carlo's play toy whenever he desired.

******

Tommy walked into the dark living room. The house was so quiet—almost as if he were the only person left alive on the planet. As he stretched out on the old leather sofa and stared out at the nothingness, Tommy whispered, "God, what now?"

It had been nearly six months since Tommy, Sara, and little Philip had returned to the small yellow house hidden away in the wooden forest of Como. After leaving Rome in Dr. Hyder's car, they headed north toward Milan. Tommy understood that Oswald would be right on his tail. He wanted to get as far away as he could, but Tommy knew he had a mission to fulfill. It was not just a matter of survival until the return of Jesus.

There were many out there that still had a chance if only someone could reach out to them with the good news of Christ.

Once Tommy entered Milan he ditched Raymond's car and headed out on foot. It pained him to leave behind all that food and water, but he could only carry so much and Sara had her arms full with Philip.

"Where will we go now?" Sara asked.

"We need to get deep into the city. I am sure Oswald is coming after us by now," said Tommy with anxiety in his tone.

In fact, Oswald was in hot pursuit of Tommy and Sara. He quickly deduced that Hyder had given them his car. He had issued an all-points lookout for the vehicle. Additionally Oswald and a few of his Special Forces headed north as fast as they could. It was an easy choice to assume Tommy would go north considering that virtually nothing existed south of Rome any longer thanks to Mount Etna and Vesuvious. Oswald was angry and worried. He feared what Simon would do to him if he did not catch the two runaways.

Oswald had been alerted that Dr. Hyder's car had been found on the outskirts of Milan. He rushed to that location with his men and climbed through the car looking for any clue that might lead him to where Tommy had gone. When Oswald saw all the food and water in the trunk, he knew that Tommy did not have a specific location to run to. He was simply running. It was obvious that the man took what he could carry and headed into the city to hide. *But where!* Oswald wondered. There were still over a million people living in Milan, primarily because Simon limited the amount of plague virus throughout Italy after his own infection nearly took his life.

Oswald decided to leave the car alone in hopes that Tommy would return for the water that was very scarce or the food that was even more unavailable. Finally Oswald went in pursuit of Tommy and Sara. From store to store and neighborhood to neighborhood he scoured the city night and day. Six months went by and Oswald was completely frustrated. His daily reports to Simon had turned into a dreaded nightmare. "Nothing yet," he would report and then stand back to hear Simon's angry remarks and threats. Oswald made up his mind that if he found Tommy and Sara, he was going to execute them on the spot so they could not escape again.

The day finally came when he received a tip from a local that deep in the center of the city was a small faction of Christians who only came out at night to witness throughout the region. Of course, Oswald had heard this before, but what he hadn't understood until now was that there was a pattern to this ministry.

It was a clockwise ministry that started in a small suburb and stretched out rotationally from town to town every week. "Where were they last seen?" Oswald asked. The local pointed out this information on his carefully detailed map. He had pins placed in each location where he had heard of Christian witnessing. Oswald was amazed at the man's attention to detail.

"Why?" Oswald asked. "Why all this detail, and why have you waited until now to notify us?"

The man answered arrogantly, "Just call it a hobby."

Oswald did not like the man or his answer. He was a rich grocery store owner who had managed to capitalize on the state of the present world. "No," said Oswald, "just call it aiding and abetting." Oswald looked at the newly anxious man and then to his security officer. "Arrest him!"

That same evening Oswald set up a stakeout in the area he suspected the Christians to come. At least if they continued to move clockwise, this was where they would end up.

******

Tommy reached for his coat. It was unlikely that it would be cool, but better to be safe than sorry. For months Tommy had been on the witness tour with a dozen other men and women that he and Sara had met on the third night in Milan. These people gratefully took the couple into their homes and provided for their needs. As a result Tommy was able to witness nightly. God anointed Tommy and when he spoke, people listened. Of course, he had a translator for his words from English to Italian, but the words were still as effective. Many made a decision for Jesus.

At Tommy's request Sara did not accompany him when he went out. This particular evening, however, Sara was determined to go with him and the other people. "I want to go too!" Sara demanded.

Tommy looked into his wife's pretty face. He knew that she had a heart for ministry just like he did, and truly he had no right to refuse her this opportunity. It was just that he wanted to protect her and Philip. Tommy remembered how Sara had demanded to go with him to Dachau and how that turned out to be a good thing.

He would have been captured, likely to never see Sara again. Just the thought caused him to shiver. "Okay, you can come. By now Oswald has probably forgotten all about us."

Sara walked next to Tommy as they rounded the corner of an old abandoned deli. In the distance Sara could hear the high toot of a train whistle. Down the street a couple more blocks, and they would be in the next community. Tommy remembered this place. It was the community he witnessed in on his first trip out with the small band of Christians. *Had that really been six months ago?* he wondered.

Sara paused. "I'm scared!" she said.

Tommy turned and looked into Sara's pretty blue eyes. She clung tightly to Philip and stood still. "Why? What's the matter?" Tommy asked.

"I don't know, but something is wrong," said Sara as she and Tommy watched the others walking toward the heart of the community.

"It will be okay. You're just a little out of practice," said Tommy with a smile.

"Maybe so," Sara sighed as Tommy led her forward. The group was already 50 yards ahead of them.

On both sides of the street staggered over four blocks were numerous Special Forces officers crouched down in their cars. Two blocks ahead of Tommy and Sara was a small blue car in which Oswald and two of his men reclined while looking out their rearview mirror. Over his radio Oswald told each vehicle to stay put until all the Christians were in the center of the neighborhood. At that point it was his intention to turn each car in towards the street blocking off any escape. The streets in this community were made of stone, and they were very narrow. Along both sides were tall rows of old apartment buildings. Occasionally a person or two could be seen moving around outside, but mainly the pedestrian traffic seemed greatly reduced compared to the average neighborhood.

Tommy and Sara walked by the first set of Special Force officers as they made their way to the second block. One of the officers spotted Sara carrying her baby. "It's her! It's them!" he said aloud. A few seconds later the officer reported this information to Oswald. A smile plastered the man's sore infested face.

"Don't anyone move until I say so," said Oswald. *Now I've got you, Tommy Glover*, thought Oswald.

Tommy and Sara made up some of the distance from the other Christians. They were now only 20 yards back and well within the second block. Up ahead one of the young Christian men walked past a small, blue car and decided for some reason to cross the street. As he did he noticed the moon's light flash against the window of the car. He quickly noted that the car's windows were all fogged up. *Somebody is in there*, he thought.

The man turned back towards the car for a closer inspection. By this time Tommy and Sara were within 30 feet of the young man. Looking into the side window of the car, the man was stunned to see three men slouched down with guns drawn. Oswald pointed his gun towards the young man and held up one finger to his lips as if to warn the man, *Say a word and I will shoot you.* The man understood the meaning, but it did not matter to him in the least.

"It's a trap. Run!" He screamed just as a bullet ripped through the side window of Oswald's car and into the chest of the young Christian man. The window exploded, covering Oswald and the other two officers with small chunks of sharp glass.

Instantly Tommy grabbed Sara's arm and began to run back the way he had come, but just as quickly two cars pulled into the middle of the street and shined their bright lights. From the other end four blocks away came other cars quickly cutting off all exits. Tommy turned to see Oswald standing over the man he had just killed. Oswald smiled at Tommy and pointed his gun directly at him. Sara saw this and grabbed Tommy in time to avoid the bullet. She had seen her man shot once before and that was enough. Sara spotted a small opening between two of the apartments. "This way!" she screamed.

"After them!" shouted Oswald as he fired again at Tommy and Sara.

Many of the Christian men and women immediately saw that Oswald was after Tommy and Sara exclusively. Without a moment's hesitation, they began to run interference for them. They tackled Special Security officers and ran in front of them as they tried to pursue Tommy and his family. Gunshots could be heard throughout the neighborhood as the officers began shooting the Christians. From windows all around the community people watched the men and women brutally abused and killed as they tried to prevent the capture of their friends. It was a remarkable witness, revealing the hearts of love that the Christians possessed and the hearts of hate that Simon's men possessed.

Tommy led Sara and Philip from backyard to backyard, heading north the whole time. From 75 yards behind Oswald and one of his men tried to follow. At the end of one long row of apartments there was a small, dry canal bed. Tommy led Sara under the small bridge as they quickly ran the length of the canal. "Give me Philip," said Tommy. Sara handed her son over which gave her to ability to continue the foot race. Tommy took Philip's little hat off and threw it up past the bridge. Again in the distance Sara could hear the distinct sound of a train whistle as she and Tommy ran on.

Oswald's officer reached the bridge first. This run was just too much for Oswald. He was too old for this. As he approached the bridge, he observed his officer pick up a small object. "It's a baby's hat. They went this way," said the man as he pointed past the bridge and down a narrow stone path. Both men ran on in pursuit of Tommy and Sara. They were, however, heading in the wrong direction.

The train whistle grew distinctly louder as Tommy continued north. Finally when he felt sure it was safe to get out of the dry canal bed he stopped and handed Philip to Sara. "You stay here for a few minutes. I'm going to climb out and see what's up there." Sara clutched Philip and prayed to God for help.

A few minutes later Tommy came back with a smile on his face. "What is it?" Sara asked.

"A train station."

They hopped the train just as before and got off in Como. Once again they walked through the forest until they came across the dirt path that led to the little yellow house where they had met Harry and Martha.

******

This morning as Tommy lay on the old leather couch he feared he would never be able to lead others to Christ again. It seemed that the Lord had led him and his family back to the safety of the little cottage outside Como. He appreciated the love and protection of God, but he also knew time was short, and he did not want any people to have their hearts deceived like his poor sister, Tina, had been. It was his passion to lead people to the Lord before it was too late.

Soon Sara entered the living room. "What's the matter?" she asked.

Tommy reached out his arms and pulled Sara down on the couch next to him. Together they lay there in the darkness holding each other.

"What's the matter?" Sara asked a second time.

"Everything!" said Tommy.

"Well, that's helpful," Sara laughed.

"There are people out there that need to hear God's Word, but at the same time we are nice and safe here. Somehow we even have cupboards full of food, but there are millions out there starving or dying from thirst or the plague, and they don't know Jesus." Tommy cried.

Sara held Tommy and stroked his hair. She had her own worries. What would happen to Philip if she and Tommy were to be captured and killed like they nearly were in Milan and Rome, not to mention all the other narrow escapes they had lived through over the years? Sara was also confused and worried about her and Tommy's life after Jesus returned. Would they still be husband and wife? Would they be changed somehow like those that went in the Rapture? Would they live through the millennium as humans in human form? Sara wondered what she would look like after a 1,000 years.

The living room of the small cottage lit up brightly. Both Sara and Tommy sat up expectantly. Soon Philip, the angel, appeared before them. "Blessings from the Lord," said Philip. "God knows your hearts. He knows that you want to spread the Good News to the lost. Tomorrow go to the city, and you will find others from the 144,000. They will welcome your help, but do not leave the city of Como. This is your home now."

Suddenly the room was black as the young couple sat back meditating on what Philip had just told them. "I guess we are home," said Tommy.

If the room had been lit, Tommy would have seen a bright smile and cheeks full of tears on his wife's pretty face.

******

Oswald was back in Rome at Simon's request. He was sure he was about to be replaced and maybe even executed after failing to capture Tommy and Sara once again. Oswald entered Carlo's old chambers which had been permanently taken over by Simon. He observed Simon sitting in the beautiful golden chair. The blank look on Simon's face told Oswald that he had not noticed him enter the room. Perhaps he was in some sort of trance, but for certain he was not the Simon that Oswald was used to.

Simon continued to stare out into space. What he was contemplating was something that he could hardly speak of even to himself. Victoria had obviously slept with Carlo once again while he was in Saudi Arabia risking his life. Neither he nor Victoria spoke about what they both knew to be true, but Simon had made up his mind. If he could not have Victoria alone, then no one would. At first he considered hiding or locking her up so that only he would know where she was at all times. This way he could lie to Carlo and say she ran off, but Simon figured Carlo would see through this deception. That only left him one option, and that was to kill Victoria in order to prevent Carlo from sleeping with her. His jealousy was now his obsession and insanity.

Oswald cleared his throat. This snapped Simon out of his trance. He looked at the old man and was embarrassed and then angry. "Why don't you knock?"

"I beg your forgiveness," said Oswald.

Simon knew the man was depressed and scared. He knew how he felt, because at that very moment he felt the same way. "Where's Glover?" Simon asked. Of course, he knew the answer, but it was necessary as the leader of the world that he let Oswald know that he had failed him once again.

"They got away," Oswald alleged as he bowed his head.

"No kidding! What a surprise," said Simon.

"Forgive me," said Oswald.

If Simon had been in a different mood, he might not have forgiven Oswald, but as it stood today Oswald was his only ally. "I want you to forget about these scientists for the time being. I have a couple of new assignments for you," Simon said wearily.

"What are they?" Oswald inquired.

"There are apparently some Christian activities happening in all 50 states in the United States. I want you to find out what is going on and put a stop to it. Additionally there is a man named Elisha Kaufman out in the desert of Israel somewhere. He has with him thousands of Jews, and Satan has asked me to find him and to kill him."

"What do you want me to do first?" Oswald asked.

Simon thought it over for a few seconds. He wanted to please Satan, but he could care less about the Jews. However, it angered him to hear that extensive Christian revivals were breaking out in the U.S.A. This had to stop right away! "Go to America first."

*****

Simon entered his apartment with a gun hidden away in his trousers. He was greeted rapidly by a number of his servants, but Victoria was nowhere to be seen. "Where's Mrs. Koch?" Simon asked.

"She's in the bath, Sir. Would you like me to get her?" one of the servants asked.

"No!" said Simon as he headed into his bedroom.

Victoria reclined in the hot, scented water. She knew Simon would be home soon, and she wanted to look her best for him. Lately he had been very distant from her, and she knew it had something to do with her and Carlo. She had hoped it would disappear as before, but this time it did not.

She was now worried that Simon was going to leave her. In fact, it had been weeks since he had requested sex from her. This was an obvious sign that she had found disfavor in his eyes. Her usual tricks were not working. She was going to have to develop a more believable plan of attack. She tried to push her desires for Carlo out of her head so she would seem more convincing to Simon.

Victoria slid into her bathrobe and walked towards Simon's bedroom. She was going to survey the room to consider how she might arrange her romantic plan for the evening. As she peeked around the corner she was surprised to see that Simon was already home.

Additionally she was very surprised to see the gun in his hand. Victoria watched carefully as Simon stroked the revolver gently. The look on his face was distant and frightening. Victoria swallowed hard. *This is worse than I thought,* she told herself.

Simon put the gun in the top drawer of his dresser and turned to leave. Victoria backed up slowly and opened her robe as if she had just come from the bathroom. Simon opened the door in time to see Victoria's perfectly shaped, unclothed body as she approached his room for the second time. Her look was very seductive and nearly more than Simon could bear. He, too, understood it had been weeks since he and Victoria had been together. A thought raced through his mind—*May as well have one more night before I kill her.*

With this thought Simon moved into Victoria without a word and began to kiss her passionately. Victoria responded in kind with all she could muster. His wife's passion and affection surprised even Simon. Maybe he had judged her unfairly. He would have to consider this carefully before pulling the trigger.

******

Chris and Joshua trudged along through the stifling heat of the jungle. It had been many months since they had left Ezra and his people at the southern tip of Indonesia. Ezra was content to set up his small village as near the sea as possible without risk of flooding. All of the smaller islands throughout the Timor Sea and all the way up to the China Sea were under water. The only portions of land that remained were in Australia, New Guinea, and southeastern Indonesia.

As Chris walked along he was amazed by what remained of the rain forest of this region. The Cloud Forest, as it was called in Maluku Archipelago, was created out of moss. This moss extended as much as 1,500 meters above the huge eucalyptus canopy. The region from Maluku, Sulawesi, to Nusa Tenggara was known as the Wallacea. This area was known for an incredible amount of rain—in excess of 2,000 millimeters per rainy season. But this was no longer the case. What Chris looked at today was a dead and startling sight. The entire forest was a massive skeleton of what used to be one huge living organism.

Joshua led Chris into Wasur Park, and the two men stopped for a quick rest. There was little concern that any Special Forces would be found in the jungle which was a relief to both of them. They still had the issue of water or the lack thereof, however. "I'm thirsty," said Chris.

"Me too!" said Joshua.

Suddenly Chris heard a dry limb crack and break. He turned quickly to see a handful of very short people rushing through the woods in pursuit of some small animal that up until now had survived the freezing cold, incredible heat, and now this terminal drought. One of the small men looked up in surprise as he spotted Chris and Joshua. With a light whistle he alerted his fellow hunters, and hastily all four men ran off in the other direction.

"I'll bet those guys have water," said Chris with a smirk.

******

A couple of hours later Joshua and Chris had finally cleared the peak of Merkele Ridge. As they stood looking down into Wasur, they noted miles and miles of trails. "Obviously someone lives here," said Joshua. About that time Chris turned to see a large pointed stick flying directly towards Joshua.

"Look out!" Chris screamed as he pulled Joshua to the ground.

"What the heck was that?" Joshua whispered.

"I don't think they want us here," said Chris.

"Well, that's too bad," said Joshua as he stood to face the direction that the spear had traveled from.

"What are you doing?" Chris asked in amazement.

"We come in peace," Joshua shouted as he raised his hands high in the air.

All of a sudden two more spears came flying in. Joshua ducked quickly.

"Maybe they don't speak English," said Chris.

If Joshua had not been so frightened at the moment, he might have found Chris' statement amusing. "God, help us!" Joshua called as another spear came flying by.

Both men looked up to see a dozen natives standing around them with spears extended. "Uh oh!" said Chris.

Just then the ground began to shake lightly, and then Philip appeared standing next to Joshua and Christopher. The native men saw this and dropped to the ground face down.

"Rise," said Philip in a language that neither Joshua nor Chris understood, but quickly each native rose to his feet. "These men have been sent here by God. They are His witnesses. Welcome them into your village," commanded Philip. Suddenly Philip was gone and the natives turned to Chris and Joshua and again they fell to the ground.

******

Billy Walker heard the plane as it approached the lake. Quickly he ran back to his wife and children who were still asleep in their small cabin hidden in the woods surrounding Lake Shasta—or what was left of it.

"Get up!" Billy shouted.

Peggy Sue rolled over and her large stomach protruded above the sheet. "Get up, Peggy!" Billy repeated.

"What's the matter?"

"There's a plane. I think someone is coming here. Maybe the owners!"

Peggy jumped up and out of bed. "Billy, get the kids."

Billy rustled his daughter, Patty, and his two sons, little Billy and baby Jerry, out of their warm beds. "What is it, Daddy?" Patty inquired.

"We have to go bye-bye," said Billy as Peggy came running into the room still trying to wrap her coat around her obviously very pregnant belly.

Suddenly there was a knock at the door. Billy turned to Peggy with a look of fear in his eyes. "What are we going to do?" she asked worriedly.

"Billy, are you in there?" a voice from outside the cabin asked.

Billy looked at Peggy with great relief and smiled.

Cory and Calvin spent the next two hours explaining to the Walker family everything that had happened over the last couple of years. Both Peggy and Billy cried when they heard that Jerry and Leasa had died, but Calvin reminded Billy that they were in Heaven with Christ and would be back very soon.

Calvin listened to Billy explain to him how he and Peggy Sue had survived the heat wave by moving into a gold mine that Billy had found. "We packed up the kids and moved into the cave. I filled every container I had with water," said Billy.

"Good thing," said Calvin. He had noted that what little water remained in the massive lake was nothing but red mud. In fact, his landing had all but buried his plane. They would never be able to fly out again.

"What are you two going to do now?" Peggy inquired.

Calvin scratched his head for a second. He and Cory had talked over many options, but the one that best fit their desires was to leave the faithful old plane on the lake and find a car to drive across the country as best they could, witnessing as they went. "We need a car," said Calvin.

Billy smiled. "What about your Jeep?"

"Is it still there?" Cory asked in surprise.

Billy nodded "Yup. At least it was last month when I hitched into

Redding."

Calvin scowled at Billy. "What are you doing hitching into a big town where you could get caught or worse yet bring the plague back to your family?"

Billy looked down as a child would who had been severely scolded by his parent. "I had to go—the baby was sick."

Calvin felt bad for reprimanding poor, simple Billy. "What was the matter with him?"

"Scarlet fever," said Peggy Sue.

"Well, how did you get help for him?" Cory inquired.

"I traded a bunch of stuff I had collected," said Billy.

"Traded with whom? How did they know what was wrong with the baby?" Calvin asked.

"I went to the pharmacy at the grocery store and told the man about little Jerry. He said he had three cases of scarlet fever this week and it sounded like Jerry had the same problem. I gave him all the stuff I had brought—food and jewelry and a gun—and he gave me the medicine. At first he said no, but when I showed him the new gun I had, he said yes quickly."

Cory started laughing. He realized that Billy didn't understand that he had scared the pharmacist into giving him the medicine. What choice would the man have had as Billy pointed the revolver towards him to show off his new gun?

"Billy, did you notice anything different about the people?" Calvin asked.

Billy nodded. "Yeah, they all had big old sores all over their faces."

"Weren't you worried that they would be concerned with the fact that you didn't have any sores?"

Billy looked at Peggy Sue and they both started laughing.

"What's so funny, Billy?" Calvin asked.

"The day before I went to town I was digging around in that old mine and I accidentally dug up a hornet's nest. About a 100 of them things stung my face real bad, so when I went to town I looked worse than all of them," he smiled dimly.

At this Cory and Calvin had a good laugh. "The Lord is taking good care of you, Billy," said Calvin.

The next day Cory and Calvin decided to go out and see if the old Jeep was still hidden in the bushes. It was only a 30-minute walk. Much to Calvin's surprise their transportation was still there even though the bushes were no more than a handful of dead weeds now. It was at the angle at which the Jeep sat that deceived people into thinking it was nothing more than a brownish-black rock. Nobody had bothered the vehicle at all, but unfortunately all four tires were flat—probably from the change in temperature from ice cold to burning hot.

******

Back in the cabin Cory lamented over the fact that the Jeep's tires were flat. "I mean we could put the plane's battery in it, but without tires it is useless, not to mention that it is parked out there because it's out of gas, and so are we."

Billy listened carefully as Cory spoke. "I wouldn't say we are out of gas," said Billy.

"What do you mean?" asked Calvin.

"At the edge of that old mine is a big fuel tank. The handle is locked with a big lock, but there might be gas there."

"Probably diesel," said Cory.

"Maybe," said Billy, "but then why is that other tank labeled diesel?"

"Are there two tanks, Billy?" Calvin asked.

Billy nodded.

"Okay, well maybe we have gas and a battery, but we still don't have air for our tires," said Cory.

Again Billy smiled, "Well, actually—"

Cory turned to Billy. "Do you have tires too?"

Billy laughed, "No, of course not. But I do have an electric air pump that runs off a cigarette lighter."

The first thing to find out was whether or not there was gas. Cory followed Billy to the mine. When he looked at the large tank, he was encouraged. There were definitely two different tanks. Cory thumped on the side of the gas tank. The sound it gave off indicated that something was inside.

"What do we do about that big lock?" Billy asked.

Cory inspected the lock and then began to look around for a tool to help him. He found a piece of steel pipe and walked back over to the tank. He slid the pipe into the hasp, and with both hands he pulled down as hard as he could. The lock did not break, but what it was clasped around did. "Dang!" said Billy. He was impressed.

******

Calvin poured the last of the gas in the Jeep's tank while Cory finished airing up the tires. It was surprising how easily the car started once they installed the battery and added some gas. Cory and Calvin drove the Jeep down into the dry lakebed and around the lake to Billy's cabin. That evening Peggy Sue made a fine supper, and as they sat down to eat Calvin prayed that God would bless her with a healthy, easy childbirth. There would be no help this time, and it would only be two months from now before she gave birth.

As it turned out Peggy did have an easy birth, and Billy did a fine job of delivering the baby all by himself. It was a little girl.

That evening Cory and Calvin said goodbye to Billy and the family for the last time. Billy had loaded the Jeep full of cans of gas, jugs of precious water, and a few crates of canned food. Calvin did not argue. He knew that Billy had turned himself into the world's finest packrat. He had plenty of supplies to last his family until the return of Jesus.

"God bless you all," said Calvin as Peggy Sue gave him a hug goodbye.

"You've done well, Billy," said Cory, "but stay away from the city."

Cory and Calvin drove Jerry's Jeep off the lake and onto I-5 heading south.

******

Bob Powell played the video one more time. On the television screen before him was Dr. Raymond Hyder. Teresa Reed entered the recreation room of the space station and floated down to the chair next to Bob. "You are watching this again?" Teresa asked. Bob had grown up in a Christian home, yet through the years he had just kind of walked away from his upbringing and started living for himself. His education in science began to pollute his mind with doubts about the creation of man. After the Rapture Bob regained his faith and made peace with God. Now six years later he found himself floating in a chair in the recreation room of the ship as it orbited the moon for the 2,000[th] time. On the television was a man that Bob did not know, but a man that he owed his life to. Raymond had made the tape and shipped it to the Jet Propulsion Laboratory to be added to the payload before lift-off. The laboratory had reviewed the tape before they added it to the payload, and it had a remarkable effect on many. Now as Bob sat back and listened once again to the tape, he heard Raymond explain all the numerous climate changes that the world had suffered. He also heard Raymond describe the plague and starvation and even the horrid war that had taken so many lives.

As the tape neared its end, Bob leaned forward to listen carefully as Raymond spoke. "Simon Koch is evil. Carlo Ventini has declared himself a god. We are all covered with these sores," said Raymond as he pointed to his face. "Only the Christians don't seem to suffer from this, although they suffer terribly at the hands of Carlo and Simon.

I think these two men are the Antichrist and the False Prophet foretold in the book of Revelation. For five months we were tortured by creatures we could not see. Finally they left, but now it is the men we can see that threaten us. There are two witnesses who claimed to be Moses and Elijah. They were very powerful and they called down many disasters, but finally Simon killed them. However, after three and a half days they rose up and floated into the air and went up to Heaven. We all watched this on television."

Raymond looked into the camera. "If you are not Christians, but have not taken the ID tag, there is still hope for you. Maybe there is even hope for me."

The tape went black and Bob looked to Teresa. "Do you believe in Jesus?"

Teresa looked deep into Bob's brown eyes. She knew that he seemed to be the only one on the ship that did not have painful sores across his body. Now that she had heard Dr. Hyder's explanation for the hundredth time, she felt a tug at her heart. She needed an answer to life. "Tell me about Him. Tell me about Jesus," she cried.

Chapter 15: Three Frog Spirits

D ay 2520, July: Simon leaned back and looked out the port window. The view from 30,000 feet did not negate the horrid sight of the blood red Mediterranean Sea. Simon considered what Dr. Hyder had said nearly two years ago—that the seas, ocean, lakes, and rivers were dying. *Well, it turned out that the weasel of a scientist was right after all.*

Not only had the world suffered the loss of nearly all its water sources, but the planet had also suffered the loss of virtually all plant and animal life. Simon's Agripods were by no means sufficient for meeting the food demands of the present world. Daily people from all four corners of the earth died from lack of nutrition. Additionally, if it had not been for the massive loss of life caused by the lengthy oil war in the Middle East, millions more would have died from hunger.

In all, the world had suffered greatly from the cold, stifling heat, ominous darkness, earthquakes, plagues, natural disasters, and three monstrous asteroids, not to mention the many meteoroids that had bombarded the planet along with tormenting demons and the painful sores that still covered the bodies of all those who served Carlo. Simon considered the last seven years to have been less than desirable. None of this was what he had expected it to be.

As he looked over to where Victoria lay curled up in her seat, he considered the torment she had put him through as well. His decision not to shoot her was a difficult one. He couldn't stand the idea of her sleeping with Carlo ever again, but still the idea of life without here was just too unimaginable for him.

Today Simon's stomach was twisted in knots as he approached

Babylon. He knew this day would come. Three weeks ago at Carlo's request Simon had flown to Babylon for a meeting. Simon feared that Carlo would want to see Victoria, as well, but to his surprise and pleasure Carlo did not mention his wife's name. Victoria held her disappointment in until Simon left for the airport. After that she became very abusive to her servants and stomped around the apartment crying. Carlo had rejected her and she knew it. As a temporary consolation, Victoria demanded that Simon's young butler sleep with her. The man was petrified by the thought, but Victoria did not give him any choice.

On the last visit to Babylon Simon had met with Carlo to discuss Simon's biggest fear— Armageddon. He and Carlo had entered his private temple at dawn and begun to pray to Satan. The two men knelt side-by-side chanting to the Lord of the Underworld. "Father, we need your guidance," said Carlo.

Abruptly the room filled with a yellow, sulfurous smoke, and that usual smell of death was all around. This time Satan appeared in full form like Simon had never seen before.

He was nearly eight feet tall and as broad as two men. Tucked behind his back were two large, dark wings—just like Simon had always imagined angels' wings would look, except for the dark color—not that Simon had ever seen or wanted to see an angel. Just the same Satan came as close as possible to meeting his expectations. However, Satan's face was far from angelic. His skin was rough and porous looking with raised bumps on his cheeks and forehead. His eyes were small and luminescent and his lips were thin and narrow placed flatly above a long, pointy chin.

"Rise!" said Satan. "The time has come to prepare for battle."

Simon rose and stood next to Carlo. His hands shook at the thought of what was coming.

"In three weeks that pretend Son of God will come back with His followers, and they will try to take this world from me. This will not happen!" Satan roared as the room shook.

"No, Father. We will not let this happen," said Carlo.

"What do we need to do to win?" Simon asked with a shaky voice.

"Simon, you go back to Rome. I will give you powers to deceive all of Europe. They will follow you back to Megiddo to do battle against Christ," said Satan.

"Why will they follow me? What should I tell them?" Simon asked.

"I have unleashed three frog-like spirits of deception. They will convince the people to follow you," said Satan.

"What about me? What do I do?" Carlo asked.

"I will give you powers to deceive the Middle East and bring them to the battlefield. I will go to Asia and throughout the world and deceive the rest to bring them across the Euphrates and into the Valley of Jezreel. With these three spirits of deception at my command, we will have the nations of the world armed and ready to destroy Christ!" Satan declared.

******

That was three weeks ago to the day, and now Simon was less than an hour away from Babylon once again only this time he had decided to bring Victoria. At first he had no intention of bringing her, but after she pleaded to be by his side as he went into battle, he reconsidered. *Besides,* he thought to himself, *Carlo will be too busy to bother Victoria, and after this war is over, I will be a god equal to Carlo and Satan.* Simon wanted his wife there to see this great transformation.

******

Chris and Joshua had been in Wasur Park for over a year now. God had blessed them so greatly with this particular ministry. Over 100 tribes from all parts of Wallacea resided within Wasur Park and the surrounding rainforest. Although not much of a rainforest, it still provided shelter from the outside world.

After Philip had shown up on the ridge of Merkele and rescued Joshua and Chris, they had become important men among the tribes. Slowly but surely both men had taught the leaders of these tribes enough English to provide an effective witness. Chris and Joshua also learned much of the native tongue from the tribe of Maluku. This enabled them to participate in much of the daily activities which created even greater acceptance for both men. Additionally Chris and Joshua were surprised to find so many children in these villages. It warmed their hearts to have an opportunity to help these young ones to develop a relationship with Jesus, thereby securing their eternity in Heaven with God.

On this particular morning Chris returned from a night of gathering mushrooms in the forest with the younger children to find the village of Sulawesia burning. Apparently while he and the children had been out in the forest, the tribe of Nusa Tenggara and many other renegades had entered the village and killed numerous people and took their food and water rations. This was not the first time Chris had observed an event like this. However, since he and Joshua had increased their witness through more effective communications, this sort of thing had been all but eliminated. Chris was saddened to see so many dead men, women, and children as he carefully entered the city.

After 30 minutes of looking around without finding a single survivor, Chris decided that he and the children should hurry down the line to the next village—their own village of Maluku. The routine Chris had developed included taking the children into the woods for the night every couple of weeks or so. They would collect all the mushrooms and truffles they could find, and then they would enter the other villages on their way back and share some of their food. This was a terrific lesson for the children and an effective witnessing tool for Chris.

Chris was near panic as he ran through the dry forest. In the past he and Joshua had offended many villagers by attacking their superstitions and pagan idols, but over time they had won over the majority of the people throughout the Wallacea. What Chris did not fully understand today was that Satan had released an evil spirit of deception throughout Asia. This deception—or frog-like spirit—whispered in the ears of those that would listen, convincing them to rebel against the Word of God, and wherever possible to join the cause and to move towards Megiddo.

As Chris and the children ran along, they began to see a small amount of smoke in the distance. He held up his hand for the children to stop and stand still. Slowly Chris worked his way towards a camp full of men and women from various tribes including the one that he lived in. They were all resting on the ground surrounded by loads of food and jugs of water. They had completely gutted Sulawesia, but there was more food here than that village could have supplied. Chris began to worry about some of the other small communities through Merkele Ridge. With over 70 miles of trails and hundreds of small communities, there was no telling how many of them had been destroyed by these evil natives. It seemed reasonable to Chris that these people had raided all night and now were resting before they entered the next village that, of course, would be Maluku in the heart of the Wasur Park. Chris backed his way out and retrieved the children. He had to get back to Joshua and the rest of his friends and warn them about the impending terrible invasion.

******

Oswald turned his car onto Colfax Avenue. Somewhere down here was a meeting about to take place, one that he had waited a year to attend. The sun would not be coming up for many hours there in the heart of the United States in Denver, Colorado. For nearly a year Oswald had followed revival after revival throughout the states. It seemed that in each state there was a number of well organized men and women who would move from city to city leading people—at least those without ID tags—into a right relationship with Jesus. This had angered Simon greatly. As a result it was Oswald's task to destroy all of these Christians.

Many times now he and his Special Forces had captured numerous Christians, and as always he executed them. He would question them for leaders and organization. Little information was ever shared, but over time Oswald was able to piece the puzzle together. Apparently many years ago a small group of people hidden away in a mine in Nevada received a call from God to witness throughout each state. A black man named Calvin Fraser led these people. In groups of three, they traveled to a specific state and lit a fire that still burned brightly today. Oswald knew that he would never be able to extinguish the flames of this movement, but if he could hinder it greatly, he would be happy.

Furthermore, there had been a rumor that the leader of this initial group, Calvin Fraser, had returned from Alaska where he had also done considerable damage to Carlo and Simon's one-world order. Oswald first heard this news about Calvin being spotted in Arizona. Since then he had a compelling desire to find this man. From place to place he and his men followed Calvin and Cory's trail. He had heard of the giant that traveled with Calvin, and he was anxious to meet this man and cut him down to size.

Finally in New Mexico Oswald had his first real encounter with Calvin, although brief. He had been tracking down a local revival when one evening he stumbled across a meeting deep in the center of an Indian reservation. For five minutes Oswald and his men sat back and listened to the speaker describe the love and grace of God. As they began to describe Christ's eminent return and His glory in the sky, the guest speaker spotted Calvin and stopped. "Now I want to introduce you to the man who started this movement in the United States—a man who led me out of Las Vegas and into the shelter of an old mine for many months—Calvin Fraser."

At the announcement of Calvin's name Oswald jumped up from where he sat to see this renegade. Calvin walked up on the platform and waved to the crowd of Indians and other Americans. "May God bless you all. Stay faithful and stand firm. Christ will return very soon. Now I want to introduce you to my friend and faithful companion, Cory Parker."

Cory stood and Oswald's mouth dropped open. He really was a giant of a man. "Okay," said Oswald, "let's take these people now!"

Officers came rushing in with guns firing as people fell to the ground bleeding or dead. Cory looked into Oswald's evil eyes for a few seconds. Anger filled his heart as he quickly grabbed Calvin and ran behind the platform and across the field to his Jeep.

Just as quickly hundreds of people rushed towards Oswald and his guards, not so much to fight but to run interference for Calvin and Cory until they could escape. This very thing had happened to Oswald over a year ago as Tommy and Sara narrowly escaped. He finally understood the lesson. *These people will die to protect their leaders. Never again will I rush in.*

Next time I'll set a trap and wait, thought Oswald to himself as he turned and fired his gun at one of the few standing Christians. In as little as two minutes over 100 Christians were dead from gunfire.

******

This evening as Oswald turned his car into a deserted alleyway he had no intention of mass murder. His was but one goal, and that was to trap Calvin Fraser and his huge buddy. He had been tracking Calvin throughout Colorado for a week, but he was always one step behind— until he captured a young Christian who had inadvertently given him information about an important meeting coming up at a specific location in downtown Denver. He had tortured the poor boy terribly until he gave out the details. Then he slit the boy's throat as he smiled and thought, *Now go meet your God.*

Oswald and two of his guards climbed out of the car and walked around the corner. He decided it was too risky to bring more than just a couple of armed supporters. He needed to be able to hide and blend in. Too many cars and people would make this impossible. Oswald and his men climbed the chain link fence and moved towards the back of the building. They would stay there and wait until they spotted Calvin.

******

For more than a year Cory had driven Calvin from place to place to witness the conversion of many to followers of Christ. It was a very moving experience for both men. After their narrow escape in New Mexico Cory took precautions to ensure that he and Calvin never found themselves trapped in a building with no way out. On this particular evening as they drove toward the site of the next meeting, Cory's thoughts were on Leasa. He missed her so much, but he knew that soon he would be with her for all eternity.

Calvin had been unusually quiet this evening. He, too, could feel that things were coming to an end, and he was grateful. But he was also troubled by the knowledge that millions of people were about to enter into a judgment that would surely send them to Hell forever.

Cory turned on to Colfax Avenue just as Calvin looked his way. "Cory, you have been a true friend. I thank God for you."

He looked at Calvin. The man had changed so greatly over the years that they had spent together. "It has been an honor to be by your side, Calvin."

"Cory, time is running out. Any moment now Christ may return. We have done all we can, and I want you to know that I could not have done any of it without you. I can't even count how many times you have saved my life over the years."

Cory smiled at his friend. "If you had not led me to Jesus, I would be dead forever. I love you, Calvin," said the big man with tears in his eyes.

Calvin smiled, "I love you too. Thank you for everything."

******

Sara looked up to the sky. *How odd*, she thought. The morning sun had been up for a few hours, but now all of a sudden the sky was turning dark. At first it was a hazy orange and then a blood red color. Finally it was as dark as night. A shiver ran down her spine.

Tommy and Sara had spent the last year commuting from their little yellow cottage into the city of Como. It turned out that this city was a perfect place to establish a Christian outpost. People moved through Como often as they traveled to other locations. Every week Tommy and Sara entered the city with their son, Philip, who was now in his terrible two's and a handful for Sara. Tommy and Sara had met others like themselves who were interested in spreading the Word of God. They moved around from place to place witnessing boldly. Often, however, they found themselves running to avoid the Special Police that wandered the city.

Lately Tommy and Sara were encountering more rejection and abuse than normal, and often Sara would suggest that she and Tommy take little Philip home before something bad happened. What both people did not understand was that Simon had released an evil frog-like spirit. This spirit was constantly sending out lies that led people further away from the truth. Over the last couple of weeks the number of people who had enlisted in Simon's army was incredible. Millions throughout Europe had joined his cause. The lie was different for each person, but it all amounted to the same thing. They needed to go to Megiddo to defeat an evil king and preserve their way of living.

Today Sara and Tommy entered the city with a new sense of fear and trepidation. The sight of the morning sky only added to their apprehension. "Weren't we supposed to meet the others by the old church?" Sara asked as she looked around.

Tommy placed Philip on the ground and looked up to the old wooden church. It had been built after World War II. The original church had been a huge cobblestone building, but unfortunately it had accidentally been blown apart. It was later rebuilt on the same site, but this particular church had also suffered damage as Simon went through Europe destroying every site that represented Christ. From this building he had taken the statue of Jesus and the cross and burned them in the center of the city, but for some reason he did not destroy the building.

"Yes! This is the place," said Tommy.

"Well, where is everyone?" Sara asked out of frustration.

"Maybe they are inside. Let's go and see," said Tommy as he bent down and picked up Philip before he could run off to play.

They crossed the deserted street hand in hand. The last seven years had been anything but relaxing for the young couple, although they had relished their time in the cottage. At least there they had felt like a real family as they rested and played with their son. Now, however, as each day passed by they both knew their life on earth was coming to an end. Tommy led his wife up the steps of the church to the large front door. He stood listening for a moment before he pushed against the door. Tommy could hear absolutely nothing. The door swung open with an ominous squeak. As he peered inside he could see nothing, as it was pitch black. Obviously the others were not inside.

"Nobody's in there," said a confused Tommy as he handed baby Philip to Sara and smiled. "I'm going to take a quick look around inside."

"Make it very quick!" said Sara. This whole scene was making her nervous.

What neither Tommy nor Sara knew was that just 50 minutes earlier a group of 30 Special Police had captured the Christians that they were supposed to meet. All of them had been hauled away for questioning which, of course, meant torture until death.

The city of Como had developed a reputation as of late as a hot spot of Christian activity. Oswald's team leaders had informed him of this. He knew Simon would be very angry if he found out, so Oswald had given directions to place as many offices as possible around the city in hopes of capturing the troublemakers. He was sure Tommy Glover had something to do with all this, but he had no intentions of going back to Italy to look for him. This young man had caused him enough trouble. Besides, he had another man whom he was very close to capturing.

Tommy walked through the dark room. There wasn't enough light from the outside to make a difference—he simply could not see anything. *This is a waste of time,* he told himself, *let's just go home.* From behind Tommy heard the door open loudly. He assumed Sara had become impatient. "I'm coming," said Tommy. "Besides, I can't see anything in this place."

Without warning, Sara let out a cry. Tommy's heart nearly stopped, and he instantly knew they were in trouble. As he turned around a bright flashlight shone in his face, blinding him momentarily. Then three men stepped forward, dragging Sara as she clutched Philip tightly. "God help us!" Sara begged.

"Shut up!" said one of the officers as he hit Sara across the face with the back of his hand. Tommy saw the impact and heard the sound as Sara let out another cry. At this anger filled his heart and he ran toward Sara's assailant with fists clenched. One of the officers pulled out his gun and fired it at Tommy, hitting him in the knee. Sara instantly started screaming as she saw Tommy drop to the ground in agonizing pain. Soon baby Philip was crying as well.

"Tie them up!" said one of the men in Italian.

Sara and Tommy had their hands tied behind their backs and their feet bound tightly as well. "What about this stupid kid?" one man asked.

"Tie him up, too, if you can—and if not, shoot him," said the other officer in English.

"No!" Sara screamed out.

Tommy looked at his son. "Philip, sit down!" he yelled.

Philip obeyed immediately and sat on the ground. The officer tied the little boy's hands behind his back and wrapped the rope around his feet. He then lifted Philip and placed him in the center of where Sara and Tommy now lay.

"Where's the gas?" one officer inquired.

"Over there," pointed another man, the one who had shot Tommy in the knee.

Soon the room was doused in gasoline and its fumes filled the air making it hard to breathe. "Okay, let's go!" said another man in Italian. He lit a match and dropped it on the wooden floor. Immediately flames ignited and spread rapidly throughout the church.

Two of the Special Police left the building as the other officer walked up to Tommy and Sara. Tommy looked up at the hateful man. "Too bad Oswald is not here to see this, but I am sure I will get my reward just the same," said the man with a smile.

"I am sure you will!" said Tommy. "I hope you like Hell because maybe even before this day is over that is where you will be for eternity."

The man shuddered at the thought and kicked Tommy in the stomach. "Enjoy the fire," he said as he walked out.

"You too!" said Sara as she spat at the man.

Sara began to cry as the door to the church closed. The flames ran up the wall and started to head across the floor. Luckily for Tommy and Sara they had not been doused with gas or they would have already been burning.

Philip began to cough and cry. Tommy leaned in toward his son to comfort him, but he was unsure of what to do next. The movement caused his knee great pain, but it did not matter. "Its okay, Philip. We are going to see Jesus in just a few minutes." The little boy nestled into his father's chest and began to whimper. Sara also scooted towards Tommy and pressed against him and Philip. "I love you two very much," said Tommy as tears fell down his cheeks.

"I love you too!" said Sara. "Mommy loves you, Philip." Sara so wanted to hold both of her men and kiss them for comfort and security.

"We love all of you," said a voice from across the room. Tommy and Sara looked up to see Harry and Martha standing with sad looks on their faces.

"You two have done such a fine job for the Lord," said Harry proudly.

"And such a sweet family too!" said Martha with her usual screechy voice.

"Can you untie us?" Tommy asked.

Martha looked to Harry and then to Tommy and Sara. The look on her face was one of pain and memory. She could still remember the day she and Harry burned to death in the makeshift Catholic Church there in Africa. "No," said Harry, "we cannot untie you."

Tommy looked at Sara and then to Harry and Martha. "Then this is it. We are to stay here and burn to death for Jesus?"

"If it is God's will," said Martha. "We have been allowed to help out many times before, but God forbids it this time. We will stay with you as long as we can," said Martha as tears streamed down her wrinkled face.

******

Bob Powell read from his Bible as the rest sat back and listened. For more than a year now he had been witnessing to every member of the space ship about Jesus Christ, the Son of God. Even Samuel Pearlman listened carefully. Numerous times he had seen the video that Dr. Hyder had smuggled up to the moon. Pearlman was a practical man. He was a man who could be convinced if the evidence was strong enough.

As for Teresa Reed and Skip Taylor, they both had nothing to lose by believing what Bob preached. Eventually Samuel, Skip, and Teresa accepted Jesus as their personal savior. However, Petra and Shila rejected all that Bob spoke as utter nonsense. Today was no different. As Bob read Petra made snide remarks that he saw as humorous. "So then I guess soon I will see a herd of white horses running across the space out here.

I guess I had better go outside and wash our windows so we can see well," Petra grinned.

Shila floated out of the room quietly. She did not want to sit through another lecture on the return of a Jesus she did not believe in.

Bob and Skip turned to watch her leave the recreation room. *What a pity,* thought both men.

Samuel watched Shila leave and followed after her. He was tired of listening to Petra make fun of something that he was now convinced would soon come to pass. "Shila," said Samuel as he entered the kitchen where she stood quietly, "why do you reject the truth of God?"

"Whose truth?" she said. "I always thought you were a smart man—probably the smartest on this ship—but now I don't know."

"Why? Because I have seen the light and now understand what is going on in our world, or because I have accepted Jesus as the only Son of God and the only way to Heaven?" Samuel asked earnestly.

"Yes! Partially anyway," said Shila.

"What else is bothering you, Shila?" Samuel inquired.

Shila paused and looked at Samuel intently. She wanted to tell him—she needed to tell someone, but it just seemed so hard to get the words to come out.

Samuel perceived that Shila had a secret—something terrible that she did not want to talk about—something that was preventing her from hearing the truth. "God sees and knows all, Shila. He is a merciful God. Christ died for our sins. We can be forgiven of anything. Anything!"

Shila began to cry. "I don't know. I don't think He will forgive me."

"Shila, listen to me! Bob read to us that if we confess our sins, God is just to forgive us and wash us clean. What have you done that is so terrible?"

Shila stared at the small man carefully. She had to tell somebody, and she greatly respected and trusted Samuel. "I sold my baby," she wept.

"What?" Samuel asked.

"Eight years ago while I was in school I got pregnant. I knew I would lose my government tuition and I would never become an astronaut, so I faked an illness and stayed out of school until the baby was born. I went on the Internet and found someone from the United States. I sold my baby girl for 20,000 American dollars!" Shila mourned aloud.

Samuel floated to Shila and wrapped his arms around the broken-hearted woman. "God will forgive you if you ask Him to."

Shila cried, "Do you really believe this to be true?"

"Yes, Shila, I do. We can ask Jesus right now if you want," said Samuel. Shila nodded.

"Okay, then let's pray," said Samuel. "Dear Jesus, hear our prayers. Please forgive all our sins and come into our hearts as the one true God. Let us live eternally with You in Heaven. We confess You as the only Son of God, raised from the cross to save us. Amen."

"Amen," said Shila as she hugged Samuel and cried unabatedly. Instantly the sores disappeared from her face and hands.

******

Simon walked into Carlo's palace with Victoria by his side. He was anxious to get this over with while Victoria was anxious to get things rekindled between her and Carlo. Simon noted the dark sky as he entered the extravagant building. An inkling of fear raced through his mind.

He and Victoria stood in the middle of the large, formal room. Victoria looked up to the mural of Carlo and admired his likeness. "It's about time you showed up," said Carlo as he entered the room. Simon turned to see a very agitated Carlo dressed in a long purple robe with a golden sash and a breastplate laden with valuable jewels.

"Sorry, Your Holiness. We got here as quickly as we could." Simon would be glad when this war was over. He had great hopes of becoming Carlo's equal with an extravagant robe all his own.

Victoria looked at Carlo and nearly blushed. He made her blood boil. Now if only she could get Simon out of the way she could be alone with Carlo and make up for lost time. After all, it had been over a year since they had been together.

Carlo did not acknowledge Victoria's presence at all. This hurt her feelings greatly, but it put Simon at ease. Obviously his leader had more important things to worry about than molesting his wife. "Simon, I need you to go to Baghdad right away!" said Carlo.

"Yes, Your Holiness. What for?" Simon asked suspiciously.

"Weeks ago," said Carlo, "I released a lying spirit among all Middle Eastern nations. Today most of them have gone to the Valley of Jezreel to prepare for war, but I also sent some to Edom to search out this Elisha Kaufman and all the Jews that he has hidden throughout Israel. I want a progress report. Take your plane and be back here in three hours."

Simon rushed out of the palace without a single concern for Victoria. He assumed that he had misjudged her, and besides, it was obvious that Carlo was no longer interested in her.

******

Elisha stood attempting to look across the desert of Edom. The ominous sky gave off the appearance of midnight except that there were no stars or moon visible. Two months earlier as Elisha and Jasmine lay side-by-side sleeping in the large cave called El Wad the Archangel Michael had appeared to them both. His splendor was overwhelming as his massive wings stood above his head some six feet. He was dressed in a shiny, white flowing robe. His face was so dazzling that Elisha and Jasmine could not look at him.

"The Lord of Heaven and earth has commanded that you go to Edom," said Michael as his voice reverberated through the cave, waking up thousands of sleeping people. God has sent a nation out to greet you. Get up and prepare to leave. Satan will send an army out to meet them and try to kill them before Christ's return."

"What about my people?" Elisha inquired as he looked around his own cave.

Instantly Elisha and Jasmine found themselves standing in the middle of the southern desert below the Dead Sea parallel to the Negev where they had led and sheltered many before. At that moment they looked up to see a swarm of people walking towards them. At least a million Jews had managed to make the journey to the original site of Edom.

Although Edom itself had been lost to history by 100 AD, this place still held significant importance to the Jews. As prophesied by Obadiah, Edom would pay for the evil deeds against Judah.

Albianus, the king of Chittim, had captured the city. This is why the people of Edom were called the Children of Chittim. Also Edom was another name for Esau, just like Israel was another name for Esau's twin brother, Jacob. Edom had been heavily influenced by Roman culture and thus was known as *Mystical Babylon*. In Daniel's vision as recorded in the Bible, the kingdoms of Rome and Edom were the fourth beast, a contemptible people hated by God.

Elisha took Jasmine's hand as they walked towards the people. The crowd was completely silent as they stood there. "What do we do with them?" Elisha whispered.

"We find them shelter before our enemies' army shows up," said Jasmine as she tugged on Elisha's arm dragging him towards the people.

******

Cory led the way as he and Calvin exited the building. It had been a spectacular time of revival and many had come to know Christ, but now it was time to leave, and Cory was nervous. "Let's take the back door out of here in case this place is being watched from the front. We can circle the block and get back to the Jeep," said Cory.

Calvin had all but lost the ability to think in terms of safety. He relied on Cory's judgment for all of these tactical decisions. "Lead the way, my friend!" said Calvin with a broad smile. He, too, was extremely pleased with the turnout tonight.

Upon exiting the rear of the building Cory led Calvin past a dumpster to a fence. "Why is it so dark out here—where did the moon go?" Cory asked as he gazed up into the eerie sky. Suddenly Cory and Calvin heard laughter from behind. The two evangelists swiftly turned around to see Oswald and two of his officers illuminated by the light above the building standing just 10 feet away with their guns pointed directly at them.

"Are you going somewhere?" Oswald asked with a grin.

Cory remembered the man's face from New Mexico, and anger filled his body like never before.

The three men approached slowly as Cory and Calvin looked on. "Well, it looks like the end for us this time," Calvin whispered to his dear friend.

Just the thought of someone hurting Calvin broke Cory's heart. Abruptly he lunged towards Oswald. Oswald fired his pistol into Cory's stomach, but it did not stop the big man from closing the distance and wrapping his arms around Oswald's moderate frame. The other two officers were not sure what to do next. If they fired their guns, it was likely they would hit their leaders as well as Cory.

Calvin stood by watching as his friend began to bend Oswald like a pretzel. Oswald's gun flew out of his hand towards Calvin. Quickly Calvin dove for the revolver just as one of the officers fired a shot. The bullet entered Calvin's back and exited his side. Calvin rolled over with the gun in his hand and pointed at one of the officers, but the pain of his wound was excruciating. Oswald looked into Cory's eyes. The light from the back door of the building gave Oswald just enough visibility to see Cory's face contort as he snapped his neck. Oswald slid out of Cory's hands and onto the asphalt, having breathed his last breath.

Both officers looked at their leader lying motionless on the ground and then back to Calvin and Cory. It was a standoff, but the guards had two guns instead of one, and both Cory and Calvin had been gravely wounded by bullets.

******

As Chris approached the village of Maluku what little light he received from the moon and the stars suddenly disappeared. Instead of getting the morning sun as he had expected, he now had total darkness very much like that which he had experienced when the entire earth had been darkened for weeks. "Light your torches," Chris whispered to all the children.

He and the children entered the village from the west. To Chris' surprise Maluku seemed deserted. *Had other evil villagers taken all the people away?* Chris wondered. Even worse yet, had Jesus returned and taken those in the village but somehow left Chris behind once again?

As he walked through the village he began to hear the happy sound of praise. *Yes, that's right,* he thought, *it's Sunday.*

Chris and the children with him hurried to the edge of the village where worship always took place. As they approached Chris saw Joshua standing between two huge eucalyptus trees leading the natives in the chorus of *Amazing Grace.* John Newton, a destitute sinner and ex-mariner, had written this song after a remarkable transformation had taken place in his life. It was an American favorite, but for Chris it was a testimony to the lives he had seen changed over the last seven years.

Joshua smiled at Chris as soon as he entered the park-like setting lit up by huge torches. Chris quickly walked towards his friend and stood beside him until the song was through.

"Did you find a lot of mushrooms?" Joshua asked as he turned toward Chris. The frown on Chris' face told Joshua that something was terribly wrong. "What is it?"

"Sulawesia has been destroyed and everyone is dead." As Chris spoke the village chief turned towards his people and repeated word for word. Soon there were many moans and loud cries among the people.

"We saw who did it, and they are on their way here!" said Chris.

"Should we run and hide?" the chief asked Joshua.

Joshua looked at Chris and then to the people. A feeling came over him—a sense of calm like never before. "No! We will not run. We will wait on the Lord to help us."

Chapter 16: His Glorious Appearance

Day 2520, July: Victoria wandered around Carlo's palace for a couple of hours. She was so depressed. All the valuable time while Simon was away to Baghdad was nearly used up. Why hadn't Carlo requested she meet him in his bedroom as before? Suddenly as Victoria walked along the dark and gloomy hanging garden, an idea came rushing into her mind. Quickly she went racing back to the palace. *Not a moment to lose,* she thought to herself.

******

Simon finished his 20-minute briefing with the head of the Iraqi military. Carlo's wishes were being carried out to Simon's satisfaction. The Iraqi military along with members of the Chinese Liberation Army and the Iranian military had been marched out in two directions. The majority of the military had been placed in Megiddo with other armies that came from every part of the world while the rest were at this moment racing through the desert on their way to Edom.

As Simon leaned back in his seat, he considered his first activity of the day well done. Now as soon as his plane landed back in Babylon he would gather his things and meet Carlo for the quick trip to the Valley of Jezreel where he would take command of the military there. After that he had no idea what would come. He would have to sit and wait for this Jesus to show up if He came at all.

******

Carlo walked past his bedroom on the way downstairs. Suddenly his eye caught sight of Victoria's blouse lying just inside the doorway. Carlo picked up the blouse and walked into his bedroom. There he found Victoria lying seductively on the bed without any clothes on. Carlo stopped and stared at her without saying a word.

"Your Holiness," Victoria whispered as she licked her lips. "I was afraid you would not come up here. We have so little time until that worm, Simon, shows up."

Carlo turned and left the room. Victoria was stunned and angered greatly. As Carlo began to walk down the stairs, Simon met him. He had just returned from Baghdad. Instantly Simon was suspicious. "Where's Victoria?" he asked angrily.

Carlo looked at his prophet closely. He was angered by Simon's tone of voice. "What did you find out in Baghdad?" Carlo growled. Simon moved past Carlo and continued up the stairs. Just then he heard Victoria call out, "It's your loss!"

Carlo yelled towards Simon, "I asked you a question!"

Simon ignored his leader and continued on as jealousy and rage filled his mind. He turned the corner and walked into Carlo's bedroom to find his wife laying on the bed naked.

Victoria was stunned to see Simon. "He made me!" she shouted out.

Simon pulled his revolver out of the holster under his coat. "You are a whore!" he screamed as he pointed the gun at Victoria. Suddenly from outside there was a great explosion and then another. The blinding light came through Carlo's bedroom window. It was lightning like never seen before. Soon the room started to shake as another bolt of lightning landed in the hanging garden just outside Carlo's palace, setting it on fire. Again more violently this time the building began to rock and sway. Victoria screamed and crawled towards the head of the bed. Another explosion and the windows in Carlo's room blew out, shattering glass all over Victoria and slicing her body terribly, causing her to scream out in pain. Just then another large piece of glass dropped down from the window and severed

Victoria's neck. Simon was stunned and horrified at the sight of his wife lying naked on Carlo's bed decapitated. Quickly he turned and ran out of the room.

Down in the center of the palace just below the great mural, Carlo called out Simon's name. Satan suddenly appeared beside his son. "It is time!" he shouted over the deafening noise of thunder from above. Simon entered the room with a horrific expression on his face. Carlo was angry to see Simon, but there was no time to discipline his disobedient prophet. "We must go to Megiddo now!" said Satan.

Instantly Carlo, Simon, and Satan disappeared from the room just as an earthquake began to shake the world violently, collapsing Carlo's precious palace. In fact, the massive force of the earthquake was so great that the entire city of Babylon began to buckle. The streets rolled like waves in the sea and soon the city fractured into three large but separate pieces.

******

The fire was within a few inches of Tommy as he lay there coughing on the thick black smoke. Sara cried out one more time, "I love you, Tommy!" In the corner Martha and Harry prayed for God to hurry to this place before Sara, Tommy, and little Philip had to endure the torture of burning to death as they had so long ago.

"You and Philip have been my joy," Tommy cried just as his pants began to burn. Abruptly the building began to quake and rock back and forth. Martha and Harry raised their hands in praise. From outside Tommy could hear great explosions unlike the lightning and thunder he and Sara had been listening to for the last few minutes. This was a different sound, but one both had heard before. It was the sound of meteorites crashing into the surface of the earth—hailstones—large ones of over 130 pounds.

The roof of the building began to collapse as the fire spread across the ceiling. Philip screamed out as large pieces of wood dropped to the ground around them. Sara wanted to hold her child and comfort him, but she could do nothing at all. "Tommy, I want to be your wife in Heaven for all eternity just like Martha and Harry."

"You will be, my love. God will take care of us," said Tommy reassuringly.

At this Martha looked to her husband and kissed him smartly on the lips. "Thank you for a lifetime as my best friend and husband," she said.

Tommy and Sara were now completely surrounded by the fire. Tommy began to feel the pain as his clothes burned. There was another sudden explosion followed by a bolt of lightning and a peal of thunder. The roof of the building caved in and fell towards Sara, Tommy, and little Philip. In an instant they were gone and all that remained was a pile of burning clothing and a handful of ropes.

******

The Nusa Tenggara people led the way as thousands followed them into the small village of Maluku. Joshua and Chris stood in front of the villagers as the mass of torch-bearing people trounced forward with spears at the ready. Chris grabbed Joshua's hand and said, "It had been my honor to work with you, Joshua."

"I thank the Lord every day for you, Chris. I love you. Soon you will see your parents and Connor again," Joshua smiled.

Suddenly lightning raced across the sky! Then came a massive boom. The evil natives stopped and looked up to the sky. Their superstitions were starting to cause them great fear. Soon the ground beneath their feet shook so fiercely that no man could stand.

"Jesus is coming!" shouted Joshua as he lay on the ground next to Christopher and hundreds of villagers.

All of a sudden a red, glowing ball of fire sped across the sky and into the canopy atop the rain forest. Quickly the entire forest was a raging fire. The dry moss and dead Eucalyptus trees were nothing more than kindling for the fiery hailstorm.

The evil natives began to rise to their feet as did the men, women, and many children from the small village. One of the Sulawesia natives gave a frightening call, and all the men and women raised their spears and pointed them towards Joshua, Chris, and the people behind them. Overhead lightning flashed as the forest fire raged on. The ground began to shake violently again just as the spears went flying towards Joshua and Chris. In a flash they were gone. All that remained were the garments they had previously worn. The spears landed forcibly into the dirt as the evil natives stood by with their mouths wide open, trapped in a burning inferno with no way out.

******

Calvin held the gun pointed towards the two officers, but his arm was getting tired. He was so weak from the loss of blood that very soon he would pass out and die. Cory staggered back to where Calvin lay and he, too, was near death as the bullet that Oswald fired into him hit its mark.

Cory fell to the ground next to his friend and took the gun from his tired hand. With his other hand he pulled Calvin in towards him as if to give him one final hug. "Calvin, what is Heaven really going to be like? Leasa asked me, but I didn't really know." Cory coughed.

The two officers stood by watching and listening as all this transpired. "I think," said Calvin, "Heaven is where all of your best dreams come true. Everything we could ever hope for will be there, and we will be in the loving presence of God for all time."

One of the two officers—the younger of the two—looked at his partner and dropped his gun. "What are you doing?" the other man asked angrily.

"I want to go to Heaven," the young man whispered.

Calvin looked up and smiled at the brave officer. The man walked towards Cory and Calvin when suddenly a round of gunfire went off. The man stumbled forward and fell at Cory's feet. This young man was dying quickly. "Have you taken Carlo's ID tag?" Cory asked.

The young officer looked up from where he lay bleeding to death. Cory held his breath waiting—the dying man's next answer was crucial. "No!" he whispered. His partner was stunned to hear that this young man had somehow avoided the mandatory insertion without getting caught.

"Do you believe in Jesus Christ?" Calvin asked with one of his few remaining breaths.

"Yes, I do now," the man whispered. Quickly his partner raised his gun to shoot the young guard before he could declare Christ as his savior.

"Do you want to ask Jesus to forgive your sins and come into your life?" Calvin choked out these last few words just as the lightning and thunder began to explode all around him.

"I do!" the young man cried as a final bullet entered his head exploding his brains all over Cory and Calvin.

"Too late!" beamed Cory. "He is in Heaven now—saved forever."

All of a sudden the ground shook violently and large fiery balls came racing in from every direction. The lone officer looked at Calvin and Cory. Both men looked pathetic—nearly dead. Cory could hardly hold the gun up, and finally he dropped it. The officer smiled at the big dying man. "Well, I guess I win," he said. He pointed his gun at Calvin. "I guess I will kill your friend first."

Again the ground shook, knocking the officer of his feet. More thunder and lightning crossed the night sky. "Cory, it is time," Calvin whispered.

Cory pulled Calvin into his arms and held him tightly as he died. Cory bent over and kissed his dear friend's forehead. "I'll see you in a few minutes!" he cried.

The officer worked his way to his knees, "Is he dead?"

"No! He is alive forever," Cory declared. "You cannot hurt him anymore."

"Yes, but I can still hurt you," said the man as he pointed his gun at Cory once again. An incredibly bright flash of light burst above both men. Cory and the officer looked up to see a massive fireball falling directly upon them. The officer yelled out in fear and turned to look towards Cory. But he was not there, nor was Calvin's lifeless body. All that remained were two sets of worn out clothing and an unoccupied guard's uniform. Looking up all the officer could do was to stare in horror as the gigantic hailstone headed straight for him and blew his body to pieces.

******

Elisha rose from his knees. He and the million other Jews and Muslims had been in prayer all morning. The sky was dark and the many torches they had lit provided the only light the camp had. Elisha knew this was a temporary situation. Soon Christ would return and fill the world with his own light and the world would never be in darkness again.

Jasmine walked up to Elisha and kissed him tenderly. "Will I be able to do this in Heaven?" she asked.

"I hope so!" Elisha grinned brightly.

From a distance Elisha could hear tanks and motorized vehicles coming quickly. "They're here!" said Elisha as he took Jasmine's hand. "You have been my strength. I thank God for you," he said as he looked into Jasmine's beautiful, dark eyes.

Jasmine hugged Elisha tightly as the people rose from the sand. "Where do we go now?" they cried aloud.

Elisha faced the people with Jasmine by his side. "We go nowhere! We wait for the Lord to deliver us."

Abruptly the sky split open and lightning ran the distance of the sky. Mighty thunderous booms reverberated through the air as the ground started to shake horribly. Soon Elisha and all the people were knocked to the ground. The fiery hail began to crash all around them.

******

Simon stood next to Satan and Carlo at the edge of the Valley of Jezreel. He could not get the image of Victoria's head lying next to her body out of his mind. His heart grieved for his cheating wife. However, a thought occurred to him that as soon as this war was over, he would be a god like Carlo and Satan. Then he could and would have any woman he wanted and as many as he wanted.

Below him were millions of soldiers. It looked like a great sea of people. Whenever the lightning exploded in the air, the sky would light up revealing the entire battlefield of Megiddo. Armageddon was about to begin. Simon did not know what to expect. He had little confidence that Satan could defeat Jesus, but if armies accounted for anything, he had amassed the biggest one the world had ever seen.

Again the ground began to shake knocking Carlo and Simon to the ground. Satan looked down in disgust. "Get up!" he ordered. Large fiery hailstones suddenly began to fall on Simon's troops. Before his eyes thousands of soldiers were either blown to pieces or running while their bodies burned as human torches lighting up the dark battlefield.

"What do we do now?" Simon asked in a panic.

"Wait!" a highly agitated Satan commanded.

What Simon did not understand was that Satan had eons of history with Christ. He had been defeated in everything he had ever attempted. Satan was far from confident in the outcome of the battle awaiting him, but he was foolish enough to believe he had a chance, even if it was a small one.

******

Elisha stood tall as the armies approached. Soon gunfire could be heard, but none of his people were wounded. The army moved into Edom and stopped before Elisha's camp. Quickly Jasmine ran to his side. The general in charge of the army stepped forward and smirked as Elisha took Jasmine's hand. "Nothing here but women and children," he laughed. "Kill them all!"

******

Bob held onto the chair as he knelt in prayer. By his side were Samuel, Teresa, Skip, and a newly converted Shila. Petra sat in the control center staring out into space. He had no interest in all this Christian nonsense. All he wanted was to get his feet on solid ground again and find a good party where there would be lots of vodka and pretty girls. The sky lit up as fire crossed in front of his glass window. The lightning out in space was incredible. This was not just an earthly phenomenon. It included the entire universe.

Petra felt the space station quake as the ripple effect of the electrical storm bombarded his craft. Soon the sky was full of orange, glowing balls as they hurled past the moon on their way to earth.

There was a tremendous shout followed by a loud trumpet blast! The blackness of the space around the ship opened wide and a dazzling white light spread across the empty sky. Quickly Petra rose and ran to the other end of the spacecraft to find Samuel. He would know what was going on. He would have an answer for Petra.

Petra entered the room only to find five empty spacesuits floating above his head. He went from room to room looking for any signs of life. Finally in a panic he went back to the command center and stood there looking out of the window. Out of nowhere millions upon millions of people could be seen riding out of Heaven on huge, beautiful, white horses. Each rider had on a flowing dazzlingly white robe. In the front was a magnificent rider whose robe was splendid—white and crimson. His eyes blazed as fire and his head was covered with many crowns. He had a name written on him that Petra did not know and another name on his thigh and robe that read *King of Kings and Lord of Lords*.

Petra began to cry and moan, for before him was the Truth of all mankind—the Creator of the world—and Petra had rejected him. The pain was too unimaginable. Petra walked to the cargo bay as tears streamed down his face. Once in the bay, he opened the outer door. Without his tether and helmet Petra was pulled out into the vacuum of space where his blood instantly boiled, exploding his body and scattering it into the brightly lit space. Petra was promptly ushered into Hell to await his judgment in God's good time.

******

The general pointed his firearm at Elisha and then reconsidered and quickly fired a shot into Jasmine's chest. Elisha caught his lovely and faithful wife before she hit the ground. Elisha looked into the hateful eyes of the general as the man smiled, pleased with his aim. Jasmine gasped for breath and looked into her husband's tear stained eyes. "I wish I could have given you many sons. I love you so much!"

Elisha knelt and held Jasmine tight. His heart broke for her. "You are my joy, wife. We will always be together. Hang on. Jesus will be here soon."

"Not soon enough," laughed the general as he gave the order to kill all the people. Unexpectedly a loud shout rippled across the valley of Edom. Then an incredible trumpet blast shattered the ears of the soldiers, forcing them to drop their guns. Jasmine looked up into Elisha's face. "He's coming!" she cried.

"Yes, Sweetheart, hang on. He's coming!" Elisha cried.

The sky split open and down rushed an incredible army dressed in white. In the front was the Lord Jesus Christ in all of His splendor and glory. Jesus raced towards Edom with millions upon millions behind him. Elisha covered Jasmine's face and bowed low before God as He approached. The general in charge of the army looked up to Christ, and his eyes melted in their sockets. Screaming out in pain he fell to the ground, as did all the soldiers.

The nation of Israel which had been led out to the desert saw Christ approach. They did not all know he was heading for Edom, but if they had studied their scripture, they would have known, because it was foretold that Jesus would come there first. "Who is this coming from Edom, from Bozrah, with his garment stained crimson?" Isaiah had prophesied about this thousands of years earlier.

Jasmine felt the wound in her chest close up. Her breathing became painless, and she was healed. She wrapped her arms around Elisha and whispered in his ears, "Seven miserable years, but we made it! The Lord has come back and He has healed me!" she cried.

Elisha kissed his beloved wife and fell prostrate on the sand, praising Jesus!

******

From every part of the world every eye saw Christ coming in the air and every voice moaned loudly, "What have we done?"

An angel could be seen standing in the blazing sun, as the sky was now clear. "'Come, birds flying in midair, come, gather together for the great supper of God, so that you may eat the flesh of kings, generals and mighty men, of horses and their riders, and the flesh of all people, free and slave, small and great.'"

******

As Simon watched in awe as Christ came to earth, fear filled every fiber in his body and he shut his eyes tightly to avoid looking at Jesus.

"Father, where is He going?" Carlo asked.

"Edom!" said Satan as he stood there rigid.

"What do we do now? Will the army in Edom defeat Him?" Simon whined.

"Shut up!" Satan commanded.

Simon fell to the ground in fear.

******

Christ swiftly defeated the soldiers in Edom with the spoken Word of God. Not a soldier dressed in white had to lift a finger. The battle was swift and complete. Soon Christ left Elisha and Jasmine kneeling in the sand as he flew to the Mount of Olives east of Jerusalem as prophesied by Zechariah. As soon as Jesus placed His foot on the Mount of Olives it split into two separate pieces, cleaving the ground and creating a new route to Jerusalem. The mountains separated north and south all the way to Azel, creating a great and wondrous valley.

Immediately Christ appeared before the Valley of Jezreel in the air. The soldiers there began to fight among each other savagely. The Valley around Megiddo turned red with the blood of evil men. Thunder and lightning shook the heavens and more hailstones crashed to the ground. Christ flew to where Satan, Carlo, and Simon stood shaking with fear. As soon as Jesus placed a foot on the ground of Megiddo the earth shook more violently than it had ever before. The mountains around the world turned to rubble. Every building small and great fell to the ground in a heap of wood, concrete, and plaster. The oceans swelled and tidal waves beyond description covered all the remaining islands on the earth and they were no more. Men and women from around the world died from the great catastrophe that surrounded them. Instantly they were ushered to Hell to await their own judgments.

Swiftly Christ moved in front of Satan and pointed a spectacular sword at him. Jesus turned his head towards Carlo, "From Hell you came, and to Hell you shall return for all times—to suffer in anguish for your blasphemy and evil deeds."

Carlo reached out towards Satan and screamed, "Father! Help me!" Instantly Michael and thousands of angels under his command stood next to Jesus and took possession of a struggling Carlo. In the blink of an eye they disappeared.

Again Jesus turned towards Simon. "You are a false prophet and butcher of men."

Simon huddled cowering on the ground. "They made me do it. Please forgive me. I can change! I can make it right. I can—" Simon began to wail. Satan looked down on his prophet. He would remember what Simon had said, and he would pay for this later.

"To Hell with you!" said Jesus as Michael appeared once again and grabbed a trembling and screaming Simon Koch—world leader, false prophet, and sorcerer. Instantly they were gone.

Jesus looked up to see a spectacular angel equivalent to Michael flying towards earth. In his hand was a shiny piece of gold. As he drew closer it was apparent that he was carrying a large golden key. Soon Gabriel landed and stood next to Christ. "Satan, your evil has gone on long enough. You cannot defeat the Creator of the heavens and earth, but for the sake of the righteous, you will be locked in Hell for 1,000 years." As Jesus spoke, the earth shook and the sky lit up with fire. Satan roared and shook the hill they stood on.

"On your knees!" commanded Jesus. Suddenly Michael stood next to

Gabriel as they encouraged Satan to the ground. "You stand judged as the creator of evil. Never again will you rule over earth and never again will you enter Heaven. In 1,000 years you will serve God by testing those on earth, but your doom is sealed."

"I am a god. I will defeat you some day!" screamed Satan as Michael and Gabriel grabbed his arms and flew away. Instantly the earth was quiet. Down below in the Valley of Jezreel, millions lay dead. From the four corners of the earth, men lay dead or hidden away until the day of their judgment, which was at hand.

******

Two days later in Bethlehem Elisha and Jasmine stood in the same spot overlooking the same city that Philip had brought them to seven years ago. They had marched through the desert once again, but this time there was no fear of evil men. Elisha and Jasmine along with their followers had been selected by God to live out the next 1,000 years in peace. A sense of accomplishment flooded Elisha's body. The judgment was over and all those found wanting had been delivered to Hell. Now for the next thousand years the earth would be populated with those that were found deserving in God's eyes. Apparently some of their offspring would somehow slide back into sin, because after the 1,000 years, another judgment awaited. Jasmine slid her small hand into Elisha's as they looked down towards the location of Benjamin's deli. The city was gone. In fact, the surface of the earth was wiped clean. God would be rebuilding it for those he loved. Suddenly Jasmine and Elisha felt a familiar presence. Philip and Barthemaus appeared before the young couple. Elisha smiled and bowed his head.

"You two did well. The Lord is pleased," Philip beamed brightly.

"We come to bring you the good news," said Barthemaus. "The Lord has made the earth new again, and you will have peace and joy for 1,000 years. Enjoy the presence of Jesus throughout your long, earthly life."

"And congratulations on your pregnancy!" said Philip as he turned to Jasmine and smiled.

Jasmine moved forward and hugged Philip tightly. "God bless you!"

"We have one more surprise for you," said Philip cheerfully. Behind Philip and Barthemaus dressed in beautiful white robes stood Joseph Bastoni, Yvette Bastoni, Peter Bastoni, Ruth Jefferson, Scott Turner, Benjamin Cohen, and little David.

The Celebration was just about to begin!

John 3:16

Printed in the United States
1387500002B/1-24